Praise for the Pr...

❦ M A R K   O F ❦

"Jessica Dotta is a phenomenal writing talent and her evocative prose draws readers in with uniquely layered characters and rich intrigues that leave you gasping and begging for more."
  SERENA CHASE, *USA Today*

"Ms. Dotta weaves a web of intricate secrets revealing one, only to expose thousands of other untold threads. Overall, this was a thrilling read, perfect for fans of Austen and Brontë, with all the intensity and tension of the Tudor court."
  RADIANT LIT

"Dotta has brought forth the complicated world of high society England and makes it understandable to readers. Her characters are charming, but she throws in a few scoundrels to even things out."
  ROMANTIC TIMES

"Dotta picks up the action right where the story left off in *Born of Persuasion*, delivering . . . richly gothic atmosphere, suspense, and tangled relationships."
  BOOKLIST

"A brooding and atmospheric tale that may appeal to readers who enjoy Charlotte Brontë."
  LIBRARY JOURNAL

"Jessica Dotta's beautiful writing and narration brought this book to life. . . . Fans of the series will be pleased with this new installment, and just as eager as I am to get their hands on the final book."
  CHRISTIAN MANIFESTO

"Readers will find themselves engulfed in a story of danger and romance. . . . In a word, the series so far is remarkable, but it is so much more than that, as it challenges readers to examine closely the world around them, the faith within them, and [the] foundation below them."
  FAMILY FICTION

"An intrepid heroine falling for two different men; a plot brimming with secrets, scandal, and suspense; and a richly atmospheric setting are the key ingredients in the first novel in Dotta's Price of Privilege trilogy. Readers who miss Victoria Holt will swoon with delight upon discovering this retro-gothic winner."

BOOKLIST

"With crossover appeal for mainstream historical romance fans of Victoria Holt, Dotta's debut novel will have readers demanding book two immediately."

LIBRARY JOURNAL

"I was delighted, enthralled, and utterly captivated by the way Jessica Dotta cleverly mixed a cast of Austen-like characters into a creative Charlotte-Brontë-meets-Victoria-Holt setting. . . . With twists, turns, and a hopeful ending that leaves so very much to be resolved, *Born of Persuasion* will no doubt make my list of top favorite debuts this year."

SERENA CHASE, *USA Today*

"Dotta's new series has something for all fans of this time period: romance, family secrets, overbearing guardians, and even a little laughter. The characters are well-rounded and the author's research on the setting shines through."

ROMANTIC TIMES

"Absolutely entertaining and brilliantly written, with lovable flawed characters. Full of witty dialogue that opened windows into a world of intriguing mystery as this author explores love, faith, and honor. Jane Austen fans will love this instant classic that dropped me into all the richness of the Victorian era. I highly recommend this book for a great read and a book club pick."

THE BOOK CLUB NETWORK INC. (BOOKFUN.ORG)

"The best Christian fiction I've read in a very long time. . . . [It] perfectly blends mystery, drama, heartbreak, and romance with just a touch of sermonizing. I believe this book could be in the running for one of my favorite Christian books of the decade."

RADIANT LIT

"*Born of Persuasion* is the sort of book in which readers of historical fiction long to lose themselves: rich with period detail and full of intrigue and deception. Fans of Philippa Gregory and Sarah Dunant will fall in love with this arresting story."

TASHA ALEXANDER, *New York Times* bestselling author

"With a voice you'll love, Jessica Dotta paints a vivid portrait in words, drawing her readers through an unexpected maze of plot twists. *Born of Persuasion* is a story of betrayal and perseverance, rich with unforgettable characters."

CINDY WOODSMALL, *New York Times* bestselling author

"A fascinating cast of characters and breathless twists and turns make this story anything but predictable. Mystery and romance, sins of the past and fears of the future all combine for a page-turning experience."

LIZ CURTIS HIGGS, *New York Times* bestselling author

"*Born of Persuasion* is among the best novels I've ever read. It is descriptive, suspenseful, and absolutely captivating. Not since *Jane Eyre* have I wanted to reread a story again and again."

GINA HOLMES, bestselling author of *Crossing Oceans*

"Filled with romantic twists, social intrigue, and beautiful writing, Dotta's *Born of Persuasion* is an alluring debut that will leave fans of Victorian fiction clamoring for more."

TOSCA LEE, *New York Times* bestselling author

"Jessica Dotta is this generation's Jane Austen but with a twenty-first-century voice, and *Born of Persuasion* is a riveting saga that will keep you turning page after page."

ANE MULLIGAN, president, *Novel Rocket*

❖❘ PRICE OF PRIVILEGE ❘❖

PRICE

of

Privilege

Tyndale House Publishers, Inc., Carol Stream, Illinois

JESSICA
DOTTA

Visit Tyndale online at www.tyndale.com.

Visit Jessica Dotta's website at www.jessicadotta.com.

TYNDALE and Tyndale's quill logo are registered trademarks of Tyndale House Publishers, Inc.

Price of Privilege

The author is represented by Chip MacGregor of MacGregor Literary Inc., 2373 NW 185th Avenue, Suite 165, Hillsboro, OR 97124.

Scripture quotations are taken from the *Holy Bible*, King James Version.

Library of Congress Cataloging-in-Publication Data
Dotta, Jessica.
   Price of Privilege / Jessica Dotta.
     pages cm. — (Price of Privilege Trilogy ; #3)
     ISBN 978-1-4143-7557-1 (sc)
1. Heiresses—Fiction 2. Upper class—England—London—Fiction. 3. London (England)—History—19th century—Fiction. 4. Christian fiction. I. Title.
   PS3604.O87P75 2014
                                      813'.6—dc23

Printed in the United States of America

20   19   18   17   16   15   14
7   6   5   4   3   2   1

To my daughter, Emily, whose worth is beyond measure

One

HOW CURIOUS IT IS, at long last, to write about the trials. Long have they been guarded, the truth kept veiled.

At first, it wasn't proper to speak of them. When so much is lost, who can bear to trample over the little that remains? One afternoon, years afterwards, sadness overtook me, and as I stood in the cool shade beneath leafy bowers, I realized my opportunity to disclose the full truth had passed. Lives were tentatively healing, and to speak would have been disruptive. By that point, my name was so besmirched by lies, accusations, and assumptions, my only defense was to allow the remainder of my life to testify to my true character.

During that period, I faced the fullness of myself and glimpsed the substance of my soul. What a strange alloy it comprised—fear intertwined with hope, cowardice lumped with bravery, innocence amassed with sin.

It is no wonder in my case God demanded a crucible. We often fail to recognize our greatest godsend simply because it comes bundled in suffering.

Thus only now, as I prepare to chronicle those fateful

months, have I reopened memories long stuffed into boxes, stored in dusty closets of forgotten chambers. Each box opened contains something precious yet equally cruel. As I bring forth the last of these remembrances, the picture finally clears, and I am able to comprehend how stunning the events actually were.

What strange nonsense I must seem to write, the babblings of an old woman, a monied dowager at that. Yet have I ever used pity as my cloak? Was I not born despised and unwanted? Only a strange twist took me from being unheeded to being one of the most influential voices of the century.

Who could have predicted such an end?

Who could have foreseen the vast power and wealth that my name would one day accrue?

But I am off point.

I begin at the end of the story that most think they understand, though in truth, they know nothing about.

The first morning I awoke in Edward's arms, I stirred in my slumber, feeling a deep sensation of lament as if something had slipped through my fingers, though I could not place what. Shivering, I shifted position and pulled the blanket higher. The nap of homespun cloth scraped my skin.

My eyes opened. No London House sheets were these.

The very first sight that greeted me was a window framing the beginnings of dawn. Only the trunk of the nearest tree could be seen in the morning fog, its branches seemingly disappearing into the mist. A grey light, thin as gruel, seeped into the cramped chambers, recalling me to my surroundings.

My breath frosted the air as I thrilled with gratitude. Of course! This was Edward's church and today was Henry and Elizabeth's wedding! I shifted onto my back and viewed the century-old slatted wood ceiling that had been resurrected as an addition to the sanctuary. The stark architecture was so unlike my father's lavish houses that I couldn't help but give a silent offering of thanks. It was as if I'd been drawn out from stormy waters and placed on the solid planking of a ship. Here, I would become myself again.

Last night, I scarcely dared to sleep, fearing that I'd wake and discover this all a dream. But now, the acceptance that this was actually true prevented all chance of returning to slumber. I turned on my stomach and propped myself on my elbows to hungrily take in every detail of our home.

To call that space a chamber was a decided compliment, yet I adored every inch of it. How much better I understood the nap of wool over the gloss of satin.

A single table served also as a desk, evidenced by the books, Bible, inkwell, and parchment laid out in orderly stacks. There were only two chairs—one shoved beneath the desk, the other in the corner where it doubled as a valet, holding Edward's extra folded clothing. Next to it, a single fireplace with a rough-hewn wood mantel provided both the kitchen and heating source. I gave the cast iron pot hanging from the crossbar a dubious look. Surely Edward wouldn't expect me to cook. I frowned, pulling the blanket over my chilled shoulder. In the past, I'd kept Sarah company while she dressed poultry, but I'd never heeded her work. And nearly six months with Pierrick, my father's world-renowned chef, hadn't extended my skills beyond choosing the proper sauce and embellishment. That knowledge hardly constituted what Edward needed in a wife.

Edward stirred, emptying the pocket of warmth trapped between us. His cold nose nuzzled through my thick hair. Sleep rusted his voice. "Awake already, Juls?"

Instead of answering, I snuggled tighter against him, savoring his warmth.

He planted a sleepy kiss on the back of my head, then slung an arm across me to pull me close. "The girls will be here soon to decorate, and I doubt our news has circulated. Besides, it's getting late. We should rise."

I squeezed my eyes shut. Clearly we needed to discuss what

constituted "late." I hitched the blanket higher. "You forget, we told Mrs. Windham we were married last night. I warrant the entire village knows by now."

"What? And risk that our news might upstage Henry and Elizabeth's wedding? Surely not!"

Smiling, I opened my eyes. "Don't you think hiding it is more of a hazard? Someone else might catch wind and spread the news first. Trust me, everyone knows."

"All right." Edward jostled the bed as he repositioned himself. "What do I get when I win?"

"*When* you win?" I turned and settled on my back, then viewed the tousled silhouette of Edward. He studied me as he propped on one elbow. Even in the semidarkness, the love in his eyes created quiescence within me. They say the ancients believed peace was a rare gift bestowed on mortals they favored. In that moment, I understood the belief. My cup couldn't have been fuller. I stretched, giving him a mischievous look.

Teasing filled his eyes. "Hmmm. How about a fair share of the blanket?"

I gave a mock pout. "That's your best demand?"

"Aye." He traced the outline of my face as he leaned forward to kiss me, but then merriment crinkled his eyes, and from my peripheral vision, I noted that his right hand inched toward the edge of the blanket.

I tilted up toward his kiss, but just before our lips met, I shrieked with laughter and yanked the blanket hard, then rolled over and cocooned myself in wool.

Edward roared with laughter. "Why, you little—" The straw in the mattress shifted as he pinioned me between his knees and searched for a seam. "That's it. As your husband, I'm taking full charge of the blanket and its distribution."

Icy air stabbed my skin as his hand found an inlet. I gave a squeal, prepared to defend my sole right to the bedclothes. "Edward! Stop! Don't you dare! It's positively freezing!"

"Trust me, I know." He continued to unwrap me, as I in turn struggled to make it more difficult. "I'm beginning to suspect," he cried, "that you, Mrs. Edward Auburn, are a cover thief! And there's only one proper punishment for thieves!"

I could scarcely breathe from laughing but still managed to keep myself enveloped by twisting every time he got the advantage. "And what . . . is that?"

He stopped wresting, triumph filling his eyes. "A thorough dunking in the horse trough."

I gave a gasp of horror as he hefted me up in the blanket and tossed me over his shoulder.

For a startled second, all I could see was my hair cascading toward the floor, where I feared it might be long enough to mingle with the crushed leaves and clods of dirt. When he started toward the chapel, however, I tried to kick free. "You wouldn't!"

"Oh, wouldn't I?"

"I'll scream," I threatened as he headed straight down the center aisle of the sanctuary.

Edward laughed, ready to answer, but then he stiffened, turned, and rushed back.

Twisting, I did my best to rise up far enough to see what had alarmed him.

Outdoors, Henry sat upon his steed. Frowning, he squinted at the row of arched windows. Though it was too dark for Henry to see inside, I had little doubt he'd heard our commotion and was debating his best course of action.

"Henry," I shouted with all my might, knowing Edward's predicament was far worse than mine, for he hadn't a stitch on, whereas I wore the blanket. "Help! Come and stop your brother from committing an evil crime!"

"Oh, you're in trouble now," Edward promised, doubling his pace as he slunk back to our chamber.

I was still laughing as he dumped me on the straw mattress and then crouched to find his trousers. The floorboards creaked as he shoved one foot through them and then the other. "Don't think I'm going to forget that!" He grinned as he pulled the shirt over his head and shoved fistfuls of it into his trousers.

My stomach ached as it hadn't in years. "That's what you get for threatening your wife."

He chuckled as he hastened back out into the sanctuary. Henry must have dismounted while Edward dressed, for in less than a minute, the brothers' voices filled the chapel.

I lay catching my breath, unable to believe that the day our foursome had dreamed about for so long was finally here. A few hours hence, Elizabeth would become my sister. After their wedding, nothing could ever separate the four of us again.

The thought gave wings to my feet. I wanted to be dressed to begin the day.

Though it was May, cold streamed up through the wooden floorboards as I planted my feet and stood. I viewed the clothing we'd carelessly discarded last night. It was impossible not to smile as I recalled our ardor, the frantic kisses, the manner in which we'd clung to each other after months of separation, and how we'd finally gone to sleep entwined together.

Henry's voice crested, recalling me to task.

I scooped up the quilted muslin underdress, slid it over my head, added drawers, then turned to my stay. With dismay I gathered the broken pieces. The previous evening as Edward undressed me layer by layer, he'd fought so much with the cording that he eventually just pulled it completely out. One aglet had snapped off the end.

I fingered the frayed cording, wondering if I could dip it in wax and fashion it to fit through the tiny ivory eyelets. I frowned, knowing that even if I managed, I'd still have to estimate how much cording to pull through the first two eyeholes. Tightening a stay by oneself was frustrating, but to start it with uneven lacing was nigh impossible.

"I'm leaving, Juls," Henry's voice carried from the sanctuary behind me. "Will you be all right?"

"Yes, I'm fine!" I called over my shoulder. "I'll see you at the wedding!"

"Don't let Ed give you any trouble."

My laughter rang through our cramped space, sounding louder than I intended. "Oh, I promise. If anything, I plan to be the handful!"

Henry rewarded me with a hearty laugh before the slap of his boots faded out of hearing.

Edward's bare feet scarcely made a sound as he approached. "We're lucky it was only Henry. Some of the girls are en route and haven't heard the felicitous news yet. He rode out to warn us, just in case."

I grinned at the imagery of Edward's female parishioners finding him frolicking au naturel with the scandalous daughter of William Elliston slung over his shoulder.

"That's humorous?"

"I'm sorry, but yes. Can't you picture their expressions had they walked into the church and seen that?"

Edward must have envisioned it too, for his eyes creased with silent mirth. Then, seeing me struggle with my stay, he wagged his fingers in a request for it.

A flush of embarrassment heightened the color of his cheeks as he realized his mistake, but presently he dimpled. "I'm sorry, Juls. I had no idea what I was doing last night."

I gave him a saucy look, rubbing the chill from my arms. "Well, thank goodness for that. I rather preferred it to finding you experienced."

He chuckled, then glanced at the empty grate. "I should have risen earlier and started the fire for you first, too." He looked at the mangled stay in his hands. "I fear I'm not much good at playing lady's maid."

I looked over the pile of my clothing, imagining how Nancy

would have made a point to grumble about our mess, and then I
gasped, stunned I hadn't thought of it beforehand.

"Nancy!" I cried. The idea caught like kindling as I clutched
Edward's sleeves. I could have danced a jig or spun in circles.
"Oh, my word! We've got to hire her! We've got to! With any luck,
she can cook too!"

"Nancy!" He shot me a look of surprise before he frowned.

Somehow that wasn't the response I expected. "I need a
maid-of-all-work, and she's skilled as an abigail. Besides, if it
wasn't for her, I never would have escaped Macy that night. Oh,
please! We must!"

Edward's eyes were his most expressive feature. His brow
furrowed, raising alarm. I pressed my nails into my palms to
keep from arguing until he'd at least answered me.

After a long while, he gave a thoughtful nod. "We can certainly offer for her to join us, but she may not wish to leave
the comforts of Am Meer. A vicarage is poor placement for a
servant." He gave me a look I couldn't quite interpret. "In all
honesty, Juls, were it anyone but you, I wouldn't dare to wed,
knowing that I'd only be pauperizing my wife. I doubt Nancy will
want part in this adventure."

I frowned, disagreeing with his assessment. My outlook was
certainly happier. I envisioned Nancy teaching me to cook and
launder clothing. Together we could tend the garden and collect
eggs. I imagined us chatting while we cleaned house. How could
she not want that?

Looking back across years of experience, I am amazed at
the fine line Edward walked that morning—joining me in my
exuberance while maintaining a deeper knowledge of reality.
For in my pipe dream, my hands weren't cracked and bleeding from hard work, nor was I frazzled with one child on hip,
another buried in skirt, hindering me as I tried to round up the
extra hours necessary to meet the demanding needs of a poor
household.

I studied Edward a moment, sensing that our views on the future were dissimilar, though I couldn't pinpoint where. To be frank, it unleashed an emotion I couldn't name. The feeling of loss from my dreams returned and crouched on the edge of my cognizance. I shook my head, desperately needing to distance myself from the sensation. "You're wrong. Of course she'll want to be with us." I picked up my petticoat. "She will. You'll see."

Ed gave a friendly nod, though it was apparent he retained his doubts. "Well, you know her best. But since we're on the topic of servants, I've something too. Henry tells me Father is about to demote Jameson. I want to offer him a place with us."

"Jameson!" Shock rippled through me. Though I'd never met Lord Auburn's valet, we were practically on visiting terms. He was part of our foursome's legacy. The energies that poor man must have expended trying to keep Henry and Edward in line—a task in which no one could have excelled—were unfathomable.

"Your father is demoting him?" I hooked my petticoat as Edward approached with my mended stay. "To what?"

"Second gardener."

I gasped at the insult. "Why?"

Displeasure tinged Edward's features as he stepped behind me. "He's well past age, and Father has no need of a second butler."

"But to make him a groundskeeper, when he's served indoors his whole life!"

"Yes, well, it'd be even less swank to make him a footman. He'd further embarrass Father by having his advanced age seen by company."

I wasn't sure how to take the news, for I still retained my childlike fear of the valet. I glanced over my shoulder. "Can we afford him and Nancy?"

With a look, Edward communicated our dire financial situation as he finished lacing me.

"What about Henry and Elizabeth? Can they take him?"

"Not likely. Father is furious over Henry's refusal to give up Elizabeth. He accepted the marriage on the condition that Henry finally buckle down and help with the estate. They're going to live at the manor, and Father has final say on estate matters, including servants."

Sympathy for Elizabeth swelled as I stooped and retrieved my massive dress from Quill's. My fingers rummaged through the billows, looking for the bodice opening. Though it was one of the simpler gowns my father purchased, still it was voluminous. Eventually, however, I located the slit. "So you wanted to hire Jameson as . . . ?"

"My own personal valet. He's . . . well, he's slipping; his hand quakes occasionally, so some of the duties I'll still do myself." Edward ran his palm over his cheek as if envisioning a sharpened razor in Jameson's hands.

I wrinkled my nose as I looked at the chair piled with his threadbare attire.

Edward understood my point. "I know, but it would gut him to take any other position, and I want him with us."

I stepped into my petticoats. "All right, one elderly valet for you. One cheeky redheaded girl for me."

"Yes." Edward's voice was muffled by the layers of my dress as he lowered it over my head. "And no extra income with which to pay them. They're going to adore working for us."

"Is my father not giving us an allowance, then?"

Edward's fingers froze as he buttoned the back of my dress. "He tried."

I lifted my hair, allowing him a better view of his work, trying to ignore the hollow sensation growing in my stomach. I had no need to inquire further. Clearly my father had set conditions, and Edward wasn't going to place any member of his family under Lord Pierson's authoritarian rule again.

All at once, joy that I had tied my fate to this man flared

within me—for in some ways, my time in London was far crueler than my childhood. The inability to bridge the gap to my father's affections was like dying from starvation and smelling the waft of food, but being unable to locate the meal. I placed my hands over my bodice, trying not to care that our relationship was even further strained. It angered me that my father believed I had purposefully used Forrester's newspaper to betray him.

Without warning, my mind flashed with Isaac Dalry's pulverized expression as he discovered the article. The same sickening emotion I felt every time I remembered Lord Dalry egressed through me.

Edward noted my silence but misunderstood it. "Believe me, we're better off managing expenses on our own."

I nodded once, knowing how deep Edward's animosity toward Isaac ran. Wanting to move back toward lighter topics, I made my voice smile. "Shall I order Nancy to marry Jameson, then? We could offer their salary as a couple."

Edward's laugh filled me with genuine warmth. "What? And hazard her tongue when she discovers she's to wed someone her grandfather's age?"

I spun. "Surely he's not that old!"

Edward shrugged. "He's nearer seventy than sixty."

"Oh no, that will never do." I sat on the bed and pulled on my stockings, happy that our banter had been restored. "Let's arrange for her to fall in love with one of your father's footmen. That might be handy."

"Shocking, Mrs. Auburn!" Pride filled Edward's voice as he used my new title for the second time. "Do you mean to tell me you're going to allow your staff to wed?"

"Oh yes!" I gave him my most mischievous look. "I want everyone to be as deliriously happy as we are."

Edward grinned as he donned his black waistcoat and started on its pewter buttons. "What sort of chap do you have in mind for her?"

"Tall and strong. A good-looking one, mind you. At least as handsome as yourself."

Edward took up his clerical collar and moved toward a small mirror. "Men such as myself are rather in shortage. Would she mind a much plainer one?"

I laughed and threw the nearest pillow at him. "In that case, let's focus instead on finding Jameson a wife. That should prove easier, at least. We'll just order him to marry—" I froze midsentence.

"Well, do tell," Edward continued as he buttoned his collar in place, unaware of the transformation happening in me. "I'm certain Jameson will be delighted to learn he's headed for wedded bliss. Who is the lucky bride?"

"Sarah," I whispered. "Oh, Edward. We must find Sarah, too!"

Forgetting that I could see his mirror image, Edward drew his brow together as if a hundredweight stone had been placed upon him. It was plain he wondered how on earth we'd manage such a large household, but he nodded.

I raced on tiptoes to him, threw my arms about his neck, and kissed his cheek. Sarah, like Jameson, was family. "We'll eat nothing but gruel if necessary, and they can sleep on pews."

He acknowledged my thanks, then took up a pocketknife, which he slid into his frock coat. "So that makes three servants, plus your father's groom, horse, and carriage, which are still under our care. There's no gruel, but as far as sleeping arrangements go, there at least I can offer our motley party better than church benches."

I arched a brow.

He retrieved a small ring with two rusty keys, which he dangled in the air. "There's Henry's wedding present to us."

For a second, I wasn't certain I'd heard him correctly.

Edward glanced out the window. "If we hurry, I could show it to you before the wedding."

"A house? But that's not—" I wanted to state that it was an impossibility, especially as Henry and Elizabeth were being forced to live at Auburn Manor. Yet all at once I remembered our garden walk at Eastbourne, where Edward had told me about Henry's early inheritance of land and the empty house he had given us.

"We have a house?" I whispered slowly.

"We have a home," Edward gently corrected. "Our home."

Only Edward could understand how that word represented the purest and most concentrated essence of belonging. I drew in a measured breath, willing myself not to cry. Like a passenger trapped inside a runaway carriage, I had spent the past year of my life in constant upheaval. I'd discovered that Mama's suicide was murder and I'd betrothed myself to the murderer. I'd learned the man who raised me wasn't my father. Overnight, still reeling from the pain of those discoveries, I'd gone from being the rejected daughter of William Elliston to the celebrated heiress of Lord Pierson. The finality of having a house—a home to grow a family and put it all behind me—nearly undid me.

Edward, thankfully, pretended not to notice that I struggled to remain self-possessed. I've since heard stories of his early pastoring days, and I can say that a truer shepherd never existed.

"Ready?" he asked.

I nodded, knowing that if I spoke, I'd cry. For the first time in my life, I was about to go home.

Two

EDWARD TOOK THE first footpath that veered into the shadowed woods. As we ducked beneath the evergreen boughs, I half closed my eyes and breathed deeply. No balm on earth compared to the healing power found there. The very woods were hallowed. Well did I recall the idle hours spent fashioning boats from birch bark, poking branches down dank foxholes, and gathering armfuls of lacy flowers with thick, syrupy smells.

I tightened my fingers around Edward's, recognizing the antechamber through which we'd been received into our woods. I rose on tiptoes, recalling the time we'd played Robin Hood on that very spot. Edward must have remembered too, but he only watched as I drank in our surroundings, imbibing their peace.

I eyed the columns of sun that slanted through the scattering branches, dispelling the vapor that hung over the carpet of pine needles. The wholesome smell of decaying pine blended with the dark, rich scent of moss. I held back happy tears, unable to believe I'd returned. The summers of our childhood were the only truth about me that hadn't yet been dismantled.

"The path might be overgrown." Edward tugged our joined hands, indicating we needed to resume our walk. "Most use the main road nowadays, and I've been gone awhile. Allow me to lead so we can avoid needlessly tearing your dress."

I nodded, eyeing the sanctum we were leaving behind. I could have spent hours there alone, basking in the peaceful solitude. Already London was becoming a distant and unhappy memory. Whether Edward felt similarly or not was impossible to tell. His face wore a vacant expression as he carefully cleared branches from our path, uprooting as little as possible.

Our dirt path wended through the heart of the woods, where trees towered over ferns like the arcade columns of a cathedral. I paused often, lifting my face in praise, amazed that I ever thought Eastbourne beautiful.

Each section of the forest was equally glorious. Moss-capped stones congregated around bubbling brooks that as children we rested beside, soaking our feet. Each step released incense—the bracing scent of balsam, the richness of dark loam, or the perfume of bluebells. Though my shoes were created to dance over polished marble floors and not root-twisted paths, I navigated with a deft step I'd rarely accomplished in the city.

Far too soon, we broke from the path and emerged on a sloping hill, where we startled grazing sheep. Their bleating reached my ears as they ran in panic from our sudden appearance.

Edward watched them flee with a shake of his head. "Can you tell me where we are, Juls?"

Ignoring the gusts of wind, I studied the breathtaking view that stretched in every direction. The grass, which I felt certain would reach our waists a few months hence, rippled in the wind like waves. As far as the eye could see, slopes of gold and green blended with borders of hawthorn and gorse. The sky was dazzling, cerulean and dotted with fleecy clouds that served to deepen the bright green of the land.

"No," I finally said but privately concluded we were on

Auburn land. As children we kept a wide berth, lest we be discovered.

Edward shielded his eyes, gazing with contentment upon the scene. "All those nights in London when the temperature dropped too low to risk slumbering, I'd sit huddled with others around their fires and picture this very spot."

I swallowed, recalling the fires that had dotted the streets as Isaac and I drove to our various engagements. Images of beggars bundled in rags, stretching raw fingers over flames, surfaced. More than once as our carriage rumbled by, I'd felt a stirring of compassion, but never had I imagined Edward sitting amongst them.

I paled, recalling how bitter those nights had been. I'd heard my father comment to one of his cronies that it was the coldest winter on record.

"Don't you dare grow sad on me." The sun warmed Edward's face as he faced me. "Dreaming of this place, of this moment, is half of what kept me alive. And I didn't envision you looking so morose."

Wind stirred strands of my hair, which I tucked behind my ear. "Why this spot?"

His smile broadened with anticipation, even as he indicated with his eyes for me to turn about. "Guess!"

I turned and London was forgotten. At the top of the hill a grey stone house sat nestled amongst a tangle of trees. It looked as if it had been spun from the substance of one of Sarah's faerie tales. Large stone walls extended behind it, enclosing a secret garden. Over the tops, budding branches of fruit trees begged to be pruned. Clouds amassed behind the gothic structure and were mirrored in its arched windows. In the scenery stretching behind it, sheep and grazing cows sprawled in every direction.

"Windhaven," Edward said. "It's been vacant for years, though I've maintained it, as Henry promised it to me the day I asked for your hand."

For a moment I was too stunned to speak. My shawl agitated in the wind as I just stared. It didn't seem possible that Henry would gift us something this extraordinary. It was extravagant, for nothing could have suited Edward and me better. It was isolated, yet a walking distance from Am Meer and the village.

My hair streamed about me like dark ribbons as I gave Edward an astonished look.

He drank in my wonderment with satisfaction, then withdrew the keys from his pocket and started toward the front door. I followed, taking care not to stumble on the slabs of stone that once served as its walkway. Everywhere I looked, I saw the future I'd dreamed of. The stone walls were in better condition than Am Meer's, and within two winters I'd have climbing roses falling in thick droves over the posts by the gate—pink, heady roses, to soften the grey.

I eyed the yard, picturing laundry lines of starched aprons, petticoats, and Edward's shirts hanging to dry above feeding hens. I viewed the side of the house and imagined strawberry beds and, when those berries were ripe, hosting parties with glowing paper lanterns that would make it look like a faerie gathering at the top of this hill.

Edward unlocked the door and opened it, inviting me to explore the interior of Windhaven when ready. As I picked my way along the overgrown walk, I glanced at the gnarled apple tree branches and imagined Nancy and myself making cider and pies. Surely, I reasoned, we could prune the branches in time for autumn fruit.

A gust of wind caught my skirt as I crossed the threshold and stood, allowing my eyes to adjust.

"Granted," Edward said, "we'll have to occupy the church until we've cleared the cobwebs. We haven't much furniture to begin with—any, really, but I warrant Abe Duncan would make us some chairs or benches if we asked."

I was too enraptured to discuss practical matters. Instead,

I marveled at my future home. A mixture of umber beams and posts stood against grey stone walls, giving the house a primitive look but with a French feel. The source of its name became evident as Edward shut the door. The structure was so well crafted that despite the blasts of wind, there wasn't a whistle.

I walked along the central hall, amazed at the layout of the chambers. Mullioned windows graced every room, promising afternoon teas with sunshine and full view of the pastures. In the back of the house, the kitchen was so low that I doubted Edward could stand upright. Yet its ceiling was the perfect height for Nancy and me. A huge arched fireplace awaited future kettles of soup and pans of fresh bread. A built-in hutch spanned the length of one wall, boasting space enough for platters and dishes to feed a large party.

"Does it please you?" Edward's voice broke my reveries of the future.

I spun, knowing that tears shone in my eyes. "You realize I shall burn every meal."

He dimpled. "As long as I'm not eating it."

I could not banter back. For the first time in months, I had a vision for my life—one with hope. Those who have never had their reality crumble cannot imagine the upheaval it wreaks on a soul. But here, here was recovery.

Edward ducked and entered the kitchen, misunderstanding my sudden tears. "I'm sorry, Juls. I swear, I'll eat everything you make."

I flung myself into his open arms and savored the kiss he planted on the top of my head, then wiped my eyes with the back of my hand. Not wanting to be looked at, I laughed to lighten the mood. "How long until we need to go to Am Meer?"

As he carried no pocket watch, Edward faced the window to gauge the time by the sun. Before he could answer, a hollow sound like a tin cup falling to the floor echoed from the next chamber.

I clutched Edward's sleeve with both hands, giving him a panic-stricken look.

He placed a finger over his mouth. Gingerly as a cat, he crept nearer the door and looked up the small set of stairs.

Like a pond slowly freezing, tingles of cold crept through my fingers and toes as I recalled Forrester's prediction that anyone I wed wouldn't last a month. I think on some level I knew then what was coming. My mouth dried as cognizance that even here I wasn't safe from Macy arose from where it rested beneath my consciousness.

A scratching noise sounded next.

"Announce yourself!" Edward's tone raised the hair along the backs of my arms. He fisted his hands in the air like a boxer. "I'm armed and will shoot."

I wanted to reach out and pull Edward away, but stood paralyzed, unable to catch my breath. The noise ceased, increasing the eeriness.

Flattening his back against the wall, Edward carefully started up the stairs, but before he managed the first step, the distinct sound of a dog's extended whine broke the tension.

White paws appeared at the top of the stairs. In excited submission, the dog rolled on its side, half-exposing its stomach, yet wagging its tail so enthusiastically it knocked the timbers of the floorboards.

"Why, it's a dog. I imagine it—" Edward stopped. I must have looked as shaken as I felt, for his face softened. "It's all right, Juls. There's no one here."

To my amazement, the scruffy dog crawled down the stairs in a strange dance. He tried to expose his belly while inching along the steps. The result was a sliding, twisting, writhing approach.

Edward's entire body relaxed as he laughed.

No other permission was needed. In two bounds the dog leaped toward Edward, who squatted in response. "Where did you come from, boy?" Edward asked as the dog squirmed with enthusiasm. "Did you follow us here?"

I stood with my hands crisscrossed over my stomach, which felt as if it'd been plunged into ice. "How did it get inside?" I demanded. "We shut the door. We did! How did it open?"

Edward frowned but stood and wiped his hands over his frock coat, looking down the dark hall. Strands of the dog's white wiry hair clung to the wool. "I don't know. I'll go check. Stay, boy."

My voice was too strained to speak, so I shook my head.

He didn't look at me, however, and left before I managed to protest. For the count of fifteen, I held my breath to ensure I could track Edward's footfalls. The dog lay sphinxlike at my feet, ears hitched, likewise tracking Edward's progress.

Within a minute Edward reappeared.

"I must not have latched it properly." He spread his hands apologetically. "We're safe."

I gave a nod, though I didn't agree with his assessment. He lacked full knowledge of our situation. Once more I debated whether now was the proper moment to confess that I'd black-mailed Macy—that Edward needed to expect retribution and that Macy had said something cryptic about still planning to collect me.

"Good boy," Edward coached as he knelt and scratched the terrier's ears; then, as the dog rolled over, he rubbed a brown patch of fur on its angled chest. "What do you think, Juls? Should we add him to our household too?"

For a second, fear vanished. The very idea that Edward, my husband and lord, awaited my opinion was dazzling. I drew in a breath, astounded at how good it felt.

I knelt next to him, resisting the dog's attempts to lick my face. I rubbed my hands over him, allowing tufts of fur to collect at the base of my fingers. I'd all but forgotten Edward's child-hood desire for a dog. I wasn't sure this was the right one. "Do you suppose he'd be protective? I mean, would he give us warning if there was an intruder?"

Edward scratched the top of the dog's head. "I suppose."

The dog entreated me with liquid brown eyes as if knowing its fate rested on me.

"Can it be taught to . . . to attack someone?"

Edward angled his head and studied me a second before taking a stab. "Macy isn't going to bother us, Juls. Forrester has him contained."

I gave a bitter laugh. "Yes, well, a truer idiot never lived. If it depends on him, we're all dead."

Edward's mouth pursed in clear disapproval. "Your father trusts him. Besides, someone is aiding Forrester, so he's not alone in his efforts."

I lifted guilty eyes. Right before me was the best opportunity to enlighten Edward. Since we'd knelt before the altar two mornings prior, I hadn't yet managed to tell him the most bone-chilling news in my repertoire. We'd travelled nonstop to arrive in time for Henry and Elizabeth's wedding. Much of the time in the carriage, Edward slept, having scarcely recovered from an illness. Thereafter, there was so much to catch up on that we'd only started exchanging our stories.

"Yes, well," I began, curling my fingers around the dog's fur, "about that . . ."

"May we speak on this later?" Edward cut me short, rising as he eyed the window behind me. His voice was tight. "We'll practically need to run to be on time as it is."

I gave him a sharp look, but he avoided eye contact, likely enough because he suspected Isaac was the person helping Forrester. Already we'd discovered that we held opposing opinions of Lord Dalry. Vehemently opposing opinions.

In less than a day, Isaac was a dead topic.

Not fully understanding at the time, I agreed to wait to discuss the matter, deciding I'd rather not cast a pall over the wedding.

At least here, I have no regret. Nothing I could have confessed to Edward in that moment would have changed the chain of events that followed. Long before the magistrates trundled up the stairs of London House and jangled the bell that sounded our death knell, the consequences of our union were unfolding. Already the clock of our happiness was winding down. Speaking sooner only would have destroyed those last happy minutes.

I gave one last look to the kitchen that turned out to be as hollow as its promises. I longed for the future hour when Nancy and I would break from work, pull chairs to its magnificent stone hearth, and take out our knitting for an hour or so, allowing the wind to howl to its content.

I didn't want to leave. It was as if I knew that by stepping foot outside those walls, our dream would shatter.

Three

※

ONCE MORE WE cut through our faerie woods. My thoughts strayed far as I harvested an assortment of wildflowers. I pondered how to broach the subject of my blackmail attempt and the resulting danger. Had I known I was experiencing the last lovely snippets of country life, I'd have stood longer, admiring the jewel-strung spiderweb that glittered with dew, or taken the time to marvel at the way sunlight danced in patches between the trees. As it was, a stone of worry settled in my stomach, making it difficult to appreciate small wonders.

Edward, thankfully, felt no such oppression. For the stretch of that walk, he reverted back to his boyhood as he played fetch with our new companion.

My outlook brightened, however, as we neared the fields flanking Am Meer. Everything I'd dreamed about since childhood was about to be sealed with Henry and Elizabeth's upcoming nuptials. I picked up my heavy skirts, made all the more cumbersome by mud coating the hem. But no fatigue could outlast me. I was steps away from seeing Elizabeth and Mrs. Windham again.

Edward ran his fingers through his curls as we stepped onto Am Meer's pebbly lane. "I'm going to look outlandish during the ceremony."

Unable to offer comfort, I gave him a look of sympathy. Unfortunately his hair did resemble a bird's nest. And to the best of my memory, I was fairly certain Mrs. Windham didn't stock men's hair wax.

"At least Henry will understand." Edward pulled out a twig and examined it before tossing it aside. "But who knows what everyone else will think."

"They'll think you've been hiding me in the woods all this time." I spread wide my skirts, showing the thorns and burs stuck to them.

Edward frowned, sticking his hands in his pockets. "Yes. We still haven't decided how to explain us yet, have we?"

I sighed, already hating this conversation. We'd yet to agree on a conclusion. Simply put, there was no acceptable explanation. The parish knew Julia Elliston had married Mr. Macy and that their vicar, Edward, unexplainably stole and hid me after the ceremony.

The only thing in our favor was that Mama had refused to visit Am Meer for three years. I'd visited alone six months ago, but thankfully an incessant rain kept everyone indoors and few had seen me. With any luck, no one yet had connected that the bitter girl they'd once known was the famed Emerald Heiress who'd been pictured on the front page of Forrester's paper only days ago.

"Let's give no explanation," I said, feeling cross.

"What? And feign deafness when asked?"

"No." I lifted my skirts higher to kick a half-rotted walnut still in its hull. "We'll stick out our tongues and tell them it's none of their business."

I have no memory of Edward's answer, but what I do remember is that the rotted walnut husk sailed through the air farther than anticipated and split apart. Curious whether the nut inside was still whole, I kept my eyes downcast until I'd reached the spot, then turned the nut about with my foot. To my disappointment, it was wormy and shrunken. I gave it one more kick before taking in the landscape surrounding me.

I dropped my skirts, unable to stop gaping.

During my absence Am Meer had altered for the worse.

It was nothing like the homey cottage I'd visited only months prior. I covered my mouth, unable to believe the scene before me. Tangles of ivy encroached over the stone walls, where they invaded the ground and throttled the thorny stalks of the climbing roses. The thatched roof bore patches of moss, and entire tufts of straw were blackish. Soot charred the brick chimney, whose gingerbread-house design I had always adored. I turned toward the gardens, which were equally disharmonious. Plants had broken rank, privates daring to mingle with brigadiers. There was no order anywhere; all manner of beds were clumped and clustered together.

I swallowed hard, unable to imagine how anything could alter so greatly in less than a year.

The scene was a beehive of activity too. Harry, the manservant, was busy setting up chairs around long tables that had been placed in the herb garden. I wrinkled my nose, assuming Mrs. Windham was planning to serve the wedding breakfast outdoors. The hall boy, Caleb, raced barefoot with a stick, trying to chase geese from the area. Next to the table, a brown cow lowed and tugged against a stake, making a racket. I nearly groaned with embarrassment. Couldn't Mrs. Windham see how positively ill-bred it was to keep kine within sight of the table? Even my father's groom had been pulled into the operation. I recognized his telltale velvet coat as he tied ribbons to tree branches.

Shouts drew my attention to the right side of the cottage, where Hannah mopped her red face with her apron as she yelled orders to a young girl dumping slop in the pigsty. What on earth possessed them to move the pigpen so near the house? It made no sense. Surely in the summer heat the stench would—

Memory awoke of a childhood game Elizabeth and I had played one day. We'd made a contest of pitching decayed apples into the pigsty from an upper window. Points were awarded for the cores that landed closest to the sleeping sow. Other memories—the sly looks of disapproval that Mama cast Sarah during our visits, the manner in which Mama would hastily run her handkerchief over a chair before sitting—rose as well.

Tingles raced the length of my spine. Am Meer hadn't changed.

I had.

We are called to cast aside all in our holy pursuit—mother, father, sisters, brothers, houses, occupations. I did likewise in pursuing my own dream. Since leaving this parish, I'd done everything in my power to ensure this very day would come. I'd spurned Isaac, blackmailed Macy, and squandered all hope of a relationship with my father. Never once had I considered that, after achieving my childhood dream, I might find I'd outgrown it.

I wrapped my shawl tightly against me, feeling misplaced and uncertain about everything. Had I not stood on this very ground last night and thought Am Meer beloved?

Edward gained my side, but he only squinted toward the cottage. "What on earth is he doing here?"

Alarm rose through me as I looked in the direction Edward had indicated.

Someone, a male to be exact, jogged down the lane. Though it should have been evident we noted him, he took off his cap and waved it wildly above his head, revealing shockingly red hair.

I laughed, both relieved he had nothing to do with Macy and grateful for the distraction. I'd met Mr. Addams only twice in my life, but already I held him in high esteem. I slid my arm through Edward's, then rose on tiptoes, willing to be cheered by one of my newer friends.

Mr. Addams waited until he was closer, then grinned. "See! All's well that ends well. Were I less polite, I might take this opportunity to say I told you so. You should have eloped months ago." He gave a spirited laugh. "I don't know whether to congratulate the pair of you or prepare for another crisis."

"Well met, my friend." I stepped forward, offering my hand. "It's good to see you."

"Devon." Edward's tone was far from welcoming. "Why are you here? I supposed you with Henry."

"Yes, well, it's very pleasant to see you, too. Hope you've had a nice journey and all that." Mr. Addams gave Edward a good-natured bow. "I *am* with Henry, only he's disappeared minutes ago in his quest to find you."

"Find me? Why? What happened?"

I nudged Edward's rib cage as a reminder to mind his manners. His body was stiff, making me wonder if he'd even registered my touch.

"What? You think I carry influence over Henry? I haven't a clue what's happening. He refused my confidences, though there was a good row at your house this morning." Mr. Addams balled his fist in his hat as if expanding its crown. "And he was ruddy set on finding you afterwards."

This news clearly angered Edward. His voice took on a tone of cold fury. "He told them! He actually told them when I expressly said not to." Then to Mr. Addams, "Where is he?"

Not following what was happening, I questioned Edward with a look.

Mr. Addams pointed toward the trees bordering Am Meer. "He went in there, looking for some oak—"

"The ancient oak," Edward murmured, shaking his arm from mine. He stalked in its direction.

Mr. Addams gave a low whistle, then chuckled. "Now there's a classic conversation with Edward Auburn for you. And to think you could have married Lord Dalry."

I made a wry face, uncertain how to take either of his statements. His evaluation of Edward alarmed and his mention of
Isaac hurt. "I didn't want Lord Dalry," I snapped back, feeling
testy. "Do you mean to tell me Edward always acts surly with
you?"

"Me?" Mr. Addams laughed in earnest. "Oh no! I at least am
able to draw conversation from him, which is better than most. I
take it you've never been on the stingy end of his temperament?"

"Once," I said absentmindedly, for Henry had emerged
from the trees and now headed toward his brother. "When Ed
thought I had broken our engagement and hired Lady Foxmore
to find me a husband. He wasn't happy then."

Mr. Addams roared with laughter, though I hadn't intended
to be humorous. "Yes, I imagine that would have managed the
trick."

Henry and Edward met with near animosity. Heads bent,
they began a heated discussion. A harrowing uncertainty filled
me as I watched.

"What do you suppose?" Mr. Addams asked quietly.

I wasn't sure I wanted to know what catastrophe warranted
the groom and the best man tearing through the countryside
looking for the vicar less than two hours before the wedding.
I glanced at the cottage, glad the turn in the lane would keep
Elizabeth from viewing the brothers. Every muscle in Edward's
body was taut. Their muffled tones carried notes of anger, but it
was Edward who looked truly dangerous.

Dread coiled through me as I picked up my skirts and
sprinted toward them. The first words I made out were
Edward's. "Do not," his strained voice choked out. "Do not ask
that of us, Henry!"

"Be reasonable," Henry pleaded, then, noting my arrival,
greeted me with a slight nod.

"I am the reasonable one!"

"Ed, please!" Henry attempted to touch his brother's arm.

Edward's face grew feral as he threw it off. "Touch me again, and we both leave now! So help me, Henry, I mean it."

Behind me, I heard Mr. Addams's footsteps stop some distance away.

Henry held up his hands. "Be fair. We sent the curate home last night. Please try to understand this."

"I understand." Edward's voice was tight. "You would have me deny my own flesh, my own wife."

Henry's nostrils flared as he threw his hands up in exasperation.

Eyes wide, I approached. "What's happening?"

"Yes, tell her, Henry." Edward's tone was antagonistic. "If this is nothing but a bit of char work that someone must do, let's see if you're beastly enough to voice it."

A slight hitch in Henry's breathing as he stared at Edward was the only indicant his anger was beginning to match his brother's. Of the two, he was more likely to remember to size up his opponent before tackling him.

"Henry," I pleaded, sensing this argument was far different from their others. "Whatever it is, it's all right. Just tell me." Then, glancing at Edward, "I swear, it doesn't matter."

"It matters," Edward countered.

"Why don't we allow her to decide." Henry angled himself forward.

"Because you know as well as I do why she'll concede." Edward's granite voice wedged between us. "This is my last warning that I'll not tolerate this."

Henry's chest heaved as he glared.

A sheet of cold rained over my body. Until that hour, I believed our foursome unbreakable, but I now saw it was a soap bubble, quivering, ready to burst at the slightest touch. The thought spurred me to action.

"It's all right," I whispered to Edward, stepping between him and Henry. With cool fingers, I reached up and touched one side of Edward's face, wooing him to look at me. Borrowing Isaac's polished expression and tone, I met his angry gaze, willing every bone in my body to communicate that I was genteel—as noble as Isaac, a lady in my own right, capable, calm, other-worldly. That whatever had him this out of sorts regarding me was unnecessary.

To my astonishment, it mellowed Edward immediately, and just as Lady Beatrice had once shrunk from Isaac's gaze, Edward drew a ragged breath and backed down from his protective stance. His face knit in grief as he moved several steps away, eschewing further eye contact. He gave us his back, where I felt certain he struggled to compose himself.

I willed my movements to remain cultured as I turned and fixed my tranquil gaze on Henry. I took care to appear serene and devoid of emotion. But in truth, fear and anguish undulated through me, further enhanced by the realization that if I could appear this unaffected while emotions raged within, what roiling turmoil might have been concealed beneath Isaac's mask?

Had I transformed into Queen Mab, Henry could not have looked more staggered. His eyes grew round, but before he could speak, I placed a finger over my lips, warning him to wait until Edward had recovered.

Henry, however, always refused instructions. "I'm sorry, Juls, but here's the short of it. I told my parents this morning about you and Ed, you know, to prepare them in advance. Only it didn't go as planned."

"Have any of your schemes?" Edward demanded.

"My parents somehow knew that your father was Lord Pierson and want to distance themselves from all knowledge about you," Henry continued, ignoring him. "And if you're in attendance at the wedding, my parents refuse to come."

And Edward won't participate in anything where I've been shunned, I mentally finished.

Edward faced us again. "Tell the whole truth. It's not only

today. They refuse to ever meet you. Today sets the precedent, and by allowing them to shun her, you're accepting it! You're taking their side!"

I struggled to maintain a placid expression. Not trusting my voice to manage the ruse, I focused on Henry, wearing the bland yet patient expression I'd seen time and again on Isaac's face. It was the one that invited the other person to expound.

"I know it's rotten." Henry's voice was low. "But if my parents refuse to be there, it means there'll be no father at the wedding."

An odd but familiar anguish crossed my soul. My throat thickened as I tried to manage the distress that his words stirred. What Henry was asking was painful but made sense. Lord Auburn was the only father Elizabeth would ever know. Like as not, she'd expressed her excitement to Henry about their relationship, and he now felt it was his duty to ensure it blossomed.

As penance to Isaac, I played his part to the hilt, allowing no emotion to ripple over my features, yet there was unending heartache within. Was it only months ago I'd practiced curtsying before a mirror, envisioning that my new position as Lord Pierson's daughter would gain Lord Auburn's approval? To keep from showing unhappiness, I clasped my hands and squeezed until my fingers smarted. Apparently I was destined never to love stepfather, father, nor father-in-law.

"Please?" Henry laid his gloved hand on my shoulder. "For me?"

I crumpled inside, knowing I had no real choice. No one could force Lord Auburn to accept me. How could I not be the one to forbear?

To plead that this event was more precious to me than they could guess—that outside of our foursome I had no family— would make me sound gluttonous. After all, my own actions brought about these horrible circumstances.

Yet I ached in an unexplored region of my soul, whose pang

kept expanding with no terminus in view. I'd given another piece of my heart to something that couldn't support it. If at the first test, the first crossroad, Henry had chosen to distance his association with me, what else loomed on the horizon?

All at once, I felt weary and chilled.

"I wouldn't ask if it weren't for Elizabeth," Henry urged.

I tucked my arms tightly about me and glanced at Edward. He stood like a pillar of marble. The decision was solely mine.

My throat aching, I nodded. "I'll stay at the cottage this morning."

Henry exhaled a breath of relief and approached to kiss my forehead. "I'll make it up to you," he promised. "Make any demand! Shall I name my firstborn son Julian?"

I was expected to laugh or tease back by telling him to name his first girl Edwina instead, but I couldn't move or speak.

"I'll perform the ceremony—" Edward's voice was flint as he approached—"but tell our parents not to approach me. I am no longer their son. Because of this, I vow to never darken the door of Auburn Manor—"

"Edward," I managed in a choked whisper, looking over my shoulder.

"Oh, that's fine coming from you." It was Henry's turn to be antagonistic. "What happened to it being our duty to honor them? Or what about not making rash vows you cannot keep?"

"Rash or not," Edward said, his words harsh, "I assure you, Henry, I *will* keep this vow."

"So what? Does that mean you'll never call on me or Elizabeth either?"

Edward crossed his arms. "I didn't insist on this; you did."

"Don't." I turned and slid my arms around his waist. "Not today. If for no other reason, for Elizabeth's sake. She's had no say in this."

But Edward did not soften. He kept his stance and glared at Henry. The pair reminded me of two bristling dogs. Henry broke away first. Keeping his mouth jutted and his eyes locked on Edward's, he retreated a couple of steps backwards, then turned and marched silently down the carriage lane. "Come on, Dev."

Mr. Addams looked as though he wished to give comfort. His mouth opened and his face was sympathetic, but he only fingered his cap and tramped after Henry.

"Edward," I whispered, a plea for him to end this.

"No, Juls." Edward clamped his hands on my shoulders as the pair turned the corner to Am Meer. "He's allowed his choices, and I'm allowed mine."

I looked down the now-empty lane, half-tempted to believe this wasn't real. "And what about me? And what I want?"

"Visit Henry and Elizabeth if you wish. Try in vain to win my parents. I'll not stop you." Edward's voice was low. "But I'll not allow my wife to be insulted and continue on as if nothing happened."

I placed my hand over my heart, hurting. Desperately I tried to think of what Isaac would do. Nothing came to mind. People like Isaac didn't get themselves entangled in messes like this. Besides, it was one thing to act like him, quite another to be him.

Within minutes, Henry and Mr. Addams rode past us. Pockets of dust kicked up beneath the hooves of their steeds.

I turned with them as they passed. "What shall I tell Elizabeth?"

Edward sighed as he crammed his hands in his pockets, following Henry's dust line. "Whatever you choose. I'm sure you'll do fine."

I wished I could feel as certain. Thus far, my past decisions had borne consequences that kept rippling out beyond anything I could have imagined. Today they'd fractured our foursome and divided my new family.

Little could I have guessed that this was just the first swing of the splintering axe.

Four

OUR MOOD WAS somber as we again approached Am Meer.

Like two monks on a pilgrimage, we trekked toward our sacred city in silence. Who could bear speech? Our merry band, our Knights Templars, had dispersed. Henry, our fearless leader, had chosen life outside our circle. My nose stung with tears I would not shed. All I could think was that on the very day our foursome should have become unbreakable, we'd shattered. I swallowed, wondering if all dreams turned to dust the moment they were nearly realized. Or if I'd been born fated to bear this painful fetter of irony.

I marveled that my feet did not stumble beneath me. Like those returning from the Crusades in the days of yore, they carried my weight, one heavy step at a time. I felt crushed that Henry had asked me to recuse myself from his wedding. Yet logic would not rest. For by the same token, had I not once abandoned our foursome too? How dare I expect Henry to behave better than I had? Did I not deserve this?

And yet my mind vehemently argued back that Henry's request must have been offensive. For I felt anguished, as if I'd come to dust, and Edward had been so affronted, he'd cut ties with his family. His anger made me wonder if I'd been wrong to agree to be left out.

As we neared the cottage, I wrapped my shawl tightly, unable to resolve anything. Was I so blind that I needed Edward's anger to recognize I'd been treated unjustly? Or had Henry been within his rights?

I drew in a breath, realizing that most people didn't seem to suffer from this malady. As a rule, Elizabeth knew exactly what she desired. Similarly, Henry would have boldly declared what he thought, whether it was offensive or not.

My thoughts were so vast and frightening, I forced myself to focus much, much smaller. I started with the way the pebbles sounded as they crunched beneath Edward's boots, and then expanded to the birdcalls that varied between two and three notes. Eventually the sound of frantic barking pricked my consciousness.

I touched Edward's arm. "Is that our dog?"

His head jerked as he awoke from his own thoughts.

We found our canine was at the rabbit hutch, where Hannah had cornered him with a broom. He was just small enough to fit beneath the wooden frame, where he alternately barked at Hannah and bared teeth at Harry, who was attempting to grab his hind legs. To my utter dismay, a bloodied rabbit lay between his paws.

Edward doubled his gait and I followed.

Hannah turned at our approach. Our faces must have communicated all she needed to know. "This your dog?"

"It is." Edward's voice was iron.

She turned and gave the dog a hard jab with the bristles of her broom. "Go on," she ordered Harry. The dog barked harder with each shove of the broom. "Go change for the wedding. If it's the *vicar's* dog, we'll let the high-and-mighty *vicar* fix his own problem."

Puzzled by the animosity with which she referred to Edward, I cast him a questioning glance.

His face was livid. "Hannah!"

Her eyes flashed as she faced him.

"If you're angry at me," Edward roared, "hit *me* with the broom! What is the meaning of this?"

Harry held on to the corner of the rabbit hutch as he hoisted himself up. Clumps of mud clung to his knees and elbows. He gave Edward and me a nod, then anxiously glanced at Hannah to see if he was in trouble for it. She paid him no mind.

"Your dog killed one of our rabbits." Hannah's face was red as she jabbed the dog again—hard.

"Oh, Hannah, I'm so—" I began wringing my hands.

"What makes you so certain it's one of your rabbits?" Edward demanded.

Hannah swelled like a toad. "Are you daft? The evidence is right there, though it's too late to save it."

"Did you count them?" Edward yelled. "Because if you're beating an animal beneath my care, you better well have counted the rabbits inside the *locked* hutch before you began. Harry, count them. How many are supposed to be there?"

Harry clutched his cloth hat, looking between Edward and Hannah, saying nothing.

Breathing hard, Hannah turned her gaze to the rusted metal lock, which was fixed in place. The hares inside skittered back and forth, but Hannah seemed able to track them as she counted beneath her breath. Her mouth pursed as she lowered her broom and turned to Harry. "Go on with you. Change, then make sure the basket of corn to throw is at the church."

Edward placed a hand on his hip and glared as Harry remorsefully passed. "Hannah?"

But Hannah did not apologize as I expected. Instead, her eyes flashed as she took in the gold bands that had once belonged to Lady Josephine and my grandfather. "So it's true? The pair of you are calling yourselves married."

Edward was frightening to behold. "It is."

"Have you not an ounce of shame? Showing up with Mrs. Macy! Ruining your brother's wedding and Miss 'Lizabeth's!"

I'd lived so long with fear of discovery that I retreated a step backwards. Edward, however, reached out and pulled me to his side with a firm grasp. "Does Mrs. Windham know you've taken it upon yourself to accost her guests and their dogs?"

Hannah's lower lip pushed out as she gave a defiant scowl.

"I thought not!" Edward's voice went from stern to fierce. "Have the kindness to go inform the lady of the house we're here; then fetch Nancy. *My wife* and I desire a word with her."

"Nancy!" Hannah glowered in disbelief. "Aye, and I'll get you an audience with an Indian raja afterwards. I can't fetch Nancy. The girl's long gone."

"Gone?" My stomach hollowed. "Where?"

Hannah gave me her blackest look, shrugging one shoulder as if I were too low to be addressed.

Edward's jaw tightened. "As the vicar responsible for placing her here, I demand to know where Nancy's gone!"

"How should I know?"

Edward's nostrils flared. "Surely you sent references."

"References!" Hannah's hands tightened over the broom handle. "What would I do a thing like that for?"

"Because it was our explicit agreement."

"Agreement!" Hannah's chest puffed out. "Reverend Auburn, when you approached me about the girl, I warned you I didn't hold with taking in rabble from the workhouse. One chance. That was the agreement. And I warrant half of the inmates would have cut off their right thumbs for that opportunity. She knew that with the first shenanigan, I'd turn her out on her ear."

Reminded that Nancy worked at Am Meer because of Edward's efforts, I moved my gaze to him.

He, however, was too roused to notice me. "And what," he ground out, "what was the reason for dismissing her without references? You yourself said she worked twice as hard as any other maid."

"You know as well as I do what she did. She helped that one there flee her husband." Here she finally faced me and unleashed her fury. "And let me tell you, missy, he was fraught with worry. Thought you had been murdered, he had. Never seen a man more shook up." Tears choked her voice. "Had you witnessed it, 'twould have broke your heart." She patted her chest. "It certainly tore right through mine."

"He is not her husband," Edward said.

"And Nancy just sat there," Hannah continued over him, "as cool as you please, while he begged and pleaded for your where-abouts." A tear escaped and trickled down her cheek. "Never in my life have I been so moved. And this—" she gestured to Edward—"this is how you treat the man who cherishes you? By taking a lover."

Normally I would have steeled off emotion, but I'd ingested more than I could handle, which somehow translated into my losing that particular ability. I intended to meet her eye with a cold look that carried the message that I didn't care, but found I was unable to do more than skate over her face, feeling shamed.

As if aware I was drowning, Edward rested his warm hand on my shoulder in a show of support.

Hannah's gaze followed the motion before her face gnarled. "But it's you," she said to Edward, her voice dropped with hus-kiness, "'tis you, Reverend Auburn, that crushed us. We never expected better from her ilk. But you! Here we all believed you. But in the end, you were worse than the whole string of vicars before you. For you preached a kingdom worth finding, worth dying for, and then yanked it all back from us!"

Edward's fingers tightened over my shoulder as Hannah turned and stormed toward the kitchen entrance. Beneath the hutch, the dog hitched its ears and watched her retreat.

I stood stock-still, believing Hannah's words were a great blow to Edward. To my surprise, he only tramped to the rabbit hutch, where he bent and easily retrieved the rabbit carcass.

He jounced it in his hands as if weighing it. "Where do you suppose . . . ?"

Unable to believe he was unaffected, I asked, "Are you not hurt?"

"Hurt?" He frowned and stood, still holding the hare. "No, and don't you be either. Did you not notice she only attacked us after her own pride was wounded?" He turned the hare over and gently probed the bite marks. "Some do that, you know. It's their way of saving face." He gave a humorless laugh. "I would become a useless vicar, though, if I allowed such people to rule my opinion of myself."

I said nothing, the idea too new to form an opinion on.

Edward tried to pocket the hare, though half of it refused to fit. His brows furrowed. "By george, I'm beginning to wish we had stuck out our tongues. Between Henry and Hannah, I've had all I'm tolerating today."

"I hate her." I blinked back tears.

"Hate? Oh no, let's not put that much effort into her." Edward worked to cram the rabbit into his pocket better. "Let's put that passion to use instead." Edward took my elbow and directed me toward the front entrance. "I vote we elevate her to head of the Women's Mission Society. By the time she's finished her first year, I warrant she'll have accomplished more than all her predecessors combined. Besides, she'll answer to you, as vicar's wife."

I smiled, but it was halfhearted.

"Are you all right?" he asked.

I eyed the peeling blue paint of Am Meer's front door, longing to say I felt unglued, unable to trust my own emotions, but an inner instinct warned me not to yet speak of it. So I nodded that I was fine, adding that discussion to our list of matters still waiting to be addressed.

Having reached the front door, Edward opened it. "Ready to encounter Mrs. Windham next?"

I raised an eyebrow at the carcass protruding from his pocket. Wondering what on earth he planned to do with it, I stepped over the threshold, doing my best to keep my swishing skirts from touching it.

Edward followed, ordering the dog to stay. To my surprise, it plopped to the ground immediately.

The interior of Am Meer at least felt like a homecoming. Water stains from two centuries prior still decorated a corner of the stone-and-plaster walls. A hodgepodge of walking canes and umbrellas poked out of the oak barrel behind the door. An assortment of capes, bonnets, and shawls filled the tarnished coat hooks, making it near impossible to pass without knocking some garment to the floor.

"Hullo?" Edward called.

"Edward?" Mrs. Windham's voice carried from the drawing room. A moment later, she rounded the corner, eyes and cheeks aglow. She wore her signature ruffled lace lappets, which flapped about her face. Arms spread, she tottered down the hall. "And Julia, too!"

"Did Hannah not inform you of our arrival?" Edward leaned forward as she tilted up to kiss his cheek.

"No, she said nothing!" Mrs. Windham released Edward and moved to me.

"Edith?" A weary voice called from the drawing room. "Whom are you speaking to now? Surely your housekeeper can attend to it."

"You'll never guess, Millicent," she shouted over her shoulder. "Word of Elizabeth's gown has already reached the village! The vicar and his bride have arrived to view it for themselves!"

"Actually," Edward interjected, "I hoped we might get a bite to eat before the wedding, and Julia needs to change her clothing. Are her trunks still on the carriage?"

Mrs. Windham ignored him but frowned at me before she spat on her handkerchief and scrubbed my cheek. "You must come and meet my sister and her husband," she whispered. "Only stand straight and tall, for she said we here in the country slouch. For heaven's sake, Julia, is this sap over your chin?"

"Your sister is here?" I glanced down the hall with a growing interest. Mrs. Windham's sister lived at a distance, and because Am Meer had a limited number of bedchambers, we'd never crossed paths.

"Why do you linger in the hall?" the woman intoned from the drawing room. "Bring them here and introduce us."

"Coming!" Mrs. Windham's voice was singsong as she grabbed our hands and pulled us toward the drawing room.

En route, she muttered, "She's spent the entire morning trying to apprise me of this season's fashion. Had you but seen the way she abused Elizabeth's dress to me, you would have been most offended. The very idea that motifs are *out*! I hope you positively refuse to act polite or put on airs for her."

"Outside of our posture," Edward amended.

"Yes, yes, whatever you do, you mustn't slouch."

"Out of curiosity," Edward asked, "did she actually see Elizabeth's dress before she told you motifs were out?"

I shot him a look telling him to behave.

"No indeed, she did not!" Mrs. Windham's expression soured as her fingers tightened on my arm. "I have not an idea how she knew to insult it."

Edward shot me a look of amusement, which I didn't return.

Outside the drawing room, Mrs. Windham paused long enough to signal for us to stand taller. Then, placing a smile on her face, she opened the door. "This," she cried with what I imagined she thought was elegance, "this is Henry's dear, dear brother!"

Edward clenched his jaw as she pulled him forward first, but then gave the chamber a stiff bow. I rose on tiptoes, trying to catch a glimpse of Mrs. Windham's sister and brother-in-law, but they sat near the windows on the far right.

"Such an interest he takes in his parishioners, too!" Mrs. Windham shoved him a step farther into the chamber and with her free hand groped blindly about for me. "Walking miles just to glimpse the bride's gown before the ceremony! And wait until you see the gown, Edward! The waist alone boasts of over a hundred pleats and each sleeve has been smocked in two places, below *and* above the elbow."

"If you ask me," the woman said, "he would do better to attend to his own appearance than tramp about the countryside worrying about Elizabeth's."

Mrs. Windham turned, revealing her profile as she blinked in earnest at Edward for the first time. Her hand stilled its search for me. Edward tried to tame his curls, which from the back looked even more like a battlefield. As he lifted his arms, the dead rabbit popped an inch or two farther from his pocket. Mrs. Windham's eyes filled with tears as she gave him a reproachful look for such a betrayal.

"I beg your pardon." Edward ran his fingers through his tangles. "But my wife is still in the hall. If you both please, may we introduce her and not leave her standing alone? Also, is there any chance there is a bit of breakfast left over?"

Mrs. Windham turned a sour face in my direction. "Oh, for heaven's sake, Julia." She reached out and pulled me toward her, stopping only to quickly shake my skirts as if to ascertain I wasn't likewise hiding rabbit carcasses. "It's rude to linger on the edges of conversation." Then, smiling to her sister, "You must not mind her. It is her mother's fault. She simply refused to correct the girl."

I gritted my teeth, suddenly reminded of what life at Am Meer was truly like.

Mrs. Windham dug her fingers into my arm, giving me a silent command to impress. "Mrs. Auburn, may I present my sister and brother-in-law, Mr. and Mrs. Smih."

A middle-aged couple sat at the gateleg table, which had been opened to its fullest extent. Mr. Smih scarcely glanced up as he concentrated on a game of peg solitaire. He could have been any country squire who was advanced in years and fat. Wispy hair framed a balding head. His red nose was bulbous and pocked. A stiff collar managed to contain his double chin, while his best frock coat stretched its might and main to reach across his stomach.

I deemed Mrs. Smih decades younger than her husband, but only years younger than Mrs. Windham, though I decided not to test that theory aloud. She sat straight as she studied me. Her hair showed little grey beneath its straw poke bonnet. Like Mrs. Windham, she favored ruffles of lace about her face and throat. Double ribbons of ivory and pale blue from her bonnet, tied beneath her chin, matched her dress and its trim.

"Hmmm," she concluded. "Already *our* vicar shows his maturity over yours. For *his* wife is the height of elegance and shows great aplomb everywhere she visits. Whatever can yours mean by lingering in halls and attending a wedding in a dirty ball gown?" The skin over her nose wrinkled as she considered Edward. "And what sort of vicar poaches on the way to perform a ceremony?"

"A hungry one," Edward complained.

"No, no, Sister!" Mrs. Windham held out her hands. "This isn't the gown she's wearing today! This is what she arrived in last night! The one she plans to wear today we have yet to see."

"Arrived only last night, did you say?" She swung her gaze back to me. "Did you leave in the middle of a ball, Mrs. Auburn?"

"No," I replied, strangely delighted by the use of my new name, for I found this woman comical, not insulting. She acted as lofty as Lady Beatrice, only without any credentials. "As a matter of fact, ma'am, I travelled from my own wedding."

"Your wedding?" She gave a disbelieving cough. "I daresay that must have been some affair." She looked at her sister. "What indecency to come to Elizabeth's wedding, still in her bridal attire, so she can put on airs."

Unable to stop myself, I spread my skirts and glanced at them. Her point became clear. In London the quality of my travel gown was intended to communicate that I was an heiress. In that parish, even mud-coated, I might as well have been wearing lavish evening attire.

"I tell you, Millicent, that is not the dress she's wearing."

"How could that not be the dress?" Mrs. Smih slapped the arm of her chair with her palm. "Look at it! Think you that she has anything better in her trunks?"

Mrs. Windham frowned at my skirts. "Julia, hurry; go and change! Your attire offends as much as Edward's hair."

"Yes, well, on that note—" Edward joined my side and gathered my arm—"if you'll excuse us both. Would you be so kind as to tell us where Julia's trunks have been stashed? And have you by any chance any hair wax?"

"As a matter of fact, I do!" Mrs. Windham squared her shoulders as she enunciated her words. "When *Lord Isaac Dalry* paid us an *extended* visit, he left a tin, which I am certain you are more than welcome to!"

I stiffened, unable to believe she'd revealed that connection.

Mrs. Smih rolled her eyes. "I tell you again, Edith, I don't care who that young man claimed he was, it was not Lord Dalry. I saw him with my own eyes not that long ago while I was in London. Now there is one of the most fashionable young gentlemen in all the empire."

"And *I* saw him a great deal while he was here," Mrs. Windham retorted. "He said that my crumpets were better than the Duchess of Kensington's, and he would know, too!"

"And you believed him? The man duped you by using false compliments."

Mrs. Windham turned toward Edward. "Wait here. I'll have Lord Dalry's own tin of hair wax fetched."

"Thank you, but no." Edward's voice was cold. "I prefer to be under no obligation to him, now or ever."

"As her vicar, you should not humor her mad fancy!" Mrs. Smih clutched the fur-trimmed bertha near her throat. "As long as we're making up things, why not claim that Lord Melbourne came for tea too?"

I glanced at Edward, feeling perspiration bead over my forehead, but he looked too angry to be nervous.

"Well, I'm not giving you a choice!" Mrs. Windham addressed Edward. "I forbid you to look as such during the wedding." She waved her lace at the rabbit. "And you'll get rid of that thing before the ceremony, too!"

"I say." Mr. Smih finally looked up from his game and squinted at Edward. "What are you planning on doing with that hare, anyway?"

"Eating it," Edward snapped, then walked to the door and jerked it open. "Raw!"

"You'd get a jolly stomachache if you tried." Mr. Smih moved his next peg. "How long has it been dead, anyhow? Hey, where do you imagine you're going?"

Edward ushered me out the door, looking wild with exasperation. Before he exited, he declared, "I'm going to pump water over my head, if you must know."

He shut the door with a bang and pinched his eyes.

Behind the door, their conversation continued. "Who was that chap, anyhow?" Mr. Smih asked.

"Upon my word, Edith!" Mrs. Smih managed. "That is Henry's brother? So ill-tempered. What on earth upset him?"

"He's no *Lord Isaac Dalry*, I'll grant you that," Mrs. Windham said.

At that, Edward lifted his head, looking ready to attack the door. Gritting his teeth, he moved us farther down the hall. Near the entrance, he pressed his palms to his forehead. "Is it just me, or is everyone acting abominably rude and out of character today?"

I shrugged. "Outside of Henry, I detect no difference."

Edward's features sharpened with something akin to pity as he studied me. Thankfully he cast off whatever his thoughts were, for I hated pity worse than anything else. He shook his head and mumbled, "I'm not sure I can handle a full day of this." Then to me, "Think you can fend off this wolf pack by yourself for a couple of hours?"

I crossed my arms and hugged them tightly to me. "Yes, I'm fine. This is Am Meer, after all. Not Eastbourne."

"All right, then I'm going to the church so I can change into my surplice and review matters with the parish clerk." His stomach growled. "Do you suppose we might get something to eat in the kitchen?"

I winced. "If we go through Hannah."

He made a noise of disgust. "No. I'll wait until the wedding breakfast. As far as that goes, it's intolerable enough that you're forced to miss the ceremony. If my parents wish to avoid you, let them not attend the reception. What will you do in the meantime?"

I glanced toward the staircase that led to Elizabeth and wet my lips.

There was still one more person who could add perspective on how to feel about Henry's request. "I'll go help Elizabeth dress. Hopefully her maid isn't as angry as Hannah."

He kissed my forehead. "Even if she is, don't allow her to bully you from the chamber. This might be your only chance to see smocking above *and* below the elbow."

My laugh was genuine. "A valet and now this! I always knew secretly you were a fop."

He displayed his threadbare elbows with a grin. "I'll see you soon."

I kept a smile pasted on my face as I tipped up and kissed his cheek. Nevertheless, I now wished we weren't about to separate, for Macy's last words to me arose in my mind:

"To spare your feelings," he'd promised, *"I'm telling you this in advance. There is no longer an easy transition back to me. . . . I fear you shan't enjoy being dangled, but know this: no matter how bad it becomes, when you're returned to me, you shall find me as doting as ever."*

As Edward turned to leave, I splayed a hand over my stomach, knowing that now was not the time to inform Edward that Macy technically never relinquished his claim on me.

It was only for a few hours of separation, and there was little sense in sending Edward off to his brother's wedding feeling the same sickening sensation that I did.

Five

❧

I LEANED AGAINST the cool plaster wall, drawing a fortifying breath as I listened to the happy cadence of Elizabeth's and Betsy's voices. Elsewhere, the occasional snatch of Mrs. Windham's peacock voice blended with Hannah's shouts. I shut my eyes. Am Meer had never seemed more squalid, nor our foursome more fractured. The idea that I might also find Elizabeth changed was so loathsome, I almost couldn't knock.

Abruptly, I decided to have this over with. I squared my shoulders and gave the door a sound rap.

The sound of trunks being scraped against the floor was followed by marbles or coins spilling and rolling everywhere. Though I couldn't distinguish what Elizabeth and Betsy were saying, their voices became hushed and hurried.

A moment later, Betsy stuck her head out the door like a frightened turtle coming out of its shell. "Why, 'tis only Miss Julia!"

"Oh, thank heavens!" Elizabeth held the corner of her vanity, where she bent, panting. Laughing in Betsy's direction, she added, "Take care you call her Mrs. Auburn now. The new vicar's wife stands before you!"

Betsy looked uncertain how to take this communication. Her cheeks filled with color as she gave me a bewildered curtsy. Avoiding calling me anything, she scurried to one of the trunks and resumed packing.

As Elizabeth wended her way through the maze of trunks, I clasped my hands over my heart. No bride ever looked bonnier.

Face flushed with excitement, her eyes shone with a rare happiness, making her all the more winsome. Elizabeth wore pale green—a bold choice, despising the superstition attached to that color. Her hair looked as though she'd stepped right out of Camelot. Thick braids wound about her head, and each tendril that escaped glinted with her unique reddish hue. Sprigs of rosemary and lily of the valley were tucked into the braids, making a gorgeous woodland crown.

"Can you believe today is finally here?" She flung herself into my arms, bringing with her the sanative fragrance from her headdress.

I leaned forward to avoid brushing the dirt on my gown against hers. Being in her presence was like eating hearty soup with wholesome bread after weeks of nothing except truffles and delicacies.

"I fear to touch you," I whispered. "You look so lovely. Your gown, it's beautiful!"

She grabbed my hands and crushed them.

I squeezed back, tapping into her delight. What did it matter whether Lord Auburn approved of me? Did I not have a lifetime to win him? And how many times had Edward and Henry fought? What was one more? So long as Elizabeth and I maintained, we'd mend this together.

"Sisters!" Elizabeth bounced on her toes. "We're to be sisters!"

Betsy frowned from where she sorted through a trunk. "What you're going to be is late."

"Fie!" Elizabeth waved her to silence. "Everything is basically packed and ready to go to Auburn Manor."

"Not the bonnet you tore apart." Betsy knelt before one of the trunks and, huffing, wrapped Elizabeth's knickknackeries in paper.

"Shh!" Elizabeth waved her to silence; then, winking at me, she lifted the lid of a nearby trunk and pulled out a deplumed bonnet. "I despised my going-away bonnet, so I'm changing it before Mama or Aunt Millicent can do a thing about it."

"They're going to have a fit," Betsy declared. "They were up until the wee hours remaking it. I'll end up in the workhouse like—" She abruptly stopped and glanced at me.

Surely Nancy hadn't been forced into a place as bad as that. I desired to ask but knew such inquiries would only dampen the wedding.

"Well, they won't know," Elizabeth rejoined, examining her untrimmed bonnet, "until it's secured to my head, ready to quit Am Meer forever. You can tell Mama I threatened to prick your feet with pins. Julia will back your story, won't you, dearest?" She grinned in my direction. "You should have seen the monstrosity. Green scaly ribbons coiled about it like a Gorgon's head. Making it even more frightful was that every inch was aquiver with ostrich feathers. I would have frightened the youngest children, making me the most gossiped-about member of the Auburn family."

I felt my eyebrows hitch as I wondered if it was reasonable to feel slighted by her statement.

"I daresay it would have become a local legend," Betsy affirmed with a stout nod.

"I tore it apart this morning," Elizabeth said, setting it on her vanity, "much to Betsy's dismay. I was planning to add that fat gauzy ribbon there so it would tie beneath the chin just so. But now I fear I should use the safer velvet one. What do you think, dearest? That's the dress there."

I looked over the maze of trunks. The room was stripped of Elizabeth's belongings, her clothing emptied from its pegs

JESSICA DOTTA   51

and drawers. My heart felt crushed as I realized the truth of her words. She really was quitting Am Meer forever. No wonder the cottage wore a mantle of desolation. It mourned the loss of Elizabeth. How on earth would life manage here without her calming hand?

"It's the green one there." Elizabeth pointed anew when I failed to note her dress.

I obliged her and looked. The dress was an intermix of moss-green velvet and *peau de soie* that were skillfully tucked and sewn in layers with ruffled ribbons. Still the dress failed to arrest my attention. Below it, resting on a chair, were four bouquets of lilies wrapped in a silk ribbon whose color Miss Moray had declared out of season last year.

I exhaled slowly, wondering who would stand as Elizabeth's maid of honor in my stead. Suddenly I felt yet more displaced. I'd sojourned in a faraway land, and though I'd pilgrimaged home, everything and everyone had changed.

"Both ribbons have merits," Elizabeth continued, unaware of the heaviness of my thoughts. With her slim fingers, she lifted the two ribbons from their spools and faced me. "Which do you think?"

Remembering her preference, I touched the wide, gauzy one. "This one."

"Oh, I thought so too," Elizabeth exclaimed, her enthusiasm rising anew. "Only Matilda Bren trimmed her bonnet with a transparent ribbon last month, and I couldn't stand the idea of her thinking I'd imitated her, but now I can say you selected it. And you never even saw her bonnet!"

"Matilda Bren?" I repeated, remembering the bossy girl we'd always shunned. "My word, it's been ages since I thought of her."

Elizabeth rolled her eyes. "Lucky you! This winter, her older sister married someone titled, and you should see the airs she puts on about it. You would never guess her brother-in-law is sixty with gout. Not that the match is any benefit to her. Mama says if she doesn't marry this year, she'll remain a wallflower for certain."

Formerly I'd have laughed and inquired whether she'd managed to attract one dance partner yet. But I found I could not command my mouth to smile. I hugged myself, feeling inexpressible grief for her. What it must feel like to know everyone secretly deemed her an old maid. How difficult it must be to enter a room and, knowing her every move was being criticized, act merry enough to capture the attention of a gentleman.

"Perhaps," I suggested, rolling up the velvet ribbon, "she hasn't yet learned the skills needed to charm. Now that you're Lord Auburn's daughter-in-law, you might make some introductions for her."

"Me?" Elizabeth gaped. "Ha! Not likely! It's her own doing she's unhappy. She made her own bed by being so overbearing. Let her sleep alone in it."

I said nothing, wondering how many people felt similarly about me. After all, Macy's missing bride was being discussed at teas, dinner tables, card games, and gatherings all across Britain. Yet which of those souls actually knew anything about me?

"Perhaps," I pressed, "she just needs a little help."

Elizabeth's nose wrinkled as she tried on her bonnet and modeled it in the mirror. "And perhaps you're speaking of yourself. You're no Matilda Bren, trust me! There's no helping her sort and there's no use trying. I most certainly won't. Take a care! You're beginning to sound just like Edward did when he came back from university."

Her words stung more than they should have. It may be that she was correct and I was internalizing it too much. Feeling dejected, I gathered my skirts and took a seat on her bed, where I privately lamented Matilda's fate. I stared at the hearth, where, as children, Elizabeth and I had sat cross-legged in our nightgowns with our cups of chamomile tea. In how many of those conversations had we verbally torn apart Matilda? It seemed so callous now. Had we treated her kindly, added her to our foursome, would her life have turned out differently?

I pressed my hands against my temples. Or was I being as judgmental as Edward had been? It wasn't like me to feel a cool anger toward Elizabeth. Were I standing in a tipping rowboat, I could not have felt more unbalanced. Today had every essence of being a bad dream.

"Are you all right?" Elizabeth's hand fluttered to my shoulder.

I jerked at her unexpected touch, then rubbed my forehead. "Yes, I'm sorry, dearest. I don't know what is wrong with me."

Elizabeth removed her bonnet and set it aside. Her face grew tender as she addressed her maid. "Betsy, go heat water for Julia to wash with, then open her trunks to air them." She lowered her voice and addressed me. "When you were missing, Mr. Macy brought your things back in case you returned. He even paid Mama to keep them here, though she said it wasn't necessary."

That was news, but I said nothing, not wanting to remind Betsy that I was supposedly Macy's missing bride.

Betsy only frowned at the clock, but she stood and obeyed.

Elizabeth waited until her footsteps retreated, then sat next to me. "Henry told me about your life in London." She placed the backs of her cool fingers against my cheek. "I can see its ill effects. Was Lord Pierson very cruel?"

Caught off guard, tears filled my eyes. Who could answer a question like that? I pictured my father's gruff indifference and compared it against the ridiculous amounts of money he'd lavished on me. I took the debt I owed him for hiding me from Macy and weighed it against the memories of his sudden tempers and the way he domineered everyone.

As with Henry's request from this morning, I lacked the ability to judge the situation. My mind and emotions disagreed, frazzling me further.

"Well, a plague on him, then," Elizabeth said when she wearied of waiting for me to reach a conclusion. "We both can claim

Lord Auburn now. Henry says he's secretly thrilled at the prospect of grandchildren."

My body froze in place as I knew I'd reached the juncture
when I needed to tell her about Lord Auburn's edict.

"Think of it, Juls." Elizabeth clapped her hands. "We might
even carry together! Can you imagine the two of us too immense
to do more than send Mama into panic with pretend labor pains?
We'll make a game of seeing who can make her faint first."

Heat flamed over my cheeks, for never in my life had someone spoken so directly about being in that condition. "For
shame, Elizabeth!"

"Oh no, you don't!" She leaned nearer. "No becoming a
prude just when I need information the most! You're going to
tell me everything! Mama's speech this morning was simply
horrid. Full of wailful tears and instructions I fear to heed. I
wanted to crawl beneath the bed and die from embarrassment
for her." She shuddered. "Give me your opinion on the matter,
Juls. What do I need to know for my wedding night? Truly?"

I dipped my head, unable to look at her as I recalled the sul-
try touch of Edward's skin against my skin. Without permission,
my mind traced over the ebullient, though sometimes-painful,
sensations from last night. Knowing I was bright red, I shielded
my face. "Elizabeth, you forget I'm a woman of scandal. I feel all
the wrong things at the wrong times."

"All the more reason to beg succor," Elizabeth pleaded. "For I
can tell just by looking at you, I'd rather repeat your experience,
by far, than Mama's."

Shocked, I gawked at her. In the next second, peals of
laughter rang from Elizabeth's chamber. We were so jubilant, I
thought Mrs. Windham took the notion to heft herself up the
stairs, for heavy footsteps outside in the hall charged toward us.

Elizabeth covered her mouth as she swallowed back laughter.
I laced my fingers in hers, recalling how often Mrs. Windham
had caught Elizabeth and me giggling in the dead of night.

The door swung open, but instead of Mrs. Windham, Betsy entered. She dipped to Elizabeth, then turned toward me. "Your water is ready."

"Would you give us another moment alone?" I scooted toward the side of the bed, ready to stand.

Betsy pressed her mouth in a firm line, likely feeling desperate to complete her duty and oversee Elizabeth packed. But she had no choice but to obey. I waited until she was out of hearing, then again slipped my fingers through Elizabeth's. "Dearest, I'm not attending your wedding."

"What?" She withdrew slightly, releasing me.

"Henry asked me not to."

Elizabeth stood, her eyes narrowed with indignation. "Why would he make such a request?"

Keeping my voice monotone and low, I explained how Lord and Lady Auburn refused to come if I was there. As I spoke, Elizabeth's face softened and she nestled back into her seat beside me. By the time I finished, I felt exposed. Pained, I waited for her to speak, waited for her to shed light on what was normal to feel or think.

She blinked several times as if slowly digesting the information. Then, gathering my hands back in hers, she said, "But you will call on us, won't you? If you do, eventually Edward will come around too."

I did not speak or move. I wanted to believe she'd misunderstood that I'd been banned from her wedding. But reason corrected me. Elizabeth grasped it. Why else would she have sought to secure my future visits?

Part of me refused to accept that Elizabeth had understood. Had she commiserated, then asked whether I would still call on her, we would have held our own handfasting, where I would have solemnly sworn we would always be inseparable. But that she'd hurtled over my rejection so easily made me want to distance myself from her.

Though I do not recall my exact words, my response was noncommittal.

It contented Elizabeth, though. The next several minutes were taken up with her asking my opinion on which feathers to add to her bonnet. I numbly assisted, feeling like a fasting monk whose attendance was required at a banquet.

I left the chamber as quickly as possible and retreated to my bedchamber, where eventually the clop of horses announced the wedding carriage. I leaned against the bedpost as the cottage filled with frantic rushing. Eyes shut, I listened to cries of "The carriage has arrived!" "What about Mrs. Auburn?" "Oh, for heaven's sakes! Let her take her own carriage!" "Elizabeth, pet, you must hasten!" "No, no, not that wrap!" "Where's my bonnet?" "Have you remembered the bouquets?" Eventually the flurry of noises distilled to Hannah and Betsy opening and shutting cupboards before hurrying off to see Elizabeth wed.

～～

Cool water trickled through my fingers into the porcelain basin as I bathed my eyes. Beneath my window, chickens and geese fussed at each other. With tired fingers I hung the dampened towel back on the washstand, then stared at my image.

Faint shadows haunted my eyes, but nothing else hinted that I felt stretched past endurance. I turned away and faced the bedchamber, grateful for the solitude.

The trunk Mr. Macy left was easy enough to locate. It sat in the corner as if forgotten. The craftsmanship, however, was impressive. Instead of slats, ingrained polished wood moved in a checkerboard pattern of stately greys. The bands and clamps were burnished nickel, and the lock, complete with an inserted key, was enamelled with mother-of-pearl.

I knelt and touched the glossy wood. No rust spotted the lock, for it clicked open with the gentlest pressure of my thumb. Likewise, the leather straps unbuckled and the lid lifted easily.

My stomach flopped as the faint scent of sandalwood and cigars tickled my nose, surfacing memories better forgotten. Stacks of folded clothing awaited me. I eyed them, fascinated. Prior to becoming Lord Pierson's daughter, these were the best gowns I'd ever owned.

I dug through the dresses, delighted by their simplicity. No pearls were sewn into their trim, and their petticoats weren't quilted with intricate coats of arms.

They were simple and straightforward but lovely. On one, I touched the cold steel buttons, recalling how Nancy wrangled over the price. Beneath it was the gown she'd insisted be trimmed in blue velvet even though I fought for red satin. Rainwater perfume, which Nancy brewed to keep the clothing fresh, imbued the garments. I shut my eyes. Was it possible to be homesick for a soul?

Making a mental note to discuss with Edward the best way to find her again, I selected a grey woollen gown that I'd yet to wear. Ten minutes sufficed to find me clothed and my tangled hair brushed and restyled.

A wan fire burned in the drawing room, left over from that morning. Glad the simplicity of my dress allowed me freedom of movement, I perched on the raised stone hearth, then took in my surroundings, realizing the pleasures of being at Am Meer had truly vanished.

My former life was like a lovely golden painting that I used to live inside, but I'd tumbled out of the frame and forever lost my world. And while I might have been able to touch the painted man playing the fiddle, I was barred from hearing his merry tune. My eyes could perceive the warm reds and oranges of the painted firelight playing over the furniture, but I no longer felt its warmth.

The knowledge was like a cold wind numbing me, yet not cold enough to deaden pain. It left behind a dull ache, one that I didn't believe I'd ever be able to subdue.

How could I mourn? Was this not what I'd fought so hard to gain? Was I not back inside Am Meer? I placed my eyes in the heels of my hands. How could the dream turn out to be so hollow and barren?

Yet the fault didn't lie with the dream. The dream was real. Henry and Elizabeth most certainly still existed within that painting. The joy brushed over Elizabeth's features this morning was proof enough. The dream hadn't failed. It was me. I'd somehow managed to mangle even this. For a moment I scarcely could breathe, but then as I lifted my gaze, it fell on the spot where Edward had stood that morning months ago, crushing his hat as I learned he'd become a vicar.

How well I remembered his rigid stance and the intensity of his gaze. I drew in a breath, the worst of the emotion passing. Now that I considered it, he too had fallen out of the picture. He'd been living in this shattered reality longer than I had.

And during that time, had he belonged anywhere? He was no longer rich, yet not poor. No longer accepted, yet not shunned. I myself had witnessed how difficult it'd been for him to participate in the easy laughter of those around us.

Yes, I decided, feeling warmth bleed back into my toes and fingers. There was still Edward.

And with that comforting thought, I tucked my feet up on the ottoman and wrapped my arms about my knees, desperately wanting him to return. At least when we were together, the loneliness was reduced from a raging tempest to a mere stirring that I could live with.

Eyes shut, I listened for the sound of wedding bells that would announce my banishment was ending, that Edward was marching back to the cottage. Having barely slept the night before, I shut my eyes, and like a rock being skipped over water, I skimmed in and out of consciousness. I was lulled so near sleep that I didn't register the sound of boots slapping down the flagstone hall until they were already at the door.

Six

"SHE'S SLEEPING. I already checked," a male voice said. "You're not to disturb her!"

"Poppycock," a second male voice retorted. "What vicar's wife sleeps while there's unfinished work in the parish? Block my path at peril to yourself."

"Sir, on Master Isaac's orders, I forbid you to open that door!"

I rose to my feet and positioned myself behind a nearby chair, feeling more curious than frightened. The first voice was most certainly Thomas, my father's groom, and the second, simply put, didn't sound frightening.

The door burst open and two men stumbled into the chamber. Thomas barely caught his balance, losing his powdered wig. The other was an elderly gentleman, wearing clothing that was outlandishly overlarge for him. Breathing heavily, he took one look at me before relief filled his eyes. "Oh, good! There you are."

I squared my shoulders and stared, astonished.

"Miss P—er, Mrs. Auburn." Thomas picked up his fallen wig from the floor and gave it a quick shake. "I beg your forgiveness. I don't know who this man is, but allow me to remove him from your presence."

"You'll have to grab hold of me first," the elderly man said, catching his breath. He pulled a handkerchief from the pocket of his frock coat and dabbed his forehead. Then, with a knobby finger, he indicated the perimeter of the chamber. "And I'm quite capable of running in circles for hours without tiring. You'd be much smarter to leave me to my business and go attend yours."

Thomas's wary expression bade me to stay put as he approached the stranger to apprehend him.

"Wait just a second," the man wheezed, holding up a finger. "Tell me, who is this Master Isaac? I might trump him."

"I highly doubt that." Thomas seized hold of the elderly man's arm.

"Then maybe I know him. If I do, I'll report you."

"Even if you could, he's not truly my master."

"Oh, how delightful!" the elderly man cried as Thomas started to drag him out the door. With a strength that surprised me, he caught the wooden door stile and managed to keep his head in the chamber. "In that case, I promised Master Barnabas that I would do the exact opposite of Master Isaac's wishes. And I win, because Barnabas comes before Isaac! We're going alphabetically, in full accordance with the rules of pitting imaginary masters one against another!"

A stunned silence followed.

"Well, come on. Save me!" the man pleaded with me. "He's far stronger than he looks."

"Wait!" I ordered, leaning forward for a better look.

I knew this game! Only I had never guessed that it originated outside of Edward and Henry. This had to be Jameson. There was no other explanation. He was playing one of our nonsensical games from childhood, ignoring that it made him appear foolish. I gave him a keen look and was delighted to find that his eyes twinkled.

Had Jameson approached me directly, I would have resented his intrusion. Had he carefully sidled his way to our acquaintance as if I were a piece of unfired porcelain, I would have despised the suggestion that I was weak. Had he ignored me, I'd have grown offended. But that Jameson wrapped his introduction in a game that only I would understand, not caring a whit what Thomas made of him, made me instantaneously approve. No, not just approve, but feel like laughing. Furthermore, he'd left the best answer for me!

"You both lose," I said, straightening. "I have my orders from Master Aaron. He says I have final say on all matters, forever, and can overthrow any rule you tack on after this."

"Ow!" Jameson let go of the wood to cover his heart, causing both men to stumble backwards. He shut his eyes as if he'd been shot. "Enslaved forever!"

It was a move I'd seen Edward mimic a hundred times before. I covered my mouth to hide a smile I could not suppress.

Jameson opened one eye and looked askance at the groom. "Quick, quick! Think of a name that alphabetically comes before Aaron."

The groom looked between us as if we were mad.

I couldn't help myself; I laughed aloud. Then asked, "Jameson?"

He removed his hat, stepped back through the door, and gave a sweeping bow. "We finally meet, O girl who has been the subject of over a thousand of my lectures."

"A thousand?" I repeated.

He bobbed his head. "At least. Since Edward was yea high, I've given him every fathomable reason why he can't marry you. It has been out of the question since the very beginning. Yet the notion formed in his head, seemingly out of nowhere—some working of your magic, I shouldn't wonder. The more I lectured him, the more headstrong he grew." He snapped his fingers, then wagged one of them at me. "Ha! Oh, now *that* was sneaky of you! You used your craft to turn my lectures against me! Then, this year, I finally won! Marriage to you became an outright impossibility. Yet here you are! Against reason. Against odds. I concede, O my most worthy foe." He gave me another deep bow. "For surely you are something elfin or faerie. Perhaps I am in the presence of a *Gwragedd Annwn*?"

Poor Thomas. Had we started speaking gibberish, he couldn't have looked more alarmed. His eyes darted between us as if he was waiting for my permission to handle Jameson while feeling uncertain about me too.

Jameson waited with merriment for my reply, and though I longed to respond just as fancifully, I feared looking foolish. I kept my reply on safe ground. "Did Edward send you? Is everything all right?"

"Yes, he sent me. And all is as right as rain." He stretched kinks from his lower back. "Well, excluding that our branch of the family no longer speaks to the rest of the tree . . . and that the congregation feels betrayed by Edward—oh, and also that her ladyship unexpectedly arrived to witness the ceremony." He pocketed his handkerchief. "But that's the risk one always takes when allowing a fair folk into their brood. Compared to the legends, I'd say we escaped with rather light consequences. I warrant they don't appreciate losing members of their court. No doubt you hold some influence over the hob king and begged him to go easy on us."

His manner was playful, but his words brought about stark dread—particularly the mention of Lady Foxmore.

I looked out the window in the general direction of the church, surmising more than he said. A valet generally would attend the wedding of the eldest son. There had to be a reason that Edward sent a servant he trusted.

Here, my sense of dread for Edward rose. While my ordeal from this morning had ended, his trial was just commencing. For how many months had he abandoned his parish to live on London streets to be near me? I could picture him standing before their hostile faces with an iron will of his own as he cut ties with his family.

"If I might make a suggestion." Jameson interrupted my thoughts and gestured to Thomas. "Why not have the carriage readied, just in case."

Alarm fluttered through me as I wondered if matters were so bad that we'd need a quick getaway.

"I don't think it's wise to leave Mrs. Auburn alone." Thomas stared pointedly at Jameson.

"Nonsense, I'll stay here the entire time." Jameson addressed me next. "Have you an apron? Let's hie to the kitchen."

"Apron?" I repeated, not able to connect how that would aid Edward.

"Yes! We have an entire wedding reception to prepare for. And I know for a fact that Hannah is short on hands."

Thomas's eyes bulged, for to him I was the Emerald Heiress, a Pierson. It was unthinkable that I'd don an apron and work.

"Is the carriage ready?" I asked him.

He frowned. "Well, no, but—"

"Do as he says," I commanded before he could object. "I'll be fine."

Dissatisfaction spread over his features, though he struggled to hide it. "I promised Master Isaac," he pleaded in a whisper, "that I would protect you if anything outside of the ordinary happened."

I felt myself blanch. "I know what Lord Dalry feared," I said quietly, feeling subdued. "It wasn't Jameson. This is my husband's lifelong servant. He's trustworthy."

Thomas looked dubious.

Annoyed that my word didn't carry weight, I dismissed him

by giving him my back and only addressing Jameson. "If you'll follow me, I'll show you the kitchen."

෴

As we entered the kitchen, my stomach grumbled at the scent of butter, parsley, and roasted pigeons. I backed against the nearest wall, curious to see what Jameson planned. To my surprise, he marched straight to the wedding cake. It stood three layers high. Each layer had been cut and was filled with Hannah's signature strawberry jam and clotted cream. Candied flowers lay atop the rim of each layer.

"Now then," Jameson declared, taking a dollop of cream and jam from the bottom layer. He added a sugared nasturtium and popped his finger in his mouth. "Let's test the most important item and . . . see . . . if . . ." He faced me and smacked his mouth, then stuck out his tongue. "Ack, no! Too peppery!" With vigor, he plucked the crimson, orange, and red flowers from the cake. "We're going to leave only the candied violets."

I half expected Hannah to charge into the kitchen. "I don't know if you should do that."

"Better and better." He stepped back, dusting his hands as he inspected his handiwork. "I'll go move the cow out of the garden; you set the table. There's a large kitchen towel, there, to pin and use as a makeshift apron. I noted that Hannah weighted the tablecloth with rocks. The weight of the flowers will keep it in place and look better." He pointed to crocks filled with buttery-yellow narcissuses. Surveying the long trundle table laden with dishes, he instructed, "Looks like Hannah created three of each, so spread them out in thirds." He grinned. "Shall we race?"

"But you're only moving a cow," I protested.

"Go!" He dashed from the kitchen.

For a moment I stood disbelievingly. I stared at the stewed oysters and molded galantines, uncertain whether or not it was demeaning to my station. Then, with a skip of my heart, I realized I was a vicar's wife. This was the life I'd wedded into.

As inexperienced as I was, I tried to carry the majority of the jars at once. Water sloshed over the crocks, soaking my dress and adding the chore of refilling them. Next I realized I didn't know what to do with the rocks on the table. My duties had never required resourcefulness. I lifted the first stone and spun slowly in two circles, trying to figure out where it would be out of the way.

"Not fair!" Jameson cried from where he tugged on a rope, trying to get the cow to move. "No faerie magic! Now the geese have wandered into the garden, giving you an unfair advantage."

It was comical, as a gaggle had indeed entered and made a fuss at him, hissing and beating their wings. Jameson tethered the cow in a new spot and then started herding the geese from the garden.

When finished, he joined me in the kitchen. "I won!"

Grinning, I shook my head, pleased to find that this servant's humor was similar to Edward's. "Good," I replied, curiously already at ease with him. "Now you can help me set the table."

From there, my thoughts returned to my new husband as I picked up a platter of mayonnaise of fowl. Knowing he wasn't having as good a time as I was, I determined to pray for him. But that in itself presented a problem.

My religious training was scant, born of my own experiences and conclusions I'd drawn from Edward's notations in his Bible. Therefore no one had yet taught me how to pray. Thus, as I reset the hard-boiled eggs decorating the edge of the platter, I mentally composed and memorized a formal prayer that I intended to verbalize when I had time alone, as though it were a spell to be cast.

My stomach cramped for want of food as I directed my course back into the cottage. Yet I considered my hunger to my benefit. For prayer and fasting certainly accompanied each other in the Bible. Surely it would advance rather than hinder the process.

The tang of smoke stung my eyes as I lifted my skirts and stepped back into the heat of the kitchen.

To my surprise, Jameson had rearranged all of Hannah's garnishes. My mouth dropped, but before I could rebuke him, the merry sound of church bells rang over the country, announcing Henry and Elizabeth's vows were completed.

I bent my head, trying to picture them as they walked down the aisle, taking care to keep their eyes straight ahead lest they acknowledge anyone, lest they give offense. Mrs. Windham would leave the church next. How well I pictured the teary way she'd draw attention to herself as she clung to her sister's arm. I envisioned Edward dutifully standing, arms stiffly at his side, as he waited for the church to empty. Mr. Addams would leave last, after paying Edward. As far as I was concerned, that moment couldn't come soon enough.

Realizing I'd sunk deep into my thoughts, I wiped my hands over the tea towel pinned about my waist. When I turned, I found that Jameson was carefully considering me, forming his opinion.

Feeling the need to fill the silence, I spread my hands over the remaining food and said the first thing that came to mind. "We're never going to manage this before they arrive."

He grinned, losing the ken that filled his eyes only seconds before. "Why couldn't the boy fall in love with an ordinary fay, one who hides in pantry shadows and sweetens the honey, or something else of that ilk? No! He insists on wooing none other than one of the royalty. One who knows nothing about humans." He shook his head. "I am to be pitied amongst men, for it's my task to turn you into a vicar's wife, and there's no telling what happens to a soul when he angers one of your folk." He moved his hands like a costermonger, keeping his crowd enthralled. "Watch, O most virtuous queen." From their ledge behind the soapstone sink, he took down two large trays. "Since we lack thousands of wee folk to run each dish separately to the banquet table, we use these."

Had I not seen him trying to puzzle me out a moment earlier, I would have laughed. But knowing his mannerism was solely for my benefit, I only smiled. I felt weary and simply wanted Edward back.

"Here, why don't I take that one?" I said, starting to lift one of the trays, but before I'd even placed it on the table to fill, hooves pounded down the lane.

My breath quickened, and without meaning to, I reached out and grasped Jameson's arm. Before my thoughts progressed, the front door of the cottage banged open.

"Mrs. Auburn!" Mr. Addams's voice called and then became muffled as he ran into the drawing room. "Mrs. Auburn?"

I took a deep breath. "In the kitchen," I shouted. "At the end of the hall."

He arrived all pothered, tripping over his own feet. Breathless, he hastened across the kitchen and grabbed my wrist. "To the ancient oak! Hurry!"

Jameson gave him a curt nod as if letting Mr. Addams know he had his permission to drag me from Am Meer into the woods.

"What?" I pulled back. "Where's Edward?"

"Oh, he's fine!" Mr. Addams grinned over his shoulder. "I don't know how you two do it—or who knows, maybe it's just you. But it's all broken loose again. Come on! I've only just managed to keep ahead of them." He laughed as he flung open the kitchen door, allowing air and sunshine into the smoky kitchen. "I've never seen anything like the pair of you!"

Jameson followed and called after us, "Tell Edward I'll bring food."

"Oh, he'll thank you for it," Mr. Addams yelled over his shoulder. Then to me, "Quick, how do we get to the oak?"

I pointed to the path through the spinney. "What happened?"

He grinned, shaking his head. "Without doubt you are the most passive person I've ever had the pleasure of meeting, yet everything happens to you! It's as if life is trying to force you to act. But why would you? Adventures fling themselves at you, out of nowhere. This morning is a perfect example. You travel to attend a wedding, and that simple act divides a family, like lightning splitting a tree."

I felt my throat knot. If that was his idea of adventure, he could have it.

"And even without your attendance—" He halted, and his grip tightened over my wrist. "Quick!" He squatted in the tall grass. "Get down! Don't let them see you."

His tone compelled me to obey. I hunched next to him as the rumble of carriages and the murmur of people filled the air.

Four plumed white horses rounded the bend, pulling a travelling chariot decorated with flowers announcing its occupants were Henry and Elizabeth. Young boys ran alongside the horses, whooping and hollering. One lad in particular took it upon himself to shake the belled harness.

I watched, horrified, but the driver trusted his team, for he smiled indulgently and kept his steeds to a walk. Behind them, the mass of villagers who followed comprised men smoking pipes or carrying fiddles, and women talking hurriedly in groups. Only the youths seemed excited, though not in the manner I expected.

Normally the girls waved ribbons and hoisted banners of flowers while the boys chased each other. Instead there was an overactive quality about them—their eyes were full of some mischievous pleasure. The rowdier boys even hit and shoved each other.

I frowned. Was it the custom here for only the children to celebrate the wedding? At my village, one heard the fiddlers and singing long before the newlywed couple was spotted. I started to rise, shielding my eyes to gain a better look.

"No!" Mr. Addams yanked me back down, rather violently. "Don't allow them to see you."

I shot him an angry glance, surprised by his use of force. "Why ever not?"

"Look at their faces." He pointed to the adults. "My orders are to keep you from their clutches. I'd rather face your Macy fellow than learn what Edward would do if I allowed something to happen to you."

Angling my head, I returned my gaze to the passing party. Now that he mentioned it, they did look eerily expectant, like spectators at a hanging. The women's faces wore hard edges, and the men's brows were sculpted with angry lines as they argued amongst themselves.

"Come on!" Mr. Addams urged.

But I wouldn't move. The wedding carriage had stopped before the garden. Henry disembarked. His expression was even harder than those of his guests as he lifted up his arms. Just as Elizabeth's pale face emerged from the darkness of the carriage, Mrs. Windham released a loud, sobbing wail.

Henry's face grew a dusky red, but he continued to hold out his arms as if deaf.

Elizabeth met his eyes. Her mouth thinned, but as if determined to ignore her mother, she allowed him to lift her down.

I sucked in my breath. Her dress was blotted with dirt and dripping stains that I couldn't identify.

"They weren't aiming for her," Mr. Addams whispered in comfort. "They were pelting Edward. She just got too close. Henry blackened one of their eyes for his poor aim, let me tell you."

I was too horrified to respond. For I'd seen enough people in the pillory as they were assailed with trash to realize what had happened to Elizabeth's dress. Nevertheless, I could scarcely frame the question. It felt too unreal. "They pelted Edward?"

"I wouldn't worry about Edward." Mr. Addams chuckled.

"You should have seen him. He was frightening to behold. One of his finest moments, let me tell you! And I consider myself amongst his chief critics. Chin high, he stood like marble and allowed them to bombard him, giving no response. Then, when they finally ran out of the offal and tired of throwing dirt, he simply flicked the entrails from his face and marched to the front of the church, where, still covered in muck, he married Henry and Elizabeth."

Tears streaked Mrs. Windham's face as she wailed openly and reached out for Mr. and Mrs. Smith's assistance. When she reached the ground, she made a show of clinging to her sister as though unable to walk.

I half believed her, for I wasn't certain I could command my limbs either.

"Come on!" Mr. Addams whispered in direct response to my thoughts. "We'll crawl through the shrubs. Trust me, we don't want to know if they reserved anything just for you."

෴

I waited for Edward at the ancient oak, keeping my eyes fixed on the mossy bole, scarcely able to hold back tears as a new idea formed.

I was only grasping the beginning of it, but the implications were dire.

During my time at London House, I recalled, Isaac had pointed out an article to my father about a certain architect they knew. Apparently the man had been commissioned to build a row of houses in the West End, but the foundation had been poured crooked. He'd built several stories upwards before the error was realized.

My father frowned as he read it. "The sooner he tears the old down and replaces it with new, the better."

Isaac lightly tapped his fingers over the ivory tablecloth, the only sign the idea was distasteful to him. "Yes, but what a shame considering the marble is cut and laid, not to mention the labor already invested in those staircases. The wood panelling was transferred from a castle in Prussia, too. It's centuries old and cannot be unfastened now."

"The longer they try to save their efforts, the more money and materials they'll waste." My father returned to his own paper, indicating the discussion had ended.

Isaac wore no expression as he picked up his paper and perused the next page.

But I'd sat silently, disagreeing with my father.

Secretly I considered how Mr. Macy had maintained the ancient edifice at Eastbourne. I tapped my foot against the chair, imagining how many people would have given up on me if everyone took that philosophy. I poured tea, hoping the builder would press on and save his project. As I stirred a spoonful of sugar into the brew, I even went so far as to silently will that he not give up.

The architect was of the same mind. He redoubled his efforts. Less than a fortnight later, his houses collapsed in such a way that it devastated the next row of houses as well. It financially ruined him.

Isaac commented on that article also.

"Never try to fix a wrong foundation," was all my father said. "It's impossible."

As I awaited Edward at the ancient oak, it was that conversation that my mind continually returned to. It didn't encapsulate the entire idea I wanted to form, but it brushed against the general concept. What if I were like those row houses? My foundation was most certainly crooked, and story upon story had been added since my childhood.

I'd married Macy, lived a lie, acted heartless toward Isaac. The longer I reflected on it, I was forced to also acknowledge that I'd become wild of late too.

My vision blurred as I wiped the wetness from my eyes. At

what point, I wondered, do rationally minded people remove such a soul from their lives and focus only on that which is recoverable? My scandals, my out-of-control temper, my melancholy, all suggested that at my very core, I was crumbling and falling apart.

And at what point ought I free Edward from such humiliation?

"Never mind that rabble," Mr. Addams said cheerfully when I sniffled too loud. "They haven't even bothered to learn the elementary points of logic. If you consider it, they can't rightfully call Edward a bigamist. He only married once."

"He was called that?" I wiped my eyes with the heel of my free hand.

He chuckled as if able to see something about this situation that I couldn't. "Oh yes! He was called lots of things. Some called him a murderer, others a bigamist, and at least one—the man pelting rotten eggs—called him a Pharisee." He laughed again, rubbing his hands. "But if you think of it, that one is actually funny. I've desired to call him that myself, only I've managed to refrain, not wanting to become one."

I gritted my teeth. To hold one's tongue requires as much strength as lambasting a person. Thus it took all my energy to keep from giving Mr. Addams a show of my temper he'd never forget.

He kept watch, occasionally shaking his head and chuckling. How long we remained there is impossible to say. It felt like the entire afternoon to me, but it might have been no more than three-quarters of an hour. Eventually a noisy trampling sounded from the bush and Edward emerged.

Edward acknowledged my approach with a slight nod.

I threw myself into his arms, my heart breaking. The version of him that had emerged through the brush was a far cry from the whistling boy who'd taken leave of me that morning. I knew without asking that he'd also cut ties with his parents—of that, there was no doubt.

Later I learned his ordeal hadn't ended at the church. After the ceremony, Lady Foxmore located him as he bathed in a stream. From her carriage, she needled him with her tongue, crowing out her final victory over him.

He rubbed sand over his arms in circles, scraping the dried refuse from his skin, pretending he could neither see nor hear her.

I clung to him. "I am so sorry that happened. So sorry!"

Anger tightened his body as he looked in Mr. Addams's direction. "You told her!"

"Well, you didn't say I couldn't."

"I shouldn't have had to! Are you daft?"

Mr. Addams gave a flippant bow. "Yes, well, you're very welcome. No, no, don't thank me. It was my pleasure. If you ever need me again, please feel free to ask. Anytime, ol' chap."

Edward ignored him and took stock of me. "I'm sorry; I wanted to break it gently. Are you all right?"

I nodded, feeling tears gather.

"Did anyone see you? Should we find a different spot?"

I tucked a wisp of my hair behind my ear. "No."

"Again," Mr. Addams said behind me, "that was my doing. You're very welcome. You can thank me anytime now."

"Where's Jameson?" Edward asked.

I shrugged, not certain which one of us he was asking.

Edward heaved an annoyed sigh, then took a folded note out of his pocket and passed it to Mr. Addams. "Go find him and give that to him."

"Are you serious?" Mr. Addams demanded. "Not even a thank-you. For someone who thinks our society treats servants like chattel, you certainly could use a few lessons on how to treat your frien—"

The feral look Edward gave him made him snap his mouth shut.

"Fine!" He swiped the note from Edward's fingers, then retrieved his coat from the branch he'd hung it on. "But you really ought to learn better manners."

Edward waited until we could no longer hear him. Then, without a word, he crushed me so tightly that I suspected he fought back tears. Guilt assailed me as his right hand scrunched my chignon over and over, as if he was assuring himself that I was truly there.

I leaned against him, feeling guilty for dragging him down with me.

"We need to leave this area as soon as possible. Macy still has a reward out for you. I suspect more than one person will be hunting us tonight."

I felt my eyes widen as I wondered if anyone from this village would dare to hold me hostage, hoping to collect the five thousand pounds.

"Judging by Mrs. Windham's expression after speaking with my parents," Edward continued, loosening his hold, "I doubt even Am Meer will house us tonight, though I intend to try. It'll be a bitter night if we end up sleeping on Windhaven's floor, but I don't think we should travel during a new moon."

"Where will we go?" I asked.

He gave me a grim look.

A strong wind stirred the branches, bringing with it the mossy scent. I looked skyward, unable to believe that already Edward and I were considering my father.

Perhaps I was cursed.

Anger flared through me. If that were true, then my curse came with a name and a face.

Fisting my hands, I considered the long shadow Mr. Macy had cast over my life. When had he not haunted me? Surely he had anathematized me from the hour of my birth.

Wind stirred tendrils of my hair as I recalled how I'd been lied to and manipulated even as he romanced me. In succession my mind reviewed each Cimmerian kiss and infernal caress with disgust. Unbeknownst to me, with each one I'd quietly been surrendering my life to him, dismantling my own future.

To say that I hated Mr. Macy in that moment is an understatement. I wanted to see him toppled; I wanted him ruined. No, even more I wanted his destruction to come by my hand and for him to know it.

All at once I saw how marvelous my position truly was.

Out of the entire world, only two people held the keys to his undoing.

And I was one.

Seven

EDWARD GAVE AM MEER'S door a sound rap. I watched as blue paint lost its hold and fluttered to the ground. The bright specks reminded me of the stars studding the welkin that had stretched over the cottage only last night. I touched the peeling paint, fascinated that it disintegrated so easily beneath my fingers. Surely it hadn't always been this way, or Lady Foxmore's footman would have pounded it completely off before now.

I studied the dusting of blue over my fingertips, saddened at how soluble life was. A week ago, I'd attended a party celebrating my engagement to Isaac. Five days ago I'd blackmailed Macy. Only sixteen hours ago, I'd stood on these grounds, the vicar's bride, loved and accepted. In less than a sun's cycle, we'd been reduced to the status of outcasts with little hope of receiving any succor. Unlike Elizabeth, Mrs. Windham wasn't likely to stand up against the tide of public opinion.

"Paint," Jameson supplied behind me as I continued to stare at my fingers. "Humans use it to brighten things, though it seems to have an opposite effect on your kind."

I chuckled before I could help it. Never before had a soul so easily burst my melancholy thoughts. I dusted my hands, smiling over my shoulder at him, when the door swung open.

A haggard-looking Betsy peeked out. Her cap was askew and sleeves rolled above her elbows. "Oh, it's you." She heaved a great sigh as if her mind were on the pile of dishes still left to tackle. I wanted to ask her if Elizabeth had left me a message. If she'd cried in private, believing her wedding had been ruined. Before I could, however, Betsy said, "I'm to tell you that your effects have been moved to the stable. Mrs. Windham desires no intrusions."

I glanced toward the stable that sat beneath piling thunderheads and silently urged Thomas to make haste. I'd been in the leaky structure before when it had rained. If the clouds burst, I feared my trunks and their contents might be ruined.

Betsy made to shut the door, but Edward held it. "Tell Mrs. Windham we're not quitting this property until I've spoken with her in person. There's been too much injustice in this parish today to willingly accept more."

Betsy threw her weight against the door. "My orders are to allow no one inside."

Edward proved stronger, and within seconds he stormed down the hall. He opened the doors to the drawing room, dining room, and office before facing me. "Well, I can't intrude in her bedchamber alone. Come with me? Which one is it?"

I gave Betsy a brief, apologetic look. She'd always been kind to me during my visits, and I knew Hannah would censure her later. Facing my husband, I pointed toward Mrs. Windham's door. "It's the last one on the right."

He pounded on it, then signaled for me to hurry.

I stepped into the dark flagstone hall, aware that this was likely the last time I'd lay eyes on Am Meer's interior. The childhood ghosts of Elizabeth and me rose in visions: playing rag dolls on the bench, mothering the basket of kittens we'd rescued, sword fighting with the canes in the oak barrel. I felt tears rising, but then, like one snuffing out a candle, I banished even my hallowed memories.

I squared my shoulders, deepening my resolve to oversee Macy's downfall. I could not afford to falter here; I would not quail. If he robbed me of my childhood safe place, then I would banish any need for it. I would forbid even memories, if necessary, to cope. I met Edward's piercing gaze, overwhelmed with gladness that he was still left to me.

He noted the change in me but, outside of a slight movement of his jaw, gave no indication what he thought of the fevered coolness of my personality. His mouth set in a firm line as he banged on the bedchamber door a second time.

Behind me, Jameson said, "Come along, Betsy; I'll help you scrub the pots while the overlords squabble this out."

When I reached Edward, he pounded a third time. "Mrs. Windham, I know you're there!"

This time the door flung open, and Hannah poked out her glaring face. "Have you gone mad! This is a house of respectable folk."

Behind her, Mrs. Windham cried out in a sniffling voice, "Hannah . . . who comes?"

I shut my eyes, knowing our mission had failed, for it was impossible that she hadn't heard Edward.

Hannah narrowed her eyes and said in a composed voice, "'Tis *Mister* Edward Auburn and . . ." Something about Edward's face must have warned her not to call me Mrs. Macy. She swallowed. "And Miss Julia, ma'am."

Mrs. Windham made a hiccupping sound, followed by, "Send them in."

Hannah swung the door wide enough for entry.

The shutters had been closed and locked, so darkness enveloped the chamber. I caught sight of Mrs. Smih's disapproving eyes as she faced us. Ramrod straight, she sat in a chair with hands folded over her stomach. The angle of her head, the way she shifted her eyes, suggested she found us too disgraceful to acknowledge. Mr. Smih lounged, absorbed in a book.

Mrs. Windham lay abed, propped up by pillows. A single lamp covered by a paper shade gave off weak light. She turned toward me as large tears formed in her eyes.

"I suppose you're here to laugh at me in person," she said. "I should have known you would return only to ruin the wedding out of jealousy."

Hannah stepped forward to plump the bedding. Her face flushed, she pummeled the pillows in a manner that made me believe she wished they were Mrs. Windham. "Rest. Pay no mind to them."

Edward glowered. "Why are you in bed? Are you ill?"

"Ill?" Mrs. Windham lifted one arm and allowed it to drop back to the pillow, a deadweight. "I am dying and he asks if I'm ill!"

"Here now, such talk." Hannah moved toward a table near the bed, where a silver teapot sat next to a platter filled with meat pies. She poured a cup of tea. "Calm yourself."

Mrs. Windham let out a dramatic moan.

My mouth twitched as I struggled to keep from laughing. I felt as though I were watching a stage performance. Surely this was some deviant comedy. She couldn't truly believe we'd come home for the sole purpose of ruining the wedding. A strange hilarity came over me. I secretly planned to bring down England's foremost criminal, and my quest began here, the bedchamber of the country's silliest woman. I compressed my lips, trying to hold back a laugh.

Mrs. Windham faced me, dabbing puffy eyes. "I have not much time left, so you may as well tell me why you've tortured me and ruined my life. Did I refuse you a treat in your child-hood? Were you so envious of Elizabeth's prospects that you had to shame us?"

"Elizabeth's prospects?" I asked. "Her twenty-five pounds per annum?"

"Yes, her prospects!" Mrs. Windham shrieked, startling me. Her limbs miraculously recovered as she took a sitting position and waved her rumpled handkerchief beneath my nose. "All you've ever done is try to outshine her. When Henry fell in love with her, you clamped on to Edward. Then, when I took you to Eastbourne, you threw yourself at Mr. Macy even though his intentions toward Elizabeth couldn't have been clearer!"

"You took her to Eastbourne?" Mrs. Smih gasped, then clasped her sister's forearm. "Edith! Please tell me you're not mixed up in this . . . this . . . sordid affair with Mr. Macy and his bride."

A wailing cry was her answer.

Hannah reached into a shallow basin, withdrew a cloth, and wrung it out before attempting to place it on Mrs. Windham's head. "Lie back and rest."

Mrs. Windham sobbed all the louder.

Edward studied the room, hands in his frock coat pockets, as emotionless as an engineer surveying a river he meant to build a bridge over. Glad he wasn't being pulled into the drama, I bent my head to hide my own rising irritation.

Instinctively I knew that if I knelt by her bedside and coaxed and petted her, I might be able to earn us a night at Am Meer. She loved nothing more than audiences. However, everything that happened today had left me unsympathetic and cold.

"I even housed Lord Dalry without a single complaint after you disappeared." Mrs. Windham tore the cloth from her forehead. "I went out of my way to make certain the best foods and linens were available to him. But did you ever write and thank me? Not one letter! Not one note to tell me you were alive and well."

"I'm . . . sorry . . . but did you just say he came after she . . . ?" Mrs. Smih's fingers rose and covered her mouth.

Even Mr. Smih stopped ignoring us and looked up from his book.

I locked my fingers behind my gown and waited for her to connect that Lord Pierson's daughter had entered society just after Macy's bride was kidnapped by a vicar. The idea that I was about to be fully discovered at Am Meer by Mrs. Windham's sister was so absurd that I couldn't even muster fear.

Mrs. Smih must have relished the gossip columns, for it took her only seconds. Her gaze flew to Edward's collar before she lifted a shaky hand and pointed. "You're . . . you're the one she slighted at the opera, aren't you?"

Remorse throbbed anew as I glanced at Edward. Somehow I hadn't expected her to connect that much.

"Who slighted Edward?" Mrs. Windham frowned as she realized she had fallen behind in the conversation she'd created. "Certainly not, Julia! You forget that *he* is the son of a lord."

Mrs. Smih rose, holding her stomach. "Edith! Oh, mercy on us! This can't be happening. Please, please tell me right now you had nothing to do with her first marriage. This is very important."

"She was Julia's chaperone," Edward said quietly.

Catching on that he was supplying her with motivation to keep my secret, I nodded. "Yes. I was under your sister's direct care the entire time."

"And very rude you were, too." Tears rolled down Mrs. Windham's cheeks. "Had I known what you were doing in the middle of the night, I would have put my foot down. Your love affairs have cost me a maid, my favorite red gown, and her ladyship's friendship. She hasn't paid me one visit, not even left a calling card, since the whole affair started."

Mrs. Smih's hands flew to her cheeks as she began to pace.

"Frederick, do something! Oh, what a perfect mess everything is!"

Her husband rose. His face was difficult to discern as he studied Edward and me. But the way his eyes lingered on me with a pitying look suggested he knew something about Macy's reputation. "Leave," he said softly. "Leave my family and this cottage out of your troubles. Make no attempt to return, or I will have to write and tell him your whereabouts." He locked eyes with Edward. "There are some souls one can't afford to offend. I won't have a choice."

Edward was not easily intimidated or convinced. He fixed his eyes on Mrs. Windham, making me wonder if he planned to dust his feet of her, too. He gave Mr. Smih a curt nod. "We'll quit this place when my wife's belongings are secured in my father-in-law's carriage, which we expect back any moment." He looked at me. "Are you ready to leave?"

"But . . . but . . . ," Mrs. Smih protested to her husband. "What about the reward money? And poor Mr. Macy? Not to mention what we've just learned about Lord Pierson! We cannot allow them to get away with this."

"It's none of our affair." Mr. Smih retook his seat. "Mind your own business, woman."

"I will not! If I must, I'll write her husband myself and relieve his mental suffering."

"You'll do as I say!"

Mrs. Smih's face pinched with bitterness. "We're just going to do nothing?"

"No." Mr. Smih picked up his book. "We're going to wait for your sister to catch her untimely death so we can bury her without a bell. That way even if she's somehow not dead, we won't have to tolerate one more sound from her."

In response, Mrs. Windham shrieked garbled words as she kicked her feet beneath the covers in a full tantrum.

Here Edward took my arm. We slipped out of the chamber unnoticed.

∽

A quarter hour later we stood in Am Meer's cramped stables amidst discarded wicker beehives, shards of broken terra-cotta pots, and moldy straw, which I avoided for fear of mice.

Memories lingered here as well. The crude butterfly nets that Elizabeth and I had constructed from discarded cheese-cloths, embroidery hoops, and the broken handles of old rakes still rested in the corner. I pressed a hand against my heart, recalling our girlish laughter as we gave up the idea of capturing insects and used them in an improvised game of tag instead.

Edward's strong arms enfolded me from behind. He held me close, rocking us side to side as he whispered, "We're going to be fine. We will. I promise it."

I hooked my fingers over his arms, allowing my gaze to wander to the tin watering can with its dented spout that Mama always used. "He stole Am Meer, too. I can't believe I lost this."

"You haven't lost me." His arms squeezed in a comforting embrace. "After today, I'm inclined to think I was the best part anyway."

I smiled, but my lips felt swollen. "Yes, but I still can't believe that Henry and Elizabeth dismissed me—us—so easily." I tightened my hold on his forearm, glad he shared these memories too. "And that your parish did that. It just feels impossible."

"Are we talking about the same Henry and Elizabeth who grew up around these parts? The ones who used to race ahead of us in order to comb through the picnic basket first? Or the ones who continually gave us the villain roles when we played Robin Goodfellow, and always took the lion's share of the candy? Or the conniving pair who hid that I became a vicar because it suited their purposes, and betrayed my trust by reading through my journals?"

His description made me chuckle despite myself. I looked at him over my shoulder. "Yes, them."

"We didn't lose them, Juls; they lost us. And there's a huge difference." He ceased rocking me as I considered his interpretation. "Furthermore, let's not give Macy more credit than due. I've prayed too long and too hard that when God desired me elsewhere, he'd dry up the streambed and remove the ravens. Apparently now is the hour."

I drew a deep breath, readying myself to argue that I wasn't giving Macy more credit than due. Before I could speak, Jameson's voice sounded behind us as he entered the stable and stomped his boots. "Newlyweds! You leave them alone for ten minutes and when you find them again, they're sermonizing."

A jagged streak of lightning scarred the sky as we turned to greet him. He hastened entry as thunder shook the landscape, its full-toned rumble ebbing like the tide. "I take it we haven't been granted sanctuary, then."

"No, we haven't," Edward said, releasing me. "When Thomas returns, we'll head to Windhaven for the night."

"And after that?" I hugged myself.

"I think you already know."

I shook my head rapidly, feeling that the nightmare just got worse. "There must be somewhere else we can go. You must know somebody."

Edward's chest filled in a silent sigh as he considered my request. What I failed to say was that I didn't want to face Isaac ever again. I couldn't endure knowing I'd caused him pain. I wasn't certain how he'd feel watching Edward's and my relationship.

Edward glanced outdoors as rain began to pelt the benighted landscape, his face etched with uncertainty. His eyes were sad as they returned to me. "We won't remain there one day longer than absolutely necessary. I promise." He faced Jameson. "I imagine you want to return to Auburn Manor and see if you can retain the post offered as gardener. When the carriage returns, we can drive you there first."

Jameson removed his hat and turned its brim in a circle with his hands. "Well, now. I don't know. I happened to see your advertisement in the newspaper and I was mighty tempted, even when I didn't know it was for you."

Edward scowled. "I haven't got an advertisement in the paper."

Jameson scratched the back of his head. "Strange. There can't be two such cases in England. Let me see if I can recall it." Jameson rubbed his chin, looking at the hewn ceiling. "'One banished fay and homeless clergyman seeking the services of a highly skilled valet. Duties include teaching one how to act human, scrounging up food, dodging hostile crowds, and making sleeping accommodations in abandoned houses.' The next part is sort of blurred in my memory, but it ran like these posts typically do, something like: 'No compensation shall be provided, but benefits include the sort of adventure most only read about in books. Persons interested must make inquiries in Am Meer's stable between noon and one o'clock, etc., etc.'"

"I can't pay the meager wages I offered," Edward said. "I have nothing. I don't even know the next time we'll have food."

"I accept the terms." The old man grinned as he bowed. Then, from the shadows near his feet, he produced a bulging sack. "As far as my duties go, I've already begun. Here, at least, is the food. You'd be surprised what a maid-of-all-work will give someone who helps clean the dishes after a wedding."

Edward stared at the sack with a look of disbelief. From the way he opened his mouth as if about to speak, but then changed his mind, I deemed him unable to accept Jameson's offer but unwilling to turn it down. He finally settled on, "I don't know what to say."

"Try thank you."

"Well, I thank you," I said, sensing that Edward still struggled to accept. "If you ask me, the employment terms are rather generous. In the faerie courts we don't ask for volunteers; we simply enslave whomever we wish."

Jameson shot me a look of gratitude. "Humph. For all I know you've already cast a spell on me and I only think I'm volunteering. But if you have done so, I already forgive you. Doubtless you've come to realize I'm the exact sort of soul—" here he gave Edward a pointed look—"capable of easing your transition into an ordinary human life."

"Yes, she does respond well to you," Edward said quietly, frowning. "That much I can't argue with. All right. If you're truly willing to remain with us, we'll keep a record book of wages owed you. When I find employment, we'll work out payment then. I have no idea when that will be, though."

"Well, what will be will be." Jameson opened the sack of food, and the scent of butter and crushed herbs accompanied that of roasted chicken. "In the meantime, you should eat. Empty stomachs make poor beginnings to adventures."

Edward peered into the bag and shook it. "My word. How much food is in here?"

Jameson jammed his hands into his pockets. "I knew Mrs. Auburn was along. So I added as much as I could carry. Faeries consume enormous amounts of food. Four times their weight daily." Winking at me, he added, "So do giants, though I hardly have need to tell you that. Someday you'll have to tell me about your feasts with them and if they really prefer human meat to swine."

Edward must have been ravenous, for he took a seat on a tool chest. His stomach grumbled as his teeth gnawed on a joint.

Jameson pried off the grey wax sealing a bottle of wine, then dug out the cork with his jackknife. He offered me the first swig.

Parched, as I had not had anything to drink since the day before, I accepted. As I had never drunk from a bottle of wine, its juices trickled down my neck as well as my stomach.

Coughing and wiping my mouth with my sleeve, I handed the bottle back to Jameson.

"Ah, I should have offered it to you in a lily's throat." He glanced about as if the flower would spring from the stone floor.

Edward shook his head at our strange manner of bantering. For a minute we all tended to our hunger, scarcely paying attention to each other. All at once, Edward laughed.

Jameson and I questioned him with a look.

"My word," Edward said, rubbing his eyes. "I am never praying that prayer again."

"Uh-oh." Jameson popped a fig in his mouth. "Did you ask for patience?"

"Something worse, I think." Edward wiped his fingers on his handkerchief. "This morning I asked God to open my eyes to what life has been like for Julia." He looked at me. "I want to be a kind and merciful husband, so I asked him to help me understand you." He chuckled. "Outside of a few uncomfortable meetings with her ladyship, I've never undergone anything like today."

His tone was good-natured, but I suddenly wasn't.

"No matter what I did," Edward continued, failing to note my perturbation, "it made no difference. I tried reasoning, threatening, bullying back, complaining, joking, nagging. Nothing! Absolutely nothing stopped people from trampling over me."

Jameson did not return Edward's boyish smile, but rather he glanced at me as he carefully brushed the straw from his sleeves. "Did Edward ever tell you I've been to Africa?"

I blinked at him, wondering how on earth our topic made him think of Africa. "No."

"Well, since we're stuck here, let me tell you one of my stories." He pushed himself farther back on the ledge as the wind howled through the opening behind him.

"Yes, now that you mention it, where is Thomas, anyhow?" Edward mumbled, heading to the second window and peering out. "How long can it possibly take to load up my books and studies?"

"Ed, listen, too, for I've not told you this one yet either."

Edward gave him a gruff nod, saying he was listening, though it was apparent he wasn't any more interested than I was.

"Now then." Jameson crossed his arms, settling into the story. "This must have happened well over thirty years ago. I travelled with a small group of hunters, serving as footman. One of the most exciting times of my life. There we were, in the middle of the dry season, tempers all hot and scarcely any game to be found. That year a drought had turned even the deepest mud holes into parched ground. After four days without success, we finally chanced upon a small water hole where several prides of starving lions were in a standoff against a herd of thirty or so elephants. Because it was the only water source, they were stuck there. Every hunter was thrilled, for here was their opportunity to bring down a mighty lion and an elephant in the space of a single day."

Edward gave me a look that begged I endure for his sake, before craning his neck to see back into the storm.

"We were, of course, obliged to wait for the peer who had organized the trip." Jameson reached into his pocket and pulled out his handkerchief. "He couldn't hunt, due to dysentery. So we bided our time at a distance. Now picture, my queen, lions so starving, their rib cages look carved into their skins. They were desperate enough to attack the herd, but never with success.

"Then, without warning, one of the cleverer lionesses managed to separate an older calf from its mother. The pride descended all at once." Jameson paused for a second. "The calf trumpeted with terror and in its panic, it ran straight toward the pride with as many as twenty lions pulling it down." Jameson shook his head at the memory. "I kept thinking, *Run back to the herd! Run to your herd!* But of course it was too terrified."

I lifted a brow, wondering why he thought this story would cheer me.

Edward, however, perked up his head and gave Jameson a pleased look.

"What I mean to say, O queen," Jameson said softly, pointing between Edward and himself, "is that you're one of us now. You've got a herd to run back to. It won't be as easy for those lions to tear you down next time."

I gave the elderly valet a disbelieving stare.

Edward straightened as the carriage finally made its appearance. Beaming with approval, he crossed the distance to Jameson and patted his shoulder. "There's Thomas. I'll help load the trunks. You two stay put."

I nodded toward Edward and tightened my shawl about me.

Jameson waited until Edward withdrew, then in a quiet voice asked, "I know what Edward thought of my story, but not you." Jameson placed his elbows on his knees as he leaned forward, looking at the stone floor. "Generally when humans make an overture of friendship, they feel vulnerable when the other person sits and studies them with that mistrusting look."

I felt color rise through my cheeks as I realized how I appeared. But I had no answer to give. For to my reasoning, if I were the target of a pride of lions, they'd already proven stronger than this meager herd. Were we not sitting in a stable, banished and defeated?

Worse yet, because of Macy, I wasn't sure if it was safe for anybody to be with me.

"Let me be plain," Jameson said when I still said nothing. "Will you honor me and accept my friendship?"

I clasped my hands in my lap as I had the day I learned I had a guardian. "No."

"What?" Jameson sat up so quickly it gave the illusion he'd thrown himself backwards. "Oh, come now! That's never happened before. You at least owe me an explanation, then."

I knew better than to be drawn into answering him, yet I disliked hurting his feelings. My voice came out strained. "I like you. That's why."

He chuckled. "Well, I see our problem. No wonder humans and faeries have difficulties when mixed together. We humans tend to band together in community with those we love and who give us love back."

"You don't understand." I focused my gaze on the straw scattered about the stone floor. "I'm caught in a current I can't escape, and only a selfish person pulls someone down with them when they're drowning."

Jameson snorted. "Only if they're with people who can't swim. Where did you get a nonsensical idea like that?"

"Someone Edward knew. Churchill."

"Winthrop!" He made a noise of disgust. "Of course! He would say that to your kind, making no allowances. He lacked talent for seeing potential. Always skipping over the good and focusing on the bad. Bah! Ignore him. Trust my advice instead."

I frowned, wondering if I'd based the last six months of my life on bad advice. Before I could speak, a jagged streak of lightning rent the sky, followed by a loud crack of thunder. I turned my gaze to the window where Edward toiled to heft up one of my heavy trunks to Thomas.

"That boy," Jameson said, following my gaze, but his voice was affectionate. "It's just like him to jump in the middle of a storm and risk getting struck by lightning. Next, if we're not careful, he'll catch his death of cold."

"Don't ever say that," I warned, clutching shut Mama's shawl. "Never curse him with words of death."

As if sensing our gaze, Edward faced our direction. Rain dripped off his curls and made his heavy clothing weigh down his limbs. Grabbing an umbrella from the interior of the coach, he slogged his way back through the thickening mud. Affection swelled through me. Surely I never loved anyone more than him.

"You don't fear his friendship, I notice," Jameson said.

I reached for Mama's locket out of habit, then curled my fingers around air. "Yes, and in one day I've cost him his family, employment, and church."

"Jameson," Edward called through the door before the valet could respond. "You're first."

"You're not making allowances for his choices." Jameson moved toward the door, promising, "But we'll discuss this later."

I crossed my arms, thinking we would discuss nothing later unless I orchestrated it. I was the mistress, after all, and not him.

Nevertheless, I felt compelled to follow his progress to the carriage, wishing he'd taken me seriously when I said I was unlucky. Yet secretly I was glad he was amongst our number, for despite myself I had warmed toward him.

Next was my turn. The mud was so thick it threatened to hold fast my slipper with each step. My stomach tightened as I mounted the carriage and viewed its interior.

Though the seats were cushioned with padded leather, mire coated nearly every surface. I sank across from Jameson. Water ran down my skirts, joining the muddy lake at my feet. I eyed the mud creviced beneath each upholstery button, knowing it would take hours of the staff members' lives to clean this. Normally these carriages were kept in pristine condition. If this couldn't be restored, my father was going to be furious with me.

The scent of wet dog tingled my nose before the stray from that morning jumped on my lap to greet me.

Resigned to fate, I drew a deep breath. Sarah always said that every couple was fated to be unlucky in some aspect of daily life. Some couldn't keep their chickens alive, regardless of effort. Others excelled in buying horses that ended up lame. We knew one family that moved four times, and each time within months their well dried. Mama and William were unable to keep their dishes from chipping. Apparently Edward and I were the death of carriages. We'd done the same thing to Henry's.

The moment Edward took his seat, the dog scrambled over my skirt and jumped onto his lap. His tail thumped against my leg as Edward bent his head forward and accepted the attention. When the carriage pitched forward, Edward wrapped his arms around the dog's chest, holding him in place.

"We need to find a home for this fellow by morning too." Edward stroked the silken ears.

I rested my head against the carriage, watching. "I'm sorry. I know you wanted him."

"Do you remember that year you tried to talk your father into buying you a mastiff as a yuletide gift?" Jameson asked Edward. "You even went so far as to send inquiries to breeders." Smiling at me, he said, "He waited until his father was at lunch and then lined up their replies over his desk."

"Did it work?" I asked.

Edward made a face. "Not entirely. Father commissioned someone to paint a mastiff."

Jameson gave his knee a slight slap. "I'd forgotten that! Yes, and in your disappointment, you declared you would only hang the picture when you had a real dog to match it. Then you ordered Rupert to remove it until such a time. It was the talk of breakfast that morning belowstairs. The staff was on your side."

"Where is that painting now?" I asked.

Edward frowned. "I don't know. I haven't seen it since that morning." He scratched the dog's chin. "What about your father, Juls? Does he keep any dogs? Would he want another?"

I compressed my lips, not entirely certain. "Maybe. There used to be one in the stables."

"Used to? That doesn't sound good. What happened to him?"

I shuddered, recalling the morning my father's footman informed us our dog had been beaten to death. My cousin, Eramus, also returned to memory—his murderous face as he turned a poker in the embers. I ran my fingertips over the faint scars on my palms. My throat closed as a panicky sensation set in. "I . . . I don't think I can talk about it."

Edward's brow furrowed with concern. "Never mind it. I think I'd rather find him a home here."

"Yes," Jameson said beneath his breath, "I second that notion."

I bent my head, the memory of that night refusing to go away. I relived the horrifying moment I tumbled headlong into London's dark streets, bleeding and burnt, with Eramus in hot pursuit. I wasn't aware my facial expression bespoke my stress until Edward placed the dog on the seat next to Jameson and drew me close.

"Let's give him to Jacob Turner," he suggested. "What do you think of that?"

I snapped out of my thoughts and blinked at him. "To whom?"

"You remember. We saw him hoeing his field last fall. He was the one saving up for a blanket. Knowing how tight his finances are, I doubt he ever got that new blanket. He does, however, strike me as the type who would sleep with his dog."

"He'll get fleas." Jameson frowned.

"He already has fleas," Edward rebuked quietly. "If anything, the dog would draw some of them away. Plus, we know firsthand this dog catches rabbits. So not only would he keep Jacob warm, but he'd add meat to his diet."

"Do you think he'll want him?"

I felt Edward give a silent sigh as he viewed our stray. "There's only one way to find out. I'll walk over and see after the storm clears."

❧

Memory of that afternoon is a soft blur of musty smells, echoing chambers, and dutiful work. Thankfully our possessions were

tied to the carriage, so we were able to change into drier clothing. Jameson and I draped wet clothing over banisters, door-
knobs, protruding nails, and a few hooks that had once served
the house's previous occupants, while rain dashed against
the windows and the wind buffeted the unyielding walls of
Windhaven.

Before many minutes passed, the tarry scent of burning peat
moss filled the downstairs.

Fatigued and devoid of emotion, I sat and stared at the yellow
flames, blinking smoke from my eyes. When I yawned repeatedly, Jameson excused himself and returned with the dampened
carriage blankets and a lumpy pillow.

"Sleep," he ordered, arranging them within the ring of
warmth provided by the fire. "You won't miss anything. You look
ready to slumber standing up."

"Yes, you hardly slept last night," Edward encouraged.

"What will you do?" I asked, knowing he couldn't feel any
more rested.

"My mind is full." He gave the windows a look of dissatisfaction. "I might work on a sermon. I've been thinking of Jacob
Turner and how God doesn't always answer prayers in the way
we plan. I might research that and outline a future sermon on
the theme."

I tried to hide my look of surprise that he was still writing
sermons as if our life hadn't just been interrupted. Perhaps I
was still a vicar's wife after all.

Thomas, who hadn't eaten yet, settled next to me by the
hearth and became my quiet companion. While he withdrew
items from the sack, I mounded the blanket in such a way as
to accommodate me where my stay was unbendable. Lastly,
I wadded Mama's shawl for an additional pillow. To my complete astonishment, when I finally settled down, Jameson produced another thick, heavy blanket, which he spread over me as
though I were a small child.

"One of the benefits of belonging to a herd," he said by way of explanation when I gave him a startled look.

The same thawing sensation I'd once experienced with Nancy fluttered through me, followed by a sense of panic when I realized I couldn't shut down my desire for friendship, no matter how much I feared allowing people in.

But why wouldn't I? I shut my eyes, though sleep felt far away. My time as the Emerald Heiress had taught me that people were far more interested in using a person as a commodity than in learning who she truly was. Today was a clear demonstration that even those who loved me were quick to put their interests above mine. Betrayal always lurked round the corner.

Then I envisioned Isaac's trusting face as he sat across the breakfast table that fateful morning. Waves of despair washed over me. I was just as guilty. Though I'd tried my best, an ugly, gaping wound now existed between us. I squeezed my eyes shut, trying to force sleep to come and offer relief from these thoughts. Yet I couldn't help but consider my father next. Since that same morning when he'd lost control, he'd wanted nothing to do with me.

How many more times could I stand this? No matter whom I loved, or who loved me, it always ended the same—people becoming bruised, broken, and battered.

I grasped the blanket and pulled it closer, wondering why we didn't give the blankets to Jacob Turner. Then, forcing myself to pretend I was asleep, I eventually calmed and drifted.

I dreamed Isaac and I were attending a soiree, only we were stuck on a staircase. Above us people waited in line, as well as below us. Everywhere I looked, crowds of people surrounded the stairs. The low murmur of voices was accompanied by feminine trills of laughter and the sound of crystal glasses being toasted. I kept edging closer to Isaac, feeling I could choke on the scent of perfumes and pomades, but there was no escape. On the step below me, a very important man turned and addressed me, and though I smiled and nodded, the notion pounded against my brain that if I didn't greet him properly, I'd cause a rift between my father and all of Parliament. I looked to Isaac, our signal that I needed help, but he stared through me, wearing his urbane expression. I felt unable to breathe. All around me were hundreds and hundreds of gentry, all turning toward me, all waiting to speak to me, and I couldn't remember any one of them or their ranks.

"Juls." The important man jabbed my shoulder.

I clutched Isaac's sleeve, but he turned his head, refusing to look at me. Near crying, for he'd never treated me like this, I tugged harder, pleading for his help.

"Juls." This time it was Edward's voice, and it was close to my ear. "You're having a nightmare."

I bolted upright and blinked about the empty room, confused.

"You were having a bad dream," Edward repeated, lowering himself to the floor next to me.

I breathed in air as my heart slowed its hammering, then turned toward the window. It was late, and stars now glistened in their velvety sky as crickets throbbed.

Edward leaned forward and kissed my shoulder, the scent of bay rum clinging to him.

"How did you know I was having a bad dream?" I demanded, wiping my eyes and finding them wet. Fearing I'd called out Isaac's name, I asked, "Did I say anything?"

"No. You just kept thrashing."

I drew my knees to my chest, allowing the lingering emotions from the dream to dissipate. "Forgive me." I had to swallow. "I'm sorry. Sometimes I have nightmares. I can't help it."

Edward's expression was difficult to read, though his brow creased. "There's nothing to be sorry about."

I pushed the hair back from my forehead, glad he didn't understand that I was apologizing for dreaming about Isaac.

Edward hesitated a second, then asked, "May I join you? Or would you rather sleep alone?"

Only then did I realize he had stripped down to his drawers and shirt.

"No. Here." I scooted over, making room for him on the bottom blanket, then lifted the cover. He quickly stripped off his shirt and slipped beneath the blanket. "Shall I hold you?"

I nodded and settled against his chest, the panic from my dream fully ebbing.

He leaned his cheek against the top of my head. "Tell me your dream? Maybe I can decipher its meaning."

I shook my head, already knowing it meant I feared to be in London or near my father without Isaac's help. The chimera was my first attempt at handling the pain of having been severed so bluntly from Isaac. Knowing that Edward was insightful about these matters, it wasn't a dream I wanted to share.

He pulled the cover over my shoulder. "Was I in it?"

Instead of answering his question, I surprised myself by relinquishing the thoughts that had built all day. They came swiftly, needing release. "How can you be so kind, when you know this is all my fault?"

"What's your fault, Juls?"

I gestured to the empty chamber. "All of this. Henry and Elizabeth's wedding. Your parents. Not having a place to sleep. Your losing your living." *Isaac's broken trust.* "My father's carriage. Henry's carriage. Churchill's murder. Everything. Everywhere I go, I hurt those I love. I am tired of seeking and being rejected. I'm sorry I brought you to this place with me."

I felt the tendons over Edward's neck move as he swallowed. For a full minute he considered his response, though he held me tight. "Do you see that star, there? Angle your head a bit and look out the left side of the pane, the middle mullion. Can you tell me its name?"

I felt too miserable to answer and only gave it a fleeting

glance. Here I granted him access to my soul and he was respond-ing with astronomy lessons.

"It's Polaris," he said softly, his gaze fixed in that direction. "Every sailor knows it. Without that fixed mark they would lose their nautical direction and never find port. Worthy captains use it nightly to track their progress. By that, they then estimate the number of days until they'll make land, which determines how they ration the food and water."

I studied the blue, sphery point of light through the wavy pane.

"The way I see it, Juls, you've been on a ship with someone at the helm who disregarded the necessity of looking heavenward to navigate. He shipwrecked his life and his family. You've been afloat in the wreckage, barely able to keep your head above the billowing waves. God is rich with mercy on the castaways and smoldering brands. They are precious to him, and he's willing to cast aside all that is dirty and offensive and replace it with robes of honor."

His words were soul-stirring, painful even. "Why?"

He laughed as if I'd asked him to explain the unexplainable. "God sovereignly chooses his representatives, and I daresay he intends to use what he saves. I would even say his love is ful-filled as he takes the fragments and transforms them."

"What if I'm not chosen?"

Edward's voice smiled. "The very fact you're questioning this is proof enough he's spoken your name."

I shifted to gain a better view of Edward, feeling restrained by the layers of clothing I wore. "If that's true, then I don't think his people agree with his choices. For I know now of two par-ishes that disapprove of me."

"And who are they to judge the servant of another?"

Not yet recognizing that verse, my thoughts briefly touched on Jameson as I wondered what he had to do with this. Edward's words brought back the memory of surrender. Several minutes passed before he spoke again. "As far as your always being rejected, that's a lie. I've chosen you and fought incredible odds for the privilege of being the one here with you tonight."

I shut my eyes, nestling closer against him. Though my stomach cramped with hunger and my bladder needed relief, I wouldn't have moved for all the world. At least here, with him, I belonged. I touched his chest, amazed at how natural being husband and wife already felt. "You're my Polaris. You've always been."

"You won't feel that way once your understanding grows."

I looked up, and the pressure of my head apparently compelled Edward to adjust his arm. I marveled at the feel of sinew and muscle beneath his skin.

Sensing I wanted more of an explanation, he turned on his side so we were face-to-face. "I am only a picture, a shadow. If I do my job well, I open a fuller understanding of the real picture." He frowned, seeing my confused look. "I never told you this, but the first time I ever saw you wasn't that day Henry and I stumbled on Elizabeth and you at the creek."

I gave him a wide stare, for that day was sacred amongst my memories. That morning I'd found Mama bedridden, a malady she suffered when great sadness would overtake her. I climbed atop her, placing my cheeks on hers, hoping she'd feel my love and revive. She did not stir, however, but just stared blankly at the wall. I moved Mama's blonde hair from her brow and kissed her.

Those rare days Mama did not speak, Sarah was wont to tell me to be a good girl, leading me to believe my goodness translated into Mama's ability to shake off the heaviness. Hence, when Sarah shooed me from the chamber with the words that good little girls were outdoors soaking up sunshine, I slipped from the bed, determined to bring her alleviation.

The remedy had finally been handed to me—find sunshine and remain in it.

The day before, Elizabeth and I had started to build a dam of sticks and mud in the creek bed, hoping to turn the woods into a body of water. She was anxious to return to the project, whereas I was hesitant to head into the trees, fearing I wouldn't find sunlight. To my relief, when we arrived, a shaft of sun was awaiting me, illuminating a large stone thickly cushioned with moss.

About a half hour later, Henry and Edward crossed our path, dressed to the hilt in riding attire. We must have made an interesting sight, for by the time the boys found us, Elizabeth was half-covered in mud, her hair hanging in clumps, as she rolled a rock down the creek bed toward our dam, while I sat in a tight ball, clutching my arms around my knees, trying to keep any part of me from falling into the shadow.

I'd noted Edward immediately, for no one had ever looked at me with the intensity that he did. Whereas Henry gave Elizabeth a look of disgust.

Without comment, Edward handed his reins to his brother, then crossed over a fallen log to me. His eyes scrunched with uncertainty as I did not move or rise to greet him. He hesitated, then asked, "May I sit with you?"

I gave a slight nod, not certain what he was about.

Clearly he expected me to scoot over, for he furrowed his brow when I made no movement. His eyes darted about the scene, and he must have noted my preference for the sun because he asked, "Are you cold?"

I shook my head.

On the other side of the creek, Henry watched his brother's attempt to make friends with me with something akin to bewilderment, but it amused him enough to hitch his booted foot on a rock and cross his arms over his knee to observe.

Elizabeth stood upright from her labors and wiped her brow, smearing mire across it. "She wants to sit." Then, in a bossy tone, "And she's allowed to."

Henry gave her another look of disgust. "What are you doing?"

Elizabeth raised her chin. "I'm making a lake."

He snorted. "That's impossible. It won't work."

Elizabeth flung her head with disdain; clumps of hair stuck to her neck. "Watch me."

Henry tethered the horses to a birch tree and began to survey the dam, pointing out the flaws and explaining why, regardless of her efforts, she'd fail. Edward waited until they were thick into their first argument before perching next to me and reaching into his pocket. He withdrew a handkerchief containing wrapped treacle toffees and extended it to me.

Half-expecting him to yank it out of reach when I attempted to take a piece, I moved cautiously, eyeing him for any hint of deception. When my fingertips cooled as they touched the shade, I decided against the treat. Mama was worth more than all the toffee in the world.

Edward grinned as he figured out my oddity; then, with a smile, he thrust the toffee fully into the bright ray. "Here, take them all. I ate so many I got a bellyache last night."

Within minutes, Henry was knee-deep in the creek, carrying the rock for Elizabeth to prove that her plan wouldn't work by showing her himself. And Edward had fisted a reedy crimson dragonfly, which he pinched between his thumb and forefinger so I could admire it.

Within an hour, I'd forgotten all about Mama and was following Edward up a tree, scraping my knees in order to see a nest with baby robins.

That afternoon when we returned home, I found Mama reclining amongst the roses, watching Mrs. Windham's garden. Her mouth stretched as if smiling, but her eyes remained sad. They lit up with surprise, however, when I deposited the untouched toffees in her lap. "My word," she said. "How thoughtful you are."

My heart throbbed with gratitude toward Edward for the ability to give her something as I quickly unwrapped a piece for her.

To hear Edward's confession that I mistook that day as the one we met elevated my heart rate. It is an awful experience to have the scaffolding of your life in continual collapse. "What do you mean that wasn't the first time you saw me?"

"I caught sight of you the year prior, when you were playing alone in a field near Am Meer. My tutor was sick with grippe, and I'd fled the estate before he could wake and assign me work. You couldn't have been more than four or five winters old and you were leaning over, kissing the flowers, telling them if they were good, you'd sing them to sleep. Your hair was unbound and nearly reached your knees."

I turned completely onto my stomach to better view him. "Are you certain that was me? It doesn't sound like me."

"It was you. Your song was a shamble of childish ideas, but fascinating to listen to. Amused, I lowered myself into the tall grass to ponder you for a bit longer."

I frowned, wishing I could be certain the memory was of me. "What happened?"

"Your mother stormed out of nowhere and yanked on your arm, scolding you. I watched as your soul closed itself like a poked woolly caterpillar. I felt as I had the day I saw someone stone a dove. It was hard to watch your spirit become crushed. But I saw, Juls; I saw. Later, when we met at that stream, I recognized you. Your countenance was withdrawn, but I already had glimpsed you. It's why I could always coax you out of your shell. I've witnessed your truer self."

Why those words should have made me feel threatened and near tears, I could not say. But I did at least finally recall the incident, though vaguely. My stepfather had been particularly cruel before we took our absence, and Mama had arrived in pain and was out of sorts for the first fortnight of our visit.

Apparently I'd wandered off and Mama had spent nearly an hour searching. When she found me, she was already frantic and then discovered I'd ruined my only pair of stockings.

"Consider now." Edward's whisper distilled over the empty chamber. "Consider the One you've never been hidden from. The One who watched you while you were yet in the womb, dreaming his plan, waiting to make you his lover. His goal for you isn't me, but him. The more you understand him, Juls, the more you'll turn toward his guiding light."

I pressed as much of my body against Edward's side as I could, unable to release my need for the tangible enough to reach out and cling to the shadowy infinite. "Even so, I rather prefer you."

I chuckle now as I envision how alarming those words must have sounded to a vicar. For to any member of the church worth his salt, I'd just confessed idolatry. Thank heavens Edward had keener insight and was less judgmental with me than others. Rather than rebuke, threaten that God might remove him, or lecture me on how to think, he just pulled me tighter, though his voice grew drowsier. "I can't always be your lodestone, though God may permit it for a time." He shifted a shoulder, adjusting his position for comfort. "Ask him to mature you."

His chest rose in a deep breath, something I would learn was a sure sign he was falling into slumber. I lay with eyes open, not quite sure what conclusion to draw from today.

As Edward's body loosened with sleep, I wondered what his former parishioners would make of his tenderness toward me. How could he so firmly rebuke them, yet so patiently lead me—and yet be the same person? I stared at the wavering firelight on the ceiling, feeling secure in the warmth of Edward's presence.

The idea flitted through my head that there was a sort of holiness to this moment, that God was closer than a hairbreadth—that he hovered, waiting to see whether I would heed Edward's advice and invite maturity. All it would take was a prayer, a simple mental invitation.

I still hadn't forgotten my belief that I'd been told my path included suffering.

The invitation was like being told to reach your hand into fire without foreknowledge of whether or not it would burn.

What if I didn't want anything more than this? What if I was content to simply be a wife and not one of those radical people who shunned all else in their pursuit of God?

I shut my eyes, trying to tell myself it was all my imagination, to go to sleep. Eventually, to my quiet dismay, the sensation passed.

Eight

✦

PINPRICKS OF ALARM pierced through my sleepiness. As groggy as I felt, my first inclination was to turn onto my stomach and return to a deep slumber. But gradually I became more aware that Edward was missing. I sat up, taking stock of my surroundings. Outdoors it was still dark enough for me to view a sprinkling of stars, though they were diminishing in the tinge of light that grew over the distant hillocks. His clothing and shoes that I'd seen near the hearth were gone.

I rubbed my tired eyes. How was it possible that Edward was already awake? He'd had less sleep than I had.

Though exhausted, I mustered enough energy to stand and enter the murky hall. There, shades of night webbed the corners.

"Edward?" I whispered, praying I wouldn't wake Thomas or Jameson.

The only response was a distant creak.

"Ed?" I tried again, slightly louder.

My voice distilled throughout the hall and into the empty rooms, amplifying the unnatural silence. I pressed my lips together, not liking how creepy Windhaven was when clothed in darkness. Where was he?

Pressing my elbows against my sides, I turned, trying to decide which direction to go first. This certainly solidified the need to tell him about Macy. He needed to know that we weren't exactly safe, and if he was going to wander off, the very least he could do was tell me where he was going and when I could expect his return.

I bit my lip, imagining what his daily routine might look like. He'd been living by himself so long, he'd probably just woken and was going about his daily business. Which was what? He didn't have a parish. The unemployed have no business to tend to.

I squeezed a fistful of my skirt, trying to remember what Sarah did first thing in the morning. I had a vague notion she used to start her day in the kitchen, boiling water. I frowned. Had Thomas packed the cast-iron pot I'd seen hanging yesterday over the hearth?

Lifting my skirts, I carefully felt my way toward the back of the house. Using the stone walls to guide me, I took tentative steps. It was impossible to see, for the doors were all shut and I didn't want to open them, being uncertain which chambers Jameson and Thomas were in.

I waited until I reached the end of the hall and had started down the small flight of kitchen stairs before risking a louder call. "Edward? Are you down here?"

There was no answer, and the kitchen too was dark. Stumbling, I made my way back up the steps. In the hall, I opened the first two doors but found only the stiff garments that Jameson and I had hung to dry yesterday. I looked again in the room I'd woken in, but it contained only the blankets Edward and I used last night. The room next to ours revealed Jameson and Thomas slumbering near the hearth.

For half a moment, I lost my resolve to remain calm. All I could think was that I couldn't stand losing one more thing, one more person—especially not Edward. Drawing a deep breath, I shut my eyes and forced myself to admit how ludicrous my thoughts were. If Macy and his men were on the property, they wouldn't have just stolen Edward in his sleep without awakening me.

I carefully shut the door so as not to wake the servants and proceeded down the hall in the other direction. Already it was less dark. The next chamber I checked was larger—the one I'd have used as a parlor, for it afforded a near-panoramic view of the enfolding countryside. Here, at last, through the window, I located Edward.

I sagged against the timber of the doorframe, fearing my knees might buckle.

He stood with his arms outstretched to the rising dawn. He made motions as if pushing against the sky and exclaimed aloud with a passion I could see, if not hear. Even though I was afforded a view of only his profile, the words he lustily cried out seemed to rend his soul.

I stepped farther into the room, entranced.

Here were depths of Edward that I was helpless to plumb. Not even I, his beloved, had ever evoked such pathos. Instinctively I knew he was praying. No rote supplication was this, given by a bland-faced vicar, spoken in sibilant tones to a benign congregation. Here was a living flame on touchwood, ready to start a raging blaze.

I bit my lip, wanting to know what sort of a prayer evoked such intensity.

Before I could think better of it, I went to the window, climbed onto the bare window seat, and unlatched the brass hook holding the fixture shut. Wind purled through the chamber as I gave the window an outward push, bringing in the fresh scent of morning.

Edward had finished whatever he'd been petitioning for, and he stood as if drinking in the carmine light of the sunrise.

Then he stretched forth his arms toward the flaming sun. His face was inscribed with a tearing passion as he cried, "And this, Lord, this too I will not withhold. I lay down this parish and give it back to you. You know, O God, you know that I have faithfully served them. That I did not neglect my duty. But have mercy on me where I failed through neglect. Bind the broken and bleeding ones that I failed to see. Have mercy on me if, by my marriage, I've caused the little ones to stumble."

He remained in a posture of worship by sheer determination—Atlas holding up the sky. "And this home, Lord, and all the plans that I had for it—" anguish colored the tones of his strained vocal cords—"I lay it down. Not a mite do I withhold. I am yours. Yours to direct and to send, though this path pains me. I petition that you open the doors for us to stay here, but even if you do not, I will serve you."

One moment it seemed to me that grief devoured Edward, but in the next it was replaced with an ardor that also consumed him. To any outsider, he might have seemed like a zealot, but it roused in me memory of London House—where I'd prayed and a sense of the vastness of eternity pressed down upon me and I felt undone.

I tightened my hold on the brass fitting. How did Edward manage to remain so long in its wind-fire? For it was plain to me that it wasn't the sunrise captivating him.

"And my wife, Julia," Edward released next, "Lord, her too—"

With a swift tug, I shut the window, blocking my ability to hear his next words.

As I backed away from the window, my shoulder hit the mantel, and I placed the backs of my hands on my cheeks, which felt flushed.

That morning as we jounced in the carriage, I sat opposite Edward and studied him anew. Without expression he fixed his gaze on the pastoral views and quaint village of his boyhood home. He reposed in ease. Not even his fingers moved with restlessness.

Frustrated with him, I turned my head and forced myself to watch the brown cows pick their way through the gorse. I shifted in my seat, still unable to accept his prayer from this morning. Part of me was in complete disbelief he'd included *me*. After all we'd been through, it felt unbelievable.

God would find no such offer from me.

No Abraham was I. My number wouldn't be counted amongst those who risked the person they loved most by placing them on the altar. I would raise no knife with the brash hope an angel would cry out for me to stop. Especially not after my fright that morning.

To use Edward's image of being shipwrecked, I had been on the verge of drowning when a large enough piece of wood finally washed within my reach.

The cold, distant light of a star above was comforting—as something familiar, as a reminder that there were fixed points I could use to better navigate next time. Yet when one is floundering in the water, stars are impractical compared to the immediate hope of driftwood.

By that time, I knew the mantra that Edward could never fulfill God's place in my life. But that platitude was like commanding a drowning person to stop sinking and simply swim.

My soul possessed an edge, like a sharpened knife, and I wasn't afraid to cut through the should-be's and address what was actually there. Instead of joy abundant, I felt deep, pressing grief. Instead of peace that passed understanding, my soul screamed—every minute of every hour—with grief and loss and worry over how and when Macy planned to retaliate. I wanted to demand of Edward whether my mourning was acceptable to God as well. Or whether doubt was ever allowed to be part of the canvas of someone's life.

Nevertheless, I hungered for a taste of what Edward possessed, but I knew how extravagant that price tag was.

Thus I closely watched him as our carriage lumbered through the last remnants of his former life, and I wondered how he disentangled himself so easily. Only as we passed the region of the church did he finally show something other than acceptance. His eyes lingered briefly on the steeple, which jutted from behind the hillock. His countenance took on the very quality of sorrow before he resolutely shifted his eyes to the road, where opaque puddles reflected the cloudy sky.

⁓

At twilight, Edward found shelter with a merchant who was willing to house our party in his barn. He'd eyed Edward's collar, then my father's carriage, before giving us a curt nod. Thomas studied me with bewilderment as he and Jameson bunched together hay for bedding. Though he didn't say anything, his wonderment that I'd chosen Edward over Isaac couldn't have been clearer.

I clung to Edward that night as rats ran along the crossbeams above us, knocking straw and dust over us. The musk of manure blended with the sweet smell of hay, competing with the ammonia stench that rose from a century of dried horse urine. I shut my eyes, still able to distinguish Edward's scent, knowing I would prefer to be with him there than in any palace.

⁓

The following evening as we neared Maplecroft, I twisted my wedding ring beneath my glove, finally allowing my mind to touch upon Isaac. The thought that he might be in attendance at

Maplecroft when we arrived unstrung me. The more I reflected, the more I realized how traumatic our disunion had been. I'd left with the vague hope that in years to come we might meet again as friends. I never imagined we'd be forced back together within a week. It was horrible knowing I'd broken his heart, but I could think of nothing crueler than to intrude upon his healing. How many people who'd been jilted weeks before the wedding were forced to live with the newlyweds?

I eyed the first dim stars, realizing if Edward didn't find employment that included a living situation for us soon, I'd have to face Isaac across the breakfast table on the morning that would have been our wedding date.

"Are you ill?" Jameson asked. "Do you need fresh air?"

I clutched the side of the carriage and shook my head, feeling too heavy to speak.

"We're nearing Eastbourne," Edward explained in a low voice. He crossed over to the seat next to mine and placed a supporting hand on my shoulder. He leaned forward and started to tug on the shade. "Shall I draw the curtain?"

"No," I said, touching his arm. "I want to see it."

Edward's lips pursed, but he released the shade.

In the darkling twilight, Eastbourne was as mesmerizing as Macy himself. My breath caught to think that I was its rightful mistress. In the only portion of the house that displayed life, yellow light poured from staggered lancet windows onto the massive lawn. Though the daylight was dimming, I clearly made out the grotesques hunched on their parapets and the various spires rising from the rooftop, adding to its grandeur. Elsewhere I traced shadowed rooflines of various edifices, stunned anew at how sprawling the ancient estate was.

Without intending to, I touched the cool glass, filled with longing. I peered at the countless windows and vast halls.

Surely the first time Macy laid eyes on this estate, it was on this very spot. Had his thoughts been similar? Had he wondered how he'd manage such an expense? Or had he started planning even then to descend upon society as a cruel and avenging angel?

Unaware I was doing so, I touched my neck where he'd given me those marks that had tipped Edward's anger.

I settled back into my seat and found Edward watching me with disappointment.

Jameson, likewise, peered from beneath tufted brows. Realizing how it must appear, I opened my mouth to explain but then snapped it shut. It was wrong to expose them to such deadly knowledge. I swallowed instead. When the silence expanded past endurance, I finally whispered, "I learned something of Eastbourne's history while living with my father, that's all."

Even to me, it sounded tinny and cheap.

Edward's chest rose and quickly fell before he turned his face to the window. In the reflection, curls framed his frustrated and hurt visage.

Jameson's continued displeasure gave me the first glimpse of our formidable childhood opponent. After a long moment, he bent forward and examined Eastbourne for himself. He gave a faint sigh through his nose, then quoted, "'He trod where none dared to gain back his bride, to the pinnacle of the mount beneath the cold light of an insane moon, where the goblins gathered and the witches shrieked.' Do you recall that poem, Edward? The one my headmaster wrote?"

"Yes." Edward's reflected face grew stonier.

Jameson sat back and crossed his hands over his stomach. "Remember how you and Henry would act out the battle between the king goblin and the young prince? Do you recall the time you rent your mother's velvet curtains?"

Edward straightened and turned his head to Jameson, his expression stony.

Jameson's eyes crinkled with warmth before he shut them. "Do you remember your favorite part of the poem?"

Edward stared into the darkness before reluctantly saying, "The final test."

"Finding a way to reverse the goblin king's enchantment over her." With the excitement of a true-born storyteller, Jameson faced me. "Edward used to question me by the hour about how one could undo an enchantment. What he didn't reveal was that he'd been bewitched by one of the fair folk. No doubt part of the spell you cast on him didn't allow him to speak of it."

Edward stared into the gloaming saying nothing, but his countenance visibly thawed. Then, after another hundred feet, he drew a long breath and loosened. He sat straight, giving his mentor a nod of thanks.

༺༻

Grooms raced across Maplecroft's lawn to greet our carriage. I clasped my hands, surprised by the rush of affection I felt upon viewing their familiar forms. Doubtless they noted the gilded coat of arms in the lamplight—a telltale sign this was a Pierson carriage. Snatches of shouted orders carried through to us. A young groom emerged from the stables last and stuck out his tongue as he raced toward us, tucking his hair beneath his wig.

I felt able to breathe again. Surely my father wasn't home. This mad scramble never occurred in his presence.

"Whoa!" Thomas called, reining in the team. Immediately he was assisted by two grooms rushing up and taking the horses' bridles before they could rear their heads.

"Your father dresses *all* his stablemen in velvet and wigs?" Jameson asked in a quiet voice, brushing off the knees of his trousers. "How is it they're ready and dressed at this hour? Is he expecting us or company?"

I gave my head a slight shake, unable to help the swell of joy as they lined up to greet us. "All my father's servants are required to be ready at a moment's notice. But look." I nudged my head toward the tallest youth. "See that square bulge in his vest pocket? Cards. I bet we interrupted their game. It's a good thing we're not my father. He'd be furious to see his stable hands rushing madly about like this."

Lamplight exposed half of Jameson's consternation as he gave Edward a concerned look.

Though he was not Hudson or Brown, the groom who opened the door looked familiar.

"Miss—er—" he coughed into his fist—"I do beg your pardon, Mrs. Auburn; welcome home. Reverend Auburn."

I gave him one of Isaac's polished nods as I offered my hand. "Thank you, John." It was the name my father called all his lower male staff, keeping him from the obligation of learning everyone's name. "Is my father home?"

The man froze as he caught sight of the interior of our carriage. For a full second, he couldn't answer. Then, blinking rapidly, "No, Mrs. Auburn. He returned to London yesterday."

I released a breath I hadn't known I was holding, then stepped onto the smooth drive. My heart burst with a lightness I didn't expect as I took in the manicured lawn. Even at dusk the scent of spring hung in the air. The heady scent of the early roses, amassed together in thick beds, fragranced the evening air. Everything was arranged in neat rows, including the groomsmen, who nodded as I looked at them.

I nearly laughed as I finally understood how Isaac moved so elegantly through society. It was a great dance, the sphere nothing more than the liquid sounds of violin and cello twining together in arpeggiated chords. When one knew the notes and the steps, how wonderfully and seamlessly they fit together.

I tugged off my gloves and surveyed the grounds, giving them a cursory inspection. This was expected, the next step in the dance. The staff worked tirelessly keeping the estate, and our appreciation of their efforts continued the rhythmic ebb and flow.

"I realize you were not expecting us, but I am pleased to find

Maplecroft in such good hands." I fisted my gloves, turning back to the grooms, pretending not to note their heavy breathing and flushed cheeks. Then, because my father and Isaac weren't present and I could, I wrinkled my nose, leaned forward, and added, "And whoever was set to win the pot, please accept my apologies for interrupting."

The men's stances loosened as they worked to keep from smiling.

I rose on tiptoes, feeling joyful. How easy, how profoundly and wonderfully easy this was.

I turned and viewed the mansion. In this season, Maplecroft possessed a sublimity that it lacked in the dead of winter. Without my father's overbearing presence, this life had a new-found appeal. No wonder Isaac felt so confident I could do this. He must have known all along that once we were free, I'd thrive on the predictability. He had been teaching me the steps of a very complicated yet simple dance.

Behind me, Edward's and Jameson's shoes crunched the gravel as the men stepped out of the carriage.

My anger toward Edward cooled. It wasn't his fault he thought me enthralled with Macy. Anyone watching me would have assumed the same thing. I faced him, smiling, feeling repentant, ready to experience the luxuries that my father's house could offer us.

Edward eyed the estate with grim determination. Clutching his hat, his hands hung before him as if weighed down by shackles. Behind him, Jameson stood looking dismayed at the sheer might of Maplecroft.

My spirits dampened slightly, for I could see they felt restrained. Trying to cheer them, I said, "Let's go inside, eat, sleep, and shed this travel weariness."

Edward nodded his thanks to my father's grooms, explained why the carriage was so mud-stained, and indicated for me to lead the way.

Someone had tipped off the indoor staff of our arrival, for the maids were assembled in the grand hall. Mrs. Coleman's eyes widened for a fraction of a second as I stepped over the threshold, though she ironed her features. Under her gaze, I grew aware of the straw in my blowsy hair and the discoloration at the bottom of my gown from rain and mud.

Behind Mrs. Coleman, maids in long starched aprons and longer black skirts dipped in unison. As they invariably stole tiny glances of bewilderment in Edward and Jameson's direction, I gritted my teeth, practically feeling their disapproval that I'd chosen what seemed like a rag sorter over Lord Dalry.

I lifted my chin and said in a firm voice, "Good evening, Mrs. Coleman."

"Mrs. Auburn." She dipped, then spread her hands apologetically. "I fear that you've arrived with the house in disorder. We've been cleaning the fireplaces and airing the chambers. No one told us you planned to spend part of your honeymoon here."

I felt my brows arch, for until that moment I hadn't considered this our honeymoon.

As I had with the grooms, I surveyed my surroundings, trying to work out how to compliment finding Maplecroft in her undergarments. White muslin was bunched and tied over the furniture and chandeliers, protecting them from ash. A glimmer of orange firelight could be seen over the polished floors of the gallery that led to the library.

My eyes lingered on the spot where Isaac had waited for me at the bottom of the stairs the night of our engagement party. Miss Moray had dressed me in so many jewels I'd glittered. James, my father's first footman, had been unable to keep a straight face. I swallowed. Above that spot, one of the larger portraits of Lady Josephine's mocking smile asked me how I enjoyed being a poor vicar's wife when she'd hand-chosen London's favorite lord for me.

Frowning, I lifted my chin, wondering how Mrs. Coleman

would have greeted Isaac and me had we suddenly shown up cold, tired, and hungry on our honeymoon. A spark of anger flared in me. "Who is in the library?"

Mrs. Coleman's gaze flickered that direction. "Simmons, m'lady."

That news didn't please me, but I resisted another frown. My father's steward always tried to pull rank on me. "Was he informed of my arrival?"

Mrs. Coleman shot a panicked look to a wide-eyed maid, who gave a slight shrug. Wringing her hands, Mrs. Coleman said, "I am uncertain."

"Very well. Have one of the maids prepare Lady Josephine's parlor and ready our bedchambers. We'll use that parlor until we join my father in London. Have supper brought on a tray for us there, then fetch us in the library. I'll greet Simmons myself."

Her mouth opened, then shut, before her voice asked an incredulous, "*All* of you?"

All at once I understood the maid's bewildered looks. Edward and I had set out as newlyweds four days ago to attend his brother's wedding. We'd returned without warning, covered in mire and straw, likely smelling like the barn we'd slept in, with a near-seventy-year-old man.

I glanced over my shoulder and found Edward intently studying me in this environment. Behind him, Jameson waited in his mismatched clothing, standing out like a sour note. Against the pedigree of Maplecroft, our doyen looked beggarly. He maintained the stance of a first-rate servant, though—hands behind his back, face expressionless, ready to serve.

It tugged my heart, for I liked him better as my comrade. I hated to send him downstairs, where they'd treat him as an inferior.

I drew a deep breath. This was ridiculous and highly improper. He wasn't my herd. Next thing I'd be inviting Nancy for tea.

"Yes, all of us," I said, shifting foot to foot. "Do not stress over our dinner. I realize you were caught unawares. Whatever the staff ate will be fine."

Mrs. Coleman breathed through her nose and spoke slowly as if I were a dull wit and she was demonstrating infinite patience. "And if you're having a tray for *three* sent up . . . how many *guest* rooms shall I prepare?"

I pressed my lips, knowing this was my second chance to amend my decision. The complexities were thick, so I glanced at Edward for his preference.

He watched stone-faced, keeping my choice independent of his wishes.

I placed a hand over my bodice, deciding to make my point clearer. "Have the guest room next to my father's bedchamber prepared, the one with the frescoes over the ceiling. My husband and I will occupy my usual chambers."

Mrs. Coleman's eyes bulged as if an insect had flown down her throat, but she gave a curt nod. As I led the retreat to the library, I noted she pinned Jameson with a long, cool stare, one that accused him of dishonoring his station and the Pierson name.

Edward waited until we were far enough away that the slap of their boots would disguise our words. He gave me a nod of approval. "Good for you, Juls! Though I don't know how we'll ever convince him to work after this."

I felt able to breathe again as the tension drained between us.

"May I ask the significance of the chamber you chose for Jameson? She looked ready to suffer an apoplexy."

I gave him a mischievous smile, feeling like us again. "I gave Jameson the room reserved solely for members of the monarchy."

Jameson emitted a soft groan and rubbed his balding spot.

"I'm sorry if I caused you embarrassment." I felt hot. "My

intention was to establish that . . ." I frowned, reminded why I didn't need anyone. I hated feeling vulnerable worse than feeling isolated or pitied. "That you were . . . well, you know, one of us . . . like with the elephants."

Jameson placed a hand over his heart, looking pained as if torn between his desire to affirm my step toward community and his desire to beg me to go back to Mrs. Coleman and revoke my order.

Now, of course, I know I'd unwittingly set him at enmity with my father's staff on his first day. Animosity between servants can run thick and ruin the atmosphere. Servants have their own code of honor, and for Jameson to assume station with us was perfidy.

Seeing my anxiety, Jameson forced a smile, though his lips remained pale. "That was marvelously done, my queen!" He chugged his arms, hopping on one foot as if he were boxing. "If that housekeeper were a lioness, you would have come trumpeting and smashed right through her. I've never been more honored." He gave Edward a look that silently tacked on *or more horrified*.

Edward's laughter rang through the marble halls before he reached over and pulled me against him in a hug that swung me off my feet. He twirled me once in a circle. "All hail Mrs. Edward Auburn! A plague on pretension!"

Jameson continued to smile, though he unfastened the top button of his shirt and tugged at his collar as we entered the library.

Simmons stood near the blazing hearth, his arms loaded with books. Before I could greet him, he tossed his armload into the fire. Hundreds of sparks flew upwards as the heat began to reduce the pages to ash.

Jameson, Edward, and I froze as if we'd just stumbled upon a parent making an offering to Moloch. I watched, horrified. In Mrs. Windham's neighborhood everyone kept a mental note of who had what book, much the same way villagers keep a tally of each other's children.

Edward recovered speech first. "You're burning my father-in-law's property! How dare you!"

Simmons gave us a snarling look over his shoulder. "Well, the ruckus is explained. What are you two doing here?"

Edward advanced three steps. "I asked you first!"

Simmons scoffed before turning his attention back to the flames, where he picked up a poker and jabbed the disintegrating books, expediting their demise. "What does it look like I'm doing?"

"On whose authority?" Edward demanded.

Simmons lifted a haughty brow in my direction as if to ask how I tolerated such a slow-witted husband.

But I scarcely registered it. My mouth dried to wool as chills pricked my arms. I'd seen those books before—red leather, so faded they'd turned a peculiar shade of orange, with copper gilt on the pages. I touched my lips as I looked at the spot where I'd last seen them. They'd been lying open on my father's desk, part of the evidence Forrester was compiling to use to blackmail Macy.

"Simmons." My voice came out half strength. "Who told you to burn those?"

He snorted through his nose. "Who do you think? I received urgent orders to do so less than an hour ago."

"Simmons." I heard tears rise in my voice. "Oh no, oh no! You're burning the wrong books!"

"I can assure you." He waved his hand toward an empty lockbox. "They're the right volumes. They, along with the other documents, were locked in the safe box specified in his letter."

"Other documents?" I intended to speak, but my voice screeched. "What documents?"

Edward's brow furrowed as he reached out to me.

I violently wrested my entire body and had to resist screaming at him not to touch me. For at that moment even a feather's stroke threatened to snap the thread holding back my full panic.

"Not that it's your business—" Simmons glowered in my direction—"but they were copies of old land records whose originals are properly filed. I am certain nothing of yours was in there."

My entire body trembled, so I gripped the back of a nearby chair. Though I intended to speak, my voice came out shouting. "Why! Think! Think! Why would my father want records burned that he *locked* away?" There was wetness on my cheeks, though I had no consciousness of crying. "Did you never even stop to question the authenticity of the order? How could you do this!"

"I've had quite enough dramatics, thank you," Simmons said dryly, jamming the poker back into its tool set. "As you can imagine, there are elements of your father's life I try my best not to peer too deeply into." He gestured to Edward and myself as an example. "Now if you'll excuse me, *Mrs. Auburn*."

Simmons stalked out of the room, and a sour taste arose in my mouth as I pressed my palms against my temples. It defied reason that we'd arrive at Maplecroft the exact moment the documentation that Forrester and I needed was being destroyed. That thought alone ordered that I becalm myself. The odds were too astronomical. I needed to breathe and collect my wits.

I forced myself to drop my hands from my face and clutch the back of the chair again. Surely, surely they weren't the same papers.

The other side of the coin, however, was sheer terror.

I returned my gaze to the fire. If those were the documents, then the only way I'd witnessed their destruction was because Macy had timed it. And if he'd timed it, then this was a demonstration of his control. Cold drenched me, and I felt like a band was tightening around my chest.

Just as Mama did after receiving that first correspondence, I began to frantically pace.

Why on earth hadn't I exposed Macy the night I learned his identity was a fraud? I should have woken my father and torn Macy from his perch immediately.

Only I didn't want to risk anything interfering with my ability to marry Edward. I grabbed a fistful of my hair. What had I been thinking? Death surrounded Macy like fog did London. What if Edward paid for my misstep with his life?

My vision blurred as I looked wildly about the library for any other paper or book I might recognize from that night. Who knew what Macy had been doing since then? Were I him, I'd most certainly be destroying evidence with a vengeance.

"Run back to us." Jameson's voice was soft.

I spun so fast, my skirts nearly made me lose my balance. Hot, angry tears spilled. "What?"

"If anyone ever looked like a pride of lions were descending upon her, it is you. Calm down and tell us what's happening. What was in those papers?"

I felt my face crumple as my mouth worked to utter the most horrible words in existence—that I'd blackmailed Macy and my evidence likely just dissolved into ash. But before I could speak, a slight movement near the door caught my eye.

Simmons stood in the shadowed hall, his hand on the doorknob, waiting.

Our eyes met, and all I could think was that I'd finally found Macy's infiltrator—that my next words held the power of life or death over Edward and Jameson, for surely everything I revealed would be repeated to Macy.

I looked at the elderly man, holding back despair. For his story from Africa was just that—a story. There was no safe group to run to. The ones I trusted heart and soul had proven capable of giving their backs over much simpler matters. Besides, who could withstand Macy? What good was an elderly valet when newspaper mongrels, MPs, and all the wealth and might of Pierson couldn't stop Macy? Even if Jameson was brave enough to stand beside me, knowledge would destroy him.

"Juls?" Edward brought my focus back to Maplecroft. A curl fell over his brow, a familiar sight.

The invisible band around my chest loosened. Here at least was someone I couldn't fault. Edward was the last person I fully trusted. His presence helped me steady my thoughts. I had no desire to drag these two into my crisis, so I needed to pull myself together.

I shifted my gaze to meet Simmons's eyes, wishing I could find words to communicate that Edward and Jameson were innocent and had no knowledge of Macy's past. I rubbed my temples. "I'm fine, Edward. I am. Jameson, my head hurts. Would you be willing to go check on the progress of supper? I . . . I think I'll feel better if I eat."

Simmons's face screwed into a look I couldn't decipher as he withdrew a piece of folded paper from his vest, consulted it, then returned it. "Never mind. I'm heading toward the kitchens next. I'll check for you." The door shut.

"What was in those papers?" Edward asked.

"I swear, I don't know." It was almost true. Now that I considered it, Forrester never told me what our most damning evidence was. I gathered my skirt and fell into a chair. Why on earth hadn't I thought this out beforehand? I'd been so relieved to wed Edward that I simply tried to forget Macy's existence. For days!

Realizing that both Jameson and Edward warily watched me, I sought a subject that might distract them. Only I couldn't think of anything that could hurtle the fact that I'd acted terror-stricken moments ago. *Ha-ha, just teasing. By the way, did either of you happen to note the color of Mrs. Windham's dress the day of the wedding? Shocking, wasn't it?*

To my relief, two upper maids turned the focus from me when they wheeled in a cart laden with dinner. Simmons followed and stood frowning, his arms akimbo. "I revoked your order to interrupt the cleaning of Lady Josephine's parlor. You'll eat here in the library, as it's already in a state of readiness."

I stiffened, knowing that Isaac would've taken great offense that he'd overridden my orders. Yet rather than battle Simmons, I decided to let him think he ruled me. Especially if he were Macy's spy. Later, if it became necessary, this might give me an advantage and he'd be easier to overthrow, as he wouldn't be expecting it.

Rubbing the back of my neck, I studied the library, wondering if there was a hidden alcove that Simmons could hide in and listen to our conversation. *Well, let him listen,* I thought as the girls set up the table. The only person I would ever speak to about this was Forrester, and I'd see him soon enough. I sank into my chair. Who would have thought the day would come when I'd actually want his company?

One of the maids, a young girl who'd helped bathe me the morning I prepared to meet my father, started to set down the plate of food in her right hand. Suddenly she hesitated, glanced nervously at Simmons—who narrowed his eyes—then gave me the plate in her left hand instead.

Before I could think, I was on my feet. I grabbed both plates and flung them into the fire, then snatched the one she was about to give Jameson. "Our food will be placed in serving dishes!" I threw Jameson's plate into the fire as one of the maids hurried from the chamber. "You will not separate them. Have new food sent! Make certain it is in serving dishes!"

Jameson cast Edward a wide-eyed look of alarm, which Edward missed as he stared at me with one of his own.

Simmons eyed the broken pieces of porcelain scattered over the hearth without emotion. "May I ask what your next set of plans are, Reverend Auburn? I'd like to keep Lord Pierson abreast of his daughter's whereabouts just now."

Edward kept a watchful gaze on me. "We're going to London

the day after tomorrow. I planned to seek Lord Pierson out for advice, as my circumstances have changed since our last meeting."

Simmons gave a nod. "Very good. I'm headed there myself at first light. Would you rather me delay my journey and travel with you? Another companion might prove beneficial."

"I'm not mad," I said in a low voice to Edward. "I'm not! But if you allow that man to travel with us, I will be."

Edward shifted his gaze to Jameson, a plea for help.

My fingers were cold as I also looked to Jameson and asked the same thing.

He considered me a second, then leaned toward Edward and whispered, "Well, any fool knows not to feed a faerie queen on china plates. How dare they! If you ask me, they deserved the broken dishes. Let's go downstairs and smash the whole set. At the very least, they could have scattered rose petals over the parts touching the food. Completely unforgivable!"

Edward, bewildered-looking, whispered, "Have you lost your senses too?"

"One can't lose something they're still searching for." Jameson gave my hand a pat. "She's no more mad than I am."

Tears of relief wet my eyes, for I could see he believed me sane even though my behavior seemed erratic.

Edward offered me a half smile, trying to follow Jameson's lead since it seemed to be working. "Thank you, but no," he said over his shoulder. "My wife and I prefer to travel alone. Please do not disturb us again tonight."

"I'll be on hand until morning," Simmons drawled in a doubtful voice before walking away, leaving the door a crack open.

"Jameson," I asked before anyone could speak, "will you tell me another story about Africa?" If Simmons did have a way of listening, I'd rather a different conversation already be rolling when he got in position to listen.

"Absolutely." Jameson sat back and crossed his legs. "Ha! It's been ages since anyone actually asked me for a story. How novel to have someone who's not heard them all before, too. Now let me think . . ."

I rested my forehead in one hand as he babbled about the delights of having an unspoiled audience. Jameson seemed to understand why I wanted him to speak, for more than once he gave me a look that asked if he were delivering what I wanted.

I relaxed and nodded. Anyone hearing us wouldn't suspect he was filling empty air. He told stories with relish. By the time new food was brought into the library, he was acting out a tale about the time he tried to jump on the back of a wild quagga to prove his horsemanship skills.

Knowing that Edward thoughtfully studied me, I took care to nod my thanks to the maids, then nibble a few bites, though I no longer had appetite.

Jameson was a capital anecdotalist. Even in my half-panicked state, by the time we reached the top of the stairs and bade each other good night, I'd felt the allure of Africa. A desire to step foot on that continent ran through me with a vein of longing. I envisioned sleeping in canvas tents with the howls of monkeys rending the air. I eyed the ancestral portraits, hugging myself, wondering if I'd feel safe from Macy even that far away.

"Good night." Jameson bowed, then started to retreat down the hall. "I'm off to sleep in a bed fit for a king."

"Jameson, wait!" Edward hastened after him.

For a moment Edward reminded me of his boyhood self. It was in the manner he stood, the expression on his face as he spoke to Jameson in whispers. He nodded agreement to whatever Jameson said in his ear, bringing to mind a boy reverently receiving instructions from his father. He looked infused with kindness and courage as he stepped away from his valet.

"Thank you," he said. "I promise, I shall."

Jameson's eyes shone with a pride that was the deepest

expression of fatherly love I'd ever beheld. It hurt to witness, the same way it is painful for victims of burns to have healing salve applied. I stood unwilling to look, yet unable to turn away. Jameson's hand twitched at his side as if he wrestled against the urge to tousle Edward's curls—something I didn't plan to resist a few minutes hence.

Jameson gave me another heartfelt bow. "Good night, O queen of queens."

The thickness in my throat restrained me from answering, so I merely nodded.

When Edward regained my side, the kindness in his expression further threatened to crumble me. I wanted to protest that it was unfair for them to unmake me with benevolence. My ability to remain aloof was temporarily impaired because of my panic.

Now I half wished they would treat me with contempt or mutter questions secretly between themselves about my sanity. Then I could have crouched safely behind my walls, clutching my secret about Macy forever. As it was, it felt like a writhing, slippery eel.

Several tapers were lit and set on their silver holders on the vanity. Their wavering flames reflected in the mirror, bathing the aureate bedchamber with a honeyed light. A fire was lit, and copper pitchers fitted with lids awaited our use. They were set near the coals to keep the water warm.

Edward gently lifted the back of my hand and kissed it before moving toward the washbasin.

I slid my arms out of the bolero I wore over my gown and set it on the bed.

Expecting Edward to pour himself a basinful of water in order to give his face and neck a good scrub, I worked on locating the hairpins that held my loose style in place. If I kept busy and didn't speak, by morning my odd behavior would be in the past. And if I were the first one out of bed and found a way to keep Mrs. Coleman with me at all times, then . . .

"Show me how," Edward requested behind me.

Hardly daring to look him in the eyes, I turned and found that he'd brought the basin of water to me.

He'd stripped off his frock coat, cravat, and vest so that he stood in trousers and wore a loose linen shirt that gleamed in the semidarkness. "Walk me through the steps of being a lady's maid. I can't afford to buy you new stays if I keep breaking them."

I glanced at the door, knowing the moment he lured me into speaking, I was lost. For I longed to pour out all the fears churning within me and to confess my manifold regrets. I pinned my arms against my stomach and sat on the bed.

"Now you look like the second time I saw you." Edward set the basin on the floor and knelt at my feet. "Making yourself as small as possible on that rock." With slow movements, he removed one shoe and then the other. "That was the real reason I asked Jameson how to undo enchantments, you know. Even then it seemed that invisible rules and codes were continuously crushing you. But they are almost impossible to unravel without understanding them. It makes me feel inadequate."

I pressed my lips together, feeling the weight in my chest grow heavier.

"Sometimes I've managed to untwist one of your funny rules, though I rarely understand why or how. I never ask, either. You're always on the verge of retreating, so instead of questioning, I've accepted. But I'm asking now, Juls. Tell me just one thing."

I started to shake my head, but instead of asking about my odd behavior in the library, he asked, "Why did you fear to step out of the sunshine that day?"

I swallowed my surprise. That was his one request?

With his thumbs he kneaded the sole of my foot as he waited.

I loosened my fingers from the knot I'd squeezed them into. "I found Mama too sad to rise from bed that morning."

He nodded encouragement to continue. As I did, he started to soak a sponge in the water and peeled off my stocking. I told him the full story, including how I gave Mama all his toffees.

When I finished, he closed his eyes as if savoring the very essence of my personality and his own swelling emotion. The picture is sharp in my mind, for that night unlocked something within me. He bent over my foot, which was supported in his lap, his face grieved, unable to contain the sorrow he felt at glimpsing the tender soul I'd once been. But then, to my surprise, cradling my foot, he bent and kissed it as if I were precious beyond measure—every part, even my feet.

Keeping his loving repose, he switched the foot he tended. He kept his eyes trained solely on his work. "Remember the condition I found you in on the night you were wandering about Eastbourne?"

I stiffened, for I'd not granted him access to this topic.

"Do you recall what you were frightened of?"

My guardian. My mind formed the words I wouldn't say. Sadness crested, though I did my best to appear unmoved.

Edward lifted his gaze. "Was there a real cause to be afraid? Or like that day in the woods, was it based on a misperception?"

I resisted arguing that it was different. I'd been lied to.

"Consider what would have happened if you explained yourself that day in the woods." He placed my foot in the towel he'd spread over his lap and gently dried it. "I would that you had trusted me to set you free, even then. Now imagine the outcome at Eastbourne if you'd not tried to handle it by yourself, but sought my aid."

"I believed my guardian murderous," I finally succumbed. "I feared it would cost you your life."

He ceased working and sat with his head bowed. "Consider the scenario from my perspective. The woman I love, isolated, in danger, and struggling to handle matters alone."

"You would have insisted on investigating."

"And would that have been a mistake?" Edward kept his posture. "What would have happened next?"

I glanced at the candlelight that shimmered on the wall. Probably Edward would have discovered that my father was Lord Pierson and Macy's manipulation would have been exposed. Edward would have petitioned my father not to send me to Scotland but to allow me to marry him instead. Likely my father would have conceded and furnished us with the money he'd set aside for me.

"This is different." I resisted tears. "I know—*I know*—this time there is danger."

"I believe you." Edward finally looked up and arrested my gaze. "But I'm asking you to allow me to lead, Juls. You may not like my choices, as my perspective is different. But I can't be a good husband unless you gift me with the trust and ability to be one. Test me. Give me this chance."

No more encouragement was needed, for my secrets were so burdensome I could scarcely carry them anyway.

My vision blurred as I nodded.

I'd like to say that I confessed all to him. But even had I wanted to, I scarcely would have found the nerve. For when Edward kissed my foot, it unleashed an emotion I wasn't certain how to handle. In that moment I felt loved and seen. Yet I feared it too good to be real. What if he only loved what he'd seen—a reflection on the water that he believed reality? For no one had ever savored my distinct personality. Not even Mama.

I feared that by revealing I was one of Macy's blackmailers, I'd throw a rock in the middle of the reflection, marring the image he loved.

My tongue swelled every time I even considered that part. My own body refused to proceed.

In the end, I told Edward as much as I deemed safe to reveal and still keep his affection—that some of my father's servants were loyal to Macy, what I knew of the books, that part of Macy's downfall had to do with land and deeds, then lastly that I'd learned Macy dabbled in poisons.

As I spoke, Edward abandoned the basin of water on the floor and took a spot beside me on the bed. When I told him why I smashed our dinner plates, he pulled me close and buried his face in my thick hair and chuckled.

"Why is that humorous?" I craned my neck.

"Because I was watching her too. Didn't you note that two of the plates had a double portion of jugged hare and potatoes? She started to give you one obviously meant for the men and then, realizing her mistake, panicked and checked to see if Simmons noted her error too."

I froze, realizing I was becoming as paranoid as Forrester. "Please tell me that you're jesting."

He parted my hair and kissed my neck, scratching me with his chin. "You should have seen her face when you snatched and threw both plates into the flames, screaming we would serve ourselves. She likely thinks you were offended she gave you the smaller portion."

His ribbing was so good-natured, I couldn't help but to join in the laugh. "That's so awful! How do these types of misunderstandings always happen to me?"

"They won't anymore," he promised, unbuttoning the back of my dress. "You're going to start trusting me. We're going to start disentangling so much more than wrong conclusions. When you're worried about Macy or Simmons, or anyone else, bring those matters to me and allow me to lead. Do we agree?"

I nodded.

Words weren't necessary thereafter. As husband and wife, there was another, deeper language we were discovering.

Nine

❦

AT SUNRISE, Edward slipped from bed, trying not to wake me.

Knowing he desired to pray in privacy, I feigned sleep until he'd dressed and gone, then moved into the spot he'd occupied, savoring its warmth. The same happiness I felt the morning I woke in the church rose afresh.

Having confessed to Edward made me feel lighter than I had in ages.

I clutched the pillow he'd used and breathed deeply of the lingering bay rum scent. So much of life is falling through dark uncertainty, but with Edward, a net had finally caught me. Until last night, I'd lacked insight on what having a partner meant. Mama and William most certainly had never been a team—in their household it was always safer to conceal yourself, your thoughts, your desires. Anything and everything learned would be used to break you.

But with Edward, everything suddenly felt fresh and alive. I'd taken a tentative first step of trust and found the planking solid.

I tossed aside the counterpane and planted my feet on the

ground. Picking up Lady Pierson's dressing gown, I examined it with disdain. Right then and there, I decided never to wear another article of my father's late wife's clothing again. I threw it to the side, choosing to wear yesterday's chemise instead. I glanced at the trunks in the corner of the chamber. Neither would I ever don one of those corpulent dresses from Quill's again.

I marched to the window and threw open the drapes, flooding the chamber with the blazing light of dawn. I lifted my chin, drinking in its warmth, then spun, gladdened that it was morning and I had a new life.

In the corner of the bedchamber, with the other luggage, Macy's trunk holding my former clothing haunted me, yet I was determined to wear my own clothing. I unlatched and lifted the lid, then grinned at how wonderfully plain the contents were. I selected a rust-brown walking dress—a color Miss Moray forbade as it made me appear pale.

A glint of gold flew out from amongst its folds and bounced off the carpet. My breath caught as I recognized it. Mama's locket. With the tenderness of a mother handling her newborn babe, I retrieved it. Inside, Mama and William's portraits were still intact. I shut my eyes and pressed Mama's image against my heart—finally feeling my past merge with my present.

～

My skirts were so light and airy, I practically skipped beneath Lady Josephine's portrait. Let her disapprove my choice of husband. While she stood forever immortalized wearing a cumbersome gown and laden with heavy chains of jewels, I would flaunt the benefit of being a poor vicar's wife—freedom.

Smiling, I slowed my pace before entering the library. A crystal bowl of shiny green apples sat on a marble-topped French table outside the chamber. Surprised they'd managed to find ripened fruit outside its season to decorate with, I grabbed one and polished it on my sleeve as I entered.

To my surprise, Eaton, Maplecroft's butler, stood at the table we'd dined at last night, rubbing silverware with a soft cloth. Near him a cart laden with dishes and roses waited.

"Eaton!" I'd all but forgotten him.

He startled, nearly dropping the knife he was polishing, but then quickly collected his dignity.

"Miss Julia. Forgive me; I didn't hear you enter."

"No, I suppose not." I couldn't help smiling. Another benefit of not wearing a lumbering gown: I didn't crinkle with every step. "When I didn't see you yesterday, I assumed my father had taken you to London."

Eaton bowed. "A new shipment of wine arrived by train yesterday. I was out selecting next season's vintage for your father's cellar. I'm sorry I missed your arrival." He glanced at the clock. "There was quite a discussion last night over whether you'd keep your father's schedule and require an early breakfast."

Unlike other English gentlemen, my father was strict about rising and breakfasting early. He had a fantastic constitution. More often than not, he stayed out until the early hours of the morning, only to rise again with but three or four hours of sleep. I glanced at the clock, wondering if I'd uncovered the reason behind his continual foul mood. Maybe he was just tired.

"I fear my husband keeps even earlier hours," I said.

Eaton's entire body froze.

I couldn't help but laugh. "Only you needn't worry about it after tomorrow morning. We're leaving for London."

"So Simmons informed me." Eaton glanced at the clock again. "What time shall I tell Cook to have breakfast ready, then?"

Not certain how long Edward prayed, I decided to give the servants enough time to reassemble. "Forty minutes from now will be suitable."

"Forty?" His eyes darted back to the clock as beads of perspiration dotted his forehead. "Very good, ma'am."

❧

"Well, we certainly have newspapers." Edward's eyes widened as Eaton set down the usual stack. He glanced at the butler before thumbing through the carefully ironed print. "My word. I think every major paper in the country is present."

Eaton gave a slight bow. "As well as two each from the United States, Prussia, and France." To me, he added, "You'll find news of your elopement still dominating the society page. In London they've even started placing bets on where you'll both make your first public appearance. I daresay there'll be a slew of invitations when you arrive."

His words dampened our entire party. Edward shot Jameson a look that I couldn't quite decipher. I doubt now that anyone ever won that bet, for no one outside of Macy could possibly have guessed where that event would take place.

"Yes, thank you," Edward finally said. "You're dismissed."

Eaton's eyes flashed in my direction as if he was only willing to accept my command. Jameson also caught the movement, for his white brows tufted. Confused, I gave Eaton a slight nod. As soon as the doors closed, Edward started to divide the papers into piles.

My teacup was suspended midair as my stomach tightened. Silently I willed Edward not to do this to me, not to disappear behind a paper wall. I ran my gaze over the opulent setting. Eaton's tablescape was magnificent. He'd chosen gilt-edged plates and matching crystal goblets. White roses, barely opened, were amassed in a gold-footed bowl. Steam fogged the silver domes that hid piles of eggs, black pudding, tomatoes, bacon, and mushrooms. I was so famished, I could identify what had been prepared by its smell. But I couldn't eat because I couldn't endure sitting through one more lavish breakfast where my presence wasn't truly required.

Edward's brow furrowed as he scanned through one of the sections he'd set apart.

I set down my teacup, my appetite diminished. Black-and-white print had come to represent an impenetrable paper-thin barrier.

Jameson lifted the first silver dome from its piping-hot dish. "I don't know what you're searching for, but eat! I can hear both your stomachs grumbling from here. Besides, your wife is languishing under your inattention. And we all saw last night what happens when you offend a faerie queen by improper table etiquette."

I laughed; once again he'd managed to scatter my clouds with a wave of his hand. That morning I'd spied Jameson and Edward standing on the open lawn, having a deep discussion. I deemed by their expressions that Edward had relayed what transpired between us last night. Jameson beamed with fatherly pride, nodding, but his face darkened toward the end of the talk. The way he'd gravely glanced over his shoulder at Eastbourne was unmistakable, tempting me to release a measure of my fears regarding Macy and place my trust in this new circle.

"I thought you had enough of London when you were beggared on its streets." Jameson frowned when Edward only bit his thumb.

Edward appeared too engrossed to answer. He strained his eyes as he trailed down one column after another.

Jameson's splayed hand smacked the paper before him. "Edward!"

Edward blinked, dazed. "Wh-what did you say?"

Jameson shoved the plate of food he'd fixed before Edward. "Whatever you're searching for can wait. Look at Mrs. Auburn. I thought you were going to maintain the Auburn tradition of gathering the family over breakfast to discuss the day's plans."

Edward did glance at me, then swiped his fingers through

his curls. Seemingly dissatisfied, he picked up a piece of toast and crunched it between his teeth. "Oh yes. Sorry, Juls."

I unfolded my napkin and placed it on my lap, aware that his gaze had already returned to the paper. This wasn't exactly the breakfast I wanted either. "It doesn't matter. Go on, read them."

Jameson shot Edward a look that forbade it.

"No, really," I said flatly. "It's fine."

"What she means to say," Jameson corrected, "is she'd rather you read the paper and ignore her than not read the paper and resent her. You must learn to use words, Mrs. Auburn." To Edward, "What's so important, anyway? I've never known you to take much interest in current happenings. Usually you're obsessed with discerning the ancient ones."

"Sorry, Juls. I didn't mean to ignore you." Edward spread his hands over the pile. "I just . . . I don't want to spend one moment longer under your father's roof than is absolutely necessary. I'm looking for work and thought to get a head start on combing through the advertisements. Though in all honesty, I haven't a clue what to do. Lady Foxmore threatened that she was petitioning for an inquiry into my misconduct, and I'm not exactly sure I'm allowed to take a position in the church. Even if I can, being a vicar might make it easier for Macy to locate us."

I lowered my chin, desiring to say that when Macy was ready, he'd find us regardless. Even arriving here, within the bastion of Maplecroft, we'd seen Macy's hand at work, destroying, controlling, subjugating. But the words stuck on my tongue.

"She seems to think it makes no difference where we go," Jameson said, using a fork and spoon to lift a heaping portion of buttered mushrooms to his plate. "If the faeries can't manage to hide her from him, then why should we humans bother trying?" Then, as I gave him a sharp look of surprise, "Words, Mrs. Auburn. I daresay the fair folk drink in their knowledge from the air, or something of that ilk, but if you insist on dwelling amongst humans, you'll have to get used to our strange manner of communicating. We have to tell each other our ideas and thoughts."

Edward gave me the same humored look he used to give me when we played with Henry and Elizabeth—one that suggested our companions were proving more fun than we anticipated.

I swallowed, knowing I ought to speak at this juncture, but felt the same painful embarrassment that always arose. "Yes, well, I tend to say all the wrong things, shocking everybody."

"What a marvelous gift!" Jameson speared his food. "But how can we celebrate it if you never use it?" He chuckled. "I'm quite looking forward to seeing you hone it. Already it's given me the best bedchamber of my life. I've never seen a house-keeper more stunned, and I warrant the downstairs buzzed like a regular wasps' nest for hours. And it's not as if we can expect you to leave all faerie mischief behind."

I laid one arm across my stomach, studying Jameson. He dangled long-denied sustenance to a malnourished soul. I'd been told so often what was wrong with me, I'd stopped believing any part of me was right. That he'd chosen my oddities—the very things that annoyed people and caused them to dislike me—felt threatening. It was like Edward with the toffees. I feared to reach for them lest I discover this nothing more than a cruel joke.

Jameson clucked his tongue twice. "I'd like to inquire the reason behind those long, distrusting glances. But I know myself too well. Nothing infuriates me more than someone being trampled over." He cast Edward a look. "I might not be able to hold my tongue later." Then to me, "Never mind it! We'll soon have you trilling as freely as every other young lady."

My expression must have indicated that I highly doubted it, for Edward laughed.

"Let's not take it that far," he told Jameson. "But trust me, you're doing exceedingly well, and you should feel proud. Outside of myself, Henry, and Elizabeth, I've never seen her open up to anyone. The very fact that she addresses you means she's accepted you."

"It's not as bad as all that," I protested, smiling as I added a piece of toast to my plate. "I talk to others too."

Jameson cracked his knuckles. "Now we're getting somewhere. Whom else does she speak to? We'll figure out the exact sorts of souls she should be around."

"There's Nancy," Edward said between a mouthful of eggs, "one of the girls I managed to keep out of the workhouse about a year back."

"Actually, she speaks to me." I tore off a piece of bread but, before popping it in my mouth, said, "I tried to ignore her, but she refused to notice."

Jameson gently drummed on the table. "I like this girl! Where did this Nancy person go?"

Edward swallowed his mouthful. "Actually, that's on my list. She ended at the workhouse regardless. I need to write and see if she'll join us." He wagged his eyebrows. "We're offering her the same salary as you. Still, to get out of the workhouse she might take it."

Jameson leaned back in his chair. "Well, tell her that despite the homelessness, the sleeping accommodations and food are superior. I think I've done my job of scrounging up provisions exceptionally well!"

"Bravo!" I dunked my next bite of toast into my teacup. "I look forward to seeing what you can produce in London. I hear there's an excellent house on Audley, with a library that exceeds even this one. They also have a famous French chef, though the lord of the house isn't always pleasant. Think you can manage accommodations there?"

Jameson snapped his fingers. "Done. That Simmons fellow should be announcing our arrival tonight."

The reminder of my father's steward turned the food in my mouth to sand. I forced myself to swallow and set down the remainder of my toast. My fingers felt so thick, I could barely clutch the tiny handle of my teacup. While I felt a wonderful sense of freedom entrusting myself to Edward, I couldn't help but wonder if I were making my worst mistake yet.

Macy had been cryptic about allowing matters to become very uncomfortable for me. I'd not told Edward that part, as Macy had said that after I'd blackmailed him. It was hard to tell one part of the story without the other.

I glanced out the window, even though Eastbourne was too far down in the ravine to see.

"Juls?"

I startled, then faced Edward.

As if guessing my thoughts, he extended his hand over the table, palm up—an invitation for me to take it. I loosened, as his wedding band winked in the light. Nodding agreement to stop worrying, I slipped my hand into his. What could Macy possibly do? We were married.

"Did you hear that?" Jameson leaned forward and faced the door.

Outside in the hall, there was a faint patter of feet.

I scooted back my chair to be prepared, though the sound was confusing. They moved too quickly to be a maid, for servants were supposed to glide in and out, unseen ghosts. The shoes weren't hard-soled, which meant the person was a female. Yet I couldn't think of a single girl who would be inside Maplecroft.

The person hesitated outside the door, piquing the interest of our entire party. For instead of knocking, she just stood there, whispering words to someone that were impossible to make out.

I placed my napkin on the table, rising. "Hello?"

"There, see! I heard her!" a familiar voice cried.

Edward likewise rose and glared at the door, ready to defend me.

The door cracked open, and Kate Dalry's grinning face peeked in near the doorknob. Her hair was in a loose bun and her cheeks in high color. She gave two tiny jumps of excitement, then called out behind her, "She is here! She really is!"

Before I could speak, she raced across the chamber and threw herself into my arms, nearly toppling me. "The grooms said you arrived and were moving on to London in a few days, but we didn't want to disturb Mrs. Coleman in case they were pulling our legs, so we let ourselves in. The front door is unlocked."

I clutched Kate's arm tightly, feeling my insides cinch like overwound gears in a clock. I hadn't considered that Isaac wasn't in London with my father. Now that the moment was upon me, I couldn't face him. I wouldn't do this. Only I couldn't think of an escape.

"You need to come grant permission for us to join you first." Kate grabbed my hand and dragged me unwillingly a couple of steps toward the door. "Though *I* wasn't worried we'd be intruding!"

I cast Edward an uncertain glance.

He knew somehow she was Isaac's sister, because his glare was fastened on the door. He waited, arms crossed, challenging.

"Come on!" Kate pulled harder. "The more you make her wait, the more nervous she'll become."

I blinked. "She?"

Kate's head bobbed. "Evelyn Greenley! Who do you think? She walked over with me this morning so I could sell my eggs." Her eyes sparkled as she pumped my hands. "Oh, Julia! You don't know! What do you think! She's started speaking again. She's come over every day since the night of the wedding. Mama says at least we can thank you for that much. When Evelyn learned that Isaac stopped sleeping as well as eating, she slipped into our house. I don't know what she said, but he finally broke down and wept. It was the most awful sound you can imagine. It was so bad, Mama rocked outside the door, crying too. Afterwards, Evelyn convinced him to go to bed and sleep. Mama clung to her next, saying she'd never felt so helpless in all her life and that Evelyn was an angel."

Each word was like a flagellum tearing flesh. It didn't seem possible that each new sentence could inflict raw agony, but it did. I stared, horrified, for no one told me Isaac had been that distraught.

Evelyn Greenley chose that exact second to tiptoe into view, a sparrow ready to take flight. Blinking back tears, she clutched a long-handled basket of brown eggs with all her might. She took one step into the chamber, glanced at the men. Then, lowering her chin, she retreated, looking wildly behind her for a place to hide.

"Evelyn!" I cried, recovering. Picking up my skirts, I hurried to her.

She pulled the basket of eggs closer to her stomach. "We only came to—I mean, I tried to stop her—"

I met her gaze; then, leaning over the basket of eggs, I squeezed her tightly about the shoulders, silently communicating my gratitude and friendship. I extended my hand. "Please, come in. I am delighted to have you. I never got to properly thank you for the wedding dress. It was so lovely."

She drew in a sharp breath at this reminder but took my hand.

I prayed Edward wouldn't be his resolute, iron-willed self when I turned. But he couldn't have been more unreadable as I gestured to him. "You've met my husband, Edward. And this here is our valet, Jameson."

Curious to see what a soul like Jameson did with a soul like Evelyn, I glanced at him too. He gave a warm smile. Everything about him appeared small and safe, as if he'd managed to reduce his very height and make his shoulders less broad for her sake.

"Breakfasting with your valet?" Kate plopped into a nearby chair uninvited and tugged on her bonnet strings. She wrinkled her freckled nose as she surveyed Edward's clothing. "Is he in training? He's not very good yet, is he?"

"Kate!" I felt like Isaac as I admonished her. "You will apologize."

Jameson shushed me with a wave of his hand from where he'd stood to greet the newcomers. "No, no! We never punish people for speaking their honest thoughts. If I were responsible for that scraggy-looking suit, she might be the only soul willing to tell you the truth. Like that new story about the emperor who is actually naked." He wagged a finger at Kate as he pulled out a chair for Evelyn. "You're a changeling if ever there was one. Doubtless you heard one of your queens was visiting. Humph. Perhaps she silently called for you. For we were just speculating whether or not Mrs. Auburn had friends, since she refuses to speak to people. Likely you're here to prove that she doesn't want our assistance."

Kate's eyebrows made a downward V. "Julia speaks. Maybe not much to me, but Isaac says you have to draw her out just right and be patient. He could do it. Some nights she and Isaac stayed up hours past bedtime just talking."

Her statement clanged through the room like a spilled tea service. Evelyn paled for me and started toward the door.

"We were studying," I quietly corrected Kate, "not talking. There's a difference."

Kate shrugged, then bent over and hiked up her drooping stocking. "Well, Miss Moray called it courting whenever she complained about the impropriety of it."

His jaw stiff, Edward fastened his gaze on the newspapers.

Evelyn's face creased as if she were aware of every quiver of hurt that pulsated through the chamber. "Sh-she talked to me too." Her voice, finespun as gossamer, was directed at Edward. "At her . . . that . . . gathering at my house. If she hadn't . . ."

Her voice choked on itself. I squeezed her hand, wondering how someone this fragile had been able to act as a ministrant to

Isaac. Perhaps she'd been so overwhelmed that, ever the gentle-man, he broke first so she wouldn't have to.

She returned my squeeze, then, glancing at Edward and Jameson, backed toward the door. "We should go. It was rude of us to just drop in."

"No, please stay." Edward woodenly stacked the papers and gathered the ones he wanted in his arm. "I was about to leave anyway. It would be good for Julia to have visitors."

Tears welled in Evelyn's eyes as if she needed to go but now feared the opportunity for escape had been cut off.

"No, no, let the girls finish their business." I shooed Evelyn out the door, where she cast me a grateful look before hasten-ing down the hall. "Kate—" I waved for her to leave—"please give your mother my greetings and my love."

She pouted, looking as if she was going to argue, but just as she opened her mouth, Edward gave her one of his stern-est gazes. She found her feet immediately—something neither Isaac nor my father had ever managed. She walked toward the door backwards, tucking her hair in place. "I might be coming to London too. Colonel Greenley spoke to Mama about it." She gave me a pleading look. "If I do and you're still there, may I call?"

"Yes. I would be honored."

In her carelessness, the door slammed shut before she raced back down the hall. The merriness that had been over our small party was gone as we retook our seats and stared at the food on our plates, which had grown cold.

❧

Two hours later, the library floor was covered in papers with inked circles, earmarking any job that might suit Edward.

After deciding which ones to apply for, he'd taken residence in Isaac's favorite seat and written letters liberally, paying no heed to his station. Posts were addressed to pewterers, furriers, booksellers, land stewards, tutors, butchers, schoolteachers—anything that had potential.

Edward refused to tout his association to my father, but privately I planned to oversee that the letters were franked, which would call attention to the fact that they'd come from the household of someone in government. Furthermore, there was no hiding that replies were to be sent to the West End of London. That, too, would raise eyebrows.

Having neither needlework nor desire to be out of Edward's sight, I ambled through the rows of books. Most of my father's volumes were dull and of little interest. Eventually I found a section of poetry and selected a volume with an eccentric-looking spine. It was black with silver-embossed thistles and pewter-colored leaves.

Slants of sun spilled into the chamber, warming my skin as I curled up in an oversized chair.

To my surprise, when I started to open the book, the spine shifted, fanning the pages. For a fraction of a second, a hidden fore-edge painting was revealed. It disappeared before I could make out its subject matter. Stunned, I sat forward to better study it, for I'd heard about books that contained a concealed image, painted on the ends of overlapped pages, invisible unless splayed just so, but I'd never seen one in real life.

It took several attempts before I managed to get the image to appear again. When I finally saw it, my blood ran cold.

The painting was of Andromeda, chained to a rock, awaiting her death. Perseus stood between his future wife, sword poised, as Cetus, the legendary monster, approached. Though Andromeda's face was turned in fear, her black hair swirled in the wind, embrangling Perseus, whose expression alone was enthralling.

His smirk was neither self-assured nor brave. The only way to describe it is to say it was like catching a glimpse of someone who's entered the fray believing their fate sealed but then, standing on the threshold of death, suddenly finds it's not all that intolerable. Perseus stood ready to hack off the first of many writhing tentacles—victor of himself, ready to embrace the battle and all its glory.

But this wasn't what stole my breath. I blinked twice, unable to believe my eyes. The painted visage was clearly Isaac's. But no cultured mask was this. The artist miraculously had guessed the crux of Isaac's soul or, like me, had once caught a rare glimpse.

Feeling ill, I shifted the book so the spine was aligned correctly and the picture disappeared into the gilt edging.

I turned the volume in my hands, feeling as though it were baneful. The eidolon was like encountering one's dream in the daytime, where phantasms had no place. I drew a deep breath, disliking the sensation of fear it pulled from deep within me.

Who on earth had commissioned this? Surely not Isaac. He was not vain, nor could he have afforded it. For this was as costly as it was disturbing. No ordinary hand painted such exquisite and tiny details. I opened to the marbleized pages, searching for a clue. I found it on the title page. Penned in a trembling, elderly, feminine hand was the inscription:

> *To Isaac on his 18th birthday.*
> *Her fate rests in your hands.*

Chills ran down my arms. Lifting my head, I scanned the library for a portrait of Lady Josephine. For the first time ever, there wasn't one around. My father apparently didn't relish conducting business beneath his mother's coy gaze.

Once more, I fanned the pages. Now that I knew how to reveal it, the slightest movement of my fingers was all it took. This time I studied the massive storm raging around the couple. Jags of lightning speared the sky over fearsome, roiling waves. The sheer size of the monster gave the impression Lady Josephine knew I had someone as formidable as Macy as a predator.

My skin tingled as the panicky sensation returned from the morning I'd awoken alone in Windhaven. The miniature painting lacked Edward. And for some reason, that made me want to flee as far from here as possible.

"Do you have any friends we can go stay with instead?" I asked.

"None that can afford to keep three," he mumbled without looking up. He pointed the top end of his pen at one of the letters. "Four if Nancy actually comes."

With a slight pressure of my thumbs, I viewed the image again. This time my heart rate increased. "What about Scotland?" My voice wavered. "I have jewelry in my possession we could sell. Or America?"

This time, Edward looked up and frowned. "What is that?"

I licked my finger and touched the top and bottom of the title page before I shut it, not caring if I was acting childish.

I would heed my worst fear and obey my baser instinct. By commissioning this, Lady Josephine set events in motion she never should have. Had not Isaac already tried to fulfill this quest, altering my life? I'd further tempted fate by finding it— oh, how I hated that out of the thousands of books in this library, *this* was the one I'd selected. Everything in me screamed that if Edward saw too, some irrevocable doom would be sealed.

I shrugged. With any luck, Edward wouldn't discover the hidden painting. "A poetry book, I think."

His brows shot up. "You *think* it's poetry?"

My mouth grew so dry, I feared to speak, lest my nervousness betray me. I shrugged again as if truly uncertain how to determine whether I was looking at prose or verse. A quick rap on the door interrupted us.

Eaton entered with a silver tray and a white card. "I beg your pardon, but Colonel Greenley has requested an audience with—" he hesitated—"well, with you, Miss Julia."

"Colonel Greenley?" Edward questioned me.

"Evelyn's father," I explained, quickly shoving the book between the chair and its cushion, then sagging with relief. At that moment, I would have welcomed even my former vicar with open arms. Anything to interrupt the storm I felt building. "Eaton, please send him in."

Unlike Edward, my father's butler noted my efforts to hide the volume. His eyes narrowed in its direction. "Shall I order refreshment also?"

"Yes." I stood to be ready to welcome my guest. "Please."

"Very well." Eaton gave the chair one last fleeting glance, then bowed and exited.

"I'm curious to see what sort of man he is, after our encounter with his daughter this morning." Edward managed to write and speak simultaneously. Then, as a boisterous voice boomed at the end of the hall, he lifted his head with surprise.

"Very good, very good! I daresay I know my way about Maplecroft as well as you," Colonel Greenley was saying as Eaton opened the door. He entered tall and straight, wearing navy serge. He spread wide his arms as if he were an uncle and I a niece. "Ah, there you are!"

I dipped, still trying to compose myself. "Colonel."

"Mrs. Auburn." He kissed both my cheeks, then pivoted in Edward's direction with arms outstretched. "And the rapscallion himself! The vicar who stole Lord Dalry's bride right out from under his nose!" He incorporated laughter into his words as he knuckled Edward's head.

"By golly, that was first-rate strategy, m'boy! Meticulously planned and executed with high merits! By Jove, I'd like to know how the pair of you pulled off that maneuver so flawlessly. I told Pierson I'd give my right arm to enlist you as my officer." He leaned over Edward's shoulder, trying to see the letter he was writing. "Working on a sermon?"

Edward covered his pursuit for employment with his forearm, then drew out a new sheet of paper and placed it on top of the letter he'd composed. "As a matter of fact, I am just beginning one."

"Well, don't let me stall you! Go on!" Colonel Greenley fisted his hands behind his back and continued leaning over Edward's shoulder, waiting.

Edward met my eye with a look that begged my aid.

"I was quite pleased to see Miss Greenley walking with Miss Dalry this morning," I said.

"Quite, quite." He rocked from heel to toe, never taking his eyes from Edward's blank sheet. "Haven't picked your topic yet, eh? Want some suggestions?"

"No. I have a topic." Edward withdrew a small Bible from his coat pocket. "Long-suffering."

Colonel Greenley frowned. "Well, no one wants to hear about that. Bah! Give us something with fire in it. Once I heard a roaring-good sermon about the military tactics of King David. Now that was worth the listen! Why not give that subject a go? I could help you, if you like!"

"No—" Edward bowed his head and gripped his hair—"thank you. I work best alone."

"Of course, of course. Pay no mind to me." Once more he fixed his stare on the blank paper.

Feeling more composed, I stepped forward. "Was there something you wished to discuss with me, Colonel?"

"Eh?" He glanced up, then grinned. "Oh yes! Confound it all. I forgot the purpose of my call. Ha-ha." He placed his hands on his stomach. "How do you like that? Here comes Eaton. Let's allow him to set up first, and then we'll get down to business. You'll not find I'm easily rushed, Mrs. Auburn. No, indeed! You'll have to cultivate your patience around me."

Edward lifted his head and gave me a look that affirmed the statement.

I waited until Eaton set down his tray and was in the process of exiting before asking, "Tea, Colonel?"

"I suppose a cup wouldn't hurt. No, indeedy." He swung his arms, catching his own fist. "Especially when you compare it to what I usually partake of here. Har-har." He accepted the cup before settling into the chair across from me. "Thank you."

While I took my seat, he frowned at the brew in his cup as if it were a foreign substance. He shifted uncomfortably with the mannerisms of a man used to action, not idleness. It seemed that his very clothing itched and rubbed his body sore, for no matter what position he tried to recline in or how he budged, he managed to look vexed and irritated.

I waited several seconds, before finally asking, "To what do I owe this honor?"

He lifted the cup and inhaled its fragrance, then clanked it back to the saucer. "Well, there's no point offending a Pierson, even if they're married and sporting another name. Pierson is Pierson, I always say."

I squinted, wondering when exactly he'd had the opportunity to use that statement before.

He lifted his left boot and then his right as if to ascertain that moss hadn't grown during their brief inactivity. "I'm just going to be blunt, so don't be minding me now. But I would greatly appreciate it if you'd be forthright and tell me straight out if you have a leftover attachment toward Isaac."

"Wh-what?" I blinked, scarcely believing my ears. From my peripheral vision, I watched as Edward looked up in complete disbelief.

Colonel Greenley stilled, appearing relieved that he'd finally addressed his topic, then sat back and crossed his legs. "What I mean to say is, what with your social standing and all, you're not planning on giving Isaac's new wife a cold shoulder, now are you? Not that I think you're mean-spirited, mind you, but Pierson blood does flow through those veins."

My hand fluttered to my heart. "I'm sorry . . . but did you just say Isaac's new wife?"

He held up his hands as though he could halt the idea, then spread them in a gesture of innocence. "Hypothetically, of course."

I shielded my face with my hands, feeling my cheeks turn scarlet. "Well, no! I mean . . . of course I wouldn't."

"Capital!" He slapped his knee. "Excellent! That's the corker I've been waiting for! Well, wait. Almost! There's one more question you can advise me on. I daresay you're probably better acquainted with Isaac by now than you are with your own husband."

I tented my hands over my mouth in complete disbelief. How could he not see the havoc he was causing?

"What I'm trying to ask—" Colonel Greenley squirmed in his chair again—"is, well, while you were in London, did Isaac show a particular preference for any young lady? Did he act sweet on, or romance, anyone in particular?"

Edward didn't look amused.

I pressed my lips together, trying to find a balanced answer that wouldn't bring discomfort to everyone. "Not that I ever particularly noticed."

Colonel Greenley's brow furrowed. Then, without warning, he shook with laughter. "Ha! The joke is on me. No, I suppose not! I daresay he's not the kind to reveal his contingency plan. He's not as rude as all that, now is he? Besides, we all ribbed him for being so smitten. After your engagement party, Bradley toasted him, noting the poor devil could hardly take his eyes off you and for his own sake ought to marry you quickly."

I blinked, unable to believe he'd said anything that crass, especially with my husband there. I glanced at Edward, but that proved a mistake, for my own pain for Isaac was plainly evident, and Edward read it accurately.

Colonel Greenley tried leaning on his elbow, apparently relieving pressure from his hip. "Worried what your new bloke thinks of this conversation! Nothing to worry about! Eh, ol' boy?" He grinned at Edward. "What's that they say? 'Love and war are all one.'" He either ignored or failed to comprehend Edward's contempt and said to me, "I highly doubt he'll sulk over Isaac, especially since the full spoils went to him."

Edward's pen struck the desk hard. He stood and gave a cold bow. "I beg you will excuse me, Juls."

"There, you see!" Colonel Greenley's cheeks upturned with approval. "He's even willing to leave the chamber to show you how comfortable he is with the subject. There's no need to leave and discomfort yourself, ol' boy. I can assure you, there's no embarrassment here."

Edward declined to answer such an insulting speech as he marched from the chamber.

"Well, that's sporting of him!" Colonel Greenley tried scooting forward in his chair. "Giving us leave to talk privately about your former beau. That's one of the things I like best about this house. I've never yet met a soul at Maplecroft with a bad motive or a hint of sulkiness!"

Only Isaac's training held me to my seat. I gave a stiff smile and set aside my teacup, wondering whether Colonel Greenley was determined to assign good motives to cross tempers, or whether he simply lied because of my father's social position.

"If I may, Mrs. Auburn, I have a favor to ask of you. I have a letter I'd like for you to hand deliver to Isaac for me."

"I'm not certain—"

"No, no! It must be you." He tapped one nostril. "Trust me, I have an instinct for reading others. Besides, if I send it through the post, your father is certain to pester him about its contents. And I want the boy to make up his own mind on this, by george! No unfair influences." He pulled out a small square of paper that had been folded to the size of one's palm. It was sealed with a wafer that bore Greenley's signature. "Will you deliver this for me?"

It was an unfair position to be placed in.

Edward's and my souls both sprang from the same empyrean region. We were aerolites, and our personalities were clustered with fragments that none outside of ourselves knew how to extract, melt, or shape. While I might not have been capable of following every nuance of Edward's reasoning, I certainly understood its rhyme and cadence. Like it or not, Isaac had offended Edward's sense of chivalry past endurance.

And this road I had no map to.

I eyed the cream square, pondering my choices. Edward might not give a whit whether or not I remained acquainted with Isaac. Yet it was entirely possible he would consider it the height of disloyalty.

"Take it already!" Colonel Greenley urged. "I daresay you're worried you'll lose it, what with having your head so crowded with the dainty morsels that fill the feminine mind. But don't allow that to stop you. I've always been one to give the weaker sex credit for their faculties. How else should they manage to keep a host of recipes in their heads or track all the ins and outs of everyone's business?"

I was not offended, as one might suppose. I was too astounded by the strange rush of contradictions coming from Colonel Greenley. Besides, I sensed his motives. He meant to compliment where he insulted. Who was I to criticize the clumsy delivery? Half of what I said seemed to insult my listeners.

But as to accepting the paper, I frowned. It was impossible to explain the complexities hanging in the balance of the decision Colonel Greenley expected me to make. To Colonel Greenley, this was just a small favor, a letter exchanging hands. But I doubted he could even conceive that there were others who operated on vastly different principles. Greenley would only laugh and assure me that he had a better handle on the situation than I did, and it was fine.

Nevertheless, I had an idea of what the note contained, and even though I knew without doubt that Isaac would refuse the request, I agreed with Colonel Greenley. My father didn't need to know of this correspondence. Furthermore, if I could shield Isaac from a personal interview with Colonel Greenley on this matter, it was the least I could do.

In a flash my mind was made. I would take the paper. It would be easy enough to slip it to Isaac. There was no telling how long we were to live at my father's. And besides, the sooner we were past this awkward stage, the better.

"I'll ensure that it reaches him," I promised. With any luck, the job could be managed without Edward even learning it had happened.

Ten

AFTER MY INTERVIEW with Greenley, I found Edward sitting beneath the ancient oak we'd discovered that first morning we arrived at Maplecroft six months ago. Massive branches corkscrewed and twisted in every direction above him, another colossal Cetus.

A hollow sensation filled my limbs as I eyed the massive branches, dismayed by their resemblance to the painted sea monster. Why I should see that book as an evil portent, I couldn't say. But I did. Forcing aside all thoughts of it, I picked up my skirts and plowed through the dead leaves, acorns, and moss.

Though my approach was as loud as a downpour on a tin roof, Edward kept his pensive gaze on the ground. His shoulders hunched forward as unknown thoughts preyed on his mind.

I settled on my knees before him.

He lifted his hazel eyes to me, looking tormented. "I'm sorry, Juls. That wasn't gentlemanly to leave you alone with Colonel Greenley, especially as I know nothing about his character. It's just . . ." His voice grew husky.

Unable to resist, I curved my hand over his cheek, then tucked a flaxen curl behind his ear.

He looked away. "I don't know. . . . It's just . . ." He turned back, his mouth pulled downward before his bottom lip trembled. "I've made such a mess of it. I hate being reminded of how much . . ." He shook his head, unwilling to voice his pain. He took a breath. His thoughts apparently shifted another direction. "There were nights I had to tell myself over and over that I would not quit, I would not leave you alone there; it would make me the worst coward ever born amongst men if I gave in to the physical hardship of vagrant living. And then to learn that . . ." He covered his mouth as if to sever the words before he could speak them.

I folded my hands in my lap, preparing for his umbrage. Early I'd formed an opinion about Edward's intense dislike of Isaac. While the average soul might have mislabelled the emotion shredding Edward as common jealousy, I didn't think there was anything common about it, for even God experiences jealousy.

Edward's feelings, I believed, weren't wrong—but rather his conclusions were.

It wasn't Isaac he detested.

It was me. Or more concretely, my disloyalty.

The very fact that I'd been betrothed to Isaac last week signified that on some level I'd given up on Edward. I'd stopped looking, stopped resisting, stopped believing we were meant to be. Subconsciously, I believed, Edward found it easier to abhor Isaac than to correctly assign the blame to me.

I shut my eyes, knowing what I needed to do. On the carriage ride to Maplecroft, I'd sworn that I was no Abraham. Nor was I. But if required to sacrifice that which I loved most in order to save the person I loved most—that I could do. To leave Edward here was past my endurance. He needed to know. Let him despise me, but I could at least set him free to walk in truth.

"It wasn't Isaac who betrayed us, Ed." I fastened my gaze on an acorn that rested in the shadowed vale of brittle leaves. "We both know it was I who gave up on us."

I waited, hearing the distant caw of a rook and the gentle rustle of dried leaves. Yet I couldn't lift my head.

Now that I'd lacerated this festering pain, more thoughts poured forth like an oozing sore. I acknowledged that I was the very worst of traitresses. I'd failed Edward, broken Isaac's heart, betrayed my father. And there was still what I felt about Macy— that twisted, serpentine emotion.

Thus, I waited for Edward to speak, willing to accept whatever well-deserved anger he unleashed.

Had Edward been a different sort of soul, my time with him might have become a living nightmare. My false guilt could have made me easy prey to someone more vengeful.

"I saw you in London, Juls," Edward finally said. "I watched from alleys and crowded streets as you disembarked from carriages, dressed like some silly doll, and I witnessed the unhappiness plaguing your eyes. I was in the shadows outside your opera box. I witnessed you being pushed and prodded. I was there when Lord Dalry asked—" Edward's vocal cords grew so harsh, they closed on themselves.

I finally looked up and found his gaze was still downcast. His right hand clutched one of the twisted roots arching from the fallen leaves, his knuckles turning white.

"He had the nerve," Edward managed through gnashed teeth, "to ask whether you'd rather face a few busybodies—people who thrive on picking apart one's dress, hair, and speech, as if those have anything to do with one's true merit—or if you'd rather go home and face your father's wrath. He used the anger of the man to whose care—" Edward released the root and thumped his chest—"*I* entrusted you. There are nights I still wake in a cold sweat, wishing I'd obeyed my instinct to pound Lord Dalry's nose to a bloody pulp right there. They took the girl I loved and had spent years coaxing to speak, to go near sunflowers, to embrace friendship, and they pressured you to reduce your value to the equivalent of some prized racehorse, to become an overdressed symbol of their status. And I am infuriated because ultimately it's my fault."

I stared, saying nothing. This was the first time Edward had revealed weaknesses to me. I knew not to be alarmed by what he said. Because he needed to be heard. He needed freedom to scrape off and expel these choking thoughts.

He shut his eyes and drew a deep breath. "I watched as you tried to save them at the opera house at cost to us, Juls. Your soul contains fire that theirs lack. But you owe them nothing. You were suffocating, and either they didn't care or they refused to see it. How badly I wanted to tell you that I wasn't angry. Every time I saw you after that night, it was clear that you thought you'd lost me. You still woodenly played your part at Lord Dalry's side. But your eyes, they were vacant."

I bit my lip. Too well did I remember those hours.

He leaned back against the trunk of the tree and closed his eyes, spent, like a sick man whose fever has left him, allowing him to finally sleep. "You're not the one who betrayed us. Shun the very thought."

His stern refusal to blame me was like a rock crashing down on a flimsy house of cards. I hated feeling so blameworthy while being exonerated. It strained the very fabric of my body, for Edward didn't yet understand Isaac, nor had he lived with my father.

"But to be called a rapscallion—" Edward buried his fingers in his curls, dredging up the next layer—"and to have it suggested that *I* stole you?" He exhibited his hands and slowly fisted them. "I could barely restrain myself. He wasn't even party to the lie you were forced to live. And to know that tomorrow, *tomorrow*, we have to go hat in hand and beg succor."

He shook his head. "It's so much worse than that, Juls. I live with the knowledge that I have nothing. Absolutely nothing to offer you, outside of an innate knowledge of who you are. And the maddening notion continuously pounds against my brain that if I had truly loved you, I would have left you in Dalry's hands. There at least you were safe from Macy, your basic needs more than met. Everywhere I go, I'm reminded of his superiority in life and in station."

This I could alleviate. I threw myself into his arms and was accepted. I rested my head against his chest. "You know on the way to that asinine engagement party, the one that everyone feels the need to bring up, Isaa—Lord Dalry and I fought in the carriage the whole way because I still and only loved you."

Edward buried his fingers in my hair and bowed his head. "I hope you socked him hard."

I laughed, unable to envision that. "No, I spent the night on Evelyn Greenley's arm instead."

Edward leaned back and rested his head against the gnarled bark. Above him were the carved initials I'd seen months ago: *BD + EG*. Benjamin Dalry and Evelyn Greenley, I now knew.

"I realize my faith is being tested," Edward continued. "I have no doubt that I was supposed to collect you. But I keep questioning what is happening now. Why did everything fall the moment we should have been free? I keep wondering if God is forcing us back here because I judged your father, or whether we missed some lesson. I've starved, slept on streets, nearly frozen to death, had to accept another man wooing you. No, make that two men! I'm tired of lessons! If I haven't yet graduated, then let me just fail. I don't understand what God is doing, and it feels like . . . like . . . we've been abandoned. All those sermons about standing firm in trials, and I'm breaking apart. We're miraculously delivered out of Egypt, against all odds, and three days into the wilderness I'm complaining about thirst. I even know to expect this. Yet it's an entirely different matter when you're the one dying of thirst. I want to scream to the heavens that we're frail and human, and that three days without water in the heat of the desert is too much for anyone. And that it doesn't make us weak; it makes him negligent!"

His conversation had wandered out of my depth, but I understood enough. He needed support, so I took up his hands, fit my fingers between them, and kissed his knuckles.

Surely by now those familiar with my story must wonder whether I would still have married Edward had I known the consequences that would unfold. Thankfully we are not allowed to see our future in advance. Suffering is bound to occur. It is often the fertile soil in which God plants seedlings of a greater end.

Which one of us, given foreknowledge, would have the strength to pick up our cup and drain it to its dregs?

⁓

I pushed my thumbs against the poetry volume, elongating the pages, revealing the concealed painting. With a slight push of my fingers in the other direction I hid it again. The more I viewed the painting, the more filled with misgivings I became.

Why on earth had the painter taken such liberties with the story? The sea monster wasn't supposed to resemble the ancient oak, but rather a serpent. How could Perseus kill it with a sword instead of a Gorgon's head? And what made Lady Josephine choose a story where the father opted to sacrifice his daughter to save his kingdom? I could scarcely form that question without feeling waves of resentment.

"This makes the third time I've passed you in my new attire," Jameson's voice interrupted. "And you've yet to comment."

I jumped from the bench, knocking my knee against one of the trunks piled about me, then quickly dropped the book on the seat I'd occupied, hiding it with my skirts.

Jameson stood clean-shaven, his hair parted and greased into place. He wore black-and-white livery that had been ironed and pressed. His gloved hands brushed off his sleeves. "Well, what do you think? Do I look presentable enough to meet your father?"

My jaw dropped, for it was the first time I actually believed he really was a servant. "Yes, you'll do very well. Where did it come from?"

He chuckled with genuine pleasure. "Simmons apparently left orders for someone to do something about me. Ha! As if there's any helping me. So Eaton passed on one of the footmen's uniforms." He bent, lifted his elbows to shoulder height, and flapped them backwards. "It fits rather well without altering, don't you think?"

London House and my father suddenly felt too real.

I nodded, not trusting my voice, and glanced up. The grey light of the approaching dawn could be seen clearly through the windows of the dome above us.

Jameson approached. Instead of stopping before me as I expected, he bent and retrieved the poetry volume from the bench. Before I could demand it back, he fanned the pages and frowned at the painting. "Well, that explains your consternation. What a strange painting. Do all books touched by faerie hands develop another story in the gilt edges?"

"I don't want to go to London," I confessed. "Can you talk Edward out of it? Something awful is on the verge of happening. Can't you feel it?"

Jameson's eyes softened as if he could guess how distressing this was, but he didn't take my premonition seriously. "What? And run from the course set before us? Hardly fitting for one of your folk!" He tapped the book's cover. "I rather liked the look on that fellow's face. Let's take a page from this book. After all, there are far worse things to face down than your father!"

"There we disagree, though only slightly." Edward's voice sounded from the front entrance. "Are we ready?"

I snatched the volume from Jameson's hands and spun to greet my husband, tucking it behind my skirts. "Nearly."

Edward nodded at us before giving private instructions to Eaton, who'd accompanied him as he inspected the carriage. Determination chiseled Edward's tight jaw and anger molded his brow, giving no hint of the deeper emotions he'd expressed yesterday.

Turning, I clutched the volume tightly against my stomach and hastened to the library to replace it on its shelf.

Already the chamber felt our absence. The hearth was empty and lifeless. I had the sensation that after we left, Mrs. Coleman would attack this room next. Every trace of our presence would be beaten from the carpets, burnished from the brass, and polished from the wood. Someday in the near future, my father would enter, and it would be as if we'd never eaten breakfast here, jested about faeries. It would be as if none of it had ever happened. I glanced at the overstuffed chair Edward had occupied yesterday and was filled with an unexplainable sadness.

"May I be of assistance?" Eaton's voice surprised me as he gained my side. His gaze locked on the book as if he remembered it from yesterday.

I hugged it against me, suddenly unwilling for any member of my father's staff to see it. That my grandmother had unfairly influenced Isaac to seek me out, to fall in love with me, was none of their business.

"No thank you. I'm finished here."

His gaze stayed fastened on the book.

"Reading material for the carriage," I finally explained.

"Isn't that one of Master Isaac's poetry books?" His hint was clear. It wasn't mine to take. Select another volume.

Heat crept up my face. "No. It's mine."

Eaton frowned, but what could he do? Call me a liar? Demand to see it?

I gave him a nod, then picked up my skirts. Knowing my

face was scarlet, I raced back down the hall. Every nerve tingled within me, telling me this book was a bane and not to bring it to London. Yet when I found Eaton's eyes were still fastened on me as I reached the end of the hall, I refused to leave it behind. Butlers were like trained hounds, able to sniff out anything.

And frankly, Isaac's heart wasn't his business.

I shoved it into the receptacle holding my toiletries, sensible that it wasn't my business either.

Eleven

SMOKE PAINTED the canvas of London's skies as we entered the city at sunset. No curtain was drawn across the window, and neither Jameson nor Edward made any attempt to censure me; thus I looked upon the throngs of London freely.

We travelled down streets near the fires of an earthenware factory, which cast an orange glow over the murky sky. We passed between shops that were not frequented by London's elite. Haggard faces extinguished candles behind windows as they closed down for the night. Rows of signs creaked in the wind as booksellers and grocers let down stalls. Crowds of lower-class citizens were pressed together as they headed home. Oily puddles of urine and waste reflected the dark sky. Though not yet summer, London already smelled worse.

"Blind Solomon begs on a corner not far from here," Edward said. "My word, but I am longing for a conversation with him. Juls, I'll have to bring you to meet him. There's no one like him. He sees souls because he can't see their faces."

I gave him an odd look, wanting him to explain that, but he tapped Jameson's knee.

"There's where I was beaten by a white cane for daring to rise on tiptoes to see into the carriage." Edward nodded to a street corner. "The crowd cheered when I pulled him down and snapped his cane over my knee." He grinned. "But I had to run because a magistrate spotted me destroying the man's property. I nearly was caught, too."

"White cane?" I asked.

Jameson's tufted brows rose in astonishment. "Oh, I know you can guess this one by the description alone."

"Not likely," Edward disagreed. "Her father's footmen use whips."

"Ah!" Jameson pointed at his own shoulder. "Hence your new scar."

Edward shot Jameson a dark look, but it was too late. My eyes widened. I had felt the angry welt over Edward's shoulder as my fingers had explored his body, but that moment hadn't been the right time to make an inquiry about the injury.

"Who whipped you?" I demanded, outraged. "James or William?"

"You're too late. It's forgiven," Edward said. "While we were at Maplecroft, after your father agreed we could wed, the poor devil took the opportunity to come and beg forgiveness."

Jameson chuckled at the thought. "Yes, I imagine that would be quite the discovery. The vagrant you've been beating is your new master. He's lucky to have come up against your temperament."

Edward laughed. "Now that's a compliment I rarely hear."

I clenched my hands, mentally reviewing each time I'd heard one of the men beating someone off our carriage. How many times had it been Edward? All I recalled was my father drawing the curtain shut and his constant commands that I was not to look upon the rabble. Had he feared we'd meet Edward on the street? I kicked the footboard of the seat across from me with vehemence. They had beaten my soul mate as though he were common rubbish. To injure him was one with injuring me.

"Juls?" Edward sounded concerned.

Rain spattered the windows then, making the stench of London yet more unbearable. Not caring that it wasn't proper, I loosened the ribbons of my bonnet and removed it. "I can't face him again," I choked out. "I'm too angry. I can't do this."

Jameson gave a low whistle as he leaned forward and peered up at the shreds of grey clouds congregating above us. "My word! It stormed when we were kicked out of Am Meer, and now it storms when you learn Edward has been whipped." He pointed skyward. "I have to say, the power to brew the weather according to your emotions was well worth keeping. Did you retain any other?"

I turned my angry glare to the streets. Having my pain ignored was just as bad. Nevertheless, my thoughts churned over all that had happened and how I seemed to curse everyone close to me. Then, "You won't appreciate that power once you've withstood one of my gales. Trust me."

"If I plead my age, will you have mercy?" Jameson's question was happily asked.

How could he continue to talk nonsense when I wasn't jesting back? Genuinely hurt, I gave him a reproachful look.

That, however, proved to be my undoing. For to meet another's gaze is an aeration of one's soul. I found that he wasn't overlooking my pain; rather he was staring directly at it, straight on, unblinkingly.

Though his eyes held only kindness and concern, they were like rays of sun piercing the eyes of a prisoner left long in darkness. Tears quickly barred him from further access. I slid my arm beneath Edward's, then touched my forehead to his shoulder, retreating into him.

"Ah, my queen of queens." Jameson's voice was sad.

"Enough," Edward said. "She obviously doesn't like being called a faerie queen. Why are you continuing, then?"

"I speak to her in parables," Jameson said quietly. "I call her forth with story. How else can I fan to embers the truth of who she is? For look, she has forgotten."

I felt Edward shift as he looked, but it was as one compelled by a boyhood habit to obey. His glance was cursory.

"You don't brew the storms," Jameson said before Edward could speak again. "Though perhaps you have an uncanny knack for flying straight into them."

"I know you mean well." Edward's voice was stern as he placed an arm about me. "But I don't follow your method. She's sadder now than before you spoke." He turned and appraised me fully. "Are you all right? Jameson's always been eccentric. Don't let him disturb you."

Jameson crossed his arms. "My goal isn't happiness but healing. Sometimes surgeons hurt their patients in order to restore them."

"He's fine," I finally managed but found I could not again look directly at Jameson. Like a flame that consumes itself in one mighty burst, my anger was gone. I huddled closer to Edward, wishing I never had to lay eyes on my father or Isaac again. For a fleeting second, I debated whether to plead one last time to flee the country instead of returning to London House.

To this day I regret that I did not at least try.

❧

By the time we reached Audley Street, the light rain had ceased and an embankment of fog enshrouded the world.

Silently I eyed the turrets that stretched high above us.

Swallowing, I lifted my hand to knock, deciding it would be unwise to ring the bell.

"One moment!" Jameson brushed off his jacket, stepping

into the dense murk that lolled over the sidewalks. "This time, my queen, I prefer to go through the back entrance. Your generosity at Maplecroft was extraordinary, but in this house I would rather we make a secret of our alliance. With your permission, that is."

"Yes, go," Edward said, taking my elbow. And as Jameson's footsteps tapped out of hearing, he tacked on, "Lucky dog. I half wish we could sneak through that way too." He frowned at the building. "I wonder why I haven't thought of that before. If I had snuck in as a delivery boy and found you, would you have dropped everything and fled with me?"

"It was more complicated than that," I said.

Edward's brows arched. "How so?"

I shrugged, knowing it would be impossible to explain that invisible chains had held me. During that time, silent commands and expectations ruled my world. I'd been so busy trying not to set off my father's temper, I'd nearly forgotten I'd existed independently. "At the opera I planned on running away with you. You saw what happened."

Edward mulled over that a moment. "Well, at least this time you've got me with you instead of Dalry. You ready?"

I nodded and gave the door a sound rap, knowing what would happen the moment we set foot inside. Our lives were about to be torn from us. My father was used to dominating others, and now that we were back on his doorstep, I saw little hope of escape.

"Should we ring the bell?" Edward asked when no servant came.

"Let's at least try the door first," I urged.

To both our surprise, it was unlocked.

The burnished floors of London House made me catch my breath. They'd been waxed until they shone like glass. The golden lights from the sconces, fastened on the mahogany walls, reflected on the glossy sheen. Despite the season, a low fire burned in the castled fireplace, adding its own path of light that was as resplendent as a moonglade.

Edward stepped forward, his mouth parting as he glanced at the dark mahogany balusters along the staircases. They gleamed on the second and third floors. I caught the scent of sweet oil and turpentine. Likely the staff here had tackled this house when we left to celebrate my engagement to Isaac at Maplecroft. Even the suits of armor were mirrors.

"Unbelievable," Edward whispered as he leaned forward and considered the stately blend of stone and lambent wood. "I can't help feeling impressed, which I suppose is the point."

My fingers were cold as I surveyed our warm surroundings. "Let's go check the library and the smoking room for my father."

"I'm yours to command."

Taking a fortifying breath, I drew up my skirts and headed toward a small door beneath an alcove. This chamber, too, I knew would stun Edward. The door looked like it might lead to a broom closet but instead opened into a massive library with velvety couches and plush rugs and rows and rows of rare and extraordinary tomes. I pressed my ear against it, hoping Edward could first experience it without my father.

To my surprise, the first voice I heard was a woman's.

"For the last time—" her voice was stern—"you will put them on before you are discovered."

"I am not under your authority." This was James, one of my father's footmen. "Besides, if you'd just leave me alone for ten more minutes, I could have this done and we'd both be satisfied."

"This is my last warning."

Intrigued by this servants' argument, I opened the door.

Three individuals clustered around my father's massive desk. The eldest, Kinsley, slept with his head tilted back, mouth ajar, polishing rag clutched between his ancient fingers. He'd aged during my short absence. His skin looked stretched over his skull and more paper-like. Next to him, James stood with streaks of perspiration running down his face as he polished the silver edging over some of the tumblers on my father's drink tray. He'd discarded his velvet coat and had rolled his sleeves above his elbows. His wig rested askew atop a marble bust of Octavian. Mrs. King, London House's venerable house-keeper, peered at him disdainfully. She pursed her mouth so hard it highlighted the lines that etched her cheeks into crack-led pottery.

"You give me no choice," Mrs. King was saying. "I shall ask Lord Pierson to deny your monthly day off."

"If you do—" James turned his head and spotted me, and his eyes widened. He threw down his polishing cloth and snatched up his wig, which he shoved on his head before starting on his sleeves. "Ah, cagmag!"

"It's all right, James," I assured. "It's only me."

"It is not all right." Green eyes bored into me as Mrs. King slowly turned my direction. "This is exactly the type of cir-cumstance I'm trying to warn him about. That a member of the upper staff should be caught without his jacket and wig is down-right shameful."

I frowned, recalling all the times I'd come upon her and Miss Moray holding a tête-à-tête in the hallway, berating the running of this household.

"Mrs. King," I said, managing what I hoped was an equally haughty expression, "in the future, when my husband and I enter a room, you will ensure that you properly greet us, or I'll personally see that you are denied your monthly day off."

Her earbobs swung as she dipped. Ice coated her voice. "Reverend Auburn. Mrs. Auburn. How unexpected."

"Did not Simmons inform you of our arrival?"

"I know not."

"Well, did he arrive yesterday and speak with my father?"

She placed her hands directly before her, a lorgnette dangling from them, her palms facing each other, fingers locked. "I can attest that both of those occurrences happened."

Realizing I'd have to word my questions perfectly in order to get any answers, I said, "Thank you; you're dismissed."

As her footsteps faded, Edward gained my side, silently studying our surroundings.

"James?" I asked when I deemed us safe from eavesdropping ears.

He frowned as he continued unrolling his sleeves. He gave Edward a glance. "Simmons was here, and he did inform your father."

"And?"

Again James glanced at Edward, not out of fear but as if pained. For a second I felt a knife twist in my soul, for I feared our informality had only been an extension of his and Isaac's relationship. It was my first taste of life in London House divided from Isaac, and it was dizzying. Normally James would at least offer a suggestion, helping me navigate what was happening. But I noted that, though James opened his mouth, he snapped it shut after glancing at Edward.

"Whatever it is," I encouraged, "just tell me. My husband won't inform on you."

The tinge of red already upon James's cheeks deepened, but at last he revealed his true self. "Your father knew you planned to arrive, but he said he didn't care what the devil you did or didn't do."

I felt the sting of his rejection but managed to keep an indifferent aspect. "And Isaa—Lord Dalry?"

Misunderstanding that I was questioning how he'd handled the news, James gave me a pitying look. "He did his best to convince your father to be here to greet you, but your father only said he had washed his hands of you, and you were your husband's problem now."

I stood unmoving—not even blinking—so that I would remain

unbreakable. Nonetheless, I felt my lips swell as I refused to acknowledge the tightness in my throat. My eyes grew watery, but I would not speak until I could command my voice. Over and over again I told myself that if my father was willing to accept only what he could control, then it was not love, and I would not mourn something false.

As if sensing my struggle, James averted his gaze and polished the tumblers.

"Does that mean we are to leave?" I finally managed.

James's eyes rose to meet mine as if he was once again uncertain whether to speak. "Mrs. King didn't tell you the full truth. Your father refused to heed your arrival, but Master Isaac ordered chambers ready for you and Reverend Auburn. You'll find beds prepared. He bids you be on time for breakfast tomorrow, where, if there are problems, he'll inform your father that you're his guests."

I shut my eyes and drew in deep breaths, not willing to betray any emotion. How did one even begin to know how to feel? Too many sensations warred. Hurt that I no longer mattered to my father. Shame that, though I deserved nothing further from Isaac, he hadn't forsaken me. Relief that my nightmare wasn't true, that he wouldn't leave me to navigate something beyond what I knew how to handle. Grief that Edward had to be subjected to any of this.

James stepped back from the tray of sparkling decanters and tumblers. "May I replace these supplies belowstairs before I wake Kinsley?"

I gave a slight nod.

"We arrived with a servant," Edward said. "He's downstairs now. Will you help oversee him?"

James looked as if we had no idea how much of a favor that was, but he agreed and gathered his supplies.

My bonnet slipped from my fingers and hit the floor, though I caught the ribbon. I swallowed, still working to regain my indifference. Here, I felt a glint of anger toward Jameson and Isaac. I knew they meant well, but their kindness hurt more than it helped. It'd pierced through my hard shell, but that now left me vulnerable. For people break if they reach for love and acceptance while still in a place where they ought to be protecting themselves.

Edward gathered me to him and whispered, "Well, we're just here for the food and beds anyway. A plague on him too."

I laughed out loud, needing some sort of a release, and anything was better than tears.

"And since you're my problem and not his, I say let's teach him a lesson he'll never forget about not caring 'what the devil you do.' Let's try out Henry and Elizabeth's personalities on him. Test how far we can really take that statement."

Again I laughed but felt the sharp pang of missing our foursome.

Edward slipped his fingers into mine, withdrawing a step. "Want to show me the rest of the house?"

I brushed aside the wisp of hair that fell over my brow. "Would you mind if I retired instead? You can explore it if you wish."

Edward scanned the fireplace, his jaw tightening. "Once you've seen one estate, you've seen them all. I'd rather retire with you." He swung his hat forward as he gestured at Kinsley. "Who's he?"

Grateful that he knew to change the subject just then, I stepped closer and took his arm. "The butler."

Confusion crossed Edward's face. "Your father keeps him?"

I nodded, glancing at the portrait of Lady Josephine, who smiled serenely upon her aged servant. I understood Edward's puzzlement. How was it that the man could act so uncaring toward one member of his household and so merciful toward another?

I crossed the chamber with awareness that we all are guilty of such erratic behavior. None of us have escaped being both good and evil, sometimes simultaneously.

I tiptoed to where Kinsley snored. I kissed my fingertips, then bent and placed them on his shoulder so as not to awaken him. Like Evelyn Greenley, here was someone safe to love, someone beyond the ability of inflicting hurt. But even that act welled sadness. His feet were tucked in mink-lined slippers and his quilted dressing robe looked brand-new. I watched the rise and fall of his chest, realizing that my father must love him dearly to have ordered such costly items.

How does one bear the ache that accompanies seeing the goodness resting in the soul of someone who denies you love because they see only your shortcomings?

It is the worst state of invisibility I have known.

Twelve

⚜

MISS MORAY PARTED my hair before braiding a length of it and looping it over my ear. Her nimble fingers made quick work of the matching loop, whose end she pinned into the knot of hair at the base of my neck. Despite the annoyance twisting her face, I watched her jerky movements, wishing this time would never end.

Careful to keep my head still, I slid my eyes to the rumpled sheets that Edward and I had slept in last night. This morning when Miss Moray shook me awake, he had already slipped from the bedchamber. Though I did my best to appear genteel, in the short amount of time it took Miss Moray to assist me, I'd harrowed my soul every imaginable way.

While I bathed my face, I had visions of Edward being hit by a carriage. While I stood to be laced, I wondered if he could be killed by one of Macy's men. And even while I argued to wear the clothing I'd recovered from Am Meer, I was plagued with an unreasonable fear that Edward might have abandoned me here, no longer willing to face the complexities. Though I knew such fears to be unfounded, I could not rid myself of the dread. I stared at my pale face in the vanity mirror, able to imagine all too well the horrors of living under my father's rule with nowhere else to go.

"There." Miss Moray stepped back, frowning at my appearance. "It's the best I can do without washing your hair."

I glanced at the clock, wondering why she hadn't attempted a wash if it offended her.

She smirked. "Oh yes, I'm to tell you that breakfast will be served an hour earlier. You best hurry. You have only minutes."

I gathered a fistful of my skirt, realizing that Edward wouldn't know about the change. My stomach plummeted at the idea of facing my father and Isaac without him. "Why did you not say something before now?"

She blinked slowly. "You can stand here and question me about how I handle my time, or hurry and not keep your father waiting."

In a flash of temper, I swept my arm over the vanity, sending the glass jars and porcelain boxes crashing to the floor. Months of her work on lotions and beauty tonics bled into each other. Her glare gave me no satisfaction, yet I crossed my arms. "There. Now I have no need to question what you intend to do with your time."

Before she could shoot another icy glance, I hastened from the chamber and down the stairs, already feeling sick and repentant.

༄

My dress practically floated as I pattered down the stairs, for gone was the weight of the more expensive gowns. As I neared the breakfast chamber, however, its layers could have been made of lead. My legs felt like stiff logs, and my palms grew clammy. I clutched Mama's shawl as my talisman. Despite its threadbare appearance, I'd insisted on wearing it as if it could take the place of Mama rushing to my side to defend me, as she used to in my stepfather's furies.

My legs quaked as I quietly slid into my usual seat and took up my napkin. Taking measured breaths and keeping my eyes downcast, I focused on the cut of the crystal goblets and the sparkle of the ornate silverware cast with figures from Greek mythology. The set must have been recently ordered, for I'd never seen it before.

I waited, head bowed, not daring to look at the clock to see if I'd made it on time. I'd not been invited to my father's or Isaac's presence since the morning they discovered the betrayal in Forrester's newspaper.

My father waited a full minute to speak, allowing the time-piece's monotonous and heavy ticks to fill the chamber. When he did speak, it was brusque and harsh. "Where is your husband?"

My cheeks felt on fire. "I know not."

His sudden exhale suggested his anger exceeded words. "Is he aware that breakfast has started?"

Beneath the table, I tightened my hold on Mama's shawl. "I know not. I have not seen him this morning."

In the blade of a knife, I could see a shadowy reflection of Isaac. He occupied his usual place, but I could not make out his expression, nor did I dare to lift my gaze. With my right hand, I felt the square of Colonel Greenley's letter, which I'd secreted in a pocket that Nancy had sewn into this dress. Now that I was in London House, I knew I'd never be able to deliver it.

"Did you inform Reverend Auburn last night of our regular breakfast hour?" my father demanded.

On the handle of the spoon, the Greek goddess Hebe dented her cheek, staring back at me. "Yes."

"Fine." The rustle of newspapers was followed by a loud crack as he snapped open the first one. "He will only eat if he arrives on time for the breakfast hour. James, you may begin."

Within minutes the clink of dishes and the waft of kidneys

and bacon filled the chamber. I adjusted Mama's shawl as if to conjure her arms about me. I studied my fork's handle, which featured a curly-haired poet, refusing to imagine what my life would look like if Edward never came back.

To my dismay, James set down the yellow teapot with roses that Isaac had purchased for me. A lavender-fragranced steam piped from its spout. For a second I nearly glanced at Isaac to see if he felt as horrified, but I recalled myself in time.

"Thank you, James." Isaac's demeanor was cultured as he dished his food; then, in an urbane tone directed at my father, "This morning I had the pleasure of bumping into Reverend Auburn's future valet. An absolutely fascinating character. I showed him your smoking chamber—"

"You showed him my smoking room?" The paper crinkled as if my father had lowered it. "Why?"

"We fell into conversation about his time in Africa, and I desired that he see your albino male lion skin. Believe it or not, sir, he claimed he glimpsed a white cat as well, while hunting with none other than Baron Beaumont."

"Beaumont? Impossible!" My father sounded incredulous. "How old is this valet?"

"Future valet," Isaac corrected. Then, taking a stab at his age, "I'd say he's a bit younger than Kinsley."

I frowned, trying to imagine why Isaac was adding years to Jameson's life.

My father's chair creaked as he sat back. "Are you certain he said Beaumont?"

Isaac's laugh was clear as rain. "Quite."

"What do you mean he's a future valet? What is he now if he's not yet employed?"

"Ah, that." Isaac's voice was polished as he reached his manicured hand within my view and picked up the mustard jar. "I think I've uncovered the reason behind your daughter's unexpected arrival, though I would rather allow Reverend Auburn to explain it. In the meantime, I was quite impressed with this Jameson fellow, and I have to give him credit. He apparently made the sacrifice of suspending his pay for a season in order to continue service to his young charge."

"Do you mean to say one of Beaumont's own men had a hand in Edward's upbringing?" My father couldn't have sounded more delighted if he'd learned that Edward came with a seat in Parliament. "Where is this Jameson fellow now?"

Isaac waited the perfect amount of time before asking, "James?"

The footman stepped forward. "Sitting on a bench downstairs, sir. Waiting for you to decide what to do with him."

My father strummed his fingers over the table; then, "And you liked this fellow?"

"Oh, I thought him quite splendid. And if you ask me, with Kinsley's condition, he might be the temporary solution we're looking for."

"Butler?" My father's glass clinked as if his ring hit it. "That's rather imprudent. What do we know of his credentials? I take it there are no references." Here I finally peeked at my father and found him staring at Isaac. "No, that's too big of a risk."

"Well," Isaac drawled as if he were completely devoid of opinion, "I'd say his credentials are top-notch. We know for a fact he was Lord Auburn's personal valet. As far as references—" All of a sudden he became too polished-sounding. "Well, what do you make of him, Mrs. Auburn? Tell us your opinion."

He used my new name effortlessly as he extended the invitation for me to join the conversation. It was impossible not to at least lift my head. He sat across from me seemingly in full possession of himself, knife poised over the rasher of bacon and oysters, fork in place, his face utterly devoid of emotion. Yet even at a glance I noted the shadows beneath his eyes and the hollowness of his cheeks.

I swallowed, lowering my gaze to my plate. "I trust him."

They were the wrong words, for the conversation fell from the air like a quail that had been shot. Traitresses, apparently, would do well to eliminate the word *trust* from their vocabulary. My father's silverware clanked loudly over his plate. He said nothing for so long that I finally stole a peek.

He glared at me, a single vein bulging over his brow, like a man straining to lift a heavy trunk. Then, turning to Isaac, he lifted his right hand, which fisted a napkin. "Arrange a time for me to meet with this valet in person." He dropped the linen on top of his breakfast. "His references are found lacking."

Abruptly he shoved back his chair and left the chamber, leaving me alone with Lord Dalry.

I turned my face toward the windows, more willing that a passerby should witness my hurt than Isaac. My eyes burned as if I'd not slept the night before, and I found that I needed to gulp in air in order to keep my countenance. But keep it I would.

He waited, perhaps to be acknowledged, perhaps too steeped in his own pain to speak. I sensed he desired me to acknowledge him—to look in his direction. But every time I even considered it, my throat ached as if I'd breathed in fire.

Eventually, as if sensing he needed to withdraw in order for me to find any sort of recovery, he quietly stood, and his soft footfall receded from the chamber, leaving behind a death-like silence.

⁓

"Juls?" Air moved next to my chair as Edward knelt.

I lifted my face from my hands, startled by his touch. I'd had no cognizance of his arrival. Struggling to keep my composure, I glanced at the clock and found James standing silently by the sideboard. Most Englishmen did not require their staff to remain with them during breakfast, but my father was so stringent in the running of his household, they were required. Swallowing, I wondered if he'd been stuck there while I silently grieved.

"Where is everyone?" Edward drew my attention back to him.

Shaking my head that I didn't know, I picked up my napkin and placed it on my plate. Speech was impossible, for to voice what was wrong would shatter me. I would continue to embrace silence, as my eyes were still dry.

Edward pressed tiny kisses into my hair, then wrapped both arms about me in silent support. I leaned my head against his shoulder for a second, the hartshorn scent on his clothing telling me he'd been walking in the less desirable parts of London that morning.

Taking his empty seat at the table, he frowned at the cold, half-eaten food. His tattered clothing and rigid posture clashed with the elegance of the table. His face clouded as he rolled the ornate handle of the knife between his forefinger and thumb. "Your father eats Greek gods for breakfast? That's not very promising for us, is it?"

I rubbed my eyes, finding release again with laughter.

Edward waited until I met his comely gaze, then jerked his head at James.

I modulated my voice. "James, thank you; you're dismissed. My apologies for keeping you so long."

He bowed and started to exit the chamber.

"Would you have Jameson sent to us too?" Edward added.

"Very good, sir."

I lifted my brows, wondering if Edward planned to force his own servant to wait on us next.

Edward's eyes drank in my father's and Isaac's plates of abandoned food before moving to the clock. "Doesn't breakfast begin at eight?"

I took up the goblet of claret with shaking fingers and sipped. "Normally, yes."

"What does that mean?"

"Not this morning, apparently." I strained to keep my voice

level. *He nearly forbade you from eating with us, and you hadn't even known about the change.*

His brows drew together, dissatisfaction deepening his every feature. "He changed the time breakfast started? Has he ever done that before?"

"No," I said. "Unless we were travelling."

Edward fastened his trenchant gaze on the table as if working to keep his anger distinct from me. "And would he have forbidden me from eating had I shown up a minute or two late?"

I gave him a sharp look, not quite sure what he was searching for, which made me hesitant to supply information. My shoulders hitched in a shrug. "It's impossible to say."

His mouth slashed in a harsh line. "Have you never been late, then?"

Still not sure what he was after, I answered, "My father is unpredictable that way. When I lived here, there were mornings I was late and wasn't allowed to eat. And then there were mornings he allowed me to remain regardless."

I did not add that usually those mornings he was anticipating a newspaper article about Isaac and myself.

"So." Edward spoke slowly, taking care not to look directly at me. "It would be fair to say his ill mood is separate from your actions."

I scrunched my nose, not certain what idea Edward was trying to express.

Jameson poked his head into the breakfast chamber. "Did you summon me?"

Edward waved him forward. "Never mind it just now, Juls. I think I have an understanding of your father's personality that you lack. The fact that you can be late for breakfast one day and not the next proves my point. Trust me on this: it's not about rules, schedules, or timelines." He gestured to Isaac's chair. "Jameson, will you join us?"

The elderly man snorted. "What did I ever do to the pair of

you? Besides occasionally interfere with your juvenile plans—" he wagged a finger at Edward—"and you should have been studying anyway. No, I will not sit! It's bad enough the staff knows that Lord Pierson summoned me for a personal audience this morning."

I couldn't help but gape. "He offered you the position of butler, didn't he?"

"So it was faerie magic!" Jameson's shining face turned in my direction. "And you did retain more powers than brewing storms! I knew it."

"No." I displayed my palms. "That was Edward's doing."

"Not me," Edward protested. "I haven't seen your father since the wedding, and he most certainly wasn't in the mood to grant me favors then."

"No, it was last night," I explained, "when you asked James to oversee Jameson. Isaac and James always work in accord. If we're a secret alliance, they're another. My guess is when Isaa—Lord Dalry came home from the clubs last night, James approached him about Jameson. Lord Dalry is the one who truly oversees matters here."

"How delightfully confusing our names are!" Jameson clapped his hands. "James and Jameson. Let's make this easier for ourselves. Just think of me as being the footman's son. Jameson. From this point forward, when I refer to him, I'll call him my father, and so can you. It will help us keep the matter straight."

Cheered, I laughed at his nonsense, feeling like a spinning diabolo that has been securely caught on its string again.

"I still don't understand." Edward frowned, then, waving aside his need to comprehend, addressed Jameson. "Are you accepting his offer?"

"Who, my new father's?" Jameson looked at me. "Is he making me an offer too?"

"No." Edward squeezed his eyes shut. "Lord Pierson's offer."

"Ah, your new father-in-law!" He clapped his hands. "How fun. We both have new fathers! I suppose we all do. How very nice of Mrs. Auburn to start the fashion and now share."

It was so nonsensical, and Jameson kept lifting his eyebrows in my direction, so I couldn't help but laugh.

Edward looked to me. "Are you following this?"

"Oh, perfectly!" I slipped my napkin out from beneath my silverware and spread it on my lap. "He's not alarming me any."

"Well, you're both alarming me," Edward said, but his voice gave away his amusement. "I go to walk and pray, and when I return, I find that the breakfast hour has changed. My valet has become a butler and the footman is his father. But most of all, my wife is upset by something that occurred at breakfast, which I still haven't ascertained."

"It's this house." Jameson gestured about the chamber. "It practically throbs with magic. I shouldn't wonder if we found a hundred years had passed us by the next time we stepped outdoors. It's a good thing you're married to a faerie queen, Ed, for protection. I don't think the house likes you much."

"Nor do I like it."

I sank against my chair, half-smiling, heartened that the three of us were still intact.

Jameson's keen gaze turned on me. "But what happened at breakfast?"

"Yes." Edward sounded annoyed. "Tell him, Juls. Please. Make him aware of the hornets' nest he's near stepping into."

I pulled Mama's shawl about me, feeling my face start to crumble as I recalled my father's words. "Nothing. It's fine."

"Her father refused to greet her last night as well." Edward's voice was wrought iron as he looked at Jameson. "Went to the club, declaring she wasn't his problem anymore. Lord Dalry, her former beau, of all people, had to order chambers for us."

Jameson's mouth looked like seagull wings as he smiled, but it was an angry smile.

I begged Jameson with my eyes to do something, to help me change the topic.

Jameson chuckled, though his eyes still wore that black look. "Mr. Addams warned me about her. Said he'd never witnessed any force like her before. 'An absolute magnet for trouble' were his exact words." He turned toward me. "Have you ever tried to act upon life instead of letting life act upon you?"

"Once." I rubbed my eyes, feeling able to breathe. "I married Mr. Macy as a result."

Jameson burst out with laughter. "Oh, no, no, no! Let's not encourage activity, then. That might prove more detrimental." He glanced at Edward. "Perhaps it quickens the process."

Even Edward chuckled and loosened before dishing himself cold kidneys and oysters. "Well, we found her, and we're not trouble. That's something, anyhow."

"Yes, Mr. Addams warned me about that part too. He said she's like a black cat and to cross paths with her is to become tangled in adventure. And here we are! London! In Lord Pierson's breakfast chamber!" Jameson looked toward the door, which was open a crack, before crossing the chamber and shutting it. "Perhaps I will sit and have a bite."

"Hear, hear!" Edward raised a glass of claret. "Lord Pierson's leftovers are a fair find for any adventurers."

I tugged Mama's shawl tighter, compelled to laugh with tears in my eyes. Outside of Christmas Day, such a thing had probably never happened at London House, but the idea that we three were breaking down all walls felt right. Like a ray of sunshine lancing a dark prison cell. It felt like even my father's angriest temper couldn't quell our merry little party.

"But only—" Jameson added a clause as he added his chair—"if Mrs. Auburn tells me what happened at her first breakfast that stole her appetite."

"Unfair!" I cried. "I haven't agreed to that!"

Jameson grinned as he tucked a napkin into his collar. "Well,

I've already sat, and you wouldn't deprive an old man of the once-in-a-lifetime chance to eat at Lord Pierson's breakfast table. Besides, it will give you practice using your words."

"As well as giving me practice at leading," Edward interjected.

Jameson gave the food a piteous look. "And I'm hungry. Starving, even."

I knew my father's words were a reflection of him and not of me, but to admit that someone thought poorly enough of me to justify demeaning me demanded a second humiliation. Ashamed, I felt my eyes blur.

"There, see it?" Edward pointed his knife as he lifted a fork-ful to his mouth. "That's the look that tells me something needs to be discussed and addressed."

"Oh yes, I do see it." Jameson emptied my father's coffee onto his plate, shook the cup, then poured tea from my yellow pot. "Rule number four of the herd, Mrs. Auburn—and keep a mind that the rules are numbered by priority, so this is the fourth most critical point about belonging to—"

"What are the first three rules?" I asked, hoping to turn the topic.

"Bad form!" Jameson chided, spreading caviar on toast. "Interruption! Though I shall allow it this morning, as I like that it was done in an attempt to communicate. As for the other rules, I'll make them up as needed."

"Then I already declare my refusal to obey them."

Jameson's eyes crinkled. "No, no! What if I make the first rule to refuse the rules—binding you to obey them? That would leave all sorts of possibilities open. I could use the second or third rules to enslave you or make you walk backwards for life."

Edward drew a deep breath, then chewed his breakfast dog-gedly as if barely able to endure more absurdity.

I gave him a sympathetic look, realizing he wasn't going to give up until he knew. "Really, it isn't that important. My father said something that hurt to hear. That's all."

Edward moved slowly, like someone trying to coax a wild animal to them. "Just tell me, then."

Rather than make the matter seem more significant than it was, I swallowed my pride and outlined the talk this morning, as well as what happened when I entered the conversation and said that I trusted Jameson.

As I expected, the air fairly sizzled with the following silence as Edward and Jameson locked eyes in a mute but determined conversation.

"When Jameson entered the chamber," Edward finally said, noting that I watched them, "we were talking about your father's bad humor. I was trying to point out that it is unconnected to you or your actions. There's no correlation between your actions and his reactions. It depends upon his mood and his need to dominate. It's not about timelines for breakfast. Even if you could manage to be exactly on time every day, he'd fault something else—the way you ate, the color of your dress. You'd never win but would always blame your own inadequacies."

"He wasn't speaking of my being late but of the fact that I betrayed him."

"How? By marrying me? So what. How many other daughters do you imagine have married outside of their fathers' choices through elopement or stubbornness? We haven't gotten into this yet, Juls, but you haven't committed any sin that isn't common to everybody. You're no better or worse than the rest of humanity."

I glanced at Jameson, who listened with a bent head. His nods of approval were nearly imperceptible.

Once, in a dream, I'd wandered down a long, narrow passage that held a mirror at its end. Each step toward that mirror filled me with dread, though I couldn't think why I should fear gazing into it. As I sat at breakfast that morning, the sensation returned. Petulant, I narrowed my eyes. "Well, there you disagree with my former vicar. He constantly threatened damnation because I needed to take responsibility for my sins and repent."

"For your sins, yes," Edward agreed. "But taking responsibility isn't allowing someone to hold you in chains over it. Besides, *your father walked you down the aisle*, Juls. What great sin are we talking about? He gave you away. If he didn't like it, he shouldn't have done it. Is he angry about your time with Macy? Then he never should have offered you protection. But to participate and then resent you for it . . . it's unconscionable."

It was agonizing not to speak. For none of us had told Edward about Forrester's newspaper article. Since the marriage was going to happen regardless, I hadn't taken issue with my father's affectations toward his future son-in-law, appearing as if he'd finally relented and agreed to the marriage. Now I saw its folly.

"If he wants to hold being human against you, that's his issue, not ours," Edward concluded.

I sighed. For I hadn't just eloped. I'd blackmailed Macy, left Isaac penniless. I'd snatched away any yield my father would have gained from the greatest risk he'd ever taken. "You don't understand."

"I do, better than you realize. He's not interested in developing rapport with you, just dominating. And I'm not interested in standing by as you devastate yourself trying to win something unattainable."

Inwardly his words agitated me. He didn't understand, and repeating it wouldn't help.

Edward flicked his eyes to the ceiling and then to the walls as if unable to believe the magnificence of this house. "I won't push further. This is something you'll have to see for yourself before you can accept it. There are people I'd like to go and visit today," Edward said quietly. "People who will rejoice to learn I won my bride. Some to whom I owe my very life. I know you dislike the awkwardness of meeting new souls, but would you come with me today?"

"Ooh! Expanding the herd," Jameson said, lifting his head and smiling. "I just remembered rule number one!"

I laughed, feeling my own tension break. "No, you didn't. You just made that up."

"No. I'd merely forgotten it until this second."

"Will you come with me?" Edward asked over us as if determined not to lapse into nonsense again.

I glanced outdoors, recalling the hours I'd stood looking longingly outside. I'd grown so used to life indoors that, now that the hour was upon me, I found myself afraid. How many times had my father preached to me the dangers of leaving London House? Even Macy had taken care to station his men outside the structure as if London were a starving cat ready to snatch up the mouse on its first appearance.

Beneath the table, I wiped my hands over my skirt. "I'm not supposed to. I *am* an emerald heiress."

"Who knows it but us? Who can forbid you from it except me?"

I bit my lip. "And if Macy is still watching?"

"What if he is?" Edward countered. "As Henry insists, bullies need to be punched in the nose. I refuse to allow Macy to hinder our life."

I touched the bottoms of my palms, feeling the scars left from my encounter with Eramus. Even if I weren't Lord Pierson's daughter or watched by Macy, there were still other dangers.

Then memory surfaced of Mr. Macy removing his black onyx ring from his finger and handing it to me as protection. It was a sign to London's criminal world that I wasn't to be touched. Thus far, I'd seen its effectiveness when two magistrates hied from my presence, leaving behind questions of Eramus's death. Like Rebekah hiding an idol in her saddlebag, I'd ripped open one of my petticoats and sewn the ring into its lining. It was an easy enough matter to retrieve it.

"I'll go," I said, rising. "But allow me to change my shoes first."

"Hurrah!" Jameson grinned approval as he pushed back his chair to stand.

Edward didn't celebrate as I expected, but rather he studied me as if sensing something had come between us. He nodded, looking thoughtful. "Come back and eat a large breakfast. We'll likely miss lunch and tea."

Thirteen

"HAVE YOU ANYTHING on your personage worth pickpocketing?" was Edward's question to me as James opened the door.

I considered Mr. Macy's ring, which hung beneath my clothing on a golden chain. Surely that wasn't worth stealing, for likely it would cost any petty thief his life. "No, nothing."

Edward turned and stepped backwards over the threshold of London House. He grinned, dimpling his chin. "Are you ready to see London as you never have?"

I smiled as if excited, but in truth, the dour expression on James's face as he held open the door behind Edward made my stomach twist with nervousness. His black brows slanted in severe disapproval and his mouth pursed angrily. His warning couldn't have been clearer—this was the height of recklessness, and as soon as he was dismissed, he planned on locating my father or Lord Dalry.

At the top of the stairs, Edward lifted his face and breathed deeply. "Ah. Can you smell that? Sewage, coal smoke, and horse urine. London at her finest!"

I started to grin, but across the street, maids were busy scrubbing the opposite house's front steps. They paused in their work, their hands so raw I could see their redness from where we stood. Their frank surprise told me they knew the Emerald Heiress was on the stoop of London House, wearing a middle-class dress and a tattered shawl. I tightened my hold on Edward's arm. "We should have taken the servants' exit."

"Why?"

I nudged my head in their direction. "They recognize me."

Edward glanced with a polite nod. "We're not the ones hiding, Juls. That's your father and Dalry."

I turned my face, glad that my bonnet had a wide brim, allowing me to block their stares. "Nevertheless, it doesn't mean I want anyone looking at me."

Edward laughed, starting us down the stairs. "Come on. This is officially our honeymoon. I do want to stop by the Holywell area. Perhaps I can find work with the booksellers and still maintain my studies. There are some friends I'd like to introduce to you near there, but other than that, the day is yours. What would you like?"

"Hyde Park!" I tugged on Edward's arm. "I asked again and again to visit it. But we never did."

His nose wrinkled. "Why not?"

"Safety."

His arm tightened with anger at the ludicrousness of that argument, but he gave a quick nod. "All right, but I'll warn you, it's not our woods. There are some pretty footpaths, though. We'll get it out of the way by going there first, as it's right around the corner. What else?"

I thought of Windhaven with a pang of regret. How much better would it be to stand on that hill, breathing air fresh with morning dew, feeling the wind ripple my shawl. I shook my head. There wasn't anywhere I wished to go outside of Hyde Park, and only there because it had long been denied me.

But then, as if the idea came from outside of me, I found myself saying, "What about the orphanage that Lord Dalry and I visited? Do you know where that is? There was a little girl there I wanted to . . ."

Visions of that courtyard with the girls marching in the freezing wind and wearing thin rags returned to mind. How well I could still envision the spark in the eyes of the little girl who had drawn me to her with a glance. She'd remained rigid with hope, stock-still, while I argued with Isaac in a bid to adopt her.

"I remember reading the article." Edward pulled on his gloves, his face frank. "With the little girl you kept in your arms? Who was she?"

I nodded, realizing how awful it was that I never thought to ask her name.

"Never mind. What were you beginning to say?"

I gave the street a hopeless look. "I've never seen anything like that place. She broke my heart. I saw her from a carriage window when she glanced in our direction. It was like . . . like I could see all her pain. But more than that, I saw *her*. She was thin and starving, but her soul was fighting to survive. And I wanted so badly to—" I surprised myself by feeling a touch of the fiery passion I experienced that day. I clamped my mouth shut and shook my head. Then followed a yearning to confess the whole truth, for I hated all the things that were gathering between Edward and me. I didn't want one more. "I . . . I even offered to marry Lord Dalry if he'd let me adopt her."

"What happened?"

I gave an embarrassed laugh, feeling the color rise in my cheeks. "It was . . . I mean, it was foolish of me, I know. Isaa— Lord Dalry got some of my father's cronies to investigate the orphanage."

Edward listened, his face stoic. "Have you ever felt anything like that sensation before?"

I felt my blush deepen. "Yes, once. Do you remember the time those boys were hurting that nest of baby robins?"

Edward tilted his chin up as he laughed. "Oh, my word! Yes! I was too far away, or I would have rushed to your aid, but you were magnificent. Your eyes blazed like Joan of Arc's as you brandished a stick and pelted at them full speed. I can still picture Jeremiah's face as he paled and raced back to Auburn Manor. He wore a velvet suit that he'd bragged about to Henry and me that morning. He looked like a complete mollycoddle running away from a girl half his size in pigtails. Do you remember how upset you were over the one they killed?"

I blinked, not remembering that part of the story. My recollection stopped with the image of four boys running away, one looking over his shoulder, aghast with fear.

"You held it in your hand and sobbed and sobbed," Edward filled in. "Then you roared to life again, and I had to grasp you about the waist, holding you in place while you screamed for me to release you. You were going to chase them down with your stick again. Don't you remember?"

Bulging eyes. Pale skin, the color of my own. Tiny white plumes that floated with the slightest current of my breath. Dead in the cupped palm of my hand.

I touched my lips. "I'd forgotten about that part." All at once I recalled the sickening feeling. "Oh, I wish I'd never remembered."

His grin was all male, half-amused that it could still upset me, half-regretful he'd brought it up. "If it cheers you, that was the day Henry finally accepted you. Before, he'd sometimes follow me about the manor, asking if I'd spent the day playing poppet with the *wittle* girl again."

I felt a pang. That sounded like Henry.

"It was the day Jameson learned about you as well."

This piqued my interest. "How?"

"When we went home, Henry kept taunting Jeremiah about

running away from a girl. Jameson caught wind and made Henry give him a full account." Edward chuckled. "I saw Jameson's eyes twinkle with interest when Henry described you. Henry also told him you were the reason I was sneaking out constantly."

"Is that when he starting playing warden?"

Edward rubbed his chin. "No, he was highly curious, now that I recall. He even went to that dance the Gardiners held and asked Hannah to point you out. You remember that day; it was the one where my tutor made me rework my translations. Jameson tramped home on foot after you left the dance. He said I'd be a knave if I didn't find you and take you back there."

This was all news to me. "So when did he start trying to prevent our relationship? And why?"

Edward's forehead creased. "You know, that's a good question, but the sun is not standing still in the sky. We can either go hunt him out and demand an answer, go to Hyde Park, or find this orphanage. Which one, Juls?"

I glanced toward Hyde Park, suddenly no longer caring to see the place where gentlemen showed off their carriages and the elite promenaded in numbers. I'd attended enough parties to have had my fill. Jameson certainly intrigued me, but it would be easy to find an opportunity to speak with him. But the orphanage—this was likely my only chance to see how it had changed. For I felt certain once my father learned Edward had taken me out of London House, he'd grow irate. For all I knew, James was already on his way.

"I want to see the orphanage," I said.

Approval only sweetened Edward's good looks. "That's my girl. That was my vote too! I am intrigued to see the lass who stirred such a degree of passion in you. Who knows, perhaps there's a reason why."

I gasped and gripped his arm, wondering if he meant what I hoped.

"No," he said, the soles of his feet tapping against the walk, "that's not a promise or even an intent. But as Jameson would say, I am highly curious."

∽

I tightened my grip on Edward's sleeve as we neared the orphanage. London on foot was a different city—one that was wilder than anything I could have imagined. Hawkers and costermongers had called to us and followed us on every street and to the mouth of every alleyway. The strong odors of sewage, horse muck, and rotting meat tossed aside from butcher shops combined with the sour scent rising from pools of human urine. I saw how clean my father's street was, in that the cobblestones were even visible. In this part, one could only catch a glimpse of brown stone between the layers of mire.

The din was never-ending. I desired to cover my ears at times, so severe was the constant noise, only I feared losing Edward too much. Dairymaids yodeled, merchants banged on pots to draw attention to their wares, bells rang, carriages clattered, hooves drummed, splashing up muck as they passed. Children beat drums, played penny flutes. Everywhere there was the neighing of horses, the bleating of goats, the sad lowing of cattle.

People jostled me without even realizing it. Having spent years shying from unforeseeable blows, my mother and I were wont to jump at the slightest brush of an arm or nudge of an elbow. And though I no longer visibly started at every touch, I registered each touch distinctly—people brushing my dress, knocking my arm, skimming too near. Children outright used me to steady themselves, making me wonder whether anything of value would have by now been picked from my pockets.

By the time we reached the gates pockmarked with rust, I felt bedraggled and spent. Edward clanged the bell, drawing stares from nearby people. The stench of ordure and rot assailed me from waste bins set near the gate. I covered my mouth and nose, but Edward caught my hand in a quick movement. "No. You'll only make them self-conscious."

I nodded agreement and tried to speak without coughing. "It wasn't this strong at Christmas."

He nodded. "Everything was frozen. Imagine how this will be a few months hence."

My foot shifted in the mire. I glanced down and studied the cart tracks in the mud and caught sight of a putrefied cabbage leaf. Surely this wasn't part of the food that had been delivered.

Before I could ask Edward for his opinion, a woman emerged holding a set of keys. Her dress of black bombazine showed no sign of fading. Swallowing, I followed the lines of the crepe veil draped over her head, barring us from seeing her. My mouth dried as I recalled the first days after Mama's funeral when I'd been similarly attired.

The matron reached the gate and stared at us through its iron bars. Up close, I could see through her veil. Dark hair was parted straight down the middle of her head and fastened into a tight bun. Because of the severity of her hairstyle, her ears stuck out on either side of her head. Her eyes looked shrunken they were so swollen.

Instinctively, I neared Edward.

"May I help you?" The woman's voice was raspy.

Edward bowed his head, removing his hat. "My name is Reverend Auburn and this is my wife, Mrs. Auburn."

The woman nodded, her mouth trembling. "Oh, bless you, sir." She could scarcely speak through her tears as she fumbled with her keys. "Bless you. We were told no one from the church would risk coming, as many have taken ill during the night. But she won't settle until she's had assurance from someone."

Edward and I stole glances at each other.

"While you're here," the woman continued, near tears with gratitude, "will you read the rites of the little ones that passed too? The teachers' corpses are gone, but we're going to bury the girls here."

Edward gave a brief nod, eyeing the building as if taking inventory. "Yes, certainly."

Trying not to lose my stomach at the stench of illness, I slowly drew in air, wondering how we'd wandered into this. With a shake of my head, I cast off thoughts of Mr. Addams's claims about me. Epidemics happened all the time. Surely this had nothing to do with me. "What sort of sickness is it?"

The woman upturned her palms in a gesture of helplessness. "Typhus, perhaps?"

"How many have died?" Edward asked.

"Seven. Five adults, two children."

"Out of how many?"

Here the woman's voice strained. "Of the six adults who contracted it, five died. One is barely alive. The one I've summoned you for. Of the fifteen children who were taken ill, two died. Four are still with fever, but the physician says there is good reason to hope. The rest are already recovering."

Edward indicated her mourning attire. "Who are you mourning for?"

I wrinkled my nose, not thinking the question particularly tactful.

Indeed, the woman's countenance twisted. "My husband. He . . . he had just been appointed director by the new committee. We ran a successful boys' school before this. We . . . we just moved from Norfolk. We hadn't even unpacked. That was three days ago."

"Have you slept?" Edward asked softly.

She shook her head, dabbing her eyes. "There wasn't time. The fever had gripped the school when we arrived. The poor teachers couldn't even rise to greet us." She blinked as if determined to dry her eyes. "Give me one more moment. The girls don't need to see me falter now. They had quite an ordeal before all this. Bad management and all."

I pulled Mama's shawl tight, unable not to study this woman, wondering if she'd dislike me if she could see the full connection between us. Had I not jumped out of a carriage five months ago and refused to leave, Isaac and my father never would have investigated, and she and her husband never would have come to London.

The woman took several deep breaths, then gestured to me. "Are you certain you wish to expose your wife, Reverend? If you have children, I'd advise that at least one of you remain here. My husband succumbed to this illness within the space of a day."

"No." I grabbed his arm. "I'm not staying out here. I'm going inside with you."

Edward started to argue, but then a look I couldn't decipher crossed his face. For five seconds, he stood immobile—as if being reminded of something or trying to pick out a specific voice in a roomful of conversation. Disbelief filled him before his face pinched with grief. "If you want to go back to London House," he said slowly, choosing each word carefully, "I will support your decision."

"I'm staying," I spoke through clenched teeth.

He glanced heavenward as if to ask why; then, placing a hand on my shoulder, he bent his mouth close to my ear. In an urgent, low whisper he communicated, "There's no shame in remaining in the courtyard."

I gave a small stamp with my foot. "You're trying to spare me, but you saw my life without you." Then, seeing my argument had no sway, I changed tactic. "I'm a vicar's wife. This is what I do now."

He ran his fingers through his curls and shut his eyes. "Yes, I know. And I'm not even allowed to stop you. Even now I am reminded of a prayer—" He stopped and glanced at the woman, remembering our audience. "All right, Juls, we go and fight sickness and death together." He grinned. "Who better to be at my side than Jameson's faerie queen."

I couldn't help but glance askance at the matron. She was not amused.

Edward, however, wasn't paying her any mind. He took me by both shoulders. "Listen carefully—this is something that was taught me by an elderly priest who survived through a nasty plague in his day. We're not physicians; we're ministering to their souls and spirits only. Drink nothing. Eat nothing. Touch no water. Touch no bedding. Let me see your hands."

I peeled off my gloves and held them out. "What are you looking for?"

"Cuts or scratches." He scrutinized them until satisfied. "If you do get a cut, do not wash it; do not allow anyone to tend it. Let it bleed." He jerked his head toward the woman. "Are they coughing?"

"Some, but only because of difficulty swallowing."

Edward nodded as if that were good news, then squeezed my hands in his.

Edward kept a firm grip on my elbow as we crossed the threshold of the orphanage, as if we were entering a dark labyrinth and he feared separation. Death became a festering reality. The putrid stench of dysentery assailed me. I gagged, unable to help it, earning a baleful glare from the matron, who led us. The malodor was so overpowering, I had to press my nose into Edward's wool coat, not certain I could suppress my stomach much longer.

We passed through a schoolroom, which temporarily had been set up to serve their laundering needs. Older girls, slightly younger than me, gagged as they plunged paddles into tubs filled with boiling water and sheets that looked soiled with bloodied excrement. Next to them, young girls sweated, one cried, as they labored to drag the dirty sheets over scrub boards. They were situated near the fire and perspiring profusely. Their brows looked like they suffered sweat rash. I released Edward's sleeve as he stepped toward them, noting their hands were cracked and bleeding. Did that mean they would become ill too?

Edward walked amongst them, placing his hand on the crown of the nearest girl, who knelt before her washtub. "I lay hands upon you in the name of the Father—" he moved his hand to the next girl—"and of the Son—" with his left hand he moved to the next—"and of the Holy Spirit, beseeching our Lord Jesus Christ to sustain you with his presence . . ."

The older girls ceased work and withdrew their steaming paddles and, after placing them over the kettles, knelt in line, closing their eyes. It was the first time I'd witnessed any group of people praying together or Edward pastoring. I marveled that he knew what to say and that the girls knew how to respond. Not recognizing the prayer for ministration to the sick, I stared at Edward, wondering by what authority he dared to utter such claims.

". . . to drive away all sickness of body and spirit," Edward continued, slowly making his way amongst them, "and to give you that victory of life and peace, which will enable you to serve him both now and forevermore. Amen."

"Amen," everyone unexpectedly intoned.

The matron gave a sidelong glance at my silence as if finding my lack of participation alarming. I swiped my brow, feeling dampness seep into all of my clothing.

"This way." Frowning, the matron gestured toward a door. "I'll take you first to Miss Rosen and then to the children who have passed."

Clotheslines were strung high above the end of the classroom and ladders placed near them so the girls could hang the washed sheets. Despite the girls' efforts, stains could still be seen. The sheets dripped continuously, creating a macabre rain through which we had to duck. I started to cover my eyes, but Edward gripped my wrist.

"No," he whispered. "Do not touch any part of your face."

My only option was to bury it against his sleeve as we walked beneath them. Water dripped down my neck and along the back of my dress. Yellow grime streaked the walls of the chamber we entered. Thick peat smoke veiled our eyes and competed with the cloying scent of death.

"Miss Rosen," the matron said, kneeling at the bed and feeling a young woman's brow with the back of her hand. "The vicar is here." Then to me, "Call for me when you're finished."

For a moment I feared the girl had already passed, for her neck was arched and her cheeks greatly sunken. One of her legs hung out from beneath the blanket. Her bones, particularly their knobby heads and ends, could be seen as if skin were only draped over them. Suddenly consciousness filled her glassy eyes, and she turned her face toward Edward with a look of fear and desperation that reminded me of Mama's anguished face from my dreams. Skeletal hands stretched through the air for Edward.

As he stepped into the light, I backed against the wall, feeling my mouth turn to wool. Gone was my playmate. This was no boy who splashed in creeks and shared his treacle toffees. A paragon of manhood stood in his place. As I blinked, I realized for the first time he truly was a grown man. It was disorienting, for like Jameson, he'd managed to keep that fact from my view as if knowing the realization would be too discomfiting for me.

Edward sat on his heels, ignoring the grime coating the floor as he enfolded her hand in his.

It became apparent why Edward took no pains toward dignity. The poor girl had no need for any pretense, for she feared her soul damned. The words she birthed from her chapped lips, uttered in dying gasps, issued from a heart that was as frozen as a Russian winter. She'd survived wretched circumstances before she was forced into the orphanage, where she later stayed on as a teacher. I won't sketch her deathbed conversation, outside of saying it was the first time I realized that the truest horrors exist outside of nightmares.

Compassion etched Edward's features even during the parts that were so unbearable I longed to cover my ears and turn toward the wall. He never flinched, but like a master surgeon extracting slivers of glass, Edward extracted confession after confession, then prayed with her. When finished, she sank against her pillow, wasted. By that time, I doubted she even realized I was there. I decided against making any noise or motion to alert her to the fact that I'd also heard those confessions.

"God the Father—" Edward's voice was tremulous. He paused, looking over the empty space around her bed, where a family would normally stand. I somehow understood that this silence was meant to be filled by an appropriate response from loved ones surrounding the deathbed. But in the burdensome silence, his eyes shut with grief before he gave the response alone. "Have mercy on your servant."

The brown of her eyes drank him in, still half-fearful, half-trusting.

He struggled to keep his composure. "God the Son, have mercy on your servant."

She blinked as if crying. The rattle in her breath grew stronger. The only support I could offer Edward was my look of loving compassion.

"God the Holy Spirit—" Edward's voice grew choked—"have mercy on your servant."

By the time he reached the fifteenth line of the traditional prayer, her soul had departed, and a holy quiescence weighted the chamber, pushing against the corners, filling it. This, too, I dared not disturb. I waited as Edward rasped out the last words: "Lord, have mercy." He wiped his nose, using the cuff of his sleeve. "Christ, have mercy." He paused, saying a silent prayer, then finished. "Lord, have mercy."

He rose. "I hate it when they die alone." His face tightened along with his voice, but whether in anger or grief I could not say. "The only things going into eternity with us are each other, yet here lay someone dying alone, with that burdening her soul. She lived day after day with something she didn't need to carry."

"But she wasn't alone," I reminded him. "We were here."

Crossing the chamber and comforting him with an embrace was an impossibility. He seemed a new creature to me—one of manly grace and strength, yes, but nonetheless one I needed more time to consider.

He sensed my change. "I am so sorry, Juls. I had no idea the sort of confessions she was going to make." He placed a hand on his hip and looked toward her body with the air of someone too stunned to know what to think. "I wouldn't have exposed you, or anyone, to that. I'm so sorry."

"Should we cover her face?" I asked.

Edward shook his head and held out his hand for me. "I know it seems crude, but no. We touch as little as possible. And when we go home, we bathe immediately."

I picked up my skirts and made my way to him. "You seemed very different."

He nodded as he opened the door. "I suppose I did."

At the threshold, I stopped and looked over my shoulder at the corpse. "Do you think the little girl we came here to see—?" I swallowed, not wanting to even think it. "Do you suppose her life has been like that?"

"There's a strong possibility."

I felt ill. "Would she be that hardened? And commit those sorts of crimes?"

Edward considered a moment. "Now you know why people rarely adopt from institutions such as this. Yes, many are very hardened at a tender age."

I felt my brow crease. Perhaps Isaac had not shared all the reasons he had been so firm about not adopting her. As I turned my thoughts back to Edward's mannerism at the bedside, it suddenly didn't seem impossible to tell him about blackmailing Macy. Comparatively, my misdeed was a fleabite.

"Were you truly not shocked by her confessions?" I asked by way of testing him further.

Immediately I felt contrite, for his countenance grew haunted. "I was grieved, deeply grieved. She spent her life not understanding she was forgiven, loved, and free because fellow man used her so harshly," he replied. "But no, not shocked."

We reached the end of the hall, but instead of leading back to the schoolroom with the laundry, it divided like a T. Edward glanced down both halls. "Did you catch the matron's name?"

"I'm not sure she ever gave it."

"Well, that makes it hard to shout for her, doesn't it?" Taking my elbow, Edward headed us back in the direction we came. As we walked, he looked over the halls. "They're going to need a new housemaster, and we already know they prefer a married couple. I have to be honest, Juls; I really want to find out who is on the committee that runs this school. What if we're called here?"

I furrowed my brow, not out of astonishment, but rather because I had knowledge that Isaac oversaw the committee. If Edward truly wanted to be a candidate, he'd have to go through Isaac. As for myself, even though I'd stopped gagging on the putrid smell, I wasn't certain what to think. A single conversation with me would decide this. If I asked, surely Isaac would hire Edward and keep his involvement confidential. On the other hand, a simple mention of Lord Dalry would be enough to make Edward abandon the idea.

This time we successfully found the schoolroom again. One of the older girls turned her head our direction, hitting the girl next to her with her plaited blonde hair.

"Right, there ya be," she said in an East London accent. "I'm to fetch ya to the mistress. This way."

Edward signalled for me to go first. I followed the girl

through a narrow passage and then down a set of stairs. Careful not to slip, I steadied myself on the cold metal handrail. "Have you been here long?"

"Aye."

"Were you here when the Emerald Heiress visited?"

The girl's plaited hair swung as she looked over her shoulder. "Oi! Why am I not surprised! It's all anyones talks 'bout. Did I see her? Was she pretty?" She picked at her threadbare skirt and mimicked a high, annoying voice. "'What did her dress look like?' Well, I'll tells ya. I could've knocked Miss Heiress flat on her bum in a fistfight, and that's all that really counts."

"I bet she's tougher than she looks," Edward said behind me.

I smiled, imagining that the odds of my being in a fistfight were rather slim. "Well, I care nothing about her dress. But I do wish to know about the little girl she visited that day. The newspapers said she carried one in her arms."

"Aye, making a right fool of herself," the girl retorted.

"Do you know which girl that was?" I pressed, growing irritated but determined not to be outlasted by ill manners.

"Maud, ya mean? Yeah, I knows her. Poor chit actually believed the heiress was coming back for her one day."

I gave Edward a concerned glance. Of course the child would indulge in such fantasies. What else did the poor thing have to look forward to in a place like this?

"Where is she now?" Edward asked.

The girl turned and gave us a smile, but it was shaped all wrong. It contained anger and hopelessness. She opened a door, and the overpowering scent of decay lambasted us. "She's in there with t'other one who died."

Fourteen

⚜

THAT NIGHT, while we waited for my father's return, I remained with Edward in his bedchamber. As Jameson brushed Edward's suit, I perched near the window, feeling an ache so fierce, I feared I might never recover. Staring at my hands, I recalled the sharp look of hope Maud had worn as I argued with Isaac.

I wondered what would have happened if I had held firm and refused to cooperate with my father or Isaac unless they'd done something for her. Even a half-decent boarding school would have been better than just setting her down and walking away—leaving her with unmet hope. Here was another life made worse for having met me. Had she died disappointed that I hadn't come back? My head clunked against the window frame as I looked skyward.

"Juls, what's troubling you?" Edward asked.

Seeing his and Jameson's concern, I sat forward. "My heart just aches and aches. I'm not sure I can take much more sadness or pain."

Jameson's smile was kind. "That's not a bad thing. It means you're still able to love and be loved."

I buried my face in my hands, thinking he didn't have to go downstairs and sit at the dinner table with the ice king next. "If this is healing, I'd rather be sick. I need my ability to shut everyone and everything out, but it's gone. I can't cope."

To my surprise, Jameson laughed, then crossed the chamber to join me on the window seat. Looking at Edward, he asked, "Does she know the story about the lame man whom Peter healed?"

Edward threw his palms up as if to say my religious training was still a mystery to him and that Jameson should leave me be.

"I know it," I said, not in the mood to hear it recited. Gritting my teeth, I looked toward the door, feeling as trapped as I used to with my former vicar. I couldn't handle people acting as though everything could be solved with the Bible.

"All right, I won't repeat it, then." Jameson held up innocent hands. "But have you ever considered how costly and painful that healing was for the man?"

I rolled my eyes, unable to hide my antagonism toward receiving a religious lecture. "Yes, how he must have hated being able to walk."

"Oh, I'm certain it was exciting at first. A huge miracle, center of attention, a great testimony, and all that." Jameson rested one foot on the bench, then laced his fingers about his knee. "But afterwards there's still the business of living to get to. What do you suppose he did for work the following morning?"

I touched my temples, not certain how I'd fallen into this conversation and wondering the quickest way out.

"Think about it, Mrs. Auburn. He was lame from birth, which meant he was a beggar by trade. He'd never been trained for any occupation, never been apprenticed. Likely he couldn't read or write. He had to learn to adjust to a half life to survive. The entire way he viewed the world, structured his life, and adapted, all gone—" Jameson snapped his fingers—"in the blink of an eye."

I said nothing but looked at him. At least he wasn't telling me what I *ought* to be feeling or thinking. And like it or not, I was now captivated enough to listen.

"Everywhere he went, he likely was stared at. Some probably suspected he'd faked being lame for pity and money. To be healed ended up costing him everything he knew. His entire world was deconstructed, leaving him the hard task of rebuilding it." Jameson's voice grew tender as I only stared. "Sounds familiar, doesn't it? I've known full-grown men to collapse under less strain than you've endured. You've been crippled from birth, too, just in a different sort of way. It hurts to be healed, but would you honestly rather be lame at the gate?"

He was serious about wanting an answer, so I gave a silent shake of my head.

He patted my hand. "For what it's worth, I think you're doing splendidly, and I'm proud of you."

"Perhaps—" Edward was closer to us than I realized—"that's why Jesus waited until people came to him, desperate to be healed. And he asked permission first." The orange light of the setting sun reflected off Edward's face as he pondered. "You know, that's not a half-bad thought." He retreated and opened his notebook of ideas, paging through it for a blank space. Finding one, he dipped his pen and began to scrawl. "I may do a series on the necessity of giving God permission to work in our lives." He glanced up. "Though who knows the next time I'll get to preach."

"Bah!" Jameson stood and motioned the idea away from him. "Logic, boy; use your logic. You can't open with a Scripture about a lame man who wanted money instead of God—and end the sermon with how God requires our permission."

Edward held up a hand for him to be quiet. Brow furrowed, he paged through a Bible.

"Change your sermon," Jameson ordered. "Why not use your wife as your starting point! For I don't think God is asking her for permission. But he just keeps shaking her world apart anyway."

I swung my legs over the window-seat ledge, unable not to smile.

"She wanted a husband—like the lame man, something to meet her immediate needs—but no!" Jameson thwacked his hand on the nightstand. "Instead God chose something completely different, something that astonished everyone. Only that part hasn't happened yet."

"Yes, well, I need to keep my text to Scripture and not to the fact that she's Macy's missing bride."

"Use Jonah, then. For here sits a Jonah if ever there was one!" Jameson rubbed his hands together. "And to think, I've always wanted to meet a Jonah! Fear rules her, she refuses to do what she ought, so a whale has to swallow her to get her attention. But again, that part is still to come."

"Will you stop saying that?" Edward frowned. "She's not Jonah, and there is no whale or disaster coming. I wish you would stop predicting dire things. You're starting to irritate me."

"And because she's married to you," Jameson continued, not heeding him, "when she's forced to do what God has planned, she'll likely be filled with self-righteousness, wrath, and indignation! How delightful! You're turning your wife into a Jonah!"

Edward set down his pen and rubbed his eyes, clearly annoyed. "Jameson, go downstairs. I'll dress myself."

"Well, don't be upset with me," he retorted. "If she's Jonah, I'm the worm. For is not my role to expose what's really there? How can that irritate you? I compare her to a prophet, one who has an entire book of the Bible all to himself, while calling myself a worm!"

Edward stood. "Now, Jameson! And don't let me catch you calling her Jonah ever again!"

"Well, right there is one of your fundamental problems." Jameson stooped and gathered Edward's shoes, which he'd polished and moved near the suit of clothing. "God uses all sorts of people and temperaments. Why should we willfully deceive ourselves into thinking God only likes Davids and Deborahs? Not everyone can walk your role, Edward. What's wrong with Jonah? God himself chose to speak with him." Jameson made a dramatic figure at the door, where he paused, pointing in the air. "God even jested with him."

"I don't agree that God jested with him." Edward stood and leaned over his desk in order to be heard as Jameson retreated. "The worm was a lesson, not intended to be a joke!"

"Jonah," Jameson bellowed down the hall, "was swallowed by a whale and had to sit in its belly while he reconsidered plans. If that doesn't show a grand sense of humor, what does?"

Edward rubbed his brow, then turned to me. "I'm sorry. Jameson sometimes thinks he's a vicar too. I told him he's not to preach at you, given your past. I'll speak to him."

Downstairs, the bell sounded that it was time to dress for dinner. I rubbed my arms, realizing it meant encountering my father.

"Don't worry yourself over Jameson," I said, rising. "He doesn't offend me. That bell means my father will be home for dinner. I'd better go dress."

Edward nodded that he'd heard as he picked up a book and searched its table of contents. "Don't fret about him. I'll be there too."

I started to leave, then turned back. "Have you heard any more about whether Jameson intends to accept my father's offer?"

Edward slowly grinned, looking up. "Trust me, it will never happen."

I rubbed my neck. "I can't imagine how he won't. He needs to make his living like everyone else."

Edward's eyes crinkled as he returned to his book. "Have better faith in our herd than that. We won't lose him after the story you told this morning. He's like us, only . . . well, friendlier. Nothing offends him deeper than seeing a soul trampled."

⌒

Edward's chair sat empty as James tipped mine back. I stared at it, dismayed, for I'd purposefully waited until the last possible second to enter so I would not be alone with my father and Isaac. Head bent, I placed my hands in my lap and waited.

My father punished me with glares that deepened every minute that passed. Five minutes after the dinner hour, I cast questioning glances at James, asking if he knew where Edward was. His shoulders lifted in the slightest motion. Once again, I avoided looking directly at Isaac. When two more minutes passed, beads of perspiration formed along my brow.

"Is your husband ill?" my father finally demanded.

I grimaced, wondering if he'd found out we'd visited the orphanage and this was his way of reprimanding us for going into an epidemic. But surely his face would be harsher than this. "He wasn't an hour ago."

My father exhaled a loud sigh of impatience. "All right. That's it. Your husband is not—"

Hearing approaching footsteps, my father cast an angry glance at Isaac as if to demand why he should tolerate this.

"Give him time, sir," was Isaac's quiet but firm reply. "Trust me, if you refuse to make allowance for him, he won't make any for you either."

Astonished by Isaac's comment, I glanced in his direction. He was giving James a significant look, rolling the blue of his eyes toward Edward's empty spot. I understood as Edward stepped into the chamber. Before anyone could speak, James rushed forward and held out Edward's chair, guaranteeing him a place at the table.

My father frowned, but the pride he took in his footmen's ability to always follow protocol exceeded his impulse to censure James.

I gripped the edge of the table as Edward nodded his thanks to the footman and took his seat. Only then did I note that he still wore his brown suit, though I knew for a fact Jameson had pressed and attended his tails. As he sat, he ascertained that his frock coat was buttoned. Horrified, I realized that ink stained his right hand. I straightened in my chair, praying my father would somehow not notice.

He noticed. "Where are your tails, Reverend Auburn?"

Edward stood slightly and offered a bow. "Forgive me, but I find I cannot wear them."

"What do you mean, you cannot wear them? Do they not fit you? We can have them altered."

A gladiator armed and ready for battle could not have looked more determined than Edward. "You mistake me, sir. What I mean to say is that when I place them on, I cease to be me."

My father shot me a look that clearly asked if Edward was touched with madness.

"To be clearer—" Edward tucked his napkin over his lap—"if I wear them, I will become that which I most detest."

Isaac loudly swallowed his wine but, with a refined movement, set aside his goblet and blotted his mouth.

Thunder developed over my father's face. "You detest the elite?"

Edward locked eyes with him. "I fear becoming like them. Yes."

To my amazement, my father narrowed his eyes at Isaac, accusing him, but then signalled for James to begin dinner. His jaw tightened as he sank against his chair. "I want to make certain I understand this. You marry *my* daughter, an heiress, but then show lack of respect by coming to dinner at my house in rags? Whatever happened to becoming Greek to the Greeks? Or not arriving at the wedding in the wrong attire?"

Even I was shocked my father was so proficient in Scripture.

Edward bowed his head, hiding his face. "I'm sorry, sir, but neither may I spar verses with you. Those words were never meant as weapons to control or to wage war on others. Your interpretation may be superior to mine, but until the Spirit shows me so, I will live by my studies and conscience."

"And how does your conscience justify offending me at my own table?"

As if purposefully avoiding eye contact, Edward straightened his flatware. "Personally, I've never imagined that when Jesus dined with the Pharisees, he changed clothing. They either took him as he was, or they were offended. If the Prince of Heaven clothed himself in the poverty of Nazareth, then surely as his disciple, I do no wrong in not rising above my master."

A look of utter fascinated disbelief crossed Isaac's face. I knew by the way his brow hitched that he practiced his logic, breaking down and rebuilding a response. I squeezed my napkin, willing him to glance at me so I could beg him not to interfere. Edward's animosity toward him was still too strong.

To my surprise, Isaac did glance in my direction. When our eyes met, a visceral shock went through me, for it was my friend and brother, not his debonair self. But quicker than thought, Isaac receded behind his veneer once more.

My father said nothing but fixed his blackest look upon Edward as if mentally pressuring him to accede to his wishes. "I'm asking you to go borrow tails from Isaac."

Edward's Adam's apple bobbed even as he stilled. "Sir, if you wish me not to dine with you, I will understand and respect that. But I cannot change clothing. I cannot live here under two identities: one that tells your staff all men are equal in the sight of God, and that as such, I have abandoned being privileged in order to better share life with all my brothers, and one that adds the clause 'unless I'm dining with Lord Pierson.'"

"My staff?" My father sank back in his chair as though thoroughly confused. "What does eating in proper dinner attire have to do with my staff?"

Edward gestured to James and William as they carried dishes into the chamber. "We're not dining in private. We never have. Every word, every action, matters."

My father smoothed out the wrinkles over his forehead. "James, William, would you please turn and show Reverend Auburn your *tails*."

My father's staff were impeccable. With fluid grace, they turned their backsides to us and bent, splitting apart their coats.

"Honestly, sir!" Isaac's eyes narrowed. "No member of your household should have to subject himself to this. James and William. You have my permission to turn about."

My father paid Isaac no mind. "And my daughter? Is that why she clutched a beggarly looking shawl this morning? Is she to join you in this strange defiance of the elite?"

I stiffened in my chair, surprised he'd noticed what I'd worn that morning.

Edward's hazel eyes moved onto me as if to imbue me with strength while he exposed my vulnerability. "If you mean her mother's shawl? No, sir. My guess is it was her attempt to feel connected somehow, someway, to one of her parents."

My father waved for his wine to be refilled, then, resting his elbow on the arm of his chair, dug his knuckles into his cheek as he considered Edward. As James bent over with the platter, he signalled for his footman to select his cut.

I crossed my feet beneath the table. If I didn't know better, I'd swear that my father nearly felt pride over his new son-in-law's insubordination. Amusement, even.

Edward sensed it too, for he frowned and added, "And as far as this being in defiance of the elite—" he gestured over the glittering table—"what makes you think that any of this is the measure of success?"

My father acknowledged his question with a respectful nod. He retrieved his utensils. "For one who claims this life is secondary to living in rags on the street, you certainly came running quickly enough when in need."

Edward reddened. "I have a wife, which means I laid down my freedom to become a servant, yes."

"Servant!" My father gave a laugh of disbelief.

"Servant," Edward affirmed, lifting his eyes for a brief second.

My father shook his head as he cut into fried sole, releasing the scent of lemons and butter. "Explain that mystery to me, and as a return favor—" he turned his angry stare on me—"I'll make certain my daughter is aware that you're the head of your household."

Isaac's chest heaved as if once again the conversation was moving past his endurance.

"And how will you manage that?" With an upturned hand, Edward declined the fish James presented. "I've already proven that my influence over Julia far surpasses yours. But let me ask, would you truly rather teach me to reign over her with a fist of iron than to serve her needs above my own?" He paused, giving my father space to answer; then, when he didn't, "So, yes, I said 'servant' because that is the role I elected to take on when I became a husband."

My father's chuckle contained anger. "You dare to preach to me by condemning my life. You insult my table by refusing to look and act the part of my son-in-law. You censure the way I treat my daughter. Yet your own household, sir, is in shambles. You need me to pay your servants, feed and clothe your wife, and provide you with food, bedding, and transportation. You're educated, which means you've reaped the benefits of being privileged. Tell me, Edward, where do you draw the line on being fanatical versus practical?"

Edward ruminated a moment, swirling, then sipping his wine. "Why do you consider your way practical? Is it so impossible to think this version of life is not the best choice? Each one of us is either building his own kingdom or God's Kingdom on earth. Which of those two realities do you suppose we're in as we sit here, putting on airs, congratulating ourselves on having figured out life to our advantages, amassing our comforts for the sole benefit of our families? While outside our doorstep people are desperate for food. Desperate to know their existence matters. Desperate for us to give them acceptance." Edward fingered the bottom of his goblet. "No. This is not practical. This is the height of being naked and blind and too witless to even know it. If experiencing starvation and homelessness has kept me disillusioned, then I shall consider myself blessed."

My father hid an incredulous smile by rubbing the receding line on his forehead. "So let me make certain I understand this. You would have us believe we should abandon position and titles—" He waved his hand as if to ask Edward if he'd left something out.

"Secondary to the Kingdom of God," Edward supplied. "Yes."

"Yet you married my daughter, an emerald heiress, and forced your way into my family?"

Edward looked askance at the table, shaking his head in disagreement. "No. I married the girl I've loved since my youth. I married Julia. Not an emerald heiress—" his teeth showed as he fairly snarled in Isaac's direction—"as some would consider her."

"And yet when she was neither my daughter nor a known heiress," my father challenged, "you wed her to someone else."

Edward always had the most stunning countenance of anyone I'd ever met. Macy was mesmerizing and enthralling in a way that eclipsed others, but Edward, though beautiful, usually managed to walk through life projecting an invisible cowl over his face, hiding his transcendence. But that night, as he lifted his gaze to my father, he was his truer self.

My breath caught, for he was formidable.

"Guilt will not work on me." He fastened his gaze on his hand, which clenched his chair. "Neither will the attraction of prestige or power. I desire neither status nor wealth. You'll have to find something new to try to lure me with. Though I should warn you, once a soul has broken free of those desires, it's much harder to coerce." He chuckled. "Actually, after that point, we tend to be pretty much useless to anyone outside of God."

Were my father a royal tailor and Edward expensive cloth on the verge of being cut, my father could not have measured him with more excitement. I'd come into his shop common serge, broadcloth, not worthy of his notice, but Edward . . . here at last was golden silk and scraps of blue taffeta for lining, with enough velvet to make cuffs. The blind purchase of materials had finally yielded something of use, just unexpectedly, at the bottom of the bag.

My father rubbed along his jawline as he considered the chandelier above. Was he thinking House of Commons? Did he envision the usefulness of Edward at clubs, or in his mind, was he grooming him to go to India and Africa, a steward of his foreign affairs? Shaking his head as if wondering how to first rid his son-in-law of such odd notions, his attention returned to the table and he gave Isaac a nod of encouragement to do something.

Here I dared look at Isaac, for he was distracted, but he remained unreadable. Aloof and detached, he considered his sip of wine before swallowing. The only sign of his true thoughts was a quick glance at me. Then, with a dispassionate gesture, he set down his wineglass. "Can you agree, Reverend Auburn, that it is equally prideful to claim that one needs nothing outside of

God, as if one somehow is spiritually above the rest of humanity? Do you not find there is danger in constantly being placed where you are the one best educated, the most privileged? How do you guard against feeling superior—not only to those, like us here, still living an advantaged life, but to those whose early deprivations make them unable to challenge you?"

Edward's eyes snapped open. He said nothing as he fastened an intense stare on his empty place setting. I held my breath, knowing he'd made the prior decision that he would never acknowledge Isaac's existence.

Isaac had masterfully played his hand, too, for he'd left Edward at the crossroads of two equally repugnant choices—speaking to him or allowing the insinuation to hang that Edward only associated with those to whom he could feel superior.

My father's eyes twinkled as he watched Isaac, telling me he likewise understood Isaac's technique. I sat on pins, pressing the tips of my fingers into the arms of my chair.

To my relief, Edward turned an angry glare on Isaac but decided he would speak. "Just as Lord Pierson failed to topple me with guilt, you cannot topple me by using my fear of being misunderstood. When you've lived on the streets of London little better than a beggar, you stop caring what others think. I do not claim that title and position are without value. How much more guilt would our country shoulder were it not for Pitt and Wilberforce? But note, even though they were in politics, they weren't working for their own kingdom. If God bids you to build a train or sponsor a poorhouse or feed the masses, then by all means do so. But let us not pretend that is what is happening here. If that were so, you would not object to my wearing a simple coat to dinner. You would not turn away an orphan simply because she does not fit into the life you've planned."

My father laughed. "Well, I can see what brought you to these circumstances. No wonder you're homeless. You cannot possibly hope to sell God to the masses with a viewpoint like that."

Edward grimaced as if experiencing a bitter taste. "Nor do I have desire to sell him, sir. Trust me, he's not concerned with whether or not he's marketable. If he were, he wouldn't dress his prophets in camels' hair or forgo giving himself good looks. No preening, strutting, hopeful suitor is he, but a King on a throne. Accept his rule or not." He faced Isaac. "Live a tidy, neat life if you wish. I won't condemn you for it. Someone must sell fish, shoe the horse, argue the law. But as for me, the only things I dare invest myself in are eternal ones—people and truth."

Isaac considered his next words with the air of someone combing them over and over for a flaw before speaking. "If you're called to invest in people, allow me to unite with those like Wilberforce. Let me introduce you to some of my friends. You would be sharpened by them—I know you would—and they by you."

"No." Edward made no attempt to veil the disdain in his voice. "I won't look for greatness amongst your peers, for I dislike fruitless searches. I tell you, it is hard to find it amongst those of title, wealth, and position. Instead I look far lower and find examples of eminence everywhere I go. Stories of courage, love, and bravery that this sphere has never dreamed existed."

"Come on then; give us an example." My father's voice was warm. "Let us hear and judge for ourselves."

"I can't." Edward's voice was empty. "For you don't have the eyes to see it."

"Bah! Riddles." My father clicked his fork against his plate. "Give me one solid example." He lifted his hand. "Bravery. You just said you'd encountered it such as I never dreamed of. Give me one example, and I'll trump it with my own story. I would like to see one of your beggarly types withstand a hostile mob of two hundred coolies, single-handedly, without a gun. Only a true born-and-bred English gentleman could manage that feat. But go on; prove me wrong."

Once again, Edward lifted his otherworldly gaze. He opened

his mouth and for a second nearly didn't speak. But then he locked eyes with me. "Once I witnessed the shyest girl I've ever known take a great risk by entering this sphere, needing to be saved, praying to win your love."

I shook my head. I did not want to be his example.

"I watched her shoved into an arena with orders to perform a role that most need a lifetime to prepare for. I watched her sacrifice her heart trying to appease the unappeasable. And when I finally managed to free her from you, she quailed at the idea of returning. But she came. Tell me, *sir*, which English gentleman friend of yours would enter a room where he had no value and no chance of redeeming himself? She wasn't even reckoned worthy enough to be personally greeted by you, sir. She sits next to you now, at this dinner, passed over, unspoken to, while you try to curry favor with me. How can I show you greater things when you refuse to see the quiet grace and bravery right before you?" He shoved back his chair and stood. "As to winning my favor, I am deaf to you until she is honored."

I turned toward Edward, feeling my face twisting, not wanting the others to see how undone I was.

He placed his napkin on his chair. "Are you ready to go to bed, Juls? We're the only ones not eating anyway."

I nodded. James must have assisted with my chair, for I found my feet before Edward made it to me. Head bent, I managed to exit the chamber and climb the stairs, clutching his hand. Tears wet my cheeks, but I didn't seem able to stop the flow of them, though I didn't know why.

Edward waited until we'd reached his bedchamber before speaking. "Forgive me. I didn't mean to—" He opened the door.

I cut him off with a kiss, feeling a fervency I scarcely understood. I pulled hard at his cravat, though my fingers shook. A sharp and acute emotion had erupted within me. Though I had never pursued him this way before, I tugged at the buttons on his frock coat, unwilling for there to be anything between us.

Why, I feebly wondered, why had I not truly known him before? Had I not searched him out as he had me? Here was the lover of my soul and my desire was insatiable.

My kisses were frantic and mingled with tears, yet he was not alarmed. No longer did I balk at the idea that he'd stepped over the threshold into manhood.

I was lovesick.

Fifteen

✦

I AWOKE WITH A START and found myself tangled in Edward. Judging by the slow rise and fall of his chest, he was in a deep slumber. Uncertain what had awakened me, I lifted my head and found it more difficult than anticipated. My hair caught in the fingers of Edward's left hand, while his right arm still pinned me against him. I collapsed back against the down mattress, no longer caring what had woken me.

Yawning, I turned on my stomach and kissed his chest before resting my head against it. His heart lub-dubbed, assuring me all was well. I planted two more kisses in succession on his shoulder, then pressed my cheek against the spot. His skin felt feverish compared to mine as I pulled up the covers.

Just before I shut my eyes, a flash of yellow light caught my attention beneath the door crack before it receded toward the staircase. I rose, causing Edward to turn over, mumbling incoherent words. Footsteps creaked near the top of the stairs, pausing.

I glanced at the mantel clock, frowning. Who was walking about at two in the morning?

Eramus's homicidal face loomed in my mind, making me shiver and consider sliding out of bed and locking the door. Yet Macy had ensured I'd never need fear my cousin again. That thought also made me feel cold, for I did not yet know what to make of Macy's continued silence since my marriage a week ago. Refusing to dwell on it, I settled against Edward's warmth, smiling at the thought that even if someone did burst through the door, Edward would teach them a lesson they'd never forget.

I cannot say how long I slept, but just as I was beginning to dream that Edward and I were searching downstairs for Jameson, the sound of glass shattering was followed by a loud thump, like that of someone falling.

I sat up. Though it was late, London House was never darker than a full-moon night due to the lampposts in this part of the city. A second thump was followed by a loud groan in the foyer downstairs. I slid from the shelter of Edward's warmth and grabbed the luxurious dressing gown within reach of his bed.

The scent of cedar and Isaac's soap tingled my nose, informing me that a servant must have pulled the gown from Isaac's closet for Edward's use. A choking sensation filled my throat. The reminder of him was like receiving a forgotten bill just as one was planning how to spend a windfall. I tied the velveteen sash with heaviness. How many times had we exchanged amused looks over the breakfast table? Less than a fortnight ago, I thought nothing of settling against him on a settee as he read to me. I missed my brother-friend, though I was loath to admit it.

I rubbed my hand over the quilted sleeve, wondering how he truly was managing. The suddenness of our separation had hurt even me. At least I had Edward, but what must it be like for him, alone and pressured to appear more polished than he felt? I forcibly shook aside the thought, for each trauma building around me was becoming heavier than I could bear. I couldn't afford to dwell any longer on Isaac.

Already I felt strained beyond endurance.

Determined only to discover who was prowling about the house in the middle of the night and why, I crossed the bed-chamber and stepped into the hall. Clothed in darkness, I dropped to my knees and peered through the nearest balustrade.

My father and James knelt beside a man who lay crumpled on the ground, groaning. He'd apparently knocked over a pedestal with a vase on it. A whale-oil lamp sat between my father and his footman. Light refracted off the polished floor, casting their features in an eerie glow.

"Well, confound it, surely it's only going to keep getting worse." My father's voice carried through the still night as it wouldn't during the busy day. "Outside of James and myself, who even knows you're here! Let me have Isaac fetched to the library, and we shall have this business aired at once."

The man groaned and turned his face upwards as James pulled off his boot. I drew a sharp breath. It was Mr. Forrester. One side of his face was swollen and nearly unrecognizable. He grimaced as he spoke through a busted lip. "You still fail to understand this. If I told, Isaac would be dead before nightfall and so would you. Especially you."

"I'm in no mood for more riddles." My father's face gnarled. "Trust me, I had my fill at dinner from my son-in-law."

Forrester cried in pain as James removed the other boot. "Your son-in-law?" A note of wildness I'd never detected in him before filled his voice. "Reverend Auburn, your daughter—they're here?"

My father made a scoffing noise. "In body, at least."

"Are they badly injured?"

"Badly injured?" My father stood and seated himself on the bench, where he rubbed his knee. "Apparently his parish pelted him with offal at his brother's wedding, though it didn't sound like it was the work of Macy."

"What?" Forrester leaned forward and spat blood on the floor, then rubbed his lip. "That's not possible. Both of my estates gone, my newspaper trashed. I barely made it here alive, and as far as I can tell, Macy's still out of the country."

I gripped the wooden spindles.

"Robert, I shall ask this only once, and I want a straight answer; so help you, don't lie to me. Simmons arrived here with a strange report. Two days ago he received my express orders to burn those papers you locked for safekeeping in my lockbox."

The noise that Forrester made was unlike any animal's—sharp, dry, and cutting. Though movement cost him, he crawled across the floor, keeping one leg straight, and reached out and grabbed the material of my father's dressing gown. "Tell me! Tell me they're not burnt!"

"They're ash." My father's tone chilled even me. "But here is the strangest part of the tale. Simmons says my daughter reacted just as you did now. She nearly went mad as they were tossed into the fire."

"What!" Forrester screamed. "She was there! She watched them burn?"

He screamed so loudly, I winced and glanced along the hall. Heat prickled my face, for I felt certain I was about to be caught eavesdropping.

"Robert." My father's voice was blacker than pitch. "What does my daughter have to do with your extortion of Macy? I want the truth!"

Forrester released a string of curses. "How can anyone be so stupid?" He bashed the wall with his fist. "Roy, hear me; really hear me! Your daughter has never been anything other than Macy's planted spy! She is going to ruin you. She—"

"Did she—" my father rose, a storm unlike any other—"help you extort from Macy?"

Forrester laughed, shaking his head. "No. She's not capable of anything but loyalty to him. I'll swear it on any Bible, if it will help."

My father heaved a deep breath, his fingers relaxing from their fists.

Forrester rested his head against the wall, tenderly touching his swollen jaw. "I've told you this before, Roy, and I'm emphasizing it now: Your daughter is the best Macy girl he's ever produced. Whatever you do, don't trust her."

My father gave a dark chuckle. "You're going to have a hard time convincing me that my son-in-law is working for Macy."

"He's a puppet." Snapping his fingers in my father's direction, Forrester cried, "You realize what's happening, don't you? We weren't giving her the freedom she needed to accomplish her task, so she bucked you and took a husband. Ha, and now the little strumpet is back in London. Who's keeping an eye on her?"

My father jammed his hands into his dressing gown. "No one, Robert. No one needs to."

"Well, what has she been doing?"

My father shook his head as if to say he could not stand having this conversation one more time. Then, with a sigh, he peered over his shoulder. "James?"

The footman couldn't have looked more expressionless. "Reverend and Mrs. Auburn spent the day out walking."

"Did they do anything out of the ordinary?" Forrester demanded. "Anything at all?"

James gave him a funny look. "Well . . . when they returned home, sir, your daughter had been crying. Reverend Auburn insisted they wash their hands four times, immediately, in the front hall, ordering new water and towels each time. He then proceeded to order the hottest baths the staff could produce and sacks for them to put their clothing inside. He insisted no one was allowed to touch their clothing until it had been boiled at least ten minutes. His orders were to wash it immediately after boiling it."

Both my father and Forrester blinked with dumb amazement.

"Why?" my father finally asked.

"I didn't inquire, sir," was James's obeisant reply.

Forrester looked at my father, gesturing toward James as if demanding a better explanation than that.

"We'll find out in the morning," my father finally said.

"Were there bloodstains on their clothes?" Forrester demanded.

"None, sir."

"May I stay here?" Forrester asked.

My father held out his hand to help Forrester rise. "What? Have London House burned to cinders next?"

"With your daughter here, we can be certain he won't touch this place." Forrester winced as he found his feet, then leaned heavily on my father's arm. "Roy, I'm begging you, give me a private audience with her. Please!"

"You never cease trying, do you? You'll have to arrange that with her husband. If I were you, I wouldn't begin my request by rousing him from his sleep, bruised and battered, asking for her company."

"Protective?"

"Humph. Deem for yourself in the morning."

Careful to keep from sight, I slid backwards, then crawled inside Edward's bedchamber. The floorboards creaked beneath the carpet, though I tiptoed across the chamber. Even sleeping, Edward accepted me, for he drew me tightly against him as I climbed back into bed. His warmth imbued me with a sense of courage as I considered Forrester's conversation.

I curled into a ball, knowing the decisions I made here in the dark alone would ripple out in unpredictable ways. Already fatal mistakes had been made. Both Mama and Eramus had paid with their lives. How badly I wished to close my eyes and pretend I had no need to think about anything more.

But I couldn't. It was like being at an elite soiree where everyone was wrapped in a delightful conversation—and being one of two people who understood that a flood was about to break loose. How does one make use of those precious few minutes, especially when they're uncertain which direction the flood is coming from?

I breathed in the scent of Edward, picturing how hurt he'd be to learn that I was still withholding vital information, that I hadn't yet truly trusted him to navigate. Yet what if telling Edward was the worst thing I could do? Forrester's words pounded against my memory—he still believed if he shared his information about Macy, the hearer would die.

I shut my eyes, a silent plea for help. Had I not already touched the untouchable? Did I not sometimes feel God's very presence? Could he not speak and direct me? What better privilege is there for his sheep than to hear his voice?

I waited in stillness, listening to the distant clop of a carriage.

Heaven chose silence.

I flopped onto my back and stared at the intricately carved oak of the massive bed frame surrounding us. I heaved a sigh, thinking anew of Forrester. Had he truly stopped trusting me? Or was that just a ruse for my father? For he'd purposefully played the antagonist toward me that morning he used his paper to betray us. Of all the souls on earth to be partnered with in this strange dance, he was the last one I'd ever have chosen. It was maddening beyond reason. For I neither liked nor trusted him. Yet our fates were tied.

But here I finally found my conclusion.

Forrester was inside London House.

There was at least a soul I could consult before taking another step.

It would be pure folly not to.

❧

The following morning, Edward woke at his usual time, dressed, then knelt by the bed. With a tender smile, he brushed the hair from my face. When he had my full attention, he said, "I'm going to walk and pray. Do you want to join me?"

I rubbed my eyes, already knowing I wouldn't accompany him.

Edward must have read my thoughts from my expression. "You can remain if you wish, Juls. I'll not require anything of you."

"I think I'll stay."

He kissed my forehead. "Don't feel obligated to attend breakfast. Jameson will bring you a tray. I'll be back soon."

I smiled and nodded, feeling a pit in my stomach. Since I'd be alone, there still might be a chance I could slip Isaac his note. And with any luck, I'd manage to have a private conversation with Forrester.

~

That morning I dressed in a gown the color of charcoal and pleated elegantly at the waist. Because I'd not worn rags in my hair the night prior, curls were not possible, but Miss Moray complied with my wish to appear simplistic and parted my hair, which she plaited in loops before adding a ribboned headband that tied across my forehead.

I nodded approval as I stared at my mirror self. Hopefully Forrester would be reminded of my nonage.

The scent of cinnamon and bacon wafted through the air as I approached the breakfast chamber. Though I could clearly hear the clink of silverware, no one spoke, making it impossible to distinguish whether Forrester was present.

Modulating my face, I crossed the threshold.

To my astonishment, Jameson stood at the sideboard wearing black tie, indicating that he was the butler. The only other occupant was Isaac. I froze, staring at Jameson, so stunned he'd accepted the position that I had to grip the doorframe.

With a rare break in his cultured expression, Isaac stood. His eyes travelled along the features of my face. Barely visible, his Adam's apple bobbed as he looked behind me. "Julia."

The tenor of his voice was enough to put me on my guard, and I wasn't the only one. Behind him, Jameson flashed me a look of warning.

I gathered my skirts, hesitating. All at once I recalled that Jameson had seen the fore-edge painting while we were at Maplecroft. Surely by now he'd connected that the figure represented was Isaac. He'd even seen me brooding over it. My cheeks tingled as I realized there was no explaining it. If I tried, it would only make me look guiltier. I glanced at the empty hall behind me, not certain what to do.

"Please." Isaac's entreaty was genuine, drawing my attention back to his pale face. He swallowed, still gripping his napkin. "Please join me. I . . ." For a moment his eyes grew pained, but in Isaac-like fashion he recovered himself. "This wall between us is torment." He lifted one hand as if what he needed to express was greater than words, but then gained possession of himself and dropped it.

My vision blurred, for I had not forgotten how isolated his world was. To walk away felt cruel, yet to stay felt like betrayal. Not certain what to do, I looked to Jameson for direction.

Jameson, to his credit, watched, displaying the same fatherly tenderness he showed Edward and me.

Isaac drew a deep breath and fixed his eyes on the table. "I know your husband does not approve of me, but I will win him over. Give me time. I swear to you, I can win him. But in the meantime, do not shut me out. I'm beg—" He squeezed shut his eyes as if to keep from uttering more. "Jameson, I know she's seeking your counsel, for I see her looking to you for help. I give you my word of honor as a gentleman, I would do nothing to harm her or her marriage. I swear it."

"I know, laddie," Jameson said. "I know."

Isaac grew very still and the blue of his eyes moved toward

Jameson with shock. But then, as if determined nothing should interfere with his request, he returned his full attention to me.

Jameson coughed into his fist, then whispered, "The first rule of the herd, Mrs. Auburn."

I pressed my fingertips against my forehead. I wasn't certain Isaac could heal in close proximity to me. And despite Isaac's belief that he could win Edward, he was wrong.

"Sit and eat breakfast." Jameson's voice travelled toward my chair. I glanced up in time to see him pulling it out. "One of the benefits of marrying a vicar—particularly Edward—is that even if he doesn't approve, he hasn't a choice but to forgive you."

Isaac's brows knit as he considered Jameson, but then, determined not to get off task, he kept his head bowed, waiting for a sign of my approval.

I folded my arms against my stomach, uncertain. One by one, I considered the pieces of Isaac's life I knew: losing his father, being torn from his family, enduring Eramus's aggression, growing up in an atmosphere thick with the bitterness that existed between my father and his wife, being jilted by me weeks before our wedding.

He lifted his eyes, waiting, making me more nervous. I squeezed my skirt, knowing I couldn't ignore Isaac, even if it was for his own benefit. Unfortunately I blurted out the first thing I could think of: "How have you been during my absence?"

Isaac hesitated, clearly searching for a truthful and polite way to bridge that.

Jameson chuckled as he held out my chair, somehow helping to alleviate the embarrassment I felt at my obvious gaffe.

I took my seat, gritting my teeth, unable to believe I'd asked that when *wretched* was the obvious answer. I drew a breath and tried anew. This was Isaac, after all. "I saw Colonel Greenley while we were at Maplecroft."

Isaac's expression was difficult to read. Perhaps he felt disappointed that I approached him only as a casual acquaintance.

Or perhaps he was so relieved we were speaking that he was once more able to discipline his features. "Yes, he calls quite regularly, though it's odd for him to do so while your father is absent."

I likewise schooled my features. "This time he desired to meet with me."

"Ah," Isaac said by way of continuing conversation, though it was like a swimmer trying to struggle against high tide. "Did he . . . Did you . . . enjoy the visit?"

In response, I withdrew the now-crumpled letter from my pocket and slid it across the table.

Isaac cocked his head, giving me a questioning look, but he picked up the note and slit it with his knife. At the sideboard, Jameson tufted his brows, apparently amazed, and perhaps a bit hurt, at how long I'd been carrying this particular secret.

Colonel Greenley must have had tiny handwriting, for it took Isaac ten minutes to finish the note. When he lifted his head, his countenance was stiff and inscrutable. In a toneless voice he asked, "How many days ago did he give this to you?"

"The day before we arrived here in London."

Isaac's pallid face was masklike as he stared at the center of the table between us. "Did he tell you its contents?"

"No."

Tormented eyes searched mine. It seemed as if, on the other side of an unreachable shore, Isaac was silently screaming and pleading for help behind his polished mask. Then his eyes went vacant as if something vital had died inside him.

Breathless, I watched, feeling helpless.

He mechanically folded the note. "If you'll excuse me. There's something I need to attend to immediately."

I cast Jameson a look, begging his help. He, however, had only seen my face and not Isaac's, which was the equivalent of hearing half a conversation. He gave a slight shake of his head, saying he didn't know what I wanted.

Isaac stood and tucked his chair under the table. Yet he remained, gripping the chair back. In a voice I doubted even Jameson heard, he asked, "But we are still friends, Julia, yes?"

I met his eyes, not missing that he'd used my first name. It was as if fate had scripted what I was to say before time began, and I was only repeating an oft-practiced line.

"Always," I found myself promising.

He nodded, and his chest filled as if he were able to breathe again. "Then it is enough. It is enough."

I shut my eyes, listening to his footfalls retreat. He went past the library, which was opposite the direction of Lady Pierson's office, where all the stationery was kept. Drawing a deep breath, I placed my hand over my heart.

"Well," Jameson said softly, "I can see why you didn't hone your conversational skills living here. He needs as much practice as you." His eyes turned in the direction Isaac had taken. "Though I bet if he were shipwrecked on an empty sea of causerie, he'd stay afloat forever, whereas you'd most definitely sink. What do you suppose was in that letter?"

Though I had an inkling, I only shook my head and changed the subject. "You're the London House butler now?"

That made him laugh. "Yes and no. I can't exactly refuse to earn my keep."

I felt all out of sorts, for something told me that Isaac felt trapped, and I was angry for him. I was tired of worrying about Mr. Macy. I wanted to know where Forrester was. And poor Jameson got the brunt of it. "What about us? The herd and all that nonsense that apparently isn't true?"

His expression was soft as he crossed his arms over the back of Isaac's empty chair. "Did you already forget, my queen, that you enslaved me forever on our first meeting?"

"That wasn't an answer," I accused.

"Mr. Jameson!" William, the second footman, poked his head inside the chamber. "You need to come to the front hall, sir."

Jameson straightened and, in a deeper tone than I'd ever heard him use, said, "Thank you, William. I'll be there in a second."

William's footsteps retreated, and though Jameson desired to say more, the slamming of doors and sounds of shoes clunking and servants exclaiming distracted him. With the dignity of a butler, he frowned, folded his hand over his jacket, and proceeded to the hall.

I pushed against the table and rose to follow. Even before we stepped into the hall, the heavy perfume of flowers, scents of chocolate, and aroma of baked goods wafted in the air.

To my amazement, maids were piling baskets over the polished foyer floor. Lilies of the valley, candy tufts, London pride, and flowers too numerous to count. Even half-farthing bundles of violets had been haphazardly tossed into a large basket. Hundreds of them, as though all the poor of London had squandered their pennies in an attempt to take part. Bandboxes of oranges, plums, and exotic fruits were stacked near the suits of armor. Over the marble hall table, presents wrapped in expensive papers, one even covered with gold leaf, were piled in a mound.

"When we opened the door," William explained, "it was piled so high, the maids couldn't get out to scrub the steps. So I had them start bringing it in here."

"What on earth?" I asked, stunned.

My father stepped out onto the third level and looked down over the balustrade. He frowned before his face grew angered. Brushing off Simmons, who'd been fastening his cravat, he pounded down the stairs, taking over the task himself. He waited until he was on the second level before speaking. "What is going on here!"

Jameson bent over, picked up one of the packages, and read its label. His mouth creased for a second before he fisted a hand behind his back and faced my father. "Wedding presents, sir."

The front door opened, and James entered cradling a mastiff

pup whose dark-grey fur wrinkled about his arm. A gold collar with a bow and tag decorated its neck.

I gasped and placed my hands over my heart.

"What is that!" my father roared.

Jameson glanced at the tag. "Zeus, apparently."

I covered my mouth, wondering if he also remembered that owning a mastiff was one of Edward's fondest wishes.

"I thought it best to bring this present indoors before the others," James explained. "It was starting to wander off."

"There's more?" My father stormed to the door and opened it.

Cheers arose from every corner of Audley Street. All down the front steps of London House, people had tossed baskets and wares over the gate.

Isaac approached behind me. "I could hear their cheering from my snuggery. What is happening?"

"Somehow London has learned that the Emerald Heiress and her new husband are here," James whispered.

Outdoors, a woman cried, "I see her!" Then, waving her hand at me, "Tell us your new name, luv!"

"Give us a name!" Others took up the call. "Show us the hubby."

"What shall I do?" I whispered to Isaac.

"Smile and wave." As he used to, Isaac directed me with a simple touch on my elbow. "Act as if you're enjoying the game of hare and hounds over who your husband is, until we figure out what is going on. Don't give his name, though. Don't linger, either. Look how they're pressing against the gate. This could turn into a riot quickly."

I glanced at Isaac, but he wore no expression. Pasting a smile on my face, I stepped toward the door and peeked out. The roar that followed stunned me.

"Come on, luv! Don't keep us guessing," a toothless man called out as he smiled. "Show us your new husband! Give us a sporting chance at least!"

His request was met with clapping approval.

Next to me, my father paled. In one of those rare moments of emergency, I suddenly realized how to draw the attention off my father. Smiling hard enough to create dimples, I shook my head in a gesture that suggested I was both shy and unwilling to ruin the fun. I blew the man a kiss, earning cheers from the crowd.

My father's smile looked skeletal as he grabbed my arm and pulled me back from the door, though he nodded his thanks to the crowd.

"I told you she was a first-rate actress," Forrester said from the third floor. "Brava, my dear. Care to tell me why you couldn't manage to pull off an act like that before now?"

Sixteen

"SO HELP ME, ROBERT—" my father gestured outdoors, his voice enraged—"do you have any knowledge about what's happening?"

"I have an idea." Mr. Forrester gripped the rail and leaned over it for a better view. In the daytime, his face looked so mangled, icy needles stabbed my stomach. The right side of his face was swollen and deeply bruised. His nose was twice its normal volume and his right eye completely forced shut. Three separate large goose eggs rose over his brow. His bottom lip was so puffy, it looked as if it would burst open if he attempted to smile.

I lifted my face and met his gaze straight on, hoping to communicate that I was still the same person who'd blackmailed Macy with him.

It was my first mistake.

Had I not eavesdropped on him and my father last night, my response would have been entirely different. I should have been living in daily dread, and I was, but one could never guess it by the calmness with which I studied Forrester's injuries. Had

I burst out in tears, given a gasp of alarm, or even covered my mouth with horror, there might have been hopes of convincing him that I, too, feared Macy.

"I see news travels fast," Forrester said while wiggling his jaw as if a tooth were loose. "Someday I'm going to figure out how he manages it."

Isaac, who'd been lost in astonishment, finally stepped forward, saying, "What on earth happened to you?"

Forrester started to hobble down the stairs. "The quicksands have grabbed hold of me, that's what."

My father stormed to the bottom of the steps and gripped the intricate newel there. "What do you have to do with that?" He jerked his finger toward the door.

Forrester kept his gaze on me. "I take it you haven't seen the *Morning Herald* yet?"

"What the devil did you do?" my father demanded yet again.

Forrester touched his lip as if in too much pain to speak.

"I'll go find and fetch it, sir." Isaac eyed Forrester as he jogged toward the breakfast chamber.

My father held his temples as he spoke. To my surprise, instead of shouting, he seemed barely capable of speech. "Robert, have you any idea how precariously close our party is to crumbling with this whole Peel affair? Isaac's entire career hinges upon the next couple of weeks, and I can't even leave my house now."

A moment later Isaac returned, carrying a copy of the *Morning Herald*. He sighed, saying, "Front page, sir."

My father snapped open the newsprint. He read, then shook his head and sagged against the newel as if words were too much. "Robert." My father's voice was weak.

"Sorry, Roy, but whether you believe me or not, I needed to curb your daughter's ability to leave London House unsupervised." He sneered at me. "No more sneaking away in the middle of the day, dearie. All of London is now at your doorstep."

My father's face looked touched with grey. "You actually offered a reward for the first person to contact your paper with her husband's identity."

Forrester tried to smirk but was in too much pain. "I'm going to keep as many people milling about these doors as possible. If you think about it, it also offers protection from its being burned down."

"And what am I to tell the queen, Melbourne, or Peel when they get caught up in the mystery of who my son-in-law is? Hope they don't connect that it's the same vicar notorious for stealing Macy's bride?"

"Why my picture?" Isaac demanded. He pinned Forrester with a gaze that asked if he hadn't suffered enough without this additional ignominy.

Forrester shrugged. "I had to stop the presses in the early hours of the morning to include this article. The only engraving we possessed with her image was the one we prepared for the engagement announcement. It's necessary that everyone knows what she looks like."

"Isaac, we're staying in today." My father dropped to the bench, the paper clutched between his fingers. Over and over he shook his head but kept his silence.

I'd said nothing until this point, trying to piece together what was happening and determine what it meant for me. Eventually my first solid thought formed. "How will Edward get back inside?"

My father rubbed his hand over his jowl, then pinched the top of his nose. When he spoke, he looked at Jameson, not me. "Do you think he'll know to keep away from this?"

Jameson inclined. "If he catches wind of why they're here, yes."

My heart pounded until I felt so light-headed that everything flashed white. Isaac must have been studying me, for in the next second he gripped my elbow and was depositing me onto the bench next to my father. I sat but had trouble focusing. Everything felt as if it were playing out at the end of a long tunnel.

"Edward will be fine." Isaac captured my hand between his.

I pulled hard from his touch and pressed the heels of my hands into my eyes, able to think of nothing but the fact that I wasn't willing to do this without Edward. That it wasn't possible to stay in these walls, in these circumstances, without him.

My father stood. "Jameson, have our breakfast transferred to the library. Have William dress in his regular clothes and prowl the edges of the crowd, looking for Reverend Auburn. When Edward makes it indoors, send him to us. Bring my brandy, all of it, from the smoking chamber." He tapped my shoulder twice. "Daughter, come with me."

I stood, but my arms and legs felt all wrong—hollow, yet tense with energy.

"All of your brandy? At this hour?" Forrester asked, following my father. "What, are we letting Julia drink with us too?"

"Breathe deep," Isaac said softly at my side as they withdrew. "The sensation you're feeling will pass. Edward will make it back to the house, sound and in one piece. He will. Don't fight the sensation; it only increases it."

I gasped, trying to get enough air, then looked at Isaac, wondering when he'd ever experienced this.

Jameson leaned into my view, wearing his crackpot smile. "Good news! I just remembered rule number two!"

It was so jolting, I blinked, staring at him.

"The herd sticks together!" He grinned. "If it becomes necessary, I shall cease being a butler and immediately transform into a faerie queen's valet." He cupped a hand over his mouth and whispered to Isaac, "Because of all the lions stalking them, the fair folk prefer to hire valets who hunt. I say the word *hire*, but it's highly inaccurate."

I gave a shaky laugh, then rested my head against the wall.

Isaac, however, stepped away, frowning as if uncertain now about Jameson.

Jameson offered me his arm. "Ready, my queen? Or shall I revert back at once and tell your father you refuse to join him unless he crawls backwards and petitions you as a faerie queen requires, in serenade?"

Amazed and touched that he was willing to look foolish to make me feel better, I accepted his arm. "I'm sorry for what I said." I felt able to breathe again. "Right now I couldn't be gladder you're the butler. At least you'll be allowed to remain in the chamber with us." My voice strained. "Will you forgive me?"

"Of course. That's rule seventy-seven."

"Seventy-seven?"

"You'll figure it out, in due course. Ready now?"

I sniffled, nodding. "Yes. I can manage."

As we passed, Isaac looked away, seemingly deflated. His very countenance bespoke frustration that he kept failing to win my trust, whereas both Jameson and Edward so easily succeeded. I dropped my gaze, wishing I could think of a way to explain it, but in truth, at that time I hardly understood it myself.

Now I better grasp it. Edward and Jameson had shown me unswerving loyalty, never asking me to betray myself. Isaac, on the other hand, was above all a peacemaker, always working to find compromise—and when it came to my father and me, I intuitively knew he'd try to convince both of us to yield. But without receiving my father's acceptance and affection, there was nothing more of myself I could offer. My father was only interested in me to the extent that I could serve his view of life.

When I entered the library, my father had already loosened his cravat and his collar buttons. He sat on the settee, legs sprawled, finger buried in his cheek, staring at Mama's sunflower painting. Near him, Forrester leaned against my father's desk, arms crossed, eyes fixed on the door.

"She's here," he announced.

My father never took his eyes off the bold hues of the painting as he gestured to the tufted sofa across from him. "Daughter, please sit." He breathed out of his nose as I obeyed. "Robert needs to know where you and your husband went yesterday."

I shifted my gaze to Forrester, wishing he weren't such an idiot. As foul as he was, I needed him. "The orphanage."

"What orphanage?" Forrester challenged.

"The one I visited at Christmas."

My father turned from Mama's painting with genuine interest. "What were you doing there?"

Jameson entered the chamber, carrying a tray with three identical decanters.

"What were you doing?" my father repeated.

My attention snapped back to him. "Edward was interested in meeting the little girl I wanted to adopt."

Mr. Forrester spat out the sip of brandy he'd been taking, then barked a sardonic laugh. "What? This is insane, Roy! She actually hopes to win favor by stating she visited orphans. Prove it. What child? Where is she?"

My stomach turned as I remembered her corpse stretched out on the floor. Then, refusing to cry again, I glanced at Isaac. "It was the girl we spoke of. Remember?"

My father looked incredulous as he faced Isaac. "You're following this?"

Isaac appeared haunted. "Yes, sir. We did discuss a little girl that day, whom Julia wished to adopt."

My father's jowls deepened. "Why was I never told this?"

Isaac wore no expression. "It wasn't a petition I took seriously, sir. I hadn't thought it warranted mentioning."

My father returned to me. "And so . . . you and Edward were just, what?" He gestured toward me. "Were going to look at her?"

I hunched my shoulders and peered down at my laced fingers. "We hadn't exactly decided what we were going to do yet."

Mr. Forrester gave another burst of laughter. "I'm sorry, Roy, but this will be tomorrow's headline. The readers will love it."

"So help me, if you do, I'll horsewhip you from my house to Macy's front door," my father growled. "I mean it, Robert. You still have no idea what you've done. After that stunt, I now need to get Simmons to forge an entirely new identity for Edward. Birth, school, marriage records. You've no idea how complicated this will grow, nor how close to disaster we already are. It was one thing for Edward to come to London, keep his head low, and start learning how to run the mines, but you made him a curiosity and offered a reward!"

I glanced at the folded newspaper between him and Isaac, wondering how much Edward's identity was worth. Already Macy had five thousand pounds hanging over me.

My father huffed and pulled sharply on his waistcoat. "For all we know, this orphanage might make the discovery." To me, "Did you give your names? Did they know you were my daughter?"

"Edward did tell her his name at the gate, but I doubt she'll read the paper, what with the outbreak happening there."

"Outbreak?" My father lifted his face.

Forrester unfolded his arms. "An outbreak of what?"

I flattened my hands over my lap, wishing this interview were over. "Typhus . . . or maybe brain fever."

A stunned silence filled the chamber while Forrester moved his hand to his neck as if to ascertain that it wasn't already stiffening. The idea that anyone might have willingly exposed themselves to sickness was so novel that my father's mouth parted as he tried to adjust his thinking.

A different emotion marked Isaac. His nose scrunched as he looked directly at me.

"Wait!" he ordered, lifting a hand as my father leaned forward, about to speak. And though Isaac's words were even, his eyes locked on mine and blazed like fire. "Did Reverend Auburn allow you to enter the orphanage?"

Stunned, I stared. He had never spoken so firmly to me. Even my father and Forrester exchanged uncomfortable glances.

And again, in a tone that silenced the chamber, Isaac asked, "Did he allow you to step foot inside the orphanage?"

My stomach tightened. "I went in of my own volition."

Isaac took a heated breath. "He knew there was an outbreak?"

I crossed my arms instead of answering. It wasn't his business.

I'd never seen Isaac angry before. He stood, clearly struggling to maintain his composure. He gave a refined bow in my father's direction. "I beg you will excuse me, sir."

My father stood to follow, then frowned, looking between Forrester and me as if uncertain he could leave the two of us alone.

I stared defiantly back, knowing it was unfair because no matter what he chose, I'd despise his decision. I wanted to talk to Forrester, desperately, but not at the cost of seeing my father leave me alone with a bully.

"Robert, stay here," my father finally said. "Let me talk to Isaac alone."

"Gladly." Forrester spread his hands innocently.

I held my sigh as I watched my father depart, then glanced at Jameson, who looked sad. I sat forward, ready to seize my opportunity of speaking with Forrester alone. "Jameson, would you please excuse us?"

Forrester frowned in his direction. "Who the devil are you, anyway?"

"Jameson, sir."

"I think I could have figured that much out," was Forrester's tart reply. "What the deuce are you doing here in London House? How did you get hired here?" Then, with a snarl, "Never mind it. I warrant you're mixed up with her. But go ahead, deny it."

"Oh, I would never deny it."

Forrester waved a hand toward him, scowling at me. "There.

No need to dismiss him." To Jameson, "I suppose you know, too, that she's Macy's missing bride?"

I gasped, stunned. Had Jameson not known it, such a statement alone could have ruined my father.

"We prefer the term *fabled* bride." Smiling, Jameson inclined his head. "But yes, I'm aware."

"And what would you say," Forrester demanded, gesturing to his face, "if I told you she'd tried to kill me?"

Jameson cocked his head and knit his brow. "I'd have to say that she wasn't very thorough. Shall I have a talk with her about being slipshod?"

I grimaced, sensing that Jameson's flippancy stemmed from a dislike of Forrester. Had not my alliance with Forrester been both necessary and shaky, I would have relished this, but I couldn't afford it today. Loyal souls have their disadvantages too. I grasped Mama's locket for strength, wondering how to calm Forrester and how to open the topic of our blackmail attempt with Jameson present.

I looked at Jameson and realized I couldn't discuss this in the chamber. Though it felt odd giving a command to him, I stood. "Jameson, please leave us alone."

His face tightened with disapproval and he shot me a look worthy of any governess as he left. I walked him to the door and shut it, counted to sixty, then opened it again to make certain we weren't being listened to.

"We need to talk," I said, turning.

Forrester gave a scoffing laugh and poured himself a drink. "What makes you think I'm going to speak with you?"

"You know what."

Forrester slurped a sip. "Sorry. I can't think of a single reason I should waste one more word in your direction."

I hugged myself, knowing how strained our alliance was. At best we were a loose dam of twigs and mud, trying to hold back the oncoming flood. Without one of the two ingredients, there was absolutely nothing in the way of the coming calamity.

Deciding I couldn't be guarded and win him, I met his eyes. "I'm sorry. Please believe me. I'm sorry about—" I nearly said "the goose egg," but feared he would think I was talking about the recent ones, so I switched. "I'm sorry about throwing pinecones at you."

Forrester slammed his drink down upon the desk and spun toward me. "That's it? You're sorry about throwing pinecones?" He pointed to his disfigurement. "You can't think of anything else you would need to confess?"

I eyed the goose eggs above his eye but again decided it would sound like I was admitting guilt for last night, so I shook my head.

"My manservant was murdered in his sleep at Eastbourne because of you. My estate is in ashes, killing my three dogs and maiming another servant. My mother and sisters are homeless and in hiding now because my father's property was ransacked, then torched. My newspaper has been looted and trashed four times since you pretended to blackmail Macy with me, and last night, for the third time, I barely escaped with my life after being kidnapped by his thugs. And you're sorry that you threw pinecones. Well, your apology," he suddenly screamed, *"is not accepted!"*

Too much depended upon our union to nurse anger or bitterness. "Please, you mustn't let what happened since that night make you believe—"

"Is there anything—" he glared at me—"anything, any little helpful tidbit, any insight about Macy, that you've not yet told me?"

Macy's fevered kisses and our stolen moments in the dark thundered back to me. Heat tingled over my cheeks, but it wasn't fair of him to want details on that. I shook my head.

"Because I searched your chamber this morning." Forrester

reached into his waistcoat and withdrew Macy's onyx ring, still strung on its chain. "Care to explain how it is that you possess Macy's passkey to the underworld?"

I rubbed the nape of my neck and was surprised to find it soaked in perspiration. "Macy gave it me."

Forrester made his face look like a simpleton's as if to say he considered me a dull wit.

"Before he killed Eramus," I continued. "He wanted me to have future protection. He said no one who recognized it would touch me, so long as I had it with me."

Mr. Forrester threw his hands wide. "Well, there apparently was my problem! When I placed my trust in you to go down that hill to blackmail Macy, I forgot to bring my secret ring that claims to the world that I'm part of his organization!" Forrester flung it hard at me. It bounced on the cushion next to me. "May it be your death. May it bring your doom. May his enemies find you in your sleep and slit your throa—"

"That's enough," I said sharply, rising.

"Tell Macy," Forrester hissed, "that my only goal now is to thwart you." And with that, he stomped from the chamber, slamming the door.

My stomach soured as his footsteps faded and I realized I was alone in our blackmail attempt now. My gaze landed on the ring. Feeling reluctant for it to end in the wrong hands, I picked up the necklace, looped it over my head, and tucked it beneath my gown.

Seventeen

FOR FOUR DAYS Edward was unable to slip back into London House. Those days were unlike the normal stream of flowing and adjusting with the current of life. Instead I'd been caught by the detritus of the broken dam I myself had constructed. Everyone around me moved and found ways to familiarize themselves with our new reality, while I floated like a pale specter—stagnant and unable to believe that Edward wasn't there.

No one except William and James came or left, and that was to carry letters and business documents for my father. The fascination over the Emerald Heiress's mysterious husband knew no bounds. They became their own cult, continually sharing theories and making conjectures about our reluctance to emerge from the shadows.

My father lived in his library, where I often heard his angry shouts and the crash of breaking glass. His party was drowning, and just when they needed him the most, he was trapped indoors, forced to dictate from a distance. The official word was that some malady had gripped London House—perhaps the idea came from my visit to the orphanage. Likely he hoped the crowds would dwindle and life would resume. He ordered one of his unmarked carriages made ready to go at a moment's notice, and I've since learned he'd prepared bags with funds he could hand off to Edward that would allow him to sustain us for years if necessary. Forrester, thankfully, remained with my father.

Isaac spent the majority of his day in the library but insisted on taking afternoon tea with me—those hours were both a blessed relief and an awkward strain. Each time he sought me out, I always felt startled, for it was a mental shift to adjust to the idea that he still remembered my existence. In my preoccupation with Edward's whereabouts, I'd crowded out everything else and perpetually found that I'd forgotten all about Isaac. When he led me to my seat, I always found myself blinking as I studied the table. Pierrick put as much effort into those teas as he had when Isaac was courting me. For some reason I particularly remember one table whose hues were meant to resemble a beach. Sand-colored sugar encrusted the tops of the round pastries, and clotted cream peaked like clouds in a wafer-thin scalloped dish. No doubt the small cakes tasted extraordinary, but I never could eat a bite.

It felt so unreal that life continued when I had so clearly given it orders to stop.

Had I been able to fully awaken from my trance, my heart would have been rent for Isaac. Despite the fact that he had to pierce the fog of my dreamworld to retrieve me—never minding that I was unable to focus on him for more than a few seconds, nor that I rarely finished any sentence—his eyes never left me during the space of that hour. It was always with great reluctance that he took his leave. He'd set aside his napkin and stare at the door looking truly harrowed, as if by stepping out of my nightmare, he was about to step into his own.

On the fourth day, I felt so fatigued that Isaac did not have to look for me. I'd retreated to the front parlor with a book and hadn't moved all day. Afternoon sun streamed through the tops of the windows, which weren't shuttered like the bottom halves. I shivered and pulled my Indian shawl tighter as his footsteps grew near.

He stepped just inside the chamber, arms laden with documents. His chestnut hair looked as if he'd run his fingers through it, forgetting it was usually waxed in place. Eyes that concealed his thoughts studied me. "I can't take tea today. There's a bit of an emergency."

"Is it Edward?" I asked, finding strength to sit forward.

He shifted the papers in his arms. "No. There's still no word on him, but do not fret. I'm certain he is fine. Are you sure you're all right? You seem a bit flushed."

"I'm fine," I said, nodding, though in truth the motion made my head spin. "Thank you."

He started to leave, then glanced back and hesitated. Even in my weakened state, I noted the intensity of his thoughts. Perhaps he wished to feel my brow but debated whether touching me was improper. Out of courtesy, I shifted my gaze and pretended not to note his struggle.

He gave a slight sigh. "If you start to feel ill—" he frowned, unable to pretend he didn't suspect—"or your condition worsens, will you have Jameson fetch me, please?"

"If it worsens," I promised, knowing I couldn't feel much sicker than I did.

I waited until he retreated down the hall before touching my forehead where it ached and burned. My joints complained with stiffness. My head swam with tiredness, blurring my thoughts. More than anything, I desired to go to bed but decided it would be too much of a climb. I returned to the book I held, though I could not concentrate on the words.

"Lord Dalry ordered me to bring you tea." William, the second footman, entered the chamber, carrying a tray. "If he hasn't located you yet, I've been asked to inform you that he doubts he'll be joining you this afternoon."

Startled by his sudden approach, I snapped my head in his direction, sending it spinning.

"William." I clasped the arm of my settee. "Help me to my bedchamber and then make sure I'm not disturbed."

"Are you feeling all right?" He set down the tray.

I nodded and pushed myself upright. Having scarcely slept, eaten, or touched any drink, I attributed my illness to Edward's absence. Sun stole across the room and crept over me, but I only shivered. "Yes, I'm just tired. Please help me to my bedchamber."

I have a vague impression that William slowly helped me climb the stairs and then at my request drew the drapes, but thankfully that long, hard climb soon left my memory.

I do, however, recall sinking to the bed, relieved I could just rest, too tired to even bother drawing back the counterpane, and then falling into a deep sleep. The chills and shaking didn't begin until hours later.

~

Cool hands gently stroked my brow and my cheeks, then felt for a pulse on my neck. I wrenched away, struggling to move, but found I couldn't.

"Shh, Juls, it's me," Edward's voice whispered.

"Ed?" I grasped through the dark, desperate to find his hand.

He gave it, then kissed my brow, smoothing back my hair. "Can you open your eyes for me?"

My head throbbed at the thought of opening my eyes, but I struggled to obey. Though a low fire burned in the hearth, my chambers were dark. A single candle sat lit on my nightstand. Illuminated in its circle of light, Edward leaned over me with a concerned gaze. His hair hadn't been combed in days, and it was apparent he'd been living on the streets.

Where tears of relief would have filled my eyes, they burned instead.

"Am I sick?" I asked, grasping his sleeves so he wouldn't turn into a dream and leave me.

"Not too badly." His eyes, however, told a different story as they scanned my features. "When was the last time you've eaten?"

I felt his arms beneath the thick material, still needing to make certain he was truly there in the flesh and not a vision. "I think Isaac made me eat something at tea. Or was that the day before yesterday? I can't remember."

"You can't remember? I thought it was just a story that the household was sick, since no physicians were seen coming or leaving." Anger tightened his jaw as he rolled back the sleeves of my dress and inspected my forearms.

"Nobody was sick," I said, shaking my head, confused.

Edward pinched my skin, and though I didn't think it possible, his eyes intensified. "Look up," he ordered in a tone that brooked no arguments. With his thumb, he tugged down on my lower eyelid. "You haven't been drinking either, have you?" He picked up my hand again, pinched the back of it, and watched my skin settle before uttering a curse.

"Can't we just sleep and talk in the morning?" I asked.

"Don't fall asleep, Juls! Stay awake!" His tone sliced through even my stupor. He stomped to the bellpull, where he demanded, "How do I get a senior staff member?"

I closed my eyes, needing to think. "Uh . . . three tugs."

Edward gave it three tugs, waited, gave it three more tugs, then slammed the nearest chair to him. "Which room is your father's?"

This woke me, for in my confused state I doubted my father would take kindly to being roused in the dead of night because Edward couldn't summon the staff. I gave Edward a warning shake of my head.

Seeing I wouldn't present him with the information, he stormed from the chamber and charged down the hall, pounding his fists on every door, screaming, "Wake up!"

Shivering, I closed my eyes.

"What the deuce!" My father's voice carried from the hall.

"Wake up!" Edward shouted as he continued his pounding. "Everyone on this floor will wake up and attend me *now*!"

"How the devil did he get back inside?" Forrester demanded next.

"The lot of you did nothing?" Edward cried. "You just left my wife lying soaked in her own clothing, on the bed, chilled with fever! Someone will fetch me a doctor, and they will fetch him *now*!"

I managed to open my eyes in time to see him storm back into the chamber. His feral gaze darted about the room, landing on the porcelain pitcher and washbasin at the other side. Struggling to maintain his composure, he placed a hand towel in the basin, then filled it with water. He set it on the nightstand. The mattress dented as he took a seat next to me and wrung out the towel.

"You're going to be all right, Juls." His words sounded slightly garbled, and he wiped his nose on the sleeve of his coat.

"I'm fine," I whispered. "Just tired."

"How long has she been ill?" My father's voice sounded near the threshold. I turned my head and found him tying the knot of his robe. Behind him, Forrester stood with hands on hips, his dressing gown untied at the top, showing a chest of black hair. Isaac arrived in nightdress and a banyan, carrying a lamp, then shouldered his way between the pair to the front.

"You mean you don't even know?" Edward shouted over his shoulder.

"May I be of service?" Jameson's voice sounded behind the group.

"Jameson." Edward threw the cloth back into the basin

and charged the gentlemen. Instead of seeking comfort, as I assumed, Edward shoved past Forrester and, facing his valet, gestured to me. "How could you let this happen? If anyone was taking care of her, I thought you were!"

"Why?" Compassion etched Jameson's features. "What's wrong with Mrs. Auburn?"

"What's wrong?" Edward pulled Jameson farther down the hall so their discussion wouldn't be heard, though the tone continued in much the same frantic fashion.

I buried my face in my hands, shutting my eyes, wanting my audience to go away. When the light brightened and I felt someone near me, however, I turned and opened them.

Isaac's face appeared before mine as he bent and studied me in the lamplight. His chestnut hair stuck straight up in the back and out on the sides. Sleep wrinkles deeply creased his cheeks, accessorizing his bohemian appearance. I smiled, amused, for he'd never looked so uncollected.

But if he didn't seem collected before, he became it next, for he expelled a deep breath. "May I see your palms, please?"

My arms felt rubbery as I displayed them. He scrutinized them carefully, then knelt at my bedside. With care he unbuckled and removed my shoes. As he reached near my calf to find the buckle holding my stocking, he seemed to recall himself and paused, staring at my shoe in his hand.

"Since you've gone this far," Forrester said, "I'd finish whatever you're doing before Edward comes back."

"Forgive me," Isaac whispered, averting his eyes. Next, he carefully examined the sole of my foot.

"It's not typhus," he said softly over his shoulder to my father. "Nor do I think brain fever, as she's moved her neck several times without wincing. Her headache would be worse, too, if it were. Can you think of any of the symptoms from that day at the orphanage?"

I started to shake my head but then recalled the laundry cauldrons. "Fever and bloodied dysentery."

"Have you suffered anything of that sort? Do your stomach or bowels feel queasy?"

My eyes widened, for I never imagined there would be a day when I'd talk of my bowels with Lord Dalry. I felt my face flood with heat. "No, not at all."

Isaac suddenly exhaled as if he'd been holding his breath. He even temporarily allowed me behind his mask, where I saw his fear change to pure, unadulterated relief.

Again I pretended not to notice. "How do you know these things?"

My father must have also felt relieved, for he chuckled and his stance loosened as he nudged Forrester. "Do you remember that fiasco?" He turned and said to me, "Isaac wanted to study medicine. It was the only time he ever truly defied me."

"Oh, my word, I'd forgotten!" Forrester crossed his arms. "For a month there, I really believed we'd lost him along with years of our work."

Whatever they spoke of was an old hurt, for traces of pain were resurrected over Isaac's countenance before he blinked and they vanished. "In Kinsley's office there's a locked cabinet with medicine that will likely bring her fever down. I'll go fetch the key and—"

I had closed my eyes; thus I wasn't aware that Edward had regained the chamber until Isaac's words were cut off, followed by a sickening thud.

When they opened again, Edward had grabbed hold of Isaac by his banyan and held him against the wall.

"Do not *ever* touch my wife again!" he yelled in Isaac's face. "Ever!"

My father placed a hand over Edward's arm and said in a gentle voice, "Release him, son. Take a deep breath and calm yourself. You're overwrought. Julia is going to be fine."

Edward tried his angry glare on my father.

"Now!" my father ordered.

"Sir, this man insulted my wife, and as such—" Edward turned and screamed at Isaac—"I am calling him out!"

My father cast Forrester a look that asked what he'd ever done to deserve such a temperamental son-in-law—though the answer seemed obvious to me. He tightened his grip on Edward's arm. "Isaac didn't insult your wife. You wanted someone to tend her *now*; well, you got what you wanted. Be more careful of your demands next time."

"I asked for a physician. He's no doctor," Edward protested. "I want to call him out!"

Isaac's face was blank, keeping any hint of his thoughts to himself as he considered Edward.

My father breathed twice as if willing himself to be patient. "Fine, but before I allow Isaac to drag you outside and kill you, I want to ascertain that Julia feels insulted he checked her feet with her father present. For make no mistake, if you duel, Isaac will win. I will get him exonerated if I have to pay a fortune to do so, and I will gain a new son-in-law in the process."

"And I'll make millions on the scandal," Forrester added with a laugh. "I vote we do it."

My father glared at him before turning and addressing me. "So, Julia, did Isaac insult you in any way? Or did you feel affronted by even the smallest degree?"

Isaac still wore no expression but kept his gaze on Edward.

"No, sir," I said.

My father faced Edward. "Release Lord Dalry now."

The tendons in Edward's neck protruded as he glowered at Isaac a second longer, then yanked his hands away so fast, Isaac nearly lost his balance.

My father steadied him by placing a hand on his shoulder. Isaac continued to study Edward.

"Jameson," my father called, releasing Isaac and heading

toward the door, "do whatever Reverend Auburn wants. If he wants my physician, fine, call him. I'm going back to bed."

"I wish you would wait, sir," Isaac finally said. "For I have yet to speak and would prefer an audience for what I'm going to say."

"Isaac," my father's voice pleaded, "it's two in the morning."

"No." Forrester hit his arm. "Let the boy speak."

Straightening his banyan, Isaac shot Forrester a look that ordered him to keep quiet. Then, taking a heated breath, he addressed Edward. "We both know the reason you're unnerved is because you allowed her to enter that orphanage. I assure you, Reverend Auburn, I did not step aside for you to destroy her with such carelessness."

"Usurpers cannot step aside." Edward's tone was flint. "They never belonged."

Isaac met his eyes. "Had I known you would be so haphazard in your care of her, I would have mended the damage from Forrester's paper and retained her as my own wife. Know that I will protect her as though she were my sister, given to you from my own household."

Edward lunged toward Isaac, but my father caught him by his shoulders. "Retain her?" Edward seethed. "Listen to yourself. You act as though she's something one owns. Unlike you, I force nothing upon her. She chose—nay, insisted—on entering the orphanage. Who am I to rule over someone else? I leave that to you cowards of the world."

"May I quote that in my paper?" Forrester asked. "Sorry, Isaac, but that would sell."

Ignoring Forrester, Isaac addressed Edward alone. "Do not try to justify your lapse of honor in your care of Julia. There's a difference between lording over your charge and guarding that with which you've been entrusted."

Chest heaving, Edward tried to lunge again but was held back by my father. "Why don't you admit that you're in love with my wife instead of attempting to remain near her by wearing a mask of honor? Even better, go find a wife of your own and leave mine alone."

"How about that?" Forrester grinned, patting himself as if looking for paper and pencil.

"You want a story?" Isaac's voice flushed with anger as he faced Forrester. "You want to exploit pain to sell more papers? Well, how about this? I'm betrothed to Evelyn Greenley, the girl who would have married my identical twin had he not gone missing! Will that sell enough copies to satisfy you?" Then, turning to Edward, "If you think I'm such a cad that I would act insultingly toward your wife while promised to another, then you know nothing about me."

At first I didn't believe I'd heard Isaac correctly. I sat forward to question him and was rewarded with white flashes of light and an increased headache.

Before I focused my thoughts, Forrester cried, "What!"

Confusion creased my father's face as he looked over his shoulder at Isaac. Edward jerked his arm from my father's grasp, then, scowling, retreated to me.

Isaac noted my father's disbelief, too, and rubbed both his eyes with long, tapered fingers. "I'm sorry, sir. I intended to tell you earlier and to discuss its implications with you. I know what you're thinking, and I have it mapped out."

"Please tell me you haven't signed an agreement yet." My father's voice was subdued. Then, "Evelyn Greenley? Son, have you any idea the pressures your future wife will be under?"

Isaac's chest swelled, and for a second he seemed to will every muscle in his body to relax. "Sir, you know I wouldn't take a step I am uncertain of. Now, if you don't mind, I'm going to bed. It's rude for us to intrude longer on Mrs. Auburn's sick chamber. And this is hardly the hour—" he glanced down—"or the appropriate dress in which to discuss this." He looked about as if trying to decide who was the most proper person to bid good night, allowing him to take his leave. His eyes swung to mine.

I swallowed, still feeling as shocked as my father.

Silently Isaac pleaded with me to aid him this time, to find the right words to mend this situation, to transition him out of this awkward moment as he always did for me.

Only this was my weakest area. I didn't know how. Especially not when I was trying to recover from my own shock.

Switch the topic, my mind supplied. Hadn't Isaac always effortlessly changed the direction of conversation for me? *Affirm him,* was the next thought. It was what Jameson kept doing. In my panic, I spoke the first affirming words that came to mind.

"Thank you for your service tonight, Isaac. You would have made a good doctor."

Forrester burst out laughing and had to grasp his rib cage. My father just winced and shook his head as if to deny I was his.

Jameson drew near to Edward and spoke in a quiet voice. "Hurry to her aid, boy, lest she retreat again."

Edward looked as if he'd rather have chewed on gravel, but he stood from the bed. His nostrils flared as he gave Isaac a stiff bow. "Yes, thank you. Perhaps I overreacted."

Strangely, my comment did help Isaac in the end. He noted my distress and slipped back into his role of being a conciliator and soothing the situation for me. He gave a liquid bow and exited the chamber.

I watched his retreating form, feeling miserable, sick, and embarrassed. As my father and Forrester closed their doors, Edward settled next to me and drew me close. I leaned against him, wondering how others transformed embarrassment while the best I ever managed was to transition it onto myself. My tearless eyes stung.

But it wasn't for myself that I tried to cry. Isaac couldn't marry Evelyn. He'd regret it for life. I had to stop him, but without taking unfair advantage of his attachment to me, I wasn't certain how I could.

Sensing that Edward studied me, I said, "I didn't mean that like it sounded."

Jameson chuckled. "Faeries are allowed to say whatever they want, and don't you forget it!"

"I owe you an apology," Edward said to him, pulling me tighter as he addressed Jameson. "I did overreact. I'm sorry."

Jameson gave a nod. "Well, we can't all be John the Beloved, such as myself."

Edward wrinkled his nose. "I thought you were a worm."

"Yes! It's the beauty of the plan." Jameson motioned for me to shift slightly over so he could pull back my counterpane. "A worm today. John the Beloved tomorrow! You must become small in order to grow big. When you have time, Edward, double-check and see what Scripture says about using wrath to accomplish the righteousness of God."

"Fine, be a worm today so you can be John the Beloved tomorrow." Edward removed himself from the bed so he could draw down the other side of the counterpane. "I'll be a son of thunder. Let's see if the path lands me at the same place."

Jameson paused, then laughed, holding up his hands. "Touché! But I still say you'll be much happier and more useful when you learn to curb that temper."

Edward's shoulders sagged. His words came out a near whisper. "I'm trying; I really am." He lifted his hands and looked at them as if amazed that only moments ago they'd pounded Isaac against the wall. "Patience and gentleness just slip out of my grasp every time I think I've finally got ahold of them."

"Stop trying and start realizing that's not who you are. That's when you'll walk in freedom. His nature has been given to you."

Frowning, Edward ran his fingers through his curls. "How do you suppose Dalry manages to keep his temper so well?"

"Never mind looking at *his* life. Trust me, that boy has his own struggles." Jameson keyed the lamp low. "Just keep your eyes on your own path and allow me to worry about Dalry."

Edward felt my brow. "She's still burning up. Lovely how her father left such vague instructions. I'm to send for his physician. Any ideas who that would be?"

"None whatsoever." Jameson touched my brow with the backs of his knobby fingers.

"Isaac said Kinsley had medicine in his office. He was about to go get the key and fetch it . . ." I glanced at Edward, trying to think of a way to soften it. "Before he was interrupted."

Jameson chuckled, finding that description humorous. "Lord Dalry is going to be delighted to discover we still need his services tonight. Funny how we continue to need the people we no longer want around, isn't it? Perhaps God is giving you a hint, Edward. I'll go rouse him."

"She needs to drink too," Edward said. "Broth, wine, claret." Then, to me, "Any idea where this illness came from?"

I shook my head.

"She suffered without you," Jameson said from the door. "She stopped eating and rarely spoke. Likely she fell ill because of her weakened state." Then quietly to Edward, though he gave me a tender look, "No doubt it's the accumulation of traumas from this past year. But in my experience, when something of this nature is highlighted, it's usually a mercy, a wind before the storm. If you'll take my advice, get to the bottom of it tonight. There's a reason God exposed this vulnerability."

Edward nodded. When Jameson closed the door, I allowed Edward to tuck me in bed. The cool, clean feel of the sheets embraced me as I rested my head against the pillow and stared at my husband. Propped on his elbow, he gently moved hair from my brow.

"You're tender and patient with me," I eventually said. "That's a start."

His laugh was husky. "And you talk to me. Personally I never understood the complaint."

Smiling, I shut my eyes, content that he was back, content to keep my world small.

"So why weren't you eating and drinking, Juls? It was a fluke I managed to get inside tonight. What if I hadn't? What if I'd been forced to live on the streets for a fortnight?"

Again my eyes burned as I shook my head. I hated having to admit that outside of Edward, I hadn't anyone else. It was too pitiful. "I just panicked and then . . ." I frowned. "I won't do this without you. It's that simple. I won't."

"And if God calls you away from me?"

I pulled the covers against my chest, feeling a vague dread numb my limbs. "Why would he call me away from my husband? That's ludicrous."

"You can't guide your life by me," Edward said. "I can't be anyone's Polaris. I can't. You'll shipwreck if you try."

There was a truth to what he said, but that picture was far too simple, like looking at a woodcut print of sailors on a boat and saying it encompassed life on the sea. That paper image will not prepare you for the cry of seagulls nor the scent of brine. It cannot give you sea legs nor callous your hands in order to hoist the lines. It cannot teach you to swim if you're thrown overboard. Nor can it convey the terror of being tossed by the wind and the waves. It was a picture; it contained a truth. But it wasn't a formula.

"You talk about being shipwrecked," I said, "but what good is Polaris when I'm adrift and foundering? I have no ship. Or if you want to say I'm the ship, then I have no crew. That is what I would be without you. What would you do if you were in the ocean, drowning, with only a cold, distant star above you?"

Jameson arrived with a tray holding a tureen of broth and a decanter of claret. For Edward there were meat pies and wine, along with various other foods that had been showered on

London House. Jameson's kindly eyes crinkled with pleasure at Edward's repose over me.

"Give her this," he ordered, pouring claret into a crystal goblet. He then emptied a packet of powder into the red liquid. The silver spoon clinked against the glass as he stirred, walking the concoction to Edward.

"Here." Carefully cradling my head, Edward pressed the glass to my lips. "Drink."

Ignoring the dryness in my throat, I swallowed. Clumps of the bitter powder broke against my tongue. I wrinkled my nose, then gagged on its taste.

"Fetch her another glass of claret," Edward ordered Jameson; then, to me, "I want you to drink so much you think your stomach will explode."

Jameson laughed, pouring the glass. "Such a romantic choice of words, Edward."

Though Edward attempted to smile, it fell short. Our minds were too full of our previous conversation. I waited until Jameson's footsteps retreated down the hall.

"You didn't answer my question," I said, determined to keep the topic from dropping.

With my eyes, I accused Edward of being trite. I wasn't satisfied to simply swallow platitudes. My silent accusation wasn't fair, though. For on one hand I knew Edward spoke the truth. He was right—I would shipwreck. There are principles that underlie life, and one cannot build lives on ideas that oppose these truths.

And yet the deepest expression of my heart was also true. Edward was all I had left. The sole member of my family. Did not our Creator himself state that it wasn't good for man to be alone? "How do you honestly expect me to continue on without you?"

Edward caught a glimmer of what I was trying to say. He most certainly felt the emotion as well, for his eyes bespoke grief and love mingled.

"'Though he slay me,'" he quoted softly after a minute, "'yet will I trust in him.' If anything happens to me, then fix your eyes on the star, Juls, and never look away, even if you sink and drown. You let God kill one life to resurrect another."

My eyes burned with tears they couldn't shed as I sank back upon the pillows and drifted into sleep, Edward's words swimming in my mind.

Eighteen

✣

MY FIRST CONSCIOUS thought was to ensure that Edward was
at my side. Eyes still closed, I reached for Edward but my fingers
found only wrinkled sheets. Not certain I hadn't dreamed him,
I sat with a gasp.

Amber light washed the chamber, for Edward had shut the
drapes and lit candles, then shielded them with screens made of
polished slices of agate fused together with copper. Combined
with the rich tones of the burled wood of my desk and furniture,
my chamber looked richer than I'd ever seen it.

Edward sat at my desk, his expression pensive as he inked
his thoughts. He wrote so quickly, the sound of scratching filled
the room. Next to him were books he'd carried upstairs from my
father's library, thick enough to require buckles over their pages.

I laughed with relief and was surprised at how dry it felt. "I
thought I dreamed you."

He blinked as if waking from a trance. Then, offering a slight
smile, he finished his sentence and tugged three times on the
bellpull. "Good, you're up. I'm famished."

"What time is it?"

"Eleven."

I looked toward the window, forgetting the drapes were shut. "You haven't eaten yet?"

Shaking his head, he took a seat near me on the bed. "I'm afraid that your father will try to befriend me. I would rather starve."

It sent a pang of hurt through me. "At least he talks to you."

Edward shrugged as if my father weren't of importance anyway. "How are you feeling?"

"Better." In spirit, at least. Bodily, however, my mouth felt dry, my head too light, and my limbs too heavy.

"Do you think you could rise?"

I nodded. "Yes, but I feel shaky."

He frowned. "Likely you need to eat too. Shall we dress and go downstairs? Or petition to have a tray brought here?"

"Let's never leave this chamber." Swinging my legs over the side of the bed, I asked, "How did you get back inside last night?"

He grinned. "There was a fight down the street. Quite a row. I was able to climb a tree near the stables, then hop the fence."

I felt my eyes widen, for I hadn't thought London House was that easy to penetrate. "Did anyone stop you?"

"I was accosted by four stable hands immediately." He winked. "But it helps being Lord Pierson's son-in-law." He turned his head as a soft knock sounded on the door. "Who is it?"

"James, sir."

"You may enter."

James opened the door. Instead of smiling, he flashed me a look. "Good morning. Lord Pierson requests both of your presence in the library immediately."

"How long ago did he give the order?" I asked, uncertain whether it was a coincidence that the footman arrived when we rang for the staff.

"This morning when the first posts arrived. He said when you rang, I was to send you to him."

I felt my brow furrow, unable to imagine why my father would desire us. "Was there something in the morning posts?"

James gave a quick glance over his shoulder. "I don't know, but he'd just finished opening a brown envelope and reading its contents when he gave the order."

"Brown?" I said, trying to imagine who would be so uncouth. "What's his mood?"

James stepped in and closed the door farther. "The queen is refusing to cooperate with Melbourne. Peel has sent two messages this morning alone, begging for your father and Lord Dalry to come support him. News of Lord Dalry's forthcoming marriage to Miss Greenley just happened to make Forrester's paper today, shocking London. Simmons has returned from the docks, looking more dour than I've ever seen him." James's eyes grew mischievous as he glanced at Edward. "And I'm under the impression his lordship didn't sleep very well last night."

I pinched my nose. "Thank you, James."

"Will there be anything else?"

"Yes," I answered. "Have tea brought to the library. Tell Mrs. King I need something for a headache as well."

❧

"Curious the way this house presses upon you," I said, looking over the other levels as we tromped down the stairs. "It's beautiful, but once inside, it's inescapable."

Edward gave a dark chuckle. "My problem is the opposite. My battle is always getting and staying inside it."

In the bottom foyer, Simmons rushed across the hall to Lady Pierson's study, where he could be heard making a ruckus. A moment later he emerged, but instead of smuggling papers to the front door, as I half expected he'd do, he rushed back to the library. Edward and I slipped in after him.

Isaac noted our presence immediately, though all he did was give us a quick glance. For a moment the way he looked at me was so benign and indifferent, I almost wondered if he truly had asked if we could be friends. My father and Simmons were looking over the documents.

Edward coughed, causing my father to glance at us, but he almost didn't seem to register our presence. Ashen, he returned to the papers. Mr. Forrester poked his head out from behind a screen.

"Aren't you overdue?" he asked.

My father looked at us again. "I want to give up," he said to Simmons. "There's so much to handle, I don't even know which problem to address first."

"There's hardly anything you can do right now about this one." Simmons shoved over what looked like a large map.

My father didn't answer.

"What's happening anyway?" Mr. Forrester stood. "You've both been acting odd since Simmons returned."

"Nothing that merits your attention." My father gripped his chin while shaking his head. "Problems with the mines' production, and it's going to cost me a lot of money, just when I'm reaping the bills from introducing an heiress into society."

"What?" Mr. Forrester strode over to the desk. "I thought you were nearest the largest vein."

"We were," my father said, "but it looks like it might be veining this way instead. And I don't own it."

Mr. Forrester tilted his head, looking at the map for a few minutes. "Have you tried buying that claim?"

"Can you imagine? Lord Pierson making an offer. They'd know."

"Just curious—when did the workers start losing the vein?"

My father consulted some papers. "October, why?"

Mr. Forrester looked at me, spreading his lips in a thin

smile. "Same month she arrived. An unlucky month all around, I'd say."

Nothing is more damaging than someone besieging you with the lie you believe about yourself. I hugged myself as I confronted Forrester's mocking eyes.

Edward's brow furrowed before he made an exaggerated mock bow to the chamber. "Well, thank you, everyone, for insisting we come join you so we could be ignored and then insulted. We had a lovely time. Let's do this again soon! Come on, Juls. Nobody is making us remain."

"Wait!" My father's tone was boorish, but once more he wore the hint of a smile.

I glanced at Isaac, curious what he thought of my father's being so smitten with Edward's unruliness, since he himself worked so hard to be genteel. His face wore nothing but a look of suavity as he carefully worked on correspondences.

My father picked up a brown piece of parchment that had been folded and sealed like an envelope. He flapped it. "I want you to tell me what the deuce this is."

"Paper?" Edward sounded sincere, though I knew he was being flippant.

Isaac noted it too, for he lifted his gaze to Edward for a fraction of a second, but what he thought was a mystery to me.

"Why is London House receiving mail for Reverend Edward Auburn—" my father's voice rose to a pitch as he stood—"when half of London is on my doorstep, trying to find your identity? What? Do you think people won't recognize the address? Why not address it to me at 10 Downing Street, and see if they notice! What were you thinking?"

Edward's nose wrinkled. "You can lower your tone, as your theatrics aren't impressive. It should be obvious that the correspondence was set in motion before Forrester's reward was posted. But since you see fit to scold me like a child, I see fit to point out your obtuseness."

Forrester chuckled, then poured himself a drink. He leaned against a chair with the air of one ready to enjoy a show at the theatre. Isaac's mouth turned down in the slightest frown. Were we still engaged, I would have taken the hint that even smiling at such behavior was beneath us.

My father struggled to keep from chuckling. "For the record, there is no Reverend Auburn living here. You're now Reverend Edison Shirley Darling."

Edward angrily looked heavenward as if petitioning for strength. "No, I'm not." Then, after a pause, "Which one of you came up with Darling?" He glared at Isaac.

"That's of no consequence to you." My father held the letter to the candle flame and allowed it to catch fire before tossing it far back in the hearth.

Edward burst into action. He raced across the chamber and, taking the most direct route, stood on a chair and jumped onto my father's desk. His feet slid over the map, sending papers everywhere as he scrambled over its surface. Despite his efforts, the page was consumed by the time he knelt by the hearth.

"What is wrong with you people?" Edward screamed.

I rubbed my thumb over the faint scars on my palm, trying not to think of Eramus screaming in that exact same spot.

Isaac rose. "Here. Take my seat. You don't look quite recovered from your illness."

I nodded and sat, gripping the edge of his desk.

"Did someone offer me a position somewhere?" Edward continued loudly.

My father glanced at Simmons, who took the hint and spoke on his behalf. "As Lord Pierson's son-in-law, you will not take that offer. I am happy to inform you that we're offering Reverend Darling a rather handsome position running his lordship's mines in South Africa."

South Africa? I gasped, recalling the allure of Jameson's stories.

"Who," Edward said very slowly, "sent that letter?"

"No one you need worry about," was my father's reply.

"So, what? You're just going to hold Julia and me hostage? Not allow me to find employment?"

"I just offered you employment, at twenty-five times the annual amount of the offer I burned." My father brushed off the top of his map as if to rid it of Edward's footprints.

"It wasn't yours to burn." Edward stalked across the library, back to me. "And you didn't offer *me* a job, but some molly-coddle named Reverend *Darling* who associates with fathers-in-law who burn letters without permission."

My father covered his mouth, hiding his smile. "The country believes you've kidnapped Macy's bride. I need something to tell my colleagues."

Edward spread his arms as he turned. "Why not the truth? Why not trust they've had their own encounters with Macy? Why not give them a chance to see if they'll assist you?"

My father made a snorting noise as though Edward had asked him to sprout wings.

Edward gave them his back. "Fine. Burn all offers of employment. I have nothing to lose by waiting." He turned at the door. "But the first time I bump into one of your cronies and they ask for my name, I'm telling them."

Seeing that Edward was prepared to leave, I likewise stood, noticing that Isaac had been corresponding with Evelyn. I placed my hand over my bodice, realizing he truly was betrothed to her. Otherwise, he would never dare to write her.

Knowing I'd placed him in this embarrassing position, I quietly searched for any hint of his true feelings.

Though he met my gaze straight on, it was like trying to find a chink missing out of a finely polished marble statue. I found nothing.

Finally I said, "James was bringing Edward and me tea here.

When he arrives, will you have him deliver it to my bedchamber instead?"

Isaac looked startled but then gave a genteel head bow. "Of course."

It wasn't until I was on the second landing that I realized our afternoon teas had ended.

～

"Are you certain?" I asked Edward upon locating him. As predicted, he'd retreated to my bedchamber.

"Yes," he said without looking up, writing hard.

"But think of it, Ed." I sank into a nearby chair, glad to rest. My legs were weak and I still felt light-headed. "Africa! Don't tell me you haven't felt its allure too? I've watched your face as Jameson recounts his travels. Consider it! We could leave here, and we could go far enough to make it difficult for Macy to find us. Plus, in the jewelry business, you'd make powerful connections who could lend us additional support if Macy gives us problems. And Jameson could see Africa again." I reached out and touched his hand. "*We* could see Africa."

"And be called Darling the rest of our lives? No thank you."

Chills swept over my body as I remembered it was Macy's pet name for me.

"For what it's worth—" Edward looked up—"I like my name. I haven't persisted in sin or done anything wrong. I'm not changing it."

"And if he wanted to hire you as Auburn?"

Edward flung his pen down and threw himself back in his seat, frowning. "Maybe. I don't know."

James knocked on the door, which had been left open a crack. I waved him inside. "How can you not be sure?" I pressed. "What better offer are we going to get? We could even save up enough money to live off the interest. We could return to Windhaven in a few years! Maybe we're supposed to do this."

"Then let it be done openly and honestly, without deceit," Edward said. "In the meantime, no. I'm not going to commit to a life of lies. Neither is your father the type of man I wish to work under. I'm not going to make decisions from the standpoint of fear, all to avoid Macy. It's a coward's solution. I want no part of it."

I glanced at James as he transferred teacups to the desk. How openly, I realized, we now spoke about Macy in his presence. Wondering if he could shed some light on how Edward's new name was chosen, I asked, "Who came up with calling us Darling?"

He grinned. "So you heard that part, did you? They spent hours deliberating. Simmons suggested Darling, as it would have a positive association in people's minds. Your father insisted on Edison, so we could explain accidentally calling him Edward or Ed."

"And Lord Dalry?" Edward demanded. "Did he come up with Shirley?"

"No. He refused to take part in the talk, saying it would only anger you."

If it were anyone except Edward, I might have been tempted to smirk that someone had thought poorly of Isaac and came out looking the worse for it. My heart, however, beat with compassion for Edward.

Edward furrowed his brow, telling me he had no intention of changing his view of Lord Dalry, despite Isaac's proving himself less of a villain than Edward had painted him.

"Edward," I intoned softly, "have you considered discussing the matter directly with my father?"

"I will," he said, "when he apologizes and returns to calling me Auburn."

Nineteen

⚜

TWO DAYS LATER Lord Dalry's engagement to Miss Evelyn Greenley had captivated London, and our house filled with visitors. Though there was scarcely need of it, both Isaac's and Evelyn's lineages were charted and explored in the *Times*. The public was properly shocked that nineteen generations back, Evelyn's ancestor had been a cousin of King Edward II. The fact that my father had donated a generously sized emerald-and-pearl ring for the engagement caused some speculation in the gossip columns that Isaac had utilized the same ring he'd planned to give me.

My mouth felt dry as I read the article. Surely, I thought, that couldn't be true.

After I finished reading the announcements, I sat back and carefully peeled an orange, wondering how Isaac truly felt. He gave no hint as he took tea and perused his appointment book. Not so much as a sigh escaped him, which I found odd, considering he'd been in love with me only weeks ago.

Yet as I divided my orange into segments and scraped off the pith, I noted that he never once acknowledged me. Even when he left the breakfast table that morning, he simply stacked his books and informed my father that his mother and Kate had arrived for his engagement celebration and he would be gone most of the day.

A grunt from behind the headlines was my father's reply.

I gave him a pitying look, certain my father's coldness had to have hurt him. But in typical fashion, he showed no expression as he took his leave.

⌇

"Do you really think he could be in love with Evelyn?" I asked a week later as I laid down a three of hearts. The candlelight caught the sheen of the illuminator's work.

"I don't really care," Edward said as he rearranged the cards in his hands.

"You won't find it there." Jameson grinned before he laid down the four and then the five of hearts.

I glanced at the clock, frowning. It was nearly midnight and we'd been playing cards in Edward's bedchamber for four hours. Downstairs, Colonel Greenley, Isaac, Simmons, my father, and a number of lawyers occupied the library. Though Evelyn didn't come with nearly the fortune that I'd have, her father had taken a week to work out the terms. From what I understood, Evelyn had to be granted an estate trust before the engagement contract was signed.

My face lowered as I shuffled through my cards looking for the six of hearts. "I don't see why she needs an estate trust. It's not like Isaac would squander her money or abandon her, even if she did become fragile again."

Edward scowled. "If you ask me, the colonel understands Dalry better than most."

I frowned, looking over my splayed cards at him. To censure Edward, however, would only escalate into an argument. We'd already exchanged sharp words last night when I'd been unable to stop speculating why Isaac was getting married to Evelyn. Edward no longer wished to speculate. He didn't care. He didn't want to care. He never wanted to talk about it again.

"Edward, Edward," Jameson rebuked quietly as he laid down a seven of hearts. "You're too harsh on the lad."

"I'll be as harsh as I want." Edward's eyes narrowed as he glanced at our manservant. "I think he's one of the most slimy politicians I've ever met. This sudden engagement to Miss Greenley only proves it. He's marrying for all the wrong reasons."

An abrupt knock on our door surprised us.

Jameson threw down his cards and quickly stood, putting on his jacket. I'd started to gather the cards from the compartments of the game board when the person knocked for the second time.

"Reverend Auburn?" Isaac's voice sounded from the other side of the door. "Mrs. Auburn?"

Frowning, Edward stomped to the door. He swung it open. "What?"

A faint scent of cigars carried from Isaac's clothing as he blinked in astonishment at Edward's greeting.

"Well, are you going to just stand there?" Edward finally demanded.

"I beg your pardon," Isaac said, giving us all a confused glance. "I heard Jameson's voice, so I assumed it wouldn't be intruding to knock."

"You're fine, laddie," Jameson said in a soothing tone. "Did you require me?"

Isaac's gaze fastened on me for a second before he swallowed. "No, I . . . Well, it's just that tomorrow evening Colonel Greenley is planning an impromptu gathering with the officers of his regiment to celebrate the contract being signed and—"

"Thank you, but no," Edward said, starting to close the door.

To my surprise, Isaac stuck his foot in the door. "You will please allow me to finish." His jaw jutted as he waited for Edward to back down. When Edward simply clamped his mouth, Isaac decided to address me. "It didn't feel right to celebrate with strangers before it was commemorated with family. So I came to ask if you and Reverend Auburn would honor me and join the tea tomorrow afternoon. Mother and Kate are coming too."

His invitation was so stunning that I could only stare. He wore no mask, and as a consequence, he looked vulnerable.

"Are you finished now?" Edward asked, starting to close the door.

Isaac looked so crestfallen that I answered before I thought.

"Yes," I found myself promising. "I'll come."

Isaac's gaze pivoted back to me as he breathed a sigh of relief.

"Well, I won't," Edward promised. Then shut the door.

"Edward!" Jameson's rebuke made me jump.

"Don't. That man has no honor, and I'll have nothing to do with him."

"Have you grown so hardened—" Jameson's tone was stricter than any headmaster's—"that you can't see what's right in front of your face? That was an earnest request for friendship."

"I'm not in such need of friends that I'd scrape the bottom of the barrel."

"Bottom of the barrel?" Jameson challenged, nearly yelling.

"He has no money of his own and lives like a leech off of Lord Pierson. I, at least, would work if her father would stop burning my correspondences! Lord Dalry tried to usurp Julia and was party to forcing her to live a lie. It's no secret to me that he's not relinquished his emotions toward Julia—"

"Poppycock!" Jameson brushed the argument from the air. "I've seen nothing improper. You can't hold him accountable to the same rules you abide by. His nature is different from yours."

"I pray that's true!" Edward opened the door in an angry gesture for Jameson to leave.

To my relief and horror, Isaac no longer stood in the hall. My father and Forrester had replaced him. Forrester snickered, then saluted Edward on his way to his bedchamber.

My father allowed his displeasure to thicken the atmosphere before taking out his pocket watch and winding it. "As someone who refuses to take the job I've offered, I'd be more careful about whom I call a leech." He nodded over Edward's shoulder. "Jameson."

"Sir." Jameson took his leave with a formal bow.

My father glanced at me with an air that asked if I was satisfied. He returned his watch to his vest, then continued toward his bedchamber.

"And as someone who prides himself on the running of his household—" Edward's tone was too soft for anyone else to hear—"you should at least try speaking with your daughter."

～

In my dream, I stood inside Maplecroft at the bottom of the great hall as sunlight slowly poured through the glass dome and stretched down the azure walls. Mouth dry, I tried to remember what I was supposed to be doing but it kept eluding me. My hands, clutching my skirt, ached as they had immediately after they'd been burned, but when I tried to look at them, it wasn't possible.

"You need to be at breakfast," Eaton said, passing me, his arms full of folded table linens.

Mrs. Coleman rounded the corner next, her apron splashed wet. "Naughty girl, why aren't you at the breakfast table?"

When I turned in the right direction, the hall stretched into pitch darkness.

"Must you always be late?" James passed me next, running headlong into the emptiness. "Make haste! There isn't much time left!"

I realized I was starving. My hands trembled as I placed them over my stomach. This time I could see them—small cuts and scratches dotted with sticky bits of sap. I stared at them, vaguely recalling they'd been like this somewhere else in a time before.

"You need to hurry!" Simmons shouted, suddenly at my side. "Or it's going to be too late!"

I ran toward the back of the dark hall and immediately found myself crossing the threshold. A serving bowl of oatmeal sat in the center of the table, surrounded by melons, pears, and oranges. A small pitcher of honey glinted in the light. Directly across the table, someone held up a newspaper. My feet felt fastened to the floor as my body had a visceral reaction to this memory—though I couldn't place what memory this was.

Then the paper lowered, revealing Isaac's afflicted expression. My gaze shifted to the front page, where Forrester's article featured us. Isaac looked at me with the fresh anguish of someone discovering a betrayal, then lowered his chin. He crumpled the newspaper against his heart as his brows pulled downward in an expression of deepest grief. I felt unconscionable as his mouth contorted with pain.

Gasping, I sat up.

Lamplight from the street below carried to Edward's open bedchamber window. The faintest stars shone through the haze of London's smoke.

"Juls?" Edward mumbled, turning in his sleep.

Breathing heavy, I checked my hands. They looked clean, but I couldn't get the image of pinesap from my mind. They still felt dirty.

"You okay?" Edward drowsily asked. "Bad dream?"

Outside, men's laughter rang out, telling me that the elite of London were still attending soirees. I nodded, though I doubted Edward could see me. "Yes, a dream."

"You want to talk?"

I sank back down and rested my head against Edward's chest, grateful that he pulled me close. "No."

Anxiety sprouted nettles in my soul as I approached the door for tea with the Dalrys.

The happy lilt of feminine voices within filled London House as pleasantries were exchanged. I ran a hand over my brow and then bodice, uncertain why I felt so nervous. After all, it was just tea. I'd had scores of them before with Kate and Isaac, separately and together.

I placed my hand on the gleaming handle but could not bring myself to turn it. Instead I glanced toward the third floor, where Edward studied. Why did this tea feel so different?

"Where is she?" Kate's impatient voice reached my ears. "You said Julia was coming too!"

"She'll come," was Isaac's bland reply.

"Is she still getting dressed?" This time Kate's voice was nearer the door. "Maybe she needs help deciding what to wear."

I stepped away from the door, hating that I was about to be caught, though I hadn't deliberately been eavesdropping.

"I said she'll come." Isaac's voice carried the weight of authority. "I don't think it wise to disturb her. She might be with Reverend Auburn."

"And her husband?" A cold pit formed in my stomach as I recognized Lady Dalry's voice. "Is he joining us too?"

"No." Isaac's laugh was mild. "I don't think he's quite ready to become acquainted with us yet."

I swallowed, realizing it was Lady Dalry making me nervous. Knowing how close Isaac was to his mother frightened me. Surely she was angry that I'd broken Isaac's heart. And surely Evelyn hadn't been thrilled to learn Isaac desired a private tea with his former fiancée. It was no wonder only Kate sounded boisterous. Surely Lady Dalry and Evelyn were sitting ramrod straight, eyeing their disapproval of Isaac's scheme to each other.

I looked toward the stairs, tempted to retreat. Before I could, the door swung open.

"She's here!" Kate screamed over her shoulder, flinging herself into my arms. "I thought you'd never arrive!"

Behind her, Isaac gave me a slight smile and nodded. Lady Dalry also smiled as she carefully removed her bonnet, using two hands. Next to her, Evelyn was still tugging off her gloves.

I stared, frozen.

"Well, don't just stand here," Kate ordered, then took my hand and tugged me inside. "Come on!"

"Kate, she needs to breathe." Lady Dalry's rebuke was mild as she placed her bonnet on the table and glided toward us. With cool fingers she lifted my chin. "How glad I am to see you again. You look lovely as always, but I think marriage suits you even better."

I swallowed as tears rose. We both knew I deserved no such acceptance from her.

"Oh, child." Her tone was one of loving-kindness as her eyes softened. "There's no need to feel nervous. Once a Dalry, always a Dalry, you know. And I must say, you do our small family proud."

Behind her, Isaac watched us with a quiet joy. His mouth curved slightly as he poured himself a cup of tea, then leaned against the back of the sofa. From there, my gaze swung to Evelyn, who smiled at me so hard, her cheeks were dimpled.

I had no words, only mild panic, for I simply could not understand them. There were no words in my emotional vocabulary to help translate this family. Gathering a fistful of my skirt, I contemplated turning and exiting. Their acceptance felt too overwhelming.

Thankfully Jameson entered, rolling a cart of delicacies.

Without expression his eyes quickly took in the chamber's occupants. They narrowed briefly in confusion as they touched on me, but then, with a look, he assured me I wasn't alone.

I found I could breathe again.

As he transferred the various confections to the table, Evelyn approached.

Though she was still birdlike and timid, there was something firmer about her footfall. "I know what you're thinking," she whispered, sliding her arm in mine. "You don't remember becoming a Dalry. It's what I thought, at any rate, after Ben disappeared. I thought them being polite. But I can attest, they're sincere."

I felt my breath quicken, though I willed myself to appear collected. But my mind screamed questions. How could they not be angry? Why had Isaac engaged himself to her? Was it only because she was family? Most panicking of all was that they treated me as if I were one of them.

"Isaac," Evelyn called softly.

He was attuned to her, for he immediately set his cup aside. But it was different from the way we'd been linked. For the first time I realized that they'd known each other as children. There was no awkwardness; they seemed capable of reading each other's mild expressions.

"Here," Isaac said softly, offering me his arm. "Come sit with Mother."

Lady Dalry made room on the settee for me by removing Kate's shawl and bonnet. I felt as though I were walking over a slippery beam as I crossed the chamber on Isaac's arm.

"I scarcely slept last night when Isaac sent a note inviting us to tea." Kate perched on the arm of the settee as I sat. "We've all been so worried about you, what with your father's moodiness."

"I've always wanted to have tea in a window seat," Evelyn said to her before anyone could speak. "What say you? Shall we take our own plate of goodies and spy back on everyone in the street? How fun it shall be. If we're careful, they'll have no idea they're being observed."

Kate rose on tiptoes, oblivious to the fact she'd just been had.

"Oh yes, let's! We can make a game of counting ostrich feathers. The passersby on this street have tons of them."

"Double points for red ones?" Evelyn suggested.

"Yes, but you won't find any that color this time of year." Kate started to select a plateful of delicacies while Evelyn poured their cups. "Guess what, Julia? Evelyn asked me to be a brides-maid. Mama says I might have a new dress and everything."

I gave a weak smile, knowing I ought to say something to her. But there were no words. This entire gathering was too confus-ing. What sort of engagement party consisted of the bride-to-be having a private tête-à-tête with a bridesmaid in the window, while the groom and his mother visited with the past fiancée?

Then my mind cast back to the day Colonel Greenley held out the note with the request that I deliver it to Isaac. It occurred to me that perhaps, in the same way Edward and I had our own brand of honor, this family had its own brand of love.

Before I could take the thought further, Isaac placed dishes of strawberry consommé before Lady Dalry and me. A pink rose floated atop the syrupy texture of each bowl. Then he returned with his own and took the seat nearest me. I wrapped my hands around my teacup and stared into it.

If my hypothesis were true, Isaac meant it when he'd said, *"I will protect her as though she were my own sister, given you from my own household."* I peeked at Isaac as he waited to see what his mother thought of the consommé.

I pressed my lips together. Isaac might live with my father, but this was true family, and against belief he still hoped to share it with me.

I observed Lady Dalry as she smiled and nodded approval of the dish, and then I considered Evelyn's chumminess as she kept Kate occupied. Kate's hair glinted red in the sunlight as she swung her feet against the wooden frame.

My throat constricted as I realized that gathered in this chamber were those whom Isaac held dearest to his heart.

I hadn't realized the caliber of Isaac's soul until that moment. His love for me had been real, and love such as this didn't corrode and dissolve with disappointment. He'd recast it and smithed something different. I met his gaze and found him unmasked.

Here sat my brother and friend. The one I thought I had lost forever. The one I never deserved.

Tears refused to stop forming, so I turned my head.

Instantly I felt Isaac's hand on my shoulder as Lady Dalry moved closer and pulled me against her. This, too, was painful, for I realized how much I missed Mama. How badly I wanted to discuss with her all the awful things that kept happening to me. How I wished I could have laid my head on her lap, as I used to do. In that moment, I sensed how much Isaac still wished to be an instrument of healing in my life, and that this was his formal invitation to help mend the damage. That he was good and trustworthy, and that despite the heartache and pain of life, he knew how to forge new paths. He finally communicated what he'd wanted to say since I'd reentered London House.

That all was well between us, if I'd have it so.

⁓

"How was *the* tea?" Edward asked as I entered his bedchamber. His expression was one of concentration as he kept his gaze fastened on the page. His tone communicated he highly doubted I'd enjoyed myself.

I crossed my arms, unable to stop the flow of tears.

When I didn't answer, he finally looked up and snapped his book shut. "What on earth?"

Before he could rise from the bed, I climbed up onto the high bed frame and started to crawl over to him. My hands and knees dented the mattress as I hastened toward him. Words remained lodged in my throat. Not that I would have released them had I been able.

The Dalrys had set free a wild and painful emotion—a branding iron in my soul.

Thankfully Edward accepted me, though his body remained taut. He glared toward the door as if ready to march downstairs and deck Isaac. "Juls, please talk to me."

I nodded to show him I would, but still only tears came.

"What happened?" Edward did his best to hold back his anger, though it bled through his voice.

"Oh, I can tell you what happened." Jameson's voice carried into the chamber. His tone was filled with delight. "The Dalry clan inflicted love and healing on her. Only they lacked the knowledge that she's not ready to accept it unless it's greatly diluted. Without intending to, they administered more than she could handle."

"What?" Edward asked, sounding thoroughly confused.

Jameson chuckled and bent into view. "Are you all right, my queen?"

I turned my head, not wanting to ever see him again. It was awful enough I'd cried before Lady Dalry and Isaac, but knowing there were more witnesses was much worse. It is one thing to pine for things to be better but quite another to experience how it would feel and how it would look. They'd meant to show me love. But in truth, they weren't my family. It wasn't their family I longed for but my own. I had a father. And today I'd tasted how love and acceptance could feel. Thus, unknowingly, they'd only deepened the ache.

"If you'll take my advice," Jameson said to Edward in a tone that lacked all playfulness, "you'll keep your wife united with the Dalrys. She needs them. She needs a larger family than just you, Edward, and they are the perfect ones for her."

Here I finally sat straight and wiped my eyes. "I don't think I can endure another meeting with them."

"That's your faerie nature talking, but our goal is to make you human, remember?"

"Well, none of it matters anyway," Edward interrupted us. "I've reached an agreement with Lord Pierson this morning. I've accepted his offer. If it's still all right with you, Juls, within a fortnight we'll be aboard a ship on our way to South Africa to oversee the emerald mines."

His statement was so shocking that I felt my mouth gape.

"Heed my voice, boy," Jameson said, his brow furrowed. "It would be a grave mistake to drag your wife to South Africa. I tell you, she needs to be here. In some ways she's tougher than whitleather, but—forgive me for saying so, Mrs. Auburn—in other ways she's more fragile than you realize, and there's only so much a soul can endure. She needs less change, not more! If you take her to an entirely different country and setting, you have no idea what it might unleash."

I gripped Edward's sleeves, shaking my head. Jameson couldn't have been more wrong. It made perfect sense to leave.

This was what needed to happen! Surely this was God's hand! We'd escape Macy, Forrester, and my father all in one move. This was the life I was meant to live—freedom from fear of Macy and the daily pain of being ignored by my father. Though I felt a slight twinge at the idea of leaving behind the Dalrys, I could see how perfectly this would all work out. Time would soften Edward's anger, enabling him to see Isaac more clearly. Besides, once a Dalry, always a Dalry. By walking away and coming back, it would enable me to bring Edward into their family too. It was the first time in a long time I saw hope at the end of this journey.

"Africa?" I said, unable to contain the rising laugh. "We're going to see Africa? Truly?"

"No, you're not," Jameson said.

Edward grinned. "We will if you're willing."

"Oh, I'm willing."

"Can neither of you hear me?" Jameson asked. "Have you both gone deaf, or am I suddenly mute? Mrs. Auburn, you're not using your magic on me, are you?"

I wiped my tears and faced him. "You'll come with us, yes?"

He opened his mouth as if to protest, then threw his hands in the air. Shaking his head, he stalked from the chamber.

"He'll come," Edward promised. "Trust me, I can't imagine anyone would choose life with your father over life with us."

Twenty

FOR A TIME, we each had a singular, myopic focus. My father fixated on the incident tearing apart his party, which later became known as the Bedchamber Crisis; Isaac on his upcoming nuptials; Edward on learning the ins and outs of the mines; and me on trying to place all my hope in moving to South Africa.

Thus we were caught up in our daily affairs like dogs running at full speed, when reality finally pulled hard on our leashes, catching us by surprise.

Other than the fact that magistrates quietly gathered outside the steps of London House, nothing marked that day as different. Edward and I had joined breakfast, which, as always, was strained. Afterwards, my father and Isaac separated into their individual worlds.

That particular morning, Edward had a stack of business correspondences he needed to respond to as Lord Pierson's new manager. To our amusement, my father had purchased sealing wax scented with bergamot.

"They're going to think I'm a milksop," Edward said as the

gold wax sizzled in its spoon. "Sending them introductions with a perfumed seal."

"Well—" I shrugged one shoulder as I studied the map of Cape Town—"even your former parish knew you were a secret fop."

His eyes sharpened with humor. "Just wait until I finish with these business correspondences."

I lifted mocking eyebrows. "Oh, how frighteningly grown-up sounding!"

"Well, you want out of here, don't you?"

I touched the Buffalo River on the map, where a settlement had been added with an ink pen. "The sooner the better."

Edward poured the wax over five letters and sealed them with the signet my father had purchased for him. "Then allow me to work."

As someone yanked hard on the bell, releasing discordant shrieks through London House, I lifted the map of the country and studied the layout of the mines, marveling that a month hence I'd step foot on another continent.

Neither of us reacted, even when the sharp cry of the bell rang again, announcing the caller's impatience.

A single set of footsteps ran down the hall. Then several feet pounded.

Edward and I gave each other a questioning look.

All at once, my father's voice roared, "How dare you enter my home! Have you any idea who I am? You will not search—"

The sound of a tussle was unmistakable as we both stood. Men grunted and the irregular slap of boots came rushing from the hall. Edward neared me as a single set of footsteps approached our door.

Isaac swung it open and entered with an expression that chilled my blood. He signalled for us to soundlessly follow him. Edward didn't hesitate. He grabbed my wrist and pulled me from the chair. My skirts swished about my legs as we tumbled through the chamber.

London House was a maze, and Isaac knew it well. He navigated us through a series of rooms. In the dining room, he removed a portrait of Lady Josephine and opened a safe. He pulled out a small satchel, which he handed to Edward.

"Is it Macy?" I begged in a whisper.

He placed a finger over his mouth, then directed us to follow him again. He pulled open the nearest door and peered about an empty room.

Catching Edward's eye, he pointed to the window, advising us to keep from view as we crossed this chamber. Edward nodded.

Instead of exiting the chamber as I expected, Isaac went to the hearth, where he reached behind another portrait. This time, instead of a safe, the panelling next to the fireplace swung open to reveal a dusty and cobwebbed passage.

Behind us, the sound of voices and footsteps were spreading.

Edward dove into the darkness, pulling me after him. I turned to give Isaac one last look of bewilderment and saw the door open behind him and a man enter.

"Here! They're here!" The man's cheeks puffed out as he sounded a police whistle. With a single shove, he knocked Isaac aside, then leaped toward me. He grabbed my ankles, sending me to the ground with a hard jolt. My chin hit the stone floor as whistles detonated all over London House.

Pain radiated through my face and knee as I tried to kick him off and caught sight of his embroidered collar. With a groan I realized these weren't Macy's thugs but Peel's bobbies.

Without thought, I reached out and grabbed Edward's calves as he turned back to fight. He tumbled and fell on top of me, winding me for a second but thankfully keeping him from punching anyone.

The constable wasted no time, pinning and securing Edward's hands behind his back. "No one is allowed to leave the premises," he ordered. "The three of you are to be questioned."

His gaze swung on me as I pushed up against the floor. "Mrs. Chance Macy?"

Knowing better than to admit it, I only stared. A drop of blood spattered and blossomed over the concrete below me. I touched my lip and found it had been cut. Dust coated my throat, so I gave a cough.

The constable swore, then withdrew a handkerchief. "I didn't mean to hurt you. You must tell him." Terror filled his voice. "Please."

Intending to use his fear to get us released, I said, "He's killed for far less. Unless you release us, I can promise you he'll hear all about this." I held out my bloodied finger. "We both know what he'll do."

"Julia!" Edward rebuked as he struggled beneath the man pushing him down.

"Can we take that as a confession of her identity?" a voice said from somewhere inside the chamber. A man appeared and signalled for someone to pull me up. A hand grasped my upper arm and yanked me to my feet.

"I heard no such confession," Isaac said in his disinterested, polite tone. "Though—" his eyes bored into mine—"I wouldn't call that speech ladylike. *And we are nothing if we are not ladylike.*"

Heat carried through my face as Edward was roughly pulled to his feet.

"Mrs. Chance Macy?" an authoritative, baritone voice queried from the doorway.

I glanced in that direction, then realized even responding to that name might implicate me.

A man in his early fifties gripped a blackthorn walking stick. He surveyed the scene with his shoulders wide apart. He was about the height of Napoleon and equally imposing. His gaze narrowed on my mouth. "Why is my client's lip bleeding?"

"She tried to run," the man holding Edward said in a tart

voice. "'Sides, how can she be your client when we ain't questioned her yet so she can be arrested?"

The man in the doorway frowned as he withdrew a silk handkerchief and extended it toward me. "No one is questioning or arresting my client, though I ask you to note how her own name sent her into a panic-stricken state."

"Panic-stricken state?" Isaac questioned blandly. "I'm sorry, but I noted no such thing. Julia was just tackled by a full-grown magistrate, cutting her lip, right before Reverend Auburn also fell on top of her. Of course she's dazed."

"Ah, young Dalry!" The man greeted Isaac with regard. "We met at Hurlingham's dinner. Remember?"

"Merrick," Isaac greeted back with a polite nod. "Of course."

"Good, you recall me. I'm surprised, given the temper Tillet was in that night. Don't suppose you've seen him lately?"

Though his arms were secured behind his back, Isaac wore his polished expression. "No, I fear not. Lord Pierson and I haven't been out much."

Merrick chuckled, then rubbed the bottom of his nose. "No, I suppose you haven't been, with a secret like this to keep." Then, to the magistrates, "It hardly does to leave the girl standing here bleeding. Take Mrs. Macy back to the front of the house."

"Her name," Edward said, spitting blood from his mouth, "is Mrs. Auburn."

Merrick gave Edward his back and continued to address Isaac. "I heard that Hamley is planning on only attending the Regent Club. That will be quite a loss for you and Pierson, considering how many Whigs are there."

Isaac shrugged. "Or perhaps Hamley plans to persuade them instead of being persuaded."

Merrick chuckled. "You should have pursued law, Dalry, but you—" he pointed to Edward—"I fear I cannot recommend you for the law or the church."

"Come on." The magistrate holding Edward shoved him toward the door.

Isaac stepped in line behind him. "May I inquire why we're being held captive by the police in Lord Pierson's house?"

"We'll ask the questions," the man securing Isaac's arms growled.

Merrick chuckled again. "And here is another problem with Peel's police for debate. They're not cultured. Have you any idea how illustrious the people you are handling are?" He gestured for me to follow. "Go on, Mrs. Macy. Your husband has given me permission to serve as your proxy, so you need not answer any questions. As far as your question, Dalry, my client Mr. Macy was out of the country on business for the last several weeks."

My mouth tasted of blood as I dabbed my lip.

"You can imagine his shock when he arrived home and learned that, despite having left her in the direct care of Lord Pierson, she'd married another. Macy is suing Pierson for damages to his conjugal happiness."

They deposited us in the same chamber that Edward and I had just occupied. Still trying to puzzle out why Macy had been abroad, I stared at the pile of posts and the maps of Africa. We had been so close. My stomach cramped as I suddenly connected everything. Of course Macy had been abroad. It made complete sense. Just as he'd somehow managed to destroy Forrester's evidence, he'd gone back to Austria to destroy any record of his childhood. And he must have succeeded; otherwise he'd never have called Forrester's and my bluff.

"Suing Pierson for damages to his conjugal happiness." Merrick's words flooded back. Surely, I thought frantically, surely he couldn't still legally claim me as his wife.

The idea was so monstrous, my heart stuttered.

"Sit and wait for Howell Ethan to question you," the man ordered.

"And the reason for the police?" Isaac asked.

Merrick retreated to the window, where he took out a small snuffbox and tapped the lid. "Naturally they caught wind of the lawsuit and are here to investigate. It's quite the scandal, let me assure you. Pierson might even face treason charges for lying to the queen."

Beneath the table, Edward tapped my foot. In my panic, I could scarcely catch my breath, much less face him. But he tapped my foot again, this time more firmly. Tears filling my eyes, I lifted my gaze. Dark-golden curls coated with dust hung over his brow. He had his own cut, a crescent-shaped gash over his left cheek. Hazel eyes fastened on mine with an expression of fearlessness I hadn't seen since our youth—the type of pluck that would jump into an adventure, dagger in hand, shouting with joy. He meant to embolden me.

I calmed enough to give a humorless laugh. Who in life was stupid enough to want adventure? I wanted Windhaven and piles of dishes and laundry.

"Though he slay us," Edward whispered. "Fix your eyes on the star."

I nodded, telling him I understood, then blotted my mouth with Merrick's handkerchief.

Isaac, however, looked puzzled as he tried to figure out Edward's mismatched statement.

"May we speak?" I asked.

"Absolutely not." Merrick took a pinch of snuff and gave it a sharp sniff.

I looked to Edward, who confirmed it.

Thus, as magistrates dumped out my father's desk drawers, ransacked Edward's meticulous studies, Edward, Isaac, and I only locked eyes, little knowing it was the last time we'd ever be all together again.

How differently each one of us was sifted too, for we had different ways of handling the world: Isaac and his ability to slip in and out of situations with the appearance of perfection, Edward with his passion and refusal to ever budge, and me and my passivity, taught young not to struggle against circumstances.

There was so much evidence that it took the police hours to document and record it. It was a hidden blessing, for otherwise I would have been arrested and immediately bailed by Mr. Macy, who waited to gather me. They had no legal right to detain my father, an MP. And by the time the magistrates were searching my bedchamber, he was already roaring like a bull in the Temple district, rousing his countersuit.

⁓

By the time my father's boots pounded up the front steps of London House, hours had passed and the afternoon sun rippled over the table we sat at, exhausting us further. I heard his arrival, but amidst the other angry noises, I scarcely registered it. Instead I swiped my damp brow, then craned my neck, swallowing as I looked over the stuffy chamber.

My mouth was parched, but asking for claret was beyond my ability. For fear had entwined and galvanized itself around every fiber of my body. Mentally I was trying to calm the storm within me by cutting short every speculation of what would happen next. Nevertheless, I repeatedly had visions of being forcibly dragged down the front steps of London House and shoved into Macy's carriage. I shut my eyes, but the image was replaced by another equally repugnant one—that of Edward being shoved into a prison cell.

I felt my face screw tight as I choked on the lump in my throat.

The door slammed open and my father barged into the chamber and threw down papers that had been trifolded, sealed, and tied with string. "She's not married to Macy."

His fingers gouged into my arm as he lifted me from the chair and pulled me against him. The smell of sweat, dust, and the manure of London's streets testified about his day. Edward's eyes narrowed at his rough manner of handling me.

As if relishing his role, Merrick smirked and strolled to the table. He paused for another pinch of snuff, then savored it with closed eyes. After tucking his walking stick beneath the crook of his arm, he untied and gathered the thick documents to him with an air of contempt. He scoffed, thumbing through the pages. "A countersuit? Contesting the marriage? Truly?"

"Leave my house." Bluish veins protruded from my father's neck.

Merrick pinched his nose and shut his eyes. "This is only going to make it worse for you, not to mention place undue stress on Mrs. Macy." He gave a slight shake of his head, then held up the packet. "Agree to negotiate a settlement, Pierson, and Mr. Macy will be merciful both in the price and with your public image." His eyes were cold as he innocently spread his hands. "After all, the only thing he truly desires is his wife's safe return."

Silence met Merrick's suggestion. My fingers growing cold, I peeked at my father to gauge his thoughts. His face was wroth with a brand of anger I hadn't seen since the night I married Mr. Macy. Dark rings of perspiration spread through his shirt and frock coat. Whereas fear coursed through my body, anger trembled through his.

"Leave." He gnashed his teeth. "Or so help me, I will beat you out with a whip."

"Fetch Mr. Ethan," one of the bobbies whispered to another one near the door.

A moment later Mr. Ethan arrived, carrying a ledger in his left hand. "What's this I hear?" He glared at my father. "Are you causing a ruckus?"

My father shoved me behind him. "I'm taking my daughter and we're leaving now!"

Mr. Ethan sneered. "With all due respect, Lord Pierson, you're under investigation for treason and—"

"You have no right to hold me or my daughter!" My father kept a tight grip on my arm. "I suggest you move from my path."

"I have every right to hold the girl, especially as I haven't questioned her yet," Mr. Ethan replied. "If you wish to leave, then you may do so, but she remains."

"She stays," Merrick agreed, "but Mrs. Macy isn't answering any questions regardless."

"Her name," Edward said from his seat, "is Mrs. Auburn."

Mr. Ethan sported a waxed mustache, which twitched as he frowned at Edward. "So you admit at least that you're Reverend Auburn? That you married Mr. Macy to Miss Julia Elliston."

"I admit nothing and everything," was Edward's circuitous response.

Mr. Ethan narrowed his eyes in my direction. "Do you deny that you're Julia Elliston Macy?"

"How many times must we do this?" Merrick removed a folded note from his vest and opened it for Mr. Ethan to see. "As I said outside, I'm serving as her proxy. Mr. Macy's wife is not to answer any questions."

"Your note carries no weight here. I'm investigating charges of bigamy and treason," was Mr. Ethan's response. "She'll either speak or be arrested."

"Plebeians in power are always the worst," Merrick muttered to himself as he dug around in the inner pocket of his frock coat. "If you want to make an arrest, you'll have to charge Mr. Macy. Hang on, I've his address in here somewhere. You'll also have to save your questions for him, for she's under coverture."

"You're claiming that she acted under Mr. Macy's direct orders?" Mr. Ethan's tone was dubious. "To commit bigamy?"

"She's been manipulated by Lord Pierson. Told outlandish lies about her husband as a continuation of an ongoing feud. In order to preserve his wife's fragile mental state, he's not torn her from her father's clutches but sanctioned for her to remain with Lord Pierson. So in that respect, yes, she's a *feme covert*."

"Her marriage to Macy isn't legal," was my father's gritty response.

"Your argument is pointless, Pierson. I have documentation that she's Macy's wife. As such, I have a carriage outside to transport her home."

"And I can prove that she isn't." My father crossed his arms, keeping his stance. "She's not going into that man's care. So help me."

Merrick spread his hand in a helpless gesture, ordering Mr. Ethan to do something. "He's standing in the way of the law. Mr. Macy has every right to demand the return of his wife."

Though I did not see his face, my father angled himself in such a way that Mr. Ethan took a small step backwards. Ethan looked askance at Merrick before lifting his hands. "I'll leave this to the courts. When they draw up the charges, you both can present your arguments. Let them decide what to do with the girl." Then, giving a nervous glance at my father, "Do I have your word not to remove your daughter from this house?"

My father gave a curt nod.

Merrick closed his eyes and shook his head. "Wouldn't like to be in your shoes, Ethan. But it's your head, not mine."

"Be glad I'm not arresting the girl." Mr. Ethan placed his hands on his hips, pushing back his frock coat. He studied me a long moment as if to say he knew I was guilty. Then he looked over his shoulder. "Are you Reverend Edward Auburn?"

"I am."

"Bring him with us."

Before the nearest magistrate could approach, Edward stood and scooted back his chair. His deep-set hazel eyes remained fixed on me as long as they were able, as if to fill me with a measure of his brand of iron will.

The slam of the front door had the ring of finality about it, and in my mind I'd never heard anything so vast, empty, and hollow.

"Go to the library," Isaac directed me in a whisper. When I made no move, he went so far as walking me to the door, where he waved for William to escort me.

Though there were magistrates in the hall questioning the staff, no one made any attempt to stop or question me. I noted the servants' wide and questioning eyes, but I pressed on.

Once in the library, I shut the door, relieved to find it was empty.

Spent, I lay on the plush carpet and stared at the empty grate, no longer bothered by memories of Eramus. Something so much worse had just happened. For a long moment I could not move, could not utter a sound, for no sound was worthy enough to express the deep ache and emptiness.

Twenty-One

THE FOLLOWING MORNING, I awoke to a silent house and opened my eyes to find Edward's shoes sitting on the chair next to the bed. I wondered what shoes he'd been wearing when he was taken. For the only ones I'd ever seen were still here.

Pushing my hair from my eyes, I pictured the sort of bed Edward had slept in. An image of him lying on a wooden pallet with fleas arose. I winced. Would prison bring on a relapse of the sickness that had nearly claimed him under the oak tree at Maplecroft?

"It should be me," I whispered. Then, realizing I was aiming my words toward God, I prayed more boldly. "We both know I'm the one who deserves prison and not him. Switch us somehow." My voice broke. "I'm begging you."

That simple prayer was all it took to find heaven's balm. As I had in the past, I felt the rich fullness of his presence. It gave the impression that during this time of deep grief I'd always find him within arm's reach, that even while one is drowning, one is never misplaced.

And with it came a flood of new ideas—that he didn't want me in prison or bondage of any sort. That this was the Goliath he'd chosen for me, and prison was the one he'd chosen for Edward. That his plan for my future was life more abundant and full than I could anticipate, not because I was strong or noble, but because of his great favor.

Like a lover hovering, he made himself known and waited for me to fix my gaze solely on him. He'd wooed me since that first day in Eastbourne's chapel, and now he was beckoning me to run to him.

I know some of my readers will think, as William Elliston maintained, that in crisis, my imagination produced the necessary sensations for me to cope. But I know it is not so, though I cannot supply tangible proofs. Perhaps it is why Jesus said his sheep will know his voice.

How Edward had known that in the hour of drowning, I'd reach out and touch God, I cannot say. For until that moment, God had seemed little more help than a far, distant star. How many countless times has humanity reached toward heaven only to find the thick veil that separates it from earth? But that morning, I found the veil rent. Like Edward stretching his arms toward the sunrise, full of passion and fire, here was manna to sustain me.

～

My attire was plain and my eyes red as I approached the breakfast chamber. The scent of croissants and eggs confirmed a meal was being served, but I was uncertain whether or not I'd find occupants, for no sound carried from the room.

Arms hugged tightly against me, I crossed the threshold. Isaac, Forrester, and my father sat in silence, sorting through the vast stack of newspapers. If my father registered me, he gave no sign. Ashen-faced, he simply continued reading.

Isaac stood and gathered me while Jameson pulled out a chair.

"Morning." Smirking, Forrester withdrew a folded paper he'd kept secured beneath his elbow. "Welcome. We're searching to see if we can discern Macy's legal strategy from the slant of the story he's telling. That, and what public opinion we need to quell about you, though so far, I can't argue with their conclusions."

Jameson's chest swelled with outrage, though he could do little more than glare. Grateful for his and Isaac's presence, I consulted the paper Forrester had reserved. The headline read:

EMERALD HEIRESS EXPOSED

Aware that Isaac carefully measured my response, I borrowed his mask as I read. It said I was a bigamist. Greedy for wealth, status, and notoriety. A vampiric spider, willing to devour anything in my path to gain power. I wasn't the only person attacked. My father had been tied to the stake next to me. His credibility was roasted and his actions torn to shreds. Every bill he was championing and every political ally he'd spoken to since my arrival were shrouded in new suspicions. Keeping my face expressionless, I picked up one paper after another. That morning it was easy to see which ones supported the Tories and which ones the Whigs. Some argued that his misdeeds needed to be separate from his party; others said the entire party's very character was tarnished. And in others there was a general outcry that people needed to hold judgment until the full truth about me came to light.

Swallowing, I turned to take measure of how my father handled the news. My stomach knotted as I found his accusing glare on me. I lowered my gaze. I alone knew that the chains of my shame were broken and I was free. For had I not just communed with God himself? Human forgiveness, however, is an entirely different matter.

The bell jangled, causing everyone to stiffen.

"Go see who it is," my father ordered Jameson.

I sat trying to regulate my breathing as I strained to hear. A moment later Jameson returned and placed a tray filled with merchant bills before my father. Jameson whispered in his ear, then stepped back.

We all watched as, frowning, my father opened one after another. Then, pinching his forehead, "James, fetch me laudanum."

"What is it?" Forrester asked.

"The full harvest of bills for introducing the Emerald Heiress into society." He picked one off the top and threw it to Forrester. "They're demanding full payment before I lose everything."

Forrester opened the note. His eyes widened before he folded it. "Why not try sending the bill to her husband and seeing if he'll pick up the tab?"

My father's black look silenced him, but not for long.

"This one remembered you, Isaac." Forrester chuckled as he perused the next newspaper, then read aloud, "'We're all left wondering how it came to pass that this whey-faced girl ever managed to fool the elite. How is it the blue bloods failed to notice her coarse manners? There are rumors that she used Lord Dalry to help with her ruse. It wouldn't be the first time a femme fatale has used her licentious nature to take advantage of a pure youth. We can only thank the heavens that he was cut loose just in time.'" He narrowed his eyes, passing the paper to Isaac. "I hope you finally believe me and see for yourself what she is now."

Frowning, Isaac took the paper and scanned the article for himself. My face burned as I waited to learn his thoughts.

"How extraordinarily faulty your memory is," he finally said. "You forget that I've always known her story was one we created. How have you already forgotten that we're the ones who pushed her into this sham? As gentlemen, instead of insulting her, we should be working on how best to assist her."

My father heaved a sigh and sat back, still pinching his brow.

"Would you all mind leaving? I desire to speak to my daughter alone."

Isaac met my gaze with a supportive look, then stood and retrieved his coat, which was slung over the back of his chair.

Jameson sailed through the background, giving me a slight nod of encouragement as Forrester gathered not only the papers but the basket of croissants. I stiffened in my chair. For the first time since Forrester published that newspaper article that broke my betrothal to Isaac, the doors of communication were open between my father and me.

My father waited until we were alone, then turned his coffee cup in a full circle, keeping its bottom on the table as he stared at it. He drew a long sigh. "I'm hiring counsel for you and Edward. The same counsel I'm hiring for myself, as our cases hinge on each other's. You're not to talk to anyone else about the investigation. Not in any way. Am I clear?"

I nodded, angry at myself for allowing a rush of hope. This was no attempt to bridge the differences between us. This was his life. He was a politician. We just found out we were in the same camp. We were speaking again. Period.

I took a careful breath weighted with sadness. Instead of relationship, I spoke his language—fact. "What happens next?"

His shoulders loosened as if he was relieved. "We plan our strategy and look for weakness in Macy's."

Not certain if I was allowed to say his name or not, now that the whole country knew the truth, I haltingly asked, "Do we know his strategy?"

"Yes and no." He leaned on an elbow and dug his finger into his cheek. "As you're aware, he's suing me for damages to his conjugal happiness. We know that Merrick attempted to make you look terrified and uncertain whom to trust. Macy is angling that I've poisoned you against him."

I allowed that thought to soak in and found I couldn't disagree with it. "Could he truly force my return?"

My father shifted his weight to his other hip. "It's not as simple as that. You're on the verge of being charged with bigamy. My first goal is to prevent that from happening before my countersuit is examined. Otherwise, as your supposed legal husband, Macy has full jurisdiction over you. As we know from Merrick, Macy is already claiming that you were acting on his orders, which makes him accountable. Thank heavens Edward performed the first ceremony, so at least there's no ability to add to your crime by saying you hid your first wedding in order to marry Edward.

"Nonetheless, you can't commit a felony as offensive as bigamy and escape under the clause that you were obeying your husband. Yet Merrick seemed absolutely certain that arresting you wouldn't stand. The most logical conclusion, therefore, is that Macy is going to claim he thought you were too emotionally fragile to snatch outright from my care. Furthermore, we know that more than once he made a point of publicizing that he and I were having meetings in private. Remember us climbing into his carriage at Lady Northrum's? I believe he's going to claim that he tried privately to negotiate with me for your safe return in order to avoid his public humiliation."

I glared at him. If that was the case, Macy was telling the truth. "That's not just an empty claim."

My father said nothing for a long moment as he looked me in the eye. "Macy did try to talk legalities to me, but in the past he's broken troth so many times, it was impossible to assign belief to anything he said."

I wrinkled my nose. "And if I am charged with bigamy before your countersuit takes place?"

The lines over my father's jowls deepened. "If he has any sense, Macy will plead guilty on your behalf. If you're guilty of bigamy, it legally establishes your marriage to Macy. In which case he'll take you into his custody and likely continue his lawsuit against me for causing detrimental harm to you."

I took a deep breath, unable to believe this was actually happening. "What if I refuse and plead innocence?"

"Since Macy is claiming this was his doing and that you're frail, you have no legal status."

This was insane, and for a moment I said nothing, trying to wrap my mind around the implications. "But what about him? Won't he go to jail, then? He can't claim he masterminded my crime and not have to pay for it!"

My father picked up a small tin of white, chalky tablets near his plate. With care he picked out two, chewed them, then pounded on his chest as he cleared his throat. "Which brings us back to why he seems to be claiming he supported your remaining where you were—because of your weak constitution. As far as Simmons can find, there's no recorded punishment for a man who accidentally cuckolded himself in this manner, so the punishment would be created uniquely. There isn't a juror or justice alive who would dare touch Macy. Adolphus is part of the reason grand juries have been nicknamed 'the hope of London thieves.'"

Rooke's lanky personage rose to mind as I twisted the cuffs of my dress. Lady Foxmore once said he should have been jailed for thuggery except for a technicality. That probably should have been my first hint something was amiss. Somehow I suspected my father did not exaggerate Macy's influence in the courts either.

My father waited to see if I had any comments, so I asked the only question I cared about. "And Edward? When are you paying his bail?"

Astonishment spread over my father's features before he glowered. "I'm not. For obvious reasons, we're leaving him in the jail until the trial."

"What!" I rose to my feet. "Why?"

"Because we're trying to stall your being charged with bigamy. London will not look kindly on Edward's being here with us. Nor Macy, for that matter."

"Can you get him a room somewhere else, then?"

"And give the papers another soul to follow everywhere? No. The next sessions are in July, and it's not that far away, considering he lived on the streets before this. Right now we want the public focused solely on Macy and me. Your marriage is now a matter of public opinion, and we don't need Edward interfering. Now if you haven't any other questions . . ." He started to remove his napkin from his lap.

"Wait." I leaned forward and gripped the table, hating our barrier. I wanted to tell him that I hadn't planned to overthrow him and Isaac with that newspaper article, but as he nailed me with an angry look, the words lodged in my throat.

"Yes?" he demanded.

I gripped Mama's shawl and kept the topic to the trial. "If Macy claims he ordered me here, wouldn't that rip shreds through his argument that you're the person who ruined his conjugal happiness?"

My father angled his head as a look of hope crossed his face. Then his eyes narrowed. "Which male servant dared speak to you about the case?"

"No one."

"You're lying." Red blotched his face as he stood. "Where else would you have come up with that idea? Was it James? Jameson? Who dared disobey me?"

"No one discussed it," I whispered.

His face contorted with anger as he tugged on his waistcoat. "I can't prove that you're lying, but we both know you are. No woman could come up with a legal argument like that on her own. So help me, if I catch any member of the staff talking about this, I'll dismiss him. Is that clear?"

A retort immediately flew to my mind. I wanted to demand that he explain how Mama found herself with child but without an offer of marriage. I wanted to scream that he had no honor—that he'd never had any, so far as I could tell—so how dare he presume to question mine. I was so angry that tears filled my eyes. But even before the words reached my lips, I saw our future stretch out.

If I screamed at him, his fury would unleash, for he looked truly angry. I doubted any crony of his had ever seen him this full of choler. Red mottled his face as he waited for me to shout back. Unlike William, his hands weren't forming fists, but there was a look of near glee in his eyes—one that said he wanted an excuse to berate someone, anyone. If I responded with anger, he'd lash out, and I'd be hurt. And in turn, I'd respond with anger. Where would it ever end?

I took a step backwards, unwilling to step foot on this path. It was far too slippery.

"Yes?" he demanded.

I studied him, not certain if I needed to stand up for myself in order to make him stop. Yet on more than one occasion I *had* stood up to him, and each time it had the opposite effect. He only grew angrier. I released my breath. Let him think me weak. I had no fight anyway. I'd simply seen too much pain in my lifetime and saw it wouldn't benefit either of us to perpetuate a never-ending cycle.

Seeing he still waited for me to react, I shook my head. "It was nothing."

Clearly he expected more, for his mouth slashed downward. He glared at me, seemingly unbalanced by my decision, mistrusting even. Then he demanded, "No disturbances today! Am I clear?"

I gave a nod, finding it odd that he'd tacked on that command. Who ever willingly disturbed him?

As his footsteps pounded away, it occurred to me that he'd made that last command out of a need to prove he had control.

I sank into my chair and heaved a sigh. What did I care if he thought me a liar? So did the rest of the country. Who knows— maybe he even believed me but just wanted something to fight about. Edward had said I needed to see my father for myself before I'd understand. I glanced at his empty seat, wondering why he was so angry anyway. I no longer believed it was me. From what I could tell, he was wick with anger long before I ever arrived.

"I saw your father stalk to his library." Jameson's voice carried from the threshold behind me.

My voice was too thick to respond, so I swallowed twice and smoothed my skirt.

Shutting the door behind him, Jameson entered. He plucked a single white rose from the bouquet arranged at the center of the table. He sat in Isaac's spot, then slid the rose across the table and bowed his head. "May I petition to speak, O queen?"

Instead of looking at him, I fastened my gaze on the dish of hard-boiled eggs nearest me. They were a soft blur of blues, greens, and browns.

"I take it your meeting with your ursine father didn't go well?"

As if determined I would acknowledge him, his aged hand crept into view as he selected the topmost egg. From across the table, the sound of his shelling it reached my ears. "Ah, well, sometimes faerie kings choose the wrong animal to transform into. Be glad he chose a bear instead of a crocodile. I know of one who accidentally ate all his children in a single night."

Despite myself, my lips twisted in a smile. "I'm not playing today."

"Well, neither am I! Good heavens, there's far too much magic in this house to let your guard down, even for a minute." He split the egg in half with Isaac's unused knife, filling the air with its pungent scent. After salting the two halves, he picked up one. "Come on. Tell me what passed."

Instead I whispered the truest desire of my heart. "I miss Edward."

His affection for Edward must have been great, for his kindly eyes radiated with love as he nodded approval. "If the boy insists on getting arrested and thrown in jail, what can we do except wait for him to finish his prison ministry?"

I smirked, then wiped aside the wetness of my eyes. "What if I'm not here when that happens? What if I truly am forced back to Macy?"

"Pshaw!" He waved half of his egg through the air. "Surely, being a vicar, Edward carries some influence with God. We'll let those two argue it out. I warrant heaven is getting its fill of Edward's prayers, even now." He bit into his egg, chewed, and swallowed before saying, "Now tell me what happened with your father. For the very air was tainted when I entered. Something happened. It is my role as your fetching butler to figure out what."

I couldn't help but laugh. "Fetching?"

His eyes twinkled. "I give you your dignity, so give me mine."

I felt my shoulders loosen. "Fine, you can be the fetching butler, so long as I'm not Jonah."

"Well, that's hardly my call." He checked his uneaten portion of egg for shells. "Tell me what passed and we can determine your role after that."

I sighed and reached into the fruit bowl, where I pinched off some grapes. It wasn't until a slight smile crossed Jameson's lips that I realized he'd hoped to coax me into eating by setting the example. I plucked off and rolled the first grape between my fingers. "Fine, I'll tell you, but only if you promise not to lecture me about using my words. I'm not going to speak and tell my father that I'm angry at him."

His white brows scrunched with concern. "Perhaps in his case we can make an exception about the need for words. Mr. Forrester tells me your aim is quite good and your arm is strong. Perhaps your father will understand what you're trying to say if you just threw a few things at his head."

I laughed outright, warmed by Jameson's presence, then

popped the grape in my mouth and crushed it in my teeth, imagining my father's shock were I to scream and pitch every dish and utensil at him. But just as before, I saw how I would feel afterwards, how the emptiness would only deepen. I shook my head, feeling pained. "No. I would ache and hurt all the more if I did that."

Jameson's eyes quickened with surprise. "Explain that."

As best I could, I tried to describe what had transpired between me and my father. Turning over the grapes in my fingers, I explained why I didn't respond. "I've seen so many versions of this path. I've seen my stepfather beating Mama, and Sarah boiling over with rage, muttering about the things she hoped would befall him. I've seen Mama, as cold as ice, resist being broken. But even that form of anger didn't work. Melancholy would utterly consume long periods of her life. But it's all the same, isn't it? I mean, none of them were ever happy." I glanced up and found Jameson's eyes riveted on me. "I don't know. It's like the more anger you drink, the thirstier you become." I lowered my eyes. "I'd rather just stop here, thirsty as I am, than continue trying to fill something bottomless."

"But you need anger," Jameson countered. "It's meant to awaken you to respond to danger."

My smile felt rueful. "Somehow it becomes a danger unto itself. If I said something hurtful in return and saw that my arrow found its mark, I would feel no satisfaction. How can anyone stand seeing the pang of hurt on someone else's face, knowing they caused it? I just can't."

Jameson sat back in his chair, looking at me anew. He considered my words a long time; then, in a half whisper, "No wonder the boy is so smitten." Looking helpless to counsel me, he asked, "So what is it you hope to achieve with your father, then?"

Feeling sad, I remembered the way my father had chucked me beneath the chin before I went to the opera, the pride in his eyes as he scanned the headlines after I came out, and the way he looked at Edward and Isaac with deep pride. I gave a sad shake of my head. "Nothing I seem to be able to keep."

Jameson sighed but nodded. Lacing his fingers behind his head, he leaned back. "Did I ever tell you about the farm I grew up on?"

I arched my brow.

He grinned, perhaps sensing he'd finally earned my trust. "Well, it was a dairy farm on which my great-great-grandfather had built a swinging bridge over a ravine with a river beneath it. It was rather high, and in its day, about a hundred years before my birth, it was used quite frequently."

"My word!" I teased. "Was it a Roman bridge?"

The wrinkles around his eyes crinkled as he covered his heart. "Spare the bear but insult the butler! No, Mrs. Auburn, it wasn't Roman. They had enough sense to build things out of stone. By the time I was ten, my great-great-grandfather's bridge was all rotted wood and frayed rope. My mother hated it because, as a young boy, it fascinated me to no end. She even demanded that my father tear it down, but he refused because it was part of our heritage."

My eyes widened, expecting a story of tragedy and why nostalgic feelings about one's family will only betray you.

Jameson surprised me with, "If you want to keep a bridge open between you and your father, go ahead. Only place no weight upon it. Have no expectations, for it will never sustain you."

I said nothing as I considered that.

"And if—" he leaned forward and placed his laced fingers on the table—"one day we see he's working to repair his half of the bridge, we can vote whether to trust the bridge again." Then, with a grin, "Edward and I will vote no and to cut down our half." His voice softened and he grew serious. "But he's not our father, and your vote will be the only one that counts."

My throat constricted as I nodded my thanks. Then, wanting

to move past how vulnerable I felt, I said, "Wait. You said the bridge was rotted by the time you were ten. Why that age? Did you actually try to cross it?"

Jameson gave me a sly smile. "Yes, and lucky for me Winthrop was home from university and was able to pull me from the rapids. Though I was half-drowned, he thrashed me and then took me home so my father could thrash me next."

Winthrop. The way he said the name roused a memory, and I angled my head.

"Churchill," I said, connecting it. "Don't tell me you're Churchill's brother?"

"Half brother," he corrected. "Our mother was widowed and remarried late in life. How else do you think Edward became acquainted with him?"

For a full second I only stared. Jameson must have known the connection between me and his brother's death. Here was another life thrown into havoc because of my actions. Yet never once had Jameson even hinted that he resented me. But how could he not?

Heavy footsteps sounded outside our door. With spry movements, Jameson stood and quickly collected the bowl of fruit and eggs, which he transferred to the buffet just as the door opened. Simmons entered and glanced at Jameson with a frown, as if suspecting he'd broken propriety, before addressing me. "I've just come from the Lady Dalry's, where I've been working on Master Isaac's wedding plans. I'm about to run over again with an updated guest list. While I'm here, Miss Greenley requested that I ask permission for her to visit you this afternoon. What shall I tell her?"

"Evelyn?" I cast him a confused glance. "Are you sure she meant me?"

His arched brows asked if I truly wanted to question him.

I emptied my hands of the grapes, then pushed the plate away. "Has she seen the newspapers and what they said?"

"I'm not a mind reader," was the curt reply.

I frowned and glanced at Jameson. He, however, remained bland-faced as he emptied the table. I tapped my fingers on my chair. Evelyn had to know that by visiting me, she was only persecuting herself. Surely every newspaperman was camped outside. Any visitors would find their way into the papers. Could she withstand that?

"Do you know what Isaac thinks of the matter?" I finally decided on. Surely he understood her best.

Simmons closed his eyes for a moment, then snapped them open and gave me a sarcastic look. "Hmm. I'm sorry, but Master Isaac's mind is closed just at the moment. Perhaps he's napping."

"Oh, Lord Dalry is all for the visit," Jameson said, smiling over his shoulder.

Simmons placed a hand on his hip. "How would you know?"

"Because I was present this morning when he wrote Miss Greenley a note and asked her to call on Mrs. Auburn this afternoon."

My stomach felt heightened and dropped as it always did with Isaac. Of course he would know how badly I needed a friend today.

"Yes," I decided, lacing my fingers together nervously. "Please tell Miss Greenley I'd be delighted to have her company this afternoon."

Twenty-Two

✦

I DOUBT EVEN ELIZABETH would have made such an ideal companion, for she had not yet been tempered by suffering. In the short time Evelyn had been engaged to Isaac, she'd become less fragile but was still highly sensitive. She seemed cognizant of her every word and, much like Isaac, modified her speech so it brought only balm, never pain.

Late in the afternoon as we partook of tea, the hurried sound of feet passed our door. Nervous that something else might have happened, I set down the cup and watched the door.

"Likely it's just a visitor?" Evelyn followed my gaze, sensing my nervousness. "What day do you normally accept callers?"

"My father doesn't."

Her brow scrunched. "How do people know when to call on you, then?"

I said nothing, for I discerned both Mrs. King's and Miss Moray's voices rising to an angry pitch. It wasn't like them to argue. Harder-soled shoes—Jameson's, for he walked faster than Kinsley but slower than James—joined their convocation. Within seconds his voice entered the fray.

Evelyn's spoon balanced on the edge of her fingers. "What on earth?"

I shook my head and stood. "I don't know, but I'm ending their nonsense now. My father will be in a tempest if he hears this."

Evelyn set down her cup and spoon with a clack, telling me she followed.

I marched into the hallway, ready to give the staff a fear they'd not forget. Just outside the door, Miss Moray, Mrs. King, and Jameson stood arguing with each other. Though they now worked to suppress their voices, their cheeks were red.

Between them stood the most beggarly person I'd seen in my life. Snarly red hair hung in clumps from beneath a sodden, dingy kerchief. Her muddy skirts were bespattered with something that looked like tar and dripped over the hardwood floors. Her coat was a red cut-up, patched blanket, which she'd obviously taken pains to sew to fashion, but she couldn't disguise it entirely.

"My word!" Evelyn whispered, joining me. "A beggar in London House." Then, in a lower voice, "Or do you think she's a gypsy?"

My body felt hollow as I wondered if she were a gypsy, if she'd be connected to Macy. Touching Evelyn's arm for support, I raised my chin and forced a steady voice. "Jameson, what is happening?"

The stench of poverty met my nose as the girl moved and lifted her face. Brown, familiar eyes met mine, though I couldn't place her yet. Then tingles of recognition swept through my body. Her cheeks were so hollow they looked excavated and her nose sharp. The slightest traces of grey tinged her pinched lips. The hand that clutched her patched coat was cadaverous, her nails ragged. It was Nancy, only a starved version of her.

My mouth parted as I wondered how one could deteriorate so much in such a short span.

Evelyn edged closer to me, breaking my trance. The upper staff stared at me in amazement as the color drained from my face.

"Do you know her?" Miss Moray demanded. My eyes fell upon the dirty note clutched in her hand. It was Edward's script on my father's stationery. I reached for the creased and dirty page. Thin, bitter lines formed around Miss Moray's mouth as she reluctantly handed it over with a flick of her wrist.

I pressed Edward's letter against my heart, wishing so badly I could talk over this event with him. How we would have celebrated her arrival.

"Well?" Miss Moray demanded.

I blinked, trying to gather my thoughts. "Well, what?"

She gestured to Nancy. "Her? Do you know her?"

Silence smothered the hall.

Nancy met my eye, her mouth twisted in irritation, before she gave the slightest nudge of her head in the direction of Miss Moray. Instantly I understood her. I wasn't to let such insolence pass.

I smoothed my brow, not caring what Nancy thought.

Nancy tightened her grip on the single bag she carried, glaring for me to address Miss Moray. I laughed because, even in rags, it was still Nancy and as bossy as ever.

Mrs. King and Miss Moray exchanged significant glances as if to suggest I was growing as finespun as Evelyn.

"Yes, yes." I gave Nancy a flippant wave. "This is my personal lady's maid. Mrs. King, take her bags, find her a bedchamber, then show her to mine." I gave Nancy an apologetic look. "She needs a bath. A maid's uniform too." I faced Miss Moray, still clutching Edward's handwriting. "I don't know what arrangement you have worked out with my father, but I'm sure something can be done."

"A mute?" Miss Moray stiffened. "You actually think you're replacing me with a mute beggar just before making court appearances? Have you no idea that history will record what you wear?" She gave a disbelieving, angry laugh. "And you think this . . . this miscreant is your *new* lady's maid?"

Jameson crossed his hands before him and met my gaze, his eyes creasing with mirth, daring me to respond how I truly wished. His expression begged, *Just once, please.*

I resisted a smile by twisting my face in a confused look. I shrugged and spread a hand in Nancy's direction. "What's wrong with her skills?"

Miss Moray looked as though she'd taken a swig of vinegar as she gathered her skirts and minced away. "Your father will hear about this."

I said nothing, for disturbing my father on a day like today could be her own punishment. Mrs. King gaped like a fish, fingering her apron, before managing, "You can't be serious, Mrs. . . ." Her cheeks turned red.

I gave her a warning look, then displayed the note. "As you can see, her services have been retained by my husband, *Reverend Auburn.*"

"Very good." Jameson stepped forward. "Thank you, Mrs. Auburn. We're sorry we disturbed you." Gesturing to Nancy, "This way, Miss . . . ?"

"She's mute!" Mrs. King protested. "There's no point in asking her last name."

Confused why everyone thought Nancy couldn't speak, I questioned her with a glance. The slightest mischievous lift of the right side of her mouth was the only hint I received. She dropped her gaze.

"Kettlefish." I crossed my arms, testing how far I could take this. "Her name is Miss Kettlefish."

Nancy's eyes narrowed.

"Welcome, Miss Kettlefish." Jameson smiled. "I've needed reinforcements in the worst way. Allow me to escort you to your chamber."

As I changed for dinner, Nancy could have been a dumb mute the way her jaw slacked as she sat in the corner working on my mending. Whenever Miss Moray asked her to fetch something, Nancy would lower her needle and thread and tilt her head with a puzzled look, slowly mouthing each word Miss Moray had spoken. Then she'd grin, nodding, and scamper to my wardrobe with all the energy of a dog playing catch.

Miss Moray fairly trembled with anger, becoming more flustered with each passing moment. Whether she had gained an audience with my father, I wasn't certain. Evelyn sat on my bed, seemingly puzzled by Nancy. I demurely went along with Nancy's performance, pretending her behavior was perfectly normal, yet inside, my heart soared. A measure of my old life had returned to me.

"When you finish with your task, take Mrs. Auburn's undergarments downstairs to the launderer." Miss Moray fairly slammed my brush on the vanity. "If you like, you have my permission to take a lemon from the kitchen. It will help remove those unsightly freckles."

I frowned at her meanness. Poor Nancy's face and arms were covered with freckles, but she only stabbed her needle in and out of stockings, blithely unconcerned.

"Would you like to freshen up in the spare bedchamber?" Miss Moray asked Evelyn.

"Would you mind?" Evelyn asked me, rising.

Suspecting she likely hadn't seen a chamber pot in hours, I shook my head. "Not at all. My father isn't joining dinner, so I'll meet you in the front parlor."

With a gentle smile, Evelyn followed Miss Moray from the room. When the door clicked shut, familiarity rushed back to me. Once again it was just Nancy and me.

For a moment neither of us spoke but just stared. Nancy

tossed her mending to the side. Then, acting as if no time had passed, she crossed the room, retrieved the brush, and with long sweeps brushed out my hair.

"I'll set thy hair in curls tonight," she said. "Tomorn, tell Miss Moray thou wants to have thy hair swept up. 'Twill lessen the leanness of thy face. Thou looks wretched."

I twisted to view her. "You should see yourself. I thought you were mute."

"Aye. To all but thee."

"How's that?"

"Think on how my testimony will sound in court. Is that what thou wants?"

Memory of Nancy finding me wearing Mr. Macy's robes, smelling of brandy and cigars, flooded my mind. No, I silently thought, it would be much better to keep her out of the courts.

"I have somewhat to give thee." Her lips compressed, as if she felt doubt, before she bent over and reached high up her skirt, then withdrew a folded, sealed letter. "Thou is suppose to 'liver it to Mr. Forrester."

The seal was a double cameo—featuring two heads of ancient Greeks. A disquiet fell over me, for I'd seen it before.

"Nancy," I whispered, fearing to touch the missive, "where did you get this?"

"Thou knows as well as I do. 'Tis from Mr. Greenham."

"You saw him?" I asked, still not willing to touch the letter.

She confirmed with a nod.

I rubbed my brow, knowing how much trouble it would cause if I tried to deliver this to Mr. Forrester. One part of me considered reading the note, but then again, would Forrester trust its contents if it wasn't sealed?

"Nancy, this is very important. You need to be the one who delivers this to him. Trust me—he won't take it from me, but it might be very important to my court case. Can you do that? Do you know what Mr. Forrester looks like?"

"Aye." Frowning, she slid the letter back across the vanity. "He's the unkempt one, right?"

෴

At nine that evening, yet another retinue trundled up the steps of London House and rang the bell. Evelyn, who'd remained with me into the evening, pricked her finger as she embroidered.

I sat forward, not certain whether I was on the verge of being arrested. "Evelyn, I don't think I can manage this day after day."

"You can." Her command brooked no refusal. She set down her embroidery hoop, then crossed the chamber. She laid her ear on the door and slowly inched it open to peek out. "They're not magistrates," she whispered over her shoulder, then angled her head for a better view. "Three of them are dressed in all black, which . . . Wait, Jameson is leaving them standing there, so he must be fetching your father. I think they're lawyers."

Emboldened by the idea that they weren't here to arrest me, I forsook my chair and joined Evelyn. Four men stood in the hall, but the one in the forefront was clearly the leader. He stood tall and sported a thick mustache. Poised, with his chest thrust out, he bit the earpiece of the spectacles in his hands as he waited. His black robe, which he'd either been too busy to remove or which he wanted others to recognize, labeled him a lawyer. Behind him, the other three men were laden with heavy satchels. Unlike their fearless leader, their expressions were animated with wonder as their gazes roamed about the hall of London House.

My father emerged from the library with Simmons at his heels.

"Pierson." The leader gave him a slight bow but eyed Simmons with a frown. "Where's the girl?"

"Entertaining a friend." My father gestured to the hall that led to the smoking room. "I'll fetch her once we're settled."

"Is it wise to allow visitors?" The man motioned for the

others to follow as he started down the hall. "Young ladies, in my experience, talk far more than they should."

"She's with Isaac's fiancée, a longtime friend of the family . . ." was all I heard before my father turned, making the rest indistinguishable.

"By all means," I whispered, glaring at their retreating backs, "lock me up again. Refuse me any company or friends. Protect yourself at all cost. What need have I for love?"

Evelyn's eyes, though sympathetic, were round with astonishment.

An hour later Simmons opened the door with a glower and informed me that my father wished to see me.

Evelyn stood with me, then, seeing my nervousness, squeezed my arm.

෨

To my surprise, every lamp in the smoking chamber was lit, washing it in light. Golden tones filled each fold of the drapery and tufted every nook of the sofas. The scent of cigars and brandy tickled my nose.

Isaac stood first and the other men followed. As they bowed, I gave them a slight curtsy.

"Daughter." My father stamped out a cigar. He indicated for me to take the seat nearest the desk.

I glanced at Isaac, for something about my father's tone made me wary. Though his face was bland, his eyes cautioned me to prepare myself.

"If you will all excuse Isaac—" my father moved in his direction—"his fiancée, Miss Greenley, is visiting. I'm certain they'd cherish the time alone."

Isaac remained rooted as my father placed a hand on his shoulder and tried to direct him from the chamber. His jaw tightened. "Thank you, sir, but I would prefer to wait until after this meeting to visit Miss Greenley."

I locked eyes with Isaac, giving him a questioning gaze. Thus I failed to see Forrester stick out his foot until I'd tripped over it.

"Upon my word!" Smirking, he jumped from his chair and dug his fingers deep into my arm, hurting me. "Pray, forgive me. I had no idea you weren't looking where you were going. Are you hurt?" He squeezed his fingers tighter.

"You are the most despicable man!" I yanked from his grasp, wondering if Nancy had delivered the letter yet and if this was why he was acting like such a dolt.

Isaac shut his eyes, looking sick for me even as Forrester made a helpless gesture of innocence and making certain the other men noted.

"Are you all right?" my father asked. He was impossible to read.

"I would be," I said, brushing off my skirts and glaring at Forrester, who grinned idiotically, "if it weren't for that buffoon."

Isaac looked so distressed, he had to cover his mouth and turn to remain composed. Next to him, Simmons carefully studied the lawyers. His reaction alerted me to the fact that the men were wearing odd expressions as they scrutinized me.

Swallowing, I took my seat.

My father started to speak, but the mustached man held up his hand and said, "My name is Goodbody. I've summoned you here in order to determine my opinion of you before agreeing to represent you. Are you willing to answer some questions?"

I glanced at Isaac for a hint of how to respond, for I trusted him the most.

He looked tenser than I'd ever seen him—on the verge of rage, even. He heaved a slight breath through his nose, but that didn't give me any indication of how to answer.

"If I don't want to?" I glanced at my father.

He remained stone-faced.

Mr. Goodbody angled his head. "Are you able to tell me with certainty whether or not you are with child?"

I placed my hand over my lower abdomen, surprised I hadn't yet considered that. "I—I don't know."

The three men behind him started writing in their ledgers, and scratching filled the air.

"If you are with child, how many potential fathers are there?"

My mouth dropped in complete shock. Behind the men, Isaac's shoulders heaved as he reared to life, but Simmons grabbed his arm and silently ordered him to remain self-possessed. Isaac's jaw clenched as he crossed his arms.

"Answer the question, please." Mr. Goodbody's eyes remained trained on me.

"One," I said angrily.

Again, scratching filled the air.

"Did you marry Mr. Macy?"

At this question, the three men lifted their gazes as if expecting my facial expression to say more than my words. Biting my lip, I glanced at Forrester. Now was the hour I needed to declare Macy an impostor.

"No," I firmly said.

The men stiffened and threw each other troubled glances. Even Isaac questioned me with his eyes.

"I beg your pardon?" Mr. Goodbody leaned back, adding distance between us. The look he gave my father was significant.

I twined my fingers. "He's not Mr. Macy, so I didn't marry him. I mean, I married Mr. Rainmayer." Seeing that they all stared at me like I was mad, I pointed to Mr. Forrester. "He can confirm what I'm saying. He knows, too."

"Robert?" my father asked.

Forrester was born for the stage, for he stared at me as though he'd never seen me before. His face was a mixture of pity and alarm. "I have no idea what gibberish the girl is speaking."

Pens furiously scratched.

Mr. Goodbody looked at my father as if unable to believe his good luck. Placing his hands on his thighs, he leaned forward. "Would you be willing to testify to that in court?"

I glanced askance at Forrester, who appeared far too glib, then at Isaac, who looked more alive than I'd seen him since the day I married Edward. He seemed ready to pummel through the chamber and pull me out of there.

"Yes," I finally decided. "Provided that you likewise put Mr. Forrester on the stand, place him under oath, and ask him to explain."

Mr. Goodbody didn't even glance at Forrester. He gave an incredulous smile. "Clearly we have a watertight case, Pierson. Do you concur that she's mentally unfit, Hutchinson?"

The man sitting behind him on the right crossed his arms. "Yes, I have not a shred of doubt."

"Are you able to make room for her at your sanitarium tonight?"

"Tonight?" Hutchinson stiffened with alarm. "Well, no, not tonight! I thought this was for assessment purposes only. I need at least a week. I'll have to transfer one of the other patients—and all our patients are amongst the elite, so that's no hasty process, let me assure you."

My ability to move finally broke through my shock. I jumped to my feet and spun accusingly toward my father. "You're going to say that I'm insane!" His impassive face enraged me. "How dare you!"

"Make a note," Goodbody intoned, "that Miss Elliston became crazed toward her father during our interview."

I rounded on him ready to unleash the fury of my full temper, but as I lunged toward him, I found that Isaac had secured my elbow. Without speaking, he dragged me to the corner of the chamber, where we stopped beneath the stuffed head of a white ram. Its empty eyes watched.

"Release me," I ordered, pulling hard against Isaac. Upon

finding him far stronger than he looked, I tried to unbalance him by giving him a quick shove in the opposite direction. His grip remained firm.

"Calm yourself," Isaac commanded in a whisper in my ear. When he backed away, his eyes radiated with a command that I obey him. "It's not helping, but making matters worse."

Tears sprang to my eyes as I glared the accusation that he was a traitor. Nevertheless his advice made sense, so I gave him a nod, showing him I was under control and he could release me.

"Take note—" Mr. Goodbody rose—"Lord Dalry alone can influence and calm her during such an outburst." He started to pace as he wagged his closed spectacles toward the gentlemen. "The marriage was never legal to begin with because she isn't mentally fit. Lord Pierson, seeing that she believes her husband murdered her mother, takes mercy and tries to shield her from the horrors that fill her mind, by providing shelter. Once she's living under his care, he quickly discovers that the meekness of Lord Dalry alone soothes her."

Mr. Goodbody paused, his brow knit in thought. I started to spin toward him to argue, but Isaac squeezed my arm, hard.

"Lord Dalry needs money to maintain his position," Mr. Goodbody continued, no longer noticing me, "and he develops a fondness for her, despite her infirmity. What else are a cash-strapped peer of the realm and a good father to do?" Mr. Goodbody spread his arms as if arguing the case. "Given enough time and a peaceful enough environment, there's hope the girl will recover her full senses. Despite the growing social pressure to see the Emerald Heiress, Lord Pierson limits her social engagements and delays announcing the engagement, just to be safe. But then, alas, the vicar who abandoned her because of her instability learns she's now an heiress and uses the knowledge of her weakness to his advantage."

The urge to scream at my father and Forrester was so

overwhelming that self-restraint was nearly impossible. Tears of utter rage filled my eyes.

Isaac met my gaze and begged me with a look to trust him and not to respond.

I shook my head, not certain whether to trust him or my own reason. For I wanted to give them all a scolding they'd never forget. At the last second, I decided to trust Isaac's opinion on the situation over my own. I turned my face and gripped his sleeve with both hands, not certain I could maintain myself.

"Even now, Dalry alone is able to calm her," Mr. Goodbody continued. He must have turned his head, for his next words were muffled. "If you want, Pierson, we could kill two birds with one stone. Not only does her mental state excuse her from the first marriage, but the fact that she married under the identity of Pierson negates her second marriage. You and Dalry did have a contract beforehand. Colonel Greenley isn't likely to cause a ruckus since you had a prior contract. Dalry can wait until your daughter is declared able-minded again."

I stiffened with suspicion. Isaac stopped breathing.

With desperation, I felt the jaws of the trap I'd finally managed to escape closing in on me again. The defense they were building fit the circumstances perfectly.

"I won't do it," I said through gritted teeth and looked at Goodbody. "We both know that I'm not insane, and I won't let you say I am for a legal defense."

"My dear girl, sitting from my position, you are the very definition of insanity. Members of your father's staff are prepared to testify they've overheard you pretending to be a faerie queen. No sane person marries someone she's known less than a week, runs away from her new husband, lies to her father to gain protection, engages herself to a peer of the realm, and then does an about-face and marries the first man she ran away with. It's self-evident that you're mentally inferior. You've made your bed; welcome to it."

"Isaac." My father stepped away from the tufted sofa he'd been standing near and headed toward the door. "Would you please remove Julia? You're welcome to come back and join us afterwards, if you wish."

Though Isaac urged me to move with a touch at my elbow, I remained where I was until my father had fully opened the door and looked in my direction to see why I hadn't obeyed.

I locked eyes with him so he'd know at least one person in the chamber saw straight through him. I waited until guilt flushed his cheeks before squaring my shoulders and leaving.

I refused to acknowledge Isaac as I stormed down the hall. The library door was open, so as I neared it, Mama's sunflower painting beckoned to me. Abruptly I turned and tore through the chamber. My father didn't deserve her painting.

Placing my hands on either side of the frame, I tried to tug it from the wall, but it didn't budge as if it were glued. I tried to shove the frame upwards in case it was caught on a nail, but it remained stuck. Screaming, I struck the wall with my fist.

I turned, ready to shove past Isaac, but the look on his face froze my blood.

His expression was a knife blow to my soul, for he wore such a look of deep grief that panic pricked my body. The only explanation I could come up with was that he truly thought me insane.

I realized how limited my options were, for I was not yet a *femme sole*, and therefore I was still under someone's legal protection. Edward was imprisoned, Macy I feared, and my father planned to have me committed to an insane asylum as his legal defense.

That left only Isaac to help me.

Here is what I have since come to understand: *failure* was not a word Isaac allowed within his psyche. Not because of his great abilities, but because early in his life fear and shame had tightly coiled around him and demanded perfection. And so rare of soul was Isaac that he'd actually managed to walk that path almost flawlessly, becoming a man worthy of regard. But no person can continue down a wrong path indefinitely without flagging. With me, however, Isaac had miscalculated. Errors were deeply painful for him, which was why he took great pains never to have them. But for him to fail *and* injure the person he'd strained himself to protect—that failure contained the means of ruining him.

Much like that night in the woods at Am Meer when I tasted Edward's rejection, something had finally rent through Isaac's carefully constructed walls. When stuck forced to choose between two evils, he started to unravel. His worldview didn't allow him to embrace a wrong choice—ever.

Such is life and such are our limited views, that I injured him further. As Isaac was disintegrating, I believed that he lost sight of who I was. I believed he grieved because, like the barristers, he thought me feebleminded. And that, in turn, deconstructed me. Unwittingly, I doubled his pain and gave him an insupportable burden.

"Don't," I begged, my knees buckling as I sank to the ground. "If you don't aid me, then I'm truly trapped." My words came out garbled. Panic rose as I envisioned the unfolding horror. "They're going to lock me up, and if you do not stop my father, who will?" I buried my face in my hands. "Please, Isaac, I'm begging you! Believe me! Help me! I am not mad; I swear it!"

"What on earth?" Evelyn's soft voice carried from the threshold.

Isaac turned his face from her, preventing her from seeing him undone.

Evelyn rushed to me, her feet pattering over the floor. As she knelt and gathered me in her frail arms, the scent of apples filled my senses. "It's going to be all right," she assured me. "Whatever it is, it will work out fine." Then to Isaac, her face white, "What happened?"

"My father is telling the court I'm unbalanced." I clutched

the sleeves of her dress. "He wants to send me to an asylum as proof."

Evelyn stared at me, horrified, before her hand tightened on my arm. Pale, she faced Isaac. "But you're not allowing it, are you?"

The pain in Isaac's eyes was unbearable. With great effort, he finally mastered his voice. "What other defense has a chance? What else can we possibly say?" Then to me, "As heartbreaking as this feels to you, would you rather go to Macy?"

"What about the truth?" I begged Edward's mantra. "What about the fact the marriage remains unconsummated? Surely that carries as much weight!"

Isaac placed his forehead in the heels of his hands. "I argued that! I did. The problem is that the defense is too flimsy. The public already believes there were improprieties before the wedding. And where do you think juries are pulled from? Jurors' minds are made up well in advance. Your case will be argued in the span of minutes, and we cannot risk trying to change something already entrenched in their minds. Furthermore, after the marriage, you spent hours alone with Macy—once when gypsies accosted Forrester and again on the night Eramus was murdered. There are witnesses willing to say you were carried into London House wearing nothing but Macy's dressing robes."

Clearly this was all news to Evelyn, for her eyes widened and she tried to appear unflappable while discussing carnal knowledge and murder. Her cheeks, however, took on a red hue.

I shook my head. It seemed impossible that anyone would believe the truth.

"You can't let them label her as being unsound." Evelyn's voice was like a slender thread of hope. "Isaac, as a gentleman, you cannot allow that."

"Do you think I have a choice? Do you think I desire to see Julia carted away to a madhouse? But what is two months living amongst lunatics compared to being handed over to Macy for life? I won't interfere with Pierson's plans." His voice came out pained. "I dare not."

"You're not condemning her to two months. This is a life sentence." Evelyn's voice blazed with anger. "I've lived it, Isaac. And it's wrong. I know what will happen. People will always treat her differently afterwards, and that will affect the way she feels about herself. Look and see for yourself. The evidence is right before your eyes. Even the idea that those men think she's unstable is making her unstable. Imagine this lie told to the world. She'll never go anywhere without feeling the stares of people upon her, judging her as mentally unfit. Who can act normal under those circumstances? How will she ever escape it when her nervous reactions will make her look abnormal? The way we treat people determines what they become." Tears filled Evelyn's eyes. "I know. It happened to me."

Her confession surprised us, for both Isaac and I shifted with discomfort.

Evelyn sensed it too, for she gave a slight sigh and braced her shoulders as she waited for us to move past our embarrassment, step over her vulnerability, and see her as our equal again. Through that one observation, I glimpsed the reality of what my future would become if I lost credibility in the eyes of others. Somehow I doubted I'd endure being seen as inferior with the same grace Evelyn did.

"I won't do it," I whispered. "I won't."

"What can you possibly expect me to do?" Isaac asked, sounding desperate. "Under no circumstances am I risking Julia's returning to Macy. And even if I supported the idea of arguing that the marriage wasn't consummated, how do you expect me to convince Lord Pierson to take that gamble? His fortune is at stake. He's not going to switch to a defense that's weak when he has a rock-solid one. He won't. I'm telling you. What do you possibly think I can do? My hands are tied."

Evelyn lifted her chin. "There must be something you overlooked."

"Tell me, then," Isaac demanded, his voice low.

"I don't know, but look at her," Evelyn rejoined. "Can you honestly claim she'll survive this? Find a solution. Just find one, somehow."

Whether he studied me or not, I cannot say, as I'd buried my eyes in my hands. For I already knew what I needed to do. Only the idea was so hateful, I needed to retreat deeper within myself, just to find strength to think it.

Twenty-Three

⬧

I THOUGHT I understood isolation.

Had I not grown up in a house where I knew how to make myself unseen and small? As a young girl, when I wandered through the market stalls, had not the villagers given us their backs? Had I not been alone after Mama's death with desperation and loneliness as my only companions? Had I not learned to survive Maplecroft's dead halls and empty chambers?

Nonetheless, the three days that followed were nothing short of harrowing.

My thoughts were painful. Each idea was a blazing-hot coal that needed to be handled in order to organize it. Only it was excruciatingly painful to hold the ideas up long enough to fully examine them. If I questioned whether to flee London House, I had to conquer the panic that I had nowhere else to go. And if I could ignore that, I had to endure the searing knowledge that my father would actually sacrifice me. And just brushing against that idea was like falling into an ocean where I was knocked under by pounding waves of grief.

Because I didn't wish to heed my father's plan, the only logical choice was to hie to Macy.

That was its own brazier of blistering coals, starting with Edward. Would he think it a betrayal? If so, could he survive that? Was it better to live with a father who cared more for himself than me, or to take refuge with Mama's murderer, who at least regarded me?

I refused to speak to anyone during that time. In the mornings I allowed Nancy to dress me. I joined the breakfasts, where I struggled to keep awake, for the toll of emotions were more wearying than labor. From there I retreated into a drawing room, where I'd curl into a large chair and pull a blanket over me.

Jameson tried the hardest. He reminded me of the herd. He attempted to make me laugh, and when that failed, he sat for hours in complete silence, wearing a look of heartfelt sympathy. I noted him but took care never to let him know. I preferred him thinking me catatonic. I feared speaking, for I might tell him what I was planning, and he might try to talk me out of turning myself over to Mr. Macy.

Isaac wasn't himself either. His normally placid features stayed cramped, plagued by his own heavy thoughts. And though he also joined us each morning at the table, he barely skimmed the articles and excused himself as quickly as possible. I learned later that he filled those hours by combing my father's library. He read and took notes for hours on end, often shoving the table in frustration or standing, arms crossed, with a dissatisfied expression as he looked over the street.

The only good thing that came to pass was that Forrester abruptly decided to leave without any explanation. My father was livid that he'd leave at such a crucial time. Forrester, however, was adamant he had to leave immediately, only saying that Isaac shouldn't marry until he'd sent further word.

❧

"What is this?" My father slammed down the first newspaper in front of Isaac, his face enraged. "What the devil is this!"

I cringed and shrank back in my seat, jolted by the sudden noise. My breath quickening, I glanced toward the door, debating whether I should flee to Macy then and there, before anything worse happened. Only my legs wouldn't move, as if my own body rejected the notion.

Isaac's gaze pivoted on me for the first time in days. His eyes bespoke that I remain calm. Then he shook out his napkin unhurriedly, though the jut of his jaw showed stubbornness. "I take it they printed my letter to Mr. Macy, then?"

My father gave an inarticulate scream as he swiped his place setting to the floor.

I jumped, covering my ears.

"How could you not have consulted me?" My father stood and fisted the tablecloth, bending forward. "Have you any idea the damage you've just caused?" My father's mouth trembled, but whether from tears, anger, or both was impossible to say. "I won't allow it! I won't!" He pounded the table with his fist.

Isaac never changed expression, though he wrapped his fingers about his teacup as if seeking warmth and comfort there. "I'm sorry, sir, but I don't think you have a choice."

With both hands, my father wrenched the cloth from the table. Dishes crashed to his feet in a mighty clatter before he kicked them and stomped from the chamber.

Isaac said nothing but kept his blue eyes trained on me. His skin was the palest I'd ever seen it. "Forgive me, Julia, for having done this without consulting you, but Evelyn is right. It would have been the breaking of you."

Jameson retrieved the paper from amongst the porcelain shards and set it before me.

I gave Isaac a questioning look, then opened the newspaper.

Isaac had sent a letter to all the papers, expressing his desire for a compromise with Mr. Macy. In his clear, precise style, he argued how the neutrality of his position, plus his privileged knowledge of me, gave him the clearest vision. He toppled the debate of who should represent me in an unexpected manner. He stated that, given the circumstances, he could see Mr. Macy's point and agree. Isaac called for a truce, arguing that without acknowledging Mr. Macy as my legal husband, an agreement could easily be reached by allowing Macy to pay for my legal defense, with a concession that Isaac alone would pick the barrister to represent me. He gave the name of one whom he trusted, but who was wholly unconnected with the case and with either party. Isaac publicly proclaimed that it would greatly reduce the stress on me, as I feared Mr. Macy but trusted Isaac. And it would relieve Mr. Macy's mind, who believed my father was poisoning me against him.

"I don't understand," I finally said.

"She's not been following the papers," Jameson said softly behind me. Then to me, "For the last couple of days, lass, Macy has declared his right to choose your legal counsel, as he's your husband. The papers have been abuzz with the argument. He claims your father's learned counsel is being too harsh in their care of you, pressuring you to change your testimony. Your father denies it, but Macy claims a sympathetic staff member has secretly come and told him you're growing fragile beneath the strain your father is placing on you."

My heart hammered as I stared at the black-and-white print. How on earth had Macy known that I was shattering? The only servants I recalled seeing were Jameson and Nancy. But then again, I hadn't exactly been paying attention.

I couldn't even speak as I looked to Isaac. Unable to help it, I confirmed, "Then you don't think me mad?"

Isaac rubbed his temples. "Oh, at this point, I think we're all mad as hatters."

Still in disbelief, I stared at the paper in my hands. "Have we any chance of winning? I mean, without the argument my father planned to use?"

Isaac's expression filled me with gravity, but he remained silent.

It was impossible to feel fear, however. For I had just been redeemed from one of the darkest pits. Like a man unexpectedly pulled out of the Bastille, I was more amazed at the glimpse of the stars than I was concerned about how to finish the escape plan. I hadn't realized how badly I wanted a chance—even an impossible one.

I clutched the paper against my chest, savoring the respite.

"With your permission, Lord Dalry, I'd like to inquire what Mrs. Auburn was thinking during the past few days," Jameson said slowly, moving back to the buffet, where he could see me. "When Edward learned you'd stopped speaking, he ordered me to keep two eyes on you at all times."

"You've seen Edward?" I faced him, hungry for news.

Jameson only frowned. "Yes, and he worried that your refusal to speak was a sign you were about to do something bullheaded and contrary." He crossed his arms. "Did the boy guess right?"

When he wished to be, Jameson could be austere. In return, I felt contrary. "Yes. If it came down to a choice between being imprisoned in a lunatic asylum or fleeing to Macy, I was going to Macy."

Both Jameson and Isaac recoiled, but for different reasons.

"Balderdash!" Jameson swung an outraged hand in the air. "Who fed you that bold lie! No one would dare send you to a place like that!" He gestured to Isaac. "Tell her!"

Isaac stared at me, aghast. "How could you even consider that? That man murdered your mother."

I felt the cords of my throat tighten as I pointed in the direction of the library. "Make no mistake; if my father would commit me into such a place, then I would do whatever is necessary to survive. *Whatever* is necessary."

Neither Jameson nor Isaac responded for a long moment. Whether my words awoke in them pity, awareness, or shame, I could not tell. It was Isaac who spoke first. "Promise me this, then. From now on, allow me to handle these matters."

I swallowed. "I can't promise. If someone comes to cart me away, I will do what I must."

"No one—" Jameson's voice shook with anger—"will take you anywhere."

Isaac held up his hands. "If I give you my troth that nothing like that will happen to you, can I get your agreement?"

I gritted my teeth but nodded.

⁓

One blessing flowed after another that day. A joyous Evelyn Greenley showed up within an hour. Apparently visitors had been prohibited from London House, preventing any chance of my father's defense being damaged. Evelyn's cheeks radiated with a pink glow as she flew across the chamber. Laughing, she ran to Isaac first and embraced him. Her skirt swished to one side as she took a step back. "I knew you would find a way!" She clapped her hands. "I just knew it! Ben would be so proud. He would! Thank you, oh, thank you!"

Isaac looked pained but gave her a slight bow.

Then, spinning and greeting me as enthusiastically, Evelyn joined me on the settee. "I can see you've suffered. How I wish I'd been allowed to be here with you, but it's over now. I won't leave you at all today. I've brought my sewing and cancelled all visits."

I felt my mouth twist into a queer smile, for allowing someone back into my life—after having shut everyone out again—was still exceedingly painful. Yet I also knew that Evelyn had played a part in helping to save me too.

Tears blurred my eyes as I decided to accept her, without walls, without defenses, to just admit I was weak too. Her fingers were long and pale compared to mine as I slipped my hand in hers. "Thank you." My voice came out soft and small. "I needed someone today."

Isaac stilled as his keen gaze fastened on us. Though his face wore no expression, his ebullient eyes were alive with an emotion I could not name.

~

That night during dinner, the bell jangled, splintering my world anew.

Twisting my napkin beneath the table, I eyed the three doors, planning which one to take if necessary. My father threw his napkin on his plate. "What the deuce now? James, answer it!" He glowered in Isaac's direction. "Are you expecting anyone?"

Isaac collected his wineglass. "No. No one."

Rain pattered against the leaded panes as I strained my ears to hear the exchange in the hall. I surmised it wasn't more magistrates, for their tones had been quite harsh. I wondered if Mr. Goodbody might have shown up, demanding to know what had happened to his case. I inched forward in my seat just in case it might be that man Hutchinson from the asylum.

A moment later James returned with a young man wearing silver spectacles. Friendly brown eyes met mine as his full lips curved in a smile. He wore side-whiskers that came halfway down his cheeks, though they didn't suit him. Thick, damp hair graced his head instead of a hat. He wore a half cape, under which was a layered cravat. The bit of frock coat that peeked through had a rolled silk collar—the combined effect made him appear top-heavy. In his hands he carried a satchel, and beneath his arms he had rolled papers that were the size of blueprints or maps. They were wrapped in waxed paper and beaded with water.

"Whitney!" Isaac found his feet. "My word, but I'm heartened to see you!"

Mr. Whitney bowed, his smile growing. "Dalry! Not as glad as I am to be alive to see you. I've had quite an adventure today. Though you shall learn more about that in a moment. What was the idea with the paper this morning?"

My father steepled his fingers. "Mr. Cudney Whitney, barrister at law, I presume." His tone was nearly guttural. "So I take it that Isaac didn't inform you of his stunt, either?"

"Both your assumptions are correct. No, I had not a clue what was coming. You should have seen the Inner Temple. The senior members were running about each other's offices aghast." Mr. Whitney bowed to my father, setting his travelling case on an empty chair. He then removed the rolled papers from beneath his arm and added them to the growing pile. "I take it I am finally standing in the presence of Lord Pierson? I do hope the stories about you *and* your famous temper turn out to be true." He smiled politely as he unbuttoned the top of his cape. "You were a legend amongst us boys at Eton, you know."

My father glared in Isaac's direction.

Mr. Whitney's fingers started on his scarf, which had been knotted in a helical fashion. "Oh no, not Isaac, sir. Ben told all the tales."

My father dug a finger into his cheek and glared at Mr. Whitney with a look of intense dislike.

With a grin, Mr. Whitney shrugged off his cape as he addressed Isaac. "And here I thought Ben exaggerated."

Isaac stood and gestured to an empty spot. "Will you join us?"

Mr. Whitney turned his smiling face in my direction and bowed. "I will if my client gives me leave."

"Client?" My father frowned. "I don't recall hiring you for the representation of my daughter."

"Well, that's an interesting story, actually." Mr. Whitney deposited his cape over the back of a chair, then tugged on the fingers of his gloves. "This morning after my name was discovered in Dalry's appeal, and right about the same hour the senior bar members were all demanding answers as to what I was about being publicly named in this case, four men arrived—brawny ones, I might add."

My father drummed his free hand on the arm of his chair.

"Shoulders of at least the width of two men." Mr. Whitney spread his hands as if to demonstrate. "There were no cards, no introductions, just the simple statement that Macy wished an audience with me. Before I could object, I was blindfolded and forcibly shoved into a carriage." Candlelight cast a sheen over his spectacles as he looked at me. "Do I have your permission to sit?"

I gave a slight nod, feeling my father's wrath turn in my direction.

Jameson pulled out a chair, while William poured the newcomer wine.

"Thank you, my good man." Mr. Whitney swirled the glass beneath his nose, inhaling. Then to Jameson, "Would you mind fetching me pen and ink too? I must begin working straightaway."

"During dinner?" My father's eyes narrowed.

"Quite right. Now where was I? Ah, yes!" He faced Isaac. "The next thing I know, I'm dragged through some blowsy tavern and pushed upstairs, where I finally meet the infamous Mr. Macy." He paused so William could set his plate and glasses. A desk mat, inkwell, and pen were also set before him, provided by Jameson. Mr. Whitney divested his waistcoat of a small packet of cigarette papers. "I don't smoke," he explained, "but I find these sheets most useful." He opened his bag, consulted a sheet of paper, scrawled a new note of several lines, then pulled out a second sheet and scrawled several more lines. He handed the first one to Jameson. "I'll need these books fetched from Lord Pierson's library. Bring them immediately, please."

My father seemed both fascinated and rebuffed. "And what makes you think I own those particular books?"

"Oh, Mr. Macy was quite thorough." Mr. Whitney pinched the tip of his nose as if to satisfy an itch. "He had a list of your books—kept track of them in a rather thick ledger, as a matter of fact. He also had made a list of books he found your library to be lacking. He wants his wife well represented—"

"His wife?" Isaac asked.

Mr. Whitney gave a soft smile. "Ah, yes, there are rather odd contingencies. One being that while in London House, I must refer to my client as his wife, though I have permission to call her Mrs. Auburn if she wishes it."

My father looked dumbstruck as he shook his head.

Before he could ask, Mr. Whitney supplied, "He feels it will help her adjust, as he is most confident you shall lose." Mr. Whitney looked directly at me. "But I always win my cases, and even though your *husband* is paying my bills, I consider myself to be working solely for you. This promises to be the trial! Likely it will define my career, so you can feel free to trust that I shall do my best to win, or at the very least, to tie it up in court indefinitely." Before anyone could speak, Mr. Whitney handed the second list to Jameson, directing him to hand it to Lord Pierson. "These are the books Mr. Macy suggests you buy to best help prove that Mrs. Auburn is not married to him." He grinned at Isaac. "All my ethics training went straight out the window today."

"Jameson, go see if the books on that first list are all in my library," my father ordered. Then to Mr. Whitney, "How the deuce would he know what's there?"

Mr. Whitney pulled a book from his bag and opened it. "Your guess is likely to be better than mine."

"And tell me why I would buy the books he recommends?"

Mr. Whitney peered over the top of his spectacles. "Would it not make sense for me to know the arguments he's already prepared to combat, rather than go in blindly planning my entire defense without them? At least he's had the decency to share his groundwork."

I picked up my wine goblet and turned my attention on Isaac. For the first time in days, he looked unburdened. He leaned back in his chair with an air of relief.

"Now then," Mr. Whitney said, smiling at my father and opening a ledger. "If you're willing, Lord Pierson, I'd like to hear your arguments. Mind, though, that our conversation will likely be repeated to Macy. Your daughter and I shall need to meet privately, of course." He glanced at Isaac, his mouth pursed. "Mr. Macy has suggested we use your snuggery, though he cautions that you'll need to cover the floor vent to keep the servants belowstairs from hearing."

"How could he possibly know about that?" Isaac asked.

Mr. Whitney gave a mild shrug. I looked at the chair Mr. Forrester usually occupied, glad he wasn't here to conjecture his theory.

My father sat back and crossed his arms, looking dismayed. "How—?" Cutting himself off, he stood. "We need to check every chamber, talk to every staff member."

Mr. Whitney's nose wrinkled. "Why are we doing that when we have so little time?"

"Isn't it obvious?" my father snapped.

"Not to me. Not when Macy has already told me which rooms to avoid when I want privacy with my client." Mr. Whitney straightened, looking to Isaac to explain it.

My father gripped the back of his chair, leaning forward. "And you trust him?" He spoke very slowly. "The man who has just proven himself unethical by admitting there are chambers in my own home where I can't have a private conversation?"

"Given the circumstances," Mr. Whitney asked as though also stating the obvious, "why wouldn't I?"

Half-smiling, Isaac leaned forward. "I fear I don't follow your thought process either, Whitney."

Mr. Whitney paused and stared as if finding it extraordinary they hadn't already bridged this idea. He looked at me. "But you understand, yes, Mrs. Auburn?"

I felt my father's displeasure that I'd been invited to speak, making me feel like a mouse charged with addressing a party of cats. I clenched my skirts. "I agree we should take the advice, though I couldn't tell you why."

"Intuitive. Good." He nodded approval. "We shall make a good team." He smiled. "That is, if you agree that I may represent you."

I gave a slight nod, as it felt right.

"Well. That's at least officially settled." He turned to Isaac. "As far as saving time by simply following Mr. Macy's instructions, it's just logical. Obviously he intends to show us his dominance and cause consternation. It would scarcely suit his purposes if his information proved faulty. What he meant to put us in a dither now simply can give us peace of mind. After we win the trial, we'll have to remember to send him thank-you notes."

Isaac's laugh was golden.

Even my father loosened and considered the list. "Fine. I'll buy the books. Use Isaac's snuggery."

Mr. Whitney again looked in my direction and nodded at me as if to say this was going much better than he'd hoped.

All at once I realized this was *my* barrister! Not Merrick nor Goodbody! A sense of relief filled me as Jameson returned with a pile of books. Mr. Whitney pointed to where he wanted them.

I sank back in my chair, stunned at how much better I felt, for he instilled confidence. Mr. Whitney had somehow managed to hurdle both Macy and my father—each an impossible feat by itself. Stunned, I looked over the books and papers spread about him. Not only that, he'd managed to intrude upon one of Lord

Pierson's impenetrable dinners as naturally as if he were dropping in for tea with his grandmother. Surely here was a prayer answered!

Swallowing, I looked toward Isaac, showing my gratitude and my apology.

A slight smile graced his lips as he raised his glass.

Twenty-Four

❦

AFTER DINNER, Isaac, Mr. Whitney, and I stood when my father did. He threw his napkin on his chair and stared angrily at Isaac for a long moment before stalking from the room.

Mr. Whitney gave a low whistle. "I say, that was rather loving, wasn't it?"

Isaac couldn't have looked more urbane as he acknowledged Mr. Whitney with a look that suggested he didn't know the half of it. "Jameson," Isaac said softly, "would you be so kind as to show Julia to my snuggery? I'd like to give Whitney a quick tour of London House."

Mr. Whitney started to gather his notes. "There's no need for that. I'd rather—"

Isaac spun toward him. His voice came out sharper. "The house is at your disposal, and you're going to need to know your way around. Allow me to show you the shortcuts to the library, if nothing else."

Mr. Whitney's brown eyes rolled in my direction for a second before he slowly said, "All right. That is, if my client agrees. After all, I'm being paid rather handsomely for my time."

Isaac loosened and turned my way. "Would you mind?"

It was obvious Isaac wished to speak to Whitney alone, and it was insulting to me that he didn't simply say so. Had it not been Isaac, and had he not gone out of his way to aid me, I'm not sure I would have been gracious. I drew a deep breath, wondering if this was how everyone had previously treated Evelyn.

"I'll meet you there," I said.

Jameson led me past the smoking chamber and down a passage I'd not yet explored. I touched the walls, remembering how Kate said she used Isaac's snuggery during the day. I hadn't even asked to see it. I sighed, realizing what little attention I had given Isaac during those long months.

When I reached the snuggery, I was amazed that Isaac had allowed me unhindered access to his private haven. For it would have been less intimate had I explored Isaac's bedchamber. I'd seen that chamber daily as I passed it in the hall. Neat, orderly, nothing ever out of place. Apart from the occasional book on his nightstand, it was nearly devoid of personal effects.

This room was different.

The scent of Isaac, a blending of his soap and musk, filled the chamber. I turned my mouth downward, surprised to find his smell brought comfort. It brought back memories of dancing in ballrooms, reading books late into the night, and the hours he'd painstakingly taught me how to walk, address fellow peers, even bow to the queen.

Acute pain washed over me.

I realized I'd not yet dealt with the grief of our prior relationship, and that being inside this room was forcing me to confront it.

A lamp, which had been keyed low, spread a weak light through the chamber. Two high-back chairs upholstered in faded material faced a hearth, but the room was so small, they barely managed to fit. I gave a laugh of disbelief. Why on earth would Isaac choose such a tiny, cramped space when he could have asked for any room in London House? Surely my father would have accommodated him with any furnishings that he wanted as well.

A stack of etiquette books for the young man were piled on his desk, found immediately on my left. I ran my finger down their spines, realizing the extent of Isaac's hardship. He must have had to make one hard choice after another since our arrival. The fact that he'd nearly vanished once he saw that Edward and my father were getting along fine only bespoke his integrity and character.

Without intending to, my eyes took in the other books on a shelf above the desk. Theology. History. Latin. Economics. Papers sat upon the desk with handwriting so tight it was scarcely legible. On the wall next to the shelves were miniatures in gilded circles. They were of his mother, Kate, and . . .

I leaned forward, gaining my first view of Ben. How could I not laugh at the bizarreness of it? There was no other way to describe this except to say it was akin to seeing Isaac's face lit up with Henry's personality. The easygoing and amused expression in the portrait did not suit Isaac's seriousness. Yet . . . there it was.

I bit my lip, wondering if I'd finally figured out how Lady Josephine had surprised Isaac with that fore-edge painting. Perhaps Ben had been the model. It could even explain why the monster looked so much like the ancient oak. Perhaps that's where Ben posed, in order to keep it a surprise. Fascinated, I removed Ben's miniature from the wall and touched his visage with my fingertip. Perhaps this was Isaac as he was born to be— carefree and happy.

I replaced it, knowing it was folly to even dwell upon it. This wasn't my business.

Shutting out my thoughts, I forced my dress to squeeze

between the chairs and took a seat to wait. I closed my eyes and gave myself permission to ache a bit.

Within a quarter hour, the pleasant voices of Mr. Whitney and Isaac approached the door. They sounded as two old friends ought—each comfortable with the other. Isaac entered first, his expression giving no hint to his thoughts as he paused to study me sitting in his snuggery. "Here, let me clear my desk for your things," he said over his shoulder, then stepped aside.

Whatever Isaac had said privately to Mr. Whitney had not changed his demeanor. He watched me with an expression of respect as he set his satchel on the floor and untucked the rolled papers from beneath his arm. "My word," he said, eyeing the low ceiling. "Perhaps we should meet in the cupboard in my chambers, as it might be less cramped." He grinned at me. "Perhaps it's the real reason why—" he leaned in the direction of the floor vent and in a loud voice said—"*your husband* suggested we meet here. So we're too packed together to plan a real defense." Then, tugging on his collar, he looked at Isaac. "It's stuffy too."

Isaac shrugged off his frock coat and piled it over the floor vent, then waved for Mr. Whitney to give him his.

"Better," Mr. Whitney said, loosening his cravat.

Next Isaac piled some of the books on top of the coats. "Think that's thick enough?"

Mr. Whitney chuckled. "This certainly promises to be one of the most interesting cases of my life. Who even conceives of taking such measures? I'm beginning to pity the poor devil. Mr. Macy's mind must never rest. How do you suppose he manages to sleep?"

My stomach dropped as I considered the ease with which Macy had interacted with me while we were in Eastbourne.

"Pick a servant whom you both agree you can trust," Mr. Whitney said after a moment's consideration. "We'll keep the coats there and give orders that no other staff member is allowed near the other end of that vent. We'll ask that servant to guard it and make certain no one is tempted to eavesdrop. I need to know that what Mrs. Auburn confides in me isn't heard by anyone without scruples."

"Jameson," I said quickly. "I trust only him."

"I was thinking James," Isaac said.

I shook my head. "Macy has told me that more than one servant here is loyal to him. Jameson served my husband and came with me. I trust him alone."

Mr. Whitney eyed Isaac.

"Someone said they were willing to testify that you pretend you're a faerie queen," Isaac said softly. "What servant except Jameson could say that? That's why I want James."

Mr. Whitney's eyes widened, though he tried to hide it.

My cheeks burned but I didn't address it, for trying to explain would make me sound nervous and more deranged. "I don't care. It wasn't Jameson. I'm certain of it. I only want him there."

"Jameson it is, then," Mr. Whitney said before Isaac could speak. Then, with a friendly smile, "This is her case. It's her decision."

Something unspoken passed between them. For Mr. Whitney's part, he seemed to be asking what on earth Isaac thought he was about. It sobered Isaac too, for he ducked his head. "Of course. I'll go find Jameson and ask if he'll sit beneath the vent and guard it for us."

Mr. Whitney's laugh was musical, infectious even. "They're never going to believe this at the Inner Temple." When alone with me, Mr. Whitney opened the middle drawer of Isaac's desk and began to search for a pen. "While he's gone, I need you to carefully review every secret you've been guarding. It is to your own detriment to hide even one, whether it seems important or not." He selected an ebony pen and studied its tip. "The law is my expertise. I am not here to judge you. It doesn't matter to me what you've done or haven't done. As far as you are concerned, I am your priest, your diary, and your dearest friend combined.

Truth alone aids you. Not Isaac. Not Reverend Auburn. Not your father." He looked at me to make sure I understood the gravity. "As far as England is concerned, you're a bigamist. Open-and-shut case. I sense, however, there is a much bigger picture behind the scenes." He arched his brows, waiting for a response.

I gave a nod.

He angled the chair at the desk so he could view me, then set out an inkwell and his pen. He gestured to them and then to the fire. "So is there anything you would like to tell me while Isaac isn't here and Jameson might not yet be listening?"

I froze, understanding him. Though I tried to look nonchalant, I felt my chest begin to rise and fall as I considered communicating the impossible.

"Think carefully," Mr. Whitney said. "I need to know if you're hiding anything *at all*."

I made my decision in the blink of an eye and acted on it before I could change my mind. Rising, I leaned over the arm of the chair, picked up the pen, and dipped it in the inkwell.

Macy is Adolphus, I scrawled, my heart racing faster. *He is also an impostor—a gypsy named Rainmayer. No proof. No one else will testify.*

Mr. Whitney understood the solemnity of accusing Macy of being Adolphus, for he stared at that word the longest before giving me a look of mute astonishment. I can only imagine how terrifying that prospect must have been to him. That week alone, a magistrate investigating a crime connected to that name had disappeared, and the prostitute he'd questioned just prior underwent a gruesome murder. The grisly way her corpse had been altered served as warning to London's underworld about double-crossing Macy's crime syndicate.

"He murdered my mother," I said softly. "I know he did."

"Hmm," was Mr. Whitney's reply before he picked up an entire stack of papers and threw them on the coals. His eyes were troubled as he retook his seat at the desk.

Over the next five hours, I learned why Mr. Whitney carried such long rolls of paper. He questioned every aspect of my life. To say that he was thorough is an understatement. He tacked one end of the paper near the doorway, and then, because Isaac's snuggery was so small, he unrolled the paper around the corner where he tacked the other end. He started with my birth. Who was present. Who witnessed it. Who visited Mama afterwards, as if I knew. Which parish book and which registry the birth was recorded in. Was I certain? Would the vicar be willing to testify I was that child? Could I have been switched at birth?

He asked about my stepfather's church attendance—and then he ordered every one of William's books and pamphlets either to be fetched from the library or to be added to the list of books he needed. He moved to Mama's church attendance, and then mine. Was I certain I was baptized? Could Sarah have lied about that point? Was I certain the vicar had truly taken orders? Was there proof he had?

He questioned every aspect of my relationship with Edward. When had we first met? Shared our first kiss? Declared our love? How many times exactly had we played together as children? How many times exactly after the age of twelve? When had we become engaged—and I needed to be more exact on the date; it was important. How many letters had passed between us? How many secret messages through Elizabeth, then?

Each subject had a different-colored thread and a matching push tack. Using his cigarette papers, Mr. Whitney would jot down every fact and add it to the timeline. He chose blue for Edward's and my relationship. Long after he'd finished questions about us and moved on to Lady Foxmore, I noticed that Isaac's eyes trailed down the blue track over and again. His eyes would fixate on certain points and he'd grow thoughtful, likely filling out his own story. For example, I know now that Edward and I had become engaged around the same time Lady Josephine gave him his eighteenth birthday present. How strange it must have felt to sit there and know that as he made pledges to find and marry me, I was betrothing myself to another. To my chagrin, when we charted my time with Isaac, he alone knew the exact dates we'd met, made our first public appearances, kissed, and the date of our engagement contract.

Once Mr. Whitney had my life charted, he stood back and examined it with his hands on his hips. The back of his shirt was soaked as he stared, waiting to see if there were any other questions he could ask.

I eyed Isaac's timeline, realizing his was the shortest one in my life. Even Macy's stretched longer than his did. Sadness filled me as I suspected that if Whitney charted Isaac's life, I would have been present in his thoughts throughout most of it because of Lady Josephine's scheming.

"Hmm," was Mr. Whitney's conclusion once he'd stared at his completed timeline for a solid half hour. He drew a deep breath. "I need to think, but my thoughts are sluggish."

Isaac chuckled and glanced at the clock. "No wonder. It's past three in the morning."

Mr. Whitney turned and gazed at the clock and made a noise of disgust, then ran his fingers through his hair. "It can't be that late! We haven't accomplished everything I needed to cover today. We only have until July before the courts are in session again."

"We'll get more accomplished if we sleep, then tackle it in the morning." Isaac rubbed his eyes. "We can't keep going like this."

Mr. Whitney frowned, walking along my timeline. He touched various tacks and papers, deep in thought. "Mrs. Auburn, can you tell me what Goodbody was preparing for the case?"

I stiffened, feeling ill.

"Insanity," Isaac supplied for me.

Mr. Whitney spun as if in disbelief. A sheen of perspiration coated his brow and caught in the light. He removed his spectacles and polished them on his untucked shirt before slumping on the hard wooden chair at the desk. "Madness? On what evidence?"

I hugged my arms to myself, unwilling even to speak this.

"Pierson was ready to claim that Macy was right, that she's unstable, but not because of his influence. Hutchinson—you know, the one who runs the asylum in Bromley Grove—was making room for her."

"Brilliant," Mr. Whitney whispered. "Absolutely, impossibly brilliant." He replaced his spectacles and leaned forward. "Does your father have the same knowledge you do?" He nudged his head toward the ebony pen, causing Isaac to narrow his eyes.

Hopelessness tingled along my spine, for I half guessed where this was going. "Half. The first part, at least."

Mr. Whitney sat back and looked at Isaac, who continued to study us with a hint of suspicion. "My word! I don't know whether to credit Lord Pierson for being the worst father or the most brilliant politician in the country. No common soul would choose that path, but it's bold and genius."

"It's not an option," Isaac said quietly.

Mr. Whitney's expression begged that he'd reconsider his stance.

"She won't survive it," Isaac said. "It's that simple. No."

"Survive it?" Mr. Whitney leaned forward and spoke so low that he formed his words carefully, allowing us to read his lips. "Is Macy Adolphus, Isaac?"

Gravely meeting his eyes, Isaac gave a single nod.

Mr. Whitney spread his hands helplessly as if to ask how Isaac thought I'd survive that.

"The answer is no," Isaac repeated, rising and placing a protective hand on the back of my chair.

Mr. Whitney studied Isaac's stance, then drew a deep breath

before rubbing the back of his neck. "All right. Give me some time to think about our case." He directed his next question at me. "It's quarter after three on the dot. Is five hours of sleep enough?" Before I could answer, Mr. Whitney raised his gaze, where Isaac must have shaken his head. "Fine. Six hours, then. I'll meet you here in the morning."

"There's a chamber next to mine that you're welcome to use." Isaac reached behind him and tugged the bell cord three times.

Mr. Whitney packed his satchel, his brow furrowed. "No. I desire to speak with other bar members. But I'll be here first thing in the morning."

Twenty-Five

❦

THE RATTLE of Miss Moray's keys woke me the following morning. Opening my eyes, I turned and squinted, prepared to tell her that I desired more sleep. Behind her, Nancy stepped into the chamber and, with a gaping mouth, surveyed the room as if she'd never seen it. Miss Moray clanked down a service for one on my nightstand. "Your lawyer has been standing in the foyer for the last seven minutes, timing your slumber." Her tone grew sarcastic. "Apparently now is the exact time to wake you."

I glanced at the clock and found it was quarter past nine.

"Because your girl is mute, I'm delivering his message. You're to meet in Master Isaac's snuggery." Her mouth pursed in anger, and she turned and minced from the chamber.

I plopped back into the feather mattress, wondering what would happen if I ignored Mr. Whitney and kept sleeping. It wasn't as if he could barge in here.

"Right." Nancy planted a hand on her hip when we were alone. "Thou best get a move on, then."

I pulled the downy comforter over my face. "One would have thought the workhouse might have given you better manners."

"Aye, just like being the Emerald Heiress has made thou less lazy." Her voice carried near my wardrobe. "If thou wants me to have better manners, thou'll have to let me play the heiress, while thou learns how to get out of bed at th' workhouse."

Despite myself, I laughed beneath the covers, feeling the air grow humid. "I'm glad we're together again."

"Aye, people without enough sense to dress themsells are always happy to see their abigails." Then, after a pause, "What's this here? Is this Reverend Auburn's?"

I shot straight out of bed, knowing exactly what she'd uncovered. "Don't touch that," I cried, snatching it from her fingers. The night of Edward's arrest, I'd found his nightshirt still tucked in the bedclothes. The maid must have missed it as she arranged the bed. It had comforted me to sleep with something that had his scent that first night. But then, not wanting it to be laundered, I'd stashed it in the wardrobe.

I dipped my head, seeing Nancy's punctured expression. "Please, just leave it be."

～～

I gathered my skirts as I raced down the stairs, once again amazed at Nancy's abilities. The ivory gown she'd picked out was one she'd commissioned at Am Meer. It mimicked a short-sleeved dress, only it had sheer sleeves—which I could have blessed her for, as close as the snuggery felt the previous night. The frills were kept at a minimum, though she'd hand-selected my jewelry pieces. Her fingers were raw and cracked, so she wore a pair of my gloves as she wove ribbons in my hair that brought the simple look together with elegance.

Both Isaac and Mr. Whitney rose as I entered the chamber.

"Are you ready to begin, Mrs. Auburn?" Mr. Whitney indicated one of the two chairs resting before the hearth. They'd been turned to face the desk and the timeline.

I gave a nod and took my seat.

"I won't need you as long today. I've a few questions I thought of during the night." He placed his hands on both his knees. "But in good conscience, I need to ask again whether you're absolutely certain Goodbody's defense isn't legitimate." He held up a hand before I could protest. "Please say nothing before I outline our position. Once I've done so, you can decide."

Isaac's face was the picture of refinement as he slowly blinked, waiting for Mr. Whitney to continue.

Mr. Whitney faced me. "First, I ought to make it clear that you're not Mr. Macy's legal wife."

I placed my hands over my heart. Had shackles fallen off my feet, I could not have felt more free. "You're certain?"

In what seemed like an absentminded gesture, Mr. Whitney picked up the pen from last night and started to tap it. "There are things about Mr. Macy that, if true, mean he is not legally married under English law. Do you understand me, Mrs. Auburn?"

My eyes were drawn to the pen. My mouth parted as I gave a slight nod. How could I not have been considering this as part of the equation beforehand? Macy had married me under a false identity. Of course we weren't married.

"This is stunning news!" Isaac grew so excited he stood. "But why the glum face, the angle to plead insanity?"

"I can't use it in court."

"What do you mean you can't use it?"

Mr. Whitney set down the pen. "It's not something that I can prove."

"Why not?"

"I'm sorry, but I can't tell you."

"On my word—" Isaac swivelled his body to look at me—"but I'm about to grow as angry as your father. I'm even considering swearing." Then, after closing his eyes and forcing a deep breath, he looked at Whitney. "Tell me what you need. If I have to walk the earth twice over, I'll find it."

"It's not that simple, Dalry."

Isaac drew in a careful breath, then slowly said, "What harm can it do to try?"

Mr. Whitney answered with a sharp look. "You'd be killed if you started asking questions. It's that simple."

"You know what?" Isaac's voice rose a pitch. "I'm sick and tired of hearing how I'll die if I defy Macy. Well, I defy him! Give me this task!"

"Fine." Mr. Whitney looked ceilingward as he loosened his cravat. "Try this one out. Will you take the stand and testify that Macy is Adolphus?"

Isaac's nose wrinkled. "How would that help? They'll think we're grasping at straws and laugh us out of court."

Mr. Whitney spread his hands. "Trust me. They'd do similarly with what I'm not telling you."

"But I'm not married to Mr. Macy," I finally managed to wedge in. "Truly! I'm not married to him."

Mr. Whitney gave me a pitying look. "Yes, according to British law, you are not married."

"I don't understand what you're about today, Whitney, but you're frustrating me." Isaac threw himself onto his seat. "Why such a coy answer? What are you not saying?"

Mr. Whitney's entire body paused as he addressed me. "What I meant to say was that you're not married *to anyone*. Julia Pierson is not your real identity, which means your marriage to Edward isn't legal either."

My hands moved of their own accord to my abdomen, for that morning I had learned I was not with child. I had been disappointed, for I'd hoped it might sway the courts. But now I was thankful at least I hadn't repeated Mama's path.

Isaac placed a supportive hand on my forearm.

"The courts, however," Mr. Whitney continued, "will likely pronounce you Macy's wife, at which time you will be recognized legally as the wife of Mr. Chance Macy. Do you understand now what a curious segment of time we're in? What we do here and now determines everything."

"Then shed light on this technicality," Isaac said.

"How can I without making her look mad or proving Macy's case that Lord Pierson poisoned her mind? Personally I think trying to bring it to light will only bolster Macy's argument that Lord Pierson used his daughter to injure him. Which leads us back to my original question: are you absolutely certain Goodbody's defense isn't legitimate? Think carefully how you answer, for I have a duty to uphold the law, which is higher than the duty of friendship."

"Then it's too late," Isaac replied. "For as you can see, she's sane! And it would be unethical for you to say otherwise."

"Or we're all mad." I twisted the linen handkerchief. "And no one has ever been sane."

Mr. Whitney looked at Isaac and spread his steepled hands slightly apart as if to say he could argue in court by holding that hypothesis in his mind.

Isaac waved to the timeline above Whitney's head. "Have we grown so ungentlemanly that we're no longer protecting the innocent? Look at her life spread over that wall behind you, Cudney. Are we now amongst those who trample over her as well? You remember Elliston's visit to the university and how he abused that poor devil for misplacing his lecture notes. *That* was the man she lived under for years. How dare we turn our backs? Can you imagine being so desperate you'd entrust yourself into the hands of Lady Foxmore?"

Mr. Whitney glanced at the timeline, then rubbed his bleary eyes. When he looked up, however, he smiled as he shook his head. "You know that you're asking me to deliver a miracle, don't you?"

"Isn't that our main forte?" Isaac's voice was rich with a tone that was new to me. "Accomplishing the impossible?"

To my surprise, Mr. Whitney instantly brightened. "You can't use my words against me! I was only thirteen. You can't hold me accountable to that!"

"Oh yes, I can!" Isaac faced me, his eyes shining. "When I reached the tender age of twelve, your father decided it was time to begin garnering support amongst the Tories for me. He wanted them to see me as a solid candidate to start grooming for the role of prime minister. He sent a note to my school saying that, instead of taking me home over the break, he'd arranged for us to go hunting with members of the party. I was instructed to prepare arguments about the bills currently before Parliament, and my instructions were that I needed to greatly impress them."

"But your father forgot to tell him which bills he meant," Mr. Whitney added with a laugh. "And Isaac only had a week's notice."

"And it was the same week as examinations!" Isaac sounded more boyish than he ever had.

"And Isaac had been sick the fortnight beforehand, so he'd not only missed the last week of lessons but the lectures intended to prepare us for examinations. It was paramount that Isaac got top-notch grades—"

"The first question they always asked on our arrival—" Isaac adjusted his sitting position as he forgot himself and interrupted—"was what grades I'd received that term. The whole party took pride in the fact that I got perfect marks."

"And," Mr. Whitney laughed, "your father demanded he brush up on his shooting skills as well."

Isaac faced me. "Because I had missed a grouse on our last trip and Lord Galway's son, Richard, took a shot and hit it."

"You mean *Dickee*." Mr. Whitney took on a tone of snobbery.

Isaac groaned, but his voice laughed. "Yes. Do you remember how Lord Galway and Pierson were always at that infernal competition as to which one of us boys was superior? And at that time I hadn't handled a rifle in months."

Mr. Whitney picked up the story. "Because Simmons delivered the letter in person, the headmaster brought it to the common room, so we all read it together. Isaac felt so ill he actually lost the contents of his sto—"

Isaac shook his head at Whitney, reminding him a lady was present. "I complained that it was impossible. Even then, Whitney was an excellent orator. He stood on the table and gave a speech about how the impossible was our forte and when we accomplished the impossible, history would carry our names until the end of time."

They laughed as they recalled how his impassioned, childish speech had motivated Isaac into action. For their sakes, I smiled. But inwardly I felt grieved at the image painted of Isaac's childhood. Somehow those memories emboldened both of them, though, for when Mr. Whitney returned to the argument of my marriage, there was a sense of adventure the two of them shared, one I was barred from.

Isaac was the first to notice and sobered instantly. "Forgive us, Julia. We did not mean to exclude you nor take more of your time than necessary." To Whitney, "So what is our plan now?"

Mr. Whitney likewise adopted a more formal position and nodded his apologies. "Well, based on everything I know, the strongest argument we have is that the marriage is unconsummated and you did not personally sign your name in the parish registry. We're weakest in that there are witnesses to the marriage and there are witnesses who can testify you and Mr. Macy spent long periods of unsupervised time together thereafter."

I crossed my arms, recalling how Macy refused to let me go home the night he murdered Eramus. Had he known he was killing two birds with one stone by keeping me there?

"Goodbody is meeting with your father this morning, and they've requested an audience with me at ten. Before I commit to a plan, I'd like to hear what they've got to say. I'd also like to meet with this Reverend Auburn fellow—"

I nearly stood. "May I go with you?"

Mr. Whitney's tone was kind. "I fear not. Right now it's nothing short of a miracle you haven't been arrested. We're not going to flaunt the fact that you're still free."

"Can I send him a message?"

"Nothing written. It could be twisted and used as evidence. Tell me what you'd like me to say instead."

I frowned, wanting to send Edward something to keep his inner fire alive. But it was too embarrassing to commit such words to Mr. Whitney. Unlike the others in our foursome, I wasn't good at cryptic messages. Usually people told *me* what was being said between the lines. Then, realizing that Mr. Whitney might deliver the devastating news that we weren't married, I decided to touch on that, to let Edward know I wasn't sinking like before. "Tell him . . . tell him . . . that I'm still me."

Mr. Whitney's laugh was hearty, yet inoffensive. "I'm fairly certain he knows that. Anything else?"

I knew Edward would be worried that I wasn't eating, as I had stopped the last time we were separated. If so, he likely hoped Jameson was stepping in. Thus I wanted to communicate something to ease his mind. "Yes, please tell him Jameson is still himself too."

Again Mr. Whitney laughed, then teased, "Shall I tell him that your father and Isaac are still themselves?"

"No!" I said too quickly. "That would only distress him."

Mr. Whitney flashed Isaac a humored look. "Very well, then. I shall deliver your message exactly as you have stated it. Are you willing to go over our timeline again? I want to test it for weaknesses."

I looked at his chart, wishing I'd never laid eyes on it. Not only was it painful to see Edward's blue line against Isaac's short yellow one and Macy's sinister black one, but it was the cigarette papers themselves that sickened me. Each one held a true fact about me. But not one spoke the truth about who I was. Yes, I had partaken of brandy and had kissed Edward while engaged to Macy. Yes, I'd run away from my husband and kissed Edward again. Yes, I'd lied to the queen and the prime minister. Yes, I'd kissed and betrothed myself to Isaac next. Yes, I'd made choice after choice based on fear.

On that timeline, I saw myself the way those without eyes of love saw me.

The depth of who I was, the dream God had spoken over me at my birth, was missing from the story and unseen.

When I looked at those papers, all the insults Lady Foxmore and Lady Beatrice had piled on me, the opinions of Mrs. Windham, the anger of my father, and the outrage of the crowds outside London House—all felt just.

And the worst part was, outside of pleading insanity, I had no defense.

"Yes," I whispered because my throat was gnarled. "We can go over it again."

Isaac turned his gaze on the timeline and studied it as if trying to guess which one of those papers had altered my mood in a matter of seconds. Then, scooting his chair closer to mine as if to reassure me by his presence, he leaned forward and said, "They're just words."

I kept my gaze fixed on my transgressions as I nodded. Rationally I agreed, but I felt their weight regardless. Now I find it ironic that, only minutes after sending a verbal message to Edward that I was still me, I lost sight of myself by focusing on my misdeeds.

Shame will unmake and warp any soul.

∽

The newspapers couldn't print fast enough to satiate public interest.

Initially I read every single one, dashing downstairs to scan them first in case there was anything particularly devastating.

My heart pounding, I'd read sensationalized versions of events and spend the remainder of the day torn between anger and hopelessness. It was Jameson who convinced me to change my habit. On the fourth morning, I rushed into the breakfast chamber and grabbed the *Times*, which for some reason was at the bottom of the stack. Jameson spun from the buffet and held out a hand to stop me.

The first headline, however, screamed before he could.

EMERALD HEIRESS OR TOILETED FILLY?

I gasped. Had a bucket of muck been thrown on me, I could not have felt more humiliated. Heat filled my cheeks, for even I understood the references—that I was an overdressed woman who galloped between men at racing speed. How well I could picture my father's coming expression when he saw this, and Isaac's tender hurt. I shook my head, knowing that even if I burned this, I couldn't stop it from being circulated throughout London. My body warming, I started to read the article, but Jameson's touch on my shoulder startled me.

"Why read it?" he gently asked.

"Because," I said, feeling my throat constrict, "I need to know what they're saying."

"Why? People are going to believe what they will. Can you change the public's view just by reading?"

Sunlight highlighted one side of his kindly face. For the first time, I noticed how aged he'd become in London House. I drew in a breath, wanting to argue that yes, the more I found out, the better prepared I'd be to counter their thoughts. But Evelyn's words carried back to me. Just knowing what people said would make it impossible to act normal, making me appear more awkward. My shyness and pain would only be interpreted as guilt.

"Do you feel more peaceful after reading those?" Jameson continued softly.

"No," I said. The idea that newspaper boys were spreading this throughout the city even now was sickening. A gleaming stack of papers, turned upside down, still awaited my father. Did they also call me a filly?

"May I offer you advice, O queen?" Jameson asked. He waited until I acknowledged him. "Don't read them. Spend your time differently."

Intense anger flashed through me. "How will I know what is happening, then? My father refuses to speak to me, and Isaac is always behind his mask." My fingers curled into fists as I tried to keep my pitch from extending outside those walls. "And Mr. Whitney hasn't stopped by once since he spoke to Goodbody! How do I know he hasn't decided to go with my father's defense?"

Though he tried to hide it, Jameson's mouth twitched as he nodded in approval.

"Why are you smiling?" I said, deflated. "I'm yelling at you."

He chuckled and brought a porcelain cup and saucer from the buffet. "Oh, I rather like a faerie in a fine temper now and then, so long as they don't unleash a plague of boils. Here, sit. I don't know how the faerie courts handle these sorts of things, but we British always find a spot of tea soothing at this point."

"You're not angry?"

"Oh, I've had much worse in my fifty years of service." He smiled, setting out a silver teapot, loose tea, and its strainer. "Once, in Africa, I angered my master so much, he threw my only boots into a mud hole with crocodiles. I had to wear shoes, which weren't made for the terrain, I might add. You wouldn't believe the blisters that week."

His story was so jarring in our setting that I didn't know which direction to take next. Knowing I looked confused, I reached for the teapot. But a glance at the headlines made it weigh a thousand pounds. I found it was beyond my ability to even pour a cup of tea.

"Do we agree you'll ignore the papers?" Jameson refolded the *Times* and stuck it at the bottom of the stack.

I swallowed, nodding, knowing those words would never be erased. They would defame me a hundred years from now. Until the end of time, perhaps. One day historians would discuss how scandalous I was.

Jameson cleared his throat.

"How am I supposed to use my time, then? There's so little I can do. At the very least I can be knowledgeable."

His eyes took on a far-off look as he glanced out the window. Sorrow encased his features. "I feel remorse for resisting the Auburn housekeeper's arguments about the lack of women's rights. The footmen used to jest behind her back that she was angry because no man wanted her. And I did not censure them as I ought have. Secretly I found her offensive too. I always believed that if everyone kept their roles perfectly, kept their proper ranks, obeyed the person set above them, everything would always run smoothly." He gave a slight chuckle. "And then you came along. I don't know how you do it, Mrs. Auburn! On the one hand, you are a perfect example of why no woman should have any say over her own affairs, for you made a perfect mess of them. Yet on the other hand, you're solid proof that women need equal rights. For you exemplify how precarious a woman's—"

The sound of my father and Isaac's arrival cut his speech short.

My cheeks burned, for Jameson's speech was probably the most radical view ever spoken aloud in London House, and I felt guilty just hearing it. It was impossible to even lift my head in greeting.

"Jameson," my father said gruffly. "Begin breakfast."

Glad my father hadn't overheard a word of Jameson's views, I spread my napkin over my lap and pondered how I would fill the weeks before the trial. Jameson was right. It would bedevil me, trying to keep up with everything that everyone was saying. Yet if I didn't read the papers, what earthly use was I?

As was his new custom, my father placed the papers in the center of the table, allowing free access. When he and Isaac selected their favorites, Jameson looked over his shoulder, curious to see if I'd take his advice. Thankfully my father hadn't noticed the *Times*. I longed to remove it from the pile and hide it beneath the table. But there was no hiding my shame for the world. It was open for all to see.

I studied the pattern on the china dishes, wondering if I should start my own campaign of exposing Macy through the newspapers. The notion was quickly rejected. It did not suit my personality. It was my father and Macy's chosen mode of battle— public opinion. I glanced at Isaac's horrified expression as he scanned pages. I was forced to look away. Surely, I thought, he deeply regretted his decision to join this fray by aligning his reputation with mine.

I cupped my chin, wondering what Edward would have done. I suspected he'd have made it his daily habit to stand on the steps of London House and preach to the crowds. But my shame was so great, I could scarcely manage to frame words to Nancy, much less angrily censure the spectators.

There was no safe place or outlet for me to take all the emotion building inside me, I realized. Had Edward or Elizabeth been there, I would have poured out my soul to them. But even that, I knew, wouldn't ease how frantic I felt. For did I not have Jameson and Nancy to talk to? I sank against the back of my chair, wondering if anyone had ever felt as trapped as I. Frowning, I envisioned the Israelites standing next to the Red Sea with Egyptian chariots rumbling toward them. Moses instructed them to stand still and not fear. To wait and see the Lord's salvation.

Mr. Whitney's words rose to mind. *"You know that asking me to deliver a miracle, don't you?"*

I nodded at Jameson, finally finding my own way of dealing with these circumstances. Since matters were outside my hands regardless, I'd seek equanimity by turning toward the Red Sea and awaiting the Lord's mighty hand.

As it turned out, there was little else I could have done.

Those who have never had their reality shattered scarcely can imagine the toll it exacts. Over the following weeks, I found it necessary to spend the majority of my time alone. Amidst the growing slander and defamation, I spent hours being tended by God. While the newspapers berated me, God told me I was the apple of his eye. While my father glared at me in stormy silence, I experienced what it meant to be enwrapped in unfailing love.

Yet this was not a spiritual experience I would wish on anyone.

More than once, panic would stab me and I'd suddenly desire to reject everything. It was as if all at once the girl I had been a year prior awoke in my body and couldn't assemble this new life into its proper proportions. I'd cover my face, uncertain this wasn't some strange and awful nightmare. Surely, I'd reason, it made more sense to declare this reality false. What were the chances that I was truly Lord Pierson's daughter? And that not only had Edward married me, but so had London's crime lord, who was really a gypsy from Austria? And that Lord Isaac Dalry, too, had sought to win my hand?

None of this was sensible, I'd realize. I wasn't even pretty, kind, generous, or any of the other qualities that attracted others. This was all wrong, I'd think. It had to be a madman's fantasy. Maybe I ought to testify that I was deranged in court, because there was no court! It was all an illusion, and I would be babbling nonsense into the air at an asylum, where the ers should have known better than to leave newspapers out for the inmates to create delusions with.

in, crying out to God not to let go, because I was fall-was no longer certain of anything. Strangely, I never questioned God, which should have been the most ludicrous part of my story. For the idea that there was a God—One who cradled me during those hours, One whose presence I could feel—is perhaps the most incoherent thought, for why would he have?

The walls of Isaac's snuggery testified that there was nothing about me worthy of loving.

It made no earthly sense that God would look down and choose to reveal himself to me when I wreaked havoc and pain on others.

Yet that slender, invisible thread of knowing him was all that kept me sound.

Twenty-Six

THOUGH I'D STOPPED reading the newspapers, they still held power over me, for I continued to join breakfast.

The morning the papers carried the news that Mr. Macy requested that he be arrested in my stead if I were going to be charged, a record number of copies were sold. I watched my father read the headlines, grab the stack of papers, and hustle to the library. He remained in meetings all day.

The next morning, I was further unsettled when my father passed his newspaper to Isaac. Even Isaac registered shock as he read it.

I did not ask as I stood and quietly left the breakfast table. I did not want to know.

The following day, Mr. Whitney arrived a half hour before breakfast. I stiffened, wondering what more could possibly happen, as the thin clang of the bell reached my bedchamber. Nancy's eyes caught mine in the mirror as she secured the plait she worked on. For the last several mornings, she'd experimented on various hairstyles for my upcoming court appearance. What exactly she hoped to achieve, I never asked, for I felt too frail for speech.

That particular morning, Nancy had divided my hair into tiny plaits which she planned to gather at the crown of my head in an elaborate bun. The scent of her almond oil pomade filled the air as she kicked the curling papers scattered about her feet.

When the bell rang again, I twisted my fingers about Mama's locket and shut my eyes.

"Likely nobbut a deliveryman," she assured me.

I nodded, though we both knew deliveries were made at the servants' entrance. Then, finding it humorous that we both pretended to believe the other, I opened my eyes and found her observing me. It brought to mind how often we'd looked at each other in the mirror at Eastbourne. Thus I found myself asking, "Nancy, if I am forced back to Mr. Macy, will you go with me?"

Her eyes flicked in the direction of the mirror as her mouth twisted. "Aye. I'll ga. And charge thee double, and all."

I released a pent-up breath I hadn't realized I'd been holding. We are not created to dwell in more than one reality at a time. Such pressure can fracture us. Thus until that day, I'd only allowed myself to handle the fact that I'd been riven from Edward again. That was unbalancing enough. But now my faith had grown, as I had chosen to anchor myself in God instead of Edward. With that first step achieved, I allowed another step, to picture what might happen if I were forced to return to Eastbourne.

Would it be possible, I wondered, to build a life there? If I were breaking apart under the strain of a court case, how on earth would I manage to live at Eastbourne, when I knew Macy was a crime lord, and still thrive? It wasn't as if I could go back to being unaware he'd orchestrated Mama's death.

How I now hated every moment at Eastbourne. What a

schoolgirl I'd been to tell Macy his past was of no concern to me. Outside of Mr. Whitney, who added clauses like: *"unless you've murdered my family."* I shuddered and pressed my hands against my temples. How differently I now saw our time together. That first night, it was so clear he'd purposefully waited until I'd ingested enough brandy to be pliable and then probed me for my knowledge, so he could adapt his story.

No wonder Lady Foxmore had scoffed. All along she'd known he was playacting. Feeling ill, I recalled how Mr. Macy challenged her ladyship by asking what it was to her if he wished to find succor from his past at my feet. No wonder she'd coughed and spat wine over the table. He was no more reformed than she was; likely he was ten times the reprobate. And no wonder Mr. Greenham had watched us so miserably. He'd murdered Mama for Macy and then personally delivered me on a silver platter to be seduced.

My stomach twisted as I realized that all along Macy had been blending half-truths. Had he not said from the very beginning never to look too closely at him, for my own happiness? Had he not coached me from the very beginning to come to him alone for explanations? He'd known I would eventually find out he was a blackguard.

Someone rapped on my door, causing us both to start.

Nancy rolled her eyes, then wiped her hands over her skirt and plodded toward the door.

"I beg your pardon," James said in a perfect lilt from the hall, "but Mr. Whitney has arrived and requested an audience with Mrs. Auburn."

Since she was playing a mute, Nancy made some sort of gesture with her hands.

I squeezed my eyes shut, blocking them from view. Now that I allowed myself to see the truth about the past, I tried again to map out a potential future. Surely Macy would sense that I no longer believed his lies. So what now?

Cold seeped through me as I recalled the day he caught me reading his mail and snatched up my wrist. His words hurtled back:

"You can either be a token wife, and after securing an heir, I'll see that your needs will be provided and leave you to your tea circles and dinner parties. Or you can stop asking questions and accept me as I am."

I stilled, truly hearing him for the first time. Either I would believe the lies he spun without questioning him, or he'd secure an heir and then abandon the guise of relationship.

I suddenly understood what my life would look like.

Whether or not I hated him or screamed or kicked and resisted, he wanted a son. Not just any son—one who was the rightful heir to Eastbourne. That had always been his objective. Of course he tried the path of least resistance first—seduction. And like a fool, an utter fool, I'd tangled myself in his web and in less than a week committed myself into his keeping.

"Mrs. Auburn?" James asked.

Angry tears shimmered in my eyes as I faced him and rose. "Yes, yes! Mr. Whitney. Where is he?"

"In the foyer, ma'am."

Crossing my arms, I started toward the door, keeping my chin tucked in, feeling fractured. Nancy thwacked James's shoulder, then pointed at my hair. Giving her an evil eye, James tugged at his waistcoat. "If I may make bold, Mrs. Auburn, your hair. I'm sure your barrister can wait until your style is finished."

I spun and consulted the large looking glass across the chamber. Under other circumstances, I might have found my appearance comical. The wild way in which the braids spread out over my head, when combined with my contorted expression, put me in mind of a Gorgon. But it was impossible to sit down and allow Nancy to do my hair while the truth about Macy thundered over me.

"What does it matter?" I cried, stalking from the chamber,

feeling the swish of my heavy skirts against my legs. In the hall I turned and screamed, "What does any of this matter!"

Isaac and Mr. Whitney were in conversation at the bottom of the steps when I emerged shouting. They both glanced upwards as I descended, wiping tears from my eyes. Whatever Isaac saw alarmed him, for he dashed up the stairs, reaching me before I set foot on the second vestibule.

He took my arm and instructed in a whisper, "Your father is in the library with Goodbody. Please comport yourself."

I shook him off, avoiding looking at him, as I lifted my skirts and started toward Mr. Whitney.

"Plead insanity," was my desperate greeting. I'm sure at that moment, my appearance and tone made it sound like a reasonable request. "Plead it. I don't care. I'm not going back to him. I'm not."

Mr. Whitney's eyes narrowed with confusion as he looked at Isaac.

"Why are you looking at him?" I protested. "*I* want to plead insanity. *I'm* the one who has to live with Macy, not him!"

Frowning, Mr. Whitney darted a glance at the library before switching his satchel between hands. "Right. Let's take this to the snuggery." To me, "Can you manage yourself until then?"

Cupping my elbows to hug myself, I nodded.

Isaac attempted to take my arm, but feeling ready to break apart, I threw him off.

Guilt assailed me as we trekked down the passage, for I could see that I'd hurt Isaac. Yet as much as I wished to apologize, I deemed it unwise to speak. Allowing myself to acknowledge the truth about Macy and my future had left me brittle, like a broken vase whose glue had not yet hardened.

Once in the snuggery, Whitney wasted no time shedding any unnecessary layers and loosening his cravat.

"I'll go ask Jameson to gather the servants and sit guard," Isaac said wearily, but at the door he turned and faced me. "Or would you rather I fetch Jameson to come speak personally with you?"

I rubbed my eyes, wanting to laugh and cry. What good was Jameson if I was about to be given into the legal custody of Macy? What could Jameson possibly say to make any of this better? And yet, even as I thought this, another part of my mind twinged with curiosity. Would he, like Nancy, also come to Eastbourne? If Edward were sent to jail, he'd have to choose between my father and Macy. "Ask him," I said with bitterness, "if he'd follow a faerie into caves of lunacy or, if she were sent there, through the very gates of hell itself."

Mr. Whitney cast Isaac a look of panicked concern.

Isaac looked torn between staying and leaving. "Just leave her alone until I get back," he commanded. Then, not trusting that Mr. Whitney understood, he added, "Say nothing."

I placed my eyes in my hands, recalling the night Macy had held me before he brutally murdered Forrester's manservant. Then I recalled the manner in which Macy had lovingly tended the burns on my hands, even as he planned out Eramus's murder in his mind. I shook my head, knowing I couldn't go back. I couldn't.

As Isaac's soft tread crossed the threshold, I looked at him.

His expression was one of perplexity. With a frown he said, "Jameson said to tell you no, but he'd be happy to bake you banana cake for the journey so you won't arrive famished."

I laughed, well able to imagine the tone in which he'd said that.

"And," Isaac added, "he said when you laughed, to tell you to stop ignoring your herd. That's what Mr. Whitney and I are here for. To help with the lions."

I nodded repeatedly, feeling the panic leave. Then I laughed twice, thinking how ridiculous this must sound to them.

As if in unison with my thoughts, Mr. Whitney's brows

scrunched before he looked over his shoulder at our timeline. "Remind me again," he said slowly, "who this Jameson is?"

"Oh, the fetching butler, of course," I said moodily, knowing it would give Jameson a chuckle later.

The expression that crossed Mr. Whitney's face is one I've encountered at least once each day since then. He stared at me as if all the facts he knew about me were incongruent with my actions, making it difficult to know how to proceed. As often happened in my earlier years, Mr. Whitney decided to parley with the person next to me instead. "Is she recovered, then?"

Isaac's blue eyes met mine as he tugged on the legs of his trousers and took a seat. He nodded.

"Enough to share what I was going to say?"

Isaac covered his mouth for a long moment in thought. When he spoke, it was to me. "What happened?"

I gave a silent chuckle, imagining how absurd it would sound to say, *I realized Macy was evil.* I clasped my hands, knowing I couldn't speak. Honor runs deep, and if I told them what I predicted, they'd feel obligated to do something rash. One shouldn't run back to the herd if it kills the herd.

"It was nothing," I said. "I'm fine."

Isaac's eyes sharpened.

"I want to use my father's defense." I turned toward Mr. Whitney.

He removed his spectacles and, using a handkerchief, wiped off the ash he'd acquired en route to London House. "I take it you haven't been reading the papers, then?"

"The papers?" I repeated dully.

"We've publicly countered Macy's claim that your father is maliciously destroying your marriage with lies. We've called Macy a sensationalist with the argument that you're not imbued with fear about your husband, but that you're calmly stating the marriage is neither legal nor consummated. And we're claiming there's far more to the story, which will come out during the trial."

My stomach was in a ferment. "Which is what, exactly?"

Isaac and Mr. Whitney exchanged glances again.

I felt a headache start. "We're bluffing? That's our defense?"

"We're not bluffing," Mr. Whitney said. "We're challenging every legal aspect of the marriage—and there are major holes, starting with the marriage license being burned and the lack of your signature in the registry. Macy, by the by, entered it, acting as your proxy."

"Fine." I kneaded my temples. "But isn't the jury going to expect something incriminating about Macy now too?"

Mr. Whitney frowned. "Well, we're also hoping that Forrester turns up with information."

"Forrester?" My laugh sounded crazed even as tears arose. I'd nearly forgotten about him. "Please, please tell me that my defense doesn't rest with that man. He would toss me to Macy if allowed." Then, before they could speak, "And if we never hear from him again?"

Mr. Whitney breathed out his nose with the air of a man telling himself to be patient, not to remind me that he already tried his hardest to get me to claim mental unsoundness. He began to unpack his satchel. "I swear to you, Mrs. Auburn, I'm doing the best with what I have."

"Can we still tie this up indefinitely in court?" I asked, recalling his statement from the first night.

He hesitated before adding a book to his stack. "Normally yes, but I've never seen anything like your case before. Every door opens for me; every petition for a legal interruption of the law is answered immediately. I've known cases that have waited years to have a single document make it from second-to-the-top of the stack to the top. But not yours. Everything is treated as though the clerk's life depends—" He clamped his mouth shut.

I stood and folded my hands over my stomach, needing

movement. Only there wasn't any space to pace. For one desperate moment, all I wanted was an audience with Edward. The desire was so overwhelming, I had to shut my eyes and wait for the fierce emotion to pass. When I opened them, both Isaac and Mr. Whitney carefully scrutinized me.

"Then why are you here?" I asked, digging my fingers into my hair, remembering too late it was in plaits. It took several seconds to untangle my fingers, and when I did, a single plait fell over my brow.

Mr. Whitney appeared unable to keep his focus off my hair as he spoke. "We believe it is a ploy to gain public sympathy, but Macy is expressing his great desire to meet with you in public."

I started to shake my head.

"Now hear me out. I think it's vital that you agree to this meeting. The longer you refuse his pleas—and they're quite heart-wrenching—the less sympathetic the jury will feel toward you. Now is the time to prove that Macy's claims are false. That you're not afraid of him and that you are open to reason."

The ringing in my ears began at a distance, but it steadily increased. "I am reasonable!" I cried. "Because it's completely unreasonable to expect me to take tea with Mama's murderer!"

"The difficulty with that argument," Mr. Whitney said, "is that the public isn't aware of it, and we must do what seems reasonable *to them*."

Again I shook my head. I understood the importance and the truth of what he was saying, but I couldn't keep track of one more reality—what other people knew or didn't know. I could only act on what I knew was true, whether that made me look rational or not. "No," I said. "No. I won't visit him."

"Once again, I'm begging for you to hear me," Mr. Whitney said. "We no longer have the option of pleading Mr. Goodbody's defense, even though now we regret it. We need to take this path while it's still open to us. This is necessary. I'm asking you to trust me."

Though he was too much of a gentleman to say, "I told you so," his message was clear.

"What about," Isaac said in a thoughtful tone, "agreeing to the meeting with Mr. Macy, but setting the date right before the courts open? That way we publicly get the credit without putting Julia through the excess strain of repeated visits."

I crossed my arms and bundled them against me. "No."

Mr. Whitney placed his hand over his mouth to restrain his mounting impatience.

"What if," Isaac attempted again, "I go with you too? If I'm with you every step of the way? Just like we used to be."

"Isaac, it's nothing like it used to be."

He leaned forward, elbows on his knees. "Please, Julia. We desperately need this. I promise, I won't leave your side once."

I gave a strained laugh, batting back the stray plait of hair. It wasn't fair of him to pressure me, but what he said was true. Isaac had risked everything to give me this shot, but already I felt as stretched as an embroidery cloth left too long in its hoop. Like the overstretched needlework, I felt misshapen, forever lopsided. "I just can't, Isaac. I just can't."

Isaac and Mr. Whitney exchanged cautious looks, which I read too well. They both feared pushing me any further.

"All right," Mr. Whitney slowly said, rubbing his brow as if stressed. "We'll ignore the request. If you change your mind, however—"

Isaac shot him a look.

"Can we go over the timeline once more?" Mr. Whitney said. "I've already memorized it, but I want to make certain your testimony is consistent."

I forced myself to take a breath. I didn't want to go over the wretched timeline. I was sick and tired of having to revisit my mistakes again and again. Nevertheless, as I caught sight of Isaac, I forced myself to become composed.

His expression was difficult to decipher as he sagged against his chair, keeping his gaze fixed on the desk. He looked for all the world as if he wished he'd not stepped in my father's path.

I felt shamed, for I'd begged him to interfere and now the case was falling apart. "Yes," I said dully, "we can cover the timeline again."

Once more we started at my birth. Oh, how weary I grew of talking about my birth and moving through each year. When we reached the point where I'd returned to Am Meer, determined to marry Edward instead of going to Scotland, Mr. Whitney wrinkled his nose and asked Isaac, "By chance do you know where Pierson was going to send her?"

"Yes, to Widow Melverton's household."

Mr. Whitney lifted his head and stared as if horrified. "I'd have gone to Lady Foxmore too." He patted his pockets and drew out his cigarette papers. Dipping his pen, he asked, "When exactly did you learn you were going to Scotland?"

"The day Mr. Graves informed me I had a guardian."

"Fancy thinking you were being sent to that wilderness." The tip of Mr. Whitney's thumb turned white as he shoved the tack into the plaster and then stood back. "My word," he said, glancing over his shoulder at Isaac, "the two of you would have crossed paths! Doesn't Widow Melverton live right next to the house you'd rented for that hunting trip?"

Isaac briefly narrowed his eyes at Mr. Whitney, a warning not to say more.

But it was too late.

My breath caught in my throat as I turned and faced Isaac. His discomfited look told me all I needed to know. He'd been planning to rescue me from Scotland all along.

I suddenly saw how my life would have turned out had I not hired her ladyship to find me a husband—had I submitted and gone to Scotland instead.

I envisioned myself, crepe clad, stepping out of the carriage and onto the springy flora to hopelessly view my new residence.

Likely I would have spent the bitterest months of my life inside those walls. I knew beforehand I was to be denied any society outside Widow Melverton's mother's sickroom. How endless would those days have felt, for my faith in Edward would have been destroyed after his becoming a vicar, and my dream of our foursome crushed.

In this story Isaac would have justly played the knight-hero. I envisioned being informed that my guardian's protégé had arrived and desired to check on me for himself. En route to meet him, likely I would have endured a lecture about showing gratitude while keeping my place. In my mind's eye, I saw how I would have entered the chamber, feeling a mixture of anger and self-consciousness, only to find Lord Dalry, London's favorite son, quietly waiting.

I pressed a hand over my heart. Without doubt, he'd have shooed all unwelcome company from the chamber, leaving just us. How quickly I would have been unmade, for I knew first-hand the benevolent manner he'd have used as we spoke. Living without even a scrap of love, how overwhelming Isaac's tender ministrations would have felt.

It wasn't hard to predict how it would have unfolded from there. Surely, all the way back to the sick chamber, I would have rebuffed myself for having been touched by his kindness. Isaac's visit would have lodged in my mind, prompting me to angrily chide myself for continuing to think upon it.

I have no doubt that Isaac planned to propose during his hunting trip or some subsequent visit—for he would not have long left Lord Pierson's daughter in those conditions. His idea of chivalry was too developed for that. Furthermore, Isaac wouldn't have seen the bitter girl who entered the chamber. He saw through eyes of hope and love what others rejected. And how madly I eventually could have loved him back. Eventually, believing that Edward had betrayed me to join the church, I'd have been able to transfer my heart from Edward to Isaac.

I ideated the story to its end, where Isaac would have sur-prised London House by arriving home with his new bride. At first glance, would my father have known who I was and arched one of those heavy brows in Isaac's direction? But under those circumstances, would he have been grateful that his protégé brought me home? Would he have choked on his words as he greeted me? Might he have spoken softly to me during that first dinner, the way he spoke to Kate and Evelyn? I wondered what life might have looked like had I not arrived on his doorstep an unchaste daughter, but rather been ushered in beneath Isaac's healing wing.

"Are you ill, Mrs. Auburn?" Mr. Whitney asked.

I placed my forehead in my palms and bent over. The phan-tasm had been so vivid, I felt as if I'd glimpsed a lost future as the door of finality shut upon it. I marveled that my subcon-scious shouted for me to make haste in my dreams. What was there to be late for? Why wasn't it screaming for me to honor Isaac and grieve that he'd lost that future too? For unlike me, he didn't have an Edward diving after him, swimming down to grab hold of his hand and then kick back to the surface.

"I beg you excuse me a moment." I stood, searching for a pretense. "I need to fetch my shawl."

Both Isaac and Mr. Whitney stood, but I gave them no time to speak or open the door. I needed to be free of that chamber. By seeing an alternative future—one where loving Isaac would have come about naturally—I finally understood.

I didn't stop until I reached my bedchamber. There, I slid to the floor and cradled my head in my hands, knowing with certainty I had just glimpsed the real Isaac. I ached that I'd hurt him, for in that single realization I understood the measure of the man I had injured, and I couldn't stand that I'd brought him pain.

Twenty-Seven

❦

THE COURT DATE arrived quietly. There was a solemnity in the air that I felt from the moment I opened my eyes. No happy sounds carried from any floor of London House. I woke before dawn and sat on the edge of my bed, quietly breathing and mentally prostrating myself before God. Even reading Scripture was too overwhelming, for the first words my eyes landed upon had been, "Oh that I had wings like a dove! for then would I fly away, and be at rest." I felt the pathos of David's lament to such a degree that even to this day I cannot look upon that psalm without growing teary.

My head bent, I cried out to God over and over that if he did not rescue me, if he did not hear my prayer, then I had no hope. I was thus as Nancy entered at dawn, shielding a candle. Strips of torn linen lay over her arm.

My fingers deepened their hold on the sheets I clutched, for it hurt to even speak when I felt this strained. "What is that?"

"Just wait, thou'll see." She placed her candle atop the vanity. "Miss Moray ordered thee a bath. Th' girls is on their way."

The maids entered my chamber with their copper pitchers of hot water. Their ministrations were a far cry from the bath I was given the first morning my father had summoned me to meet him. A measure of ruth was mixed into the expressions of the girls as they gravely upturned their pitchers, pouring water into the tub. Only one dared to peek in my direction before she tucked in her chin and hastened from the chamber. Nancy, thankfully, had managed to oversee that there were several pitchers of cooler water, as the temperature upstairs was sticky.

When alone with Nancy, I stood before the copper tub with my stomach writhing. The idea that this might be my last bath in London House, that tonight I might find myself in Macy's bed-chamber, was so repugnant to me that I nearly considered refusing to be washed. The hairs along the back of my neck tingled as I remembered the bath of rose petals that awaited me the night I arrived at Eastbourne. It hadn't been a luxury for my benefit, I realized, feeling gooseflesh rise over my body. He'd wanted me washed and fragranced before he began his seduction.

I curled my fingers into the hair at the nape of my neck, shaking my head. "No. I won't bathe for him. I won't. I won't!"

Nancy was one of those souls who managed to keep pace with my rapid thoughts and connected what I meant. "If Macy wants thou clean, he'll scrub thee himsell! Which is better? Me or him?"

Knowing it was important that I not have red eyes at my court appearance, I nodded, then disrobed and sat in the water. I fixed my gaze on the bed that Edward and I had shared, trying to keep my growing horror at bay. Now that I knew what it was to be with my husband, I could never repeat it with Macy. Never. How on earth did those forced into a lifestyle of prostitution manage to stay sane? Eventually I shut my eyes and placed my forehead on my knees, determining that if I escaped my circumstances, I would join those who made it their life's work to assist fallen women.

That morning, I learned how much planning Nancy had put into my attire. She had prepared an array of perfumed talc powders and oils in hopes of keeping me dry despite the heavy summer heat and the press of bodies in the courtroom. Once I was bathed and powdered, she used the strips of linen to bind my chest. Afterwards, she opened my wardrobe and withdrew a garment she'd assembled from three dresses she'd rent. The dress was white silk and poplin gathered to fall in soft, feminine frills. The sleeves were only slightly puffed, ending just above the elbows, where layers of tucked lace added to the lovely, soft look. After fastening the hooks, Nancy unwound my curls and gathered them on either side of my head. Lastly, she framed my face with a deep-brimmed bonnet that made my features look small. When she produced a lace parasol, I touched my lips. "Nancy, I scarcely look old enough to attend a dance."

She collapsed against the bed. "Aye. Let 'em talk 'bout thee now."

～

"Kate, you're descending from the carriage first," Isaac instructed as he peeked out the curtain he'd lifted slightly. "I'll join you next, and then I'll assist Julia."

"First?" Kate whispered, paling. "Why first? What if they think I'm Julia and throw rotten food on me? It's a brand-new dress!"

"No one is going to throw anything," Isaac assured her.

I pressed a hand to my lips, recalling Macy's plea in the papers that the crowd treat me tenderly and wishing I hadn't agreed to put Kate through this. Earlier this week, Mr. Whitney argued it would be best for my image if I entered the courts with both Kate and Isaac. That way, if any jurors were watching, they'd see that I was beneath Lord Dalry's protection and considered a sister.

"But what if they call me names?" Kate asked, her eyes tearing.

Isaac released the curtain and leaned forward to address her. His face was filled with pride. "Have you any idea how brave you are? My little sister, a fighter for justice and equality! Yes, first! Because you're Katherine Mary Jane Dalry. Nobody else can lead the way for us. Nobody else can help Julia as you can right now. Show the world that the Dalry clan has claimed Julia and we all surround her. She needs you!"

There was poignancy in Isaac's tone that touched even my heartstrings, though at the time I didn't understand it.

Kate breathed out her nose, taking on a look of fierce determination. Her chin jutted with pride, she gave a curt nod, and then she dropped out of the carriage. The crowd roared, likely spreading the news that I had arrived.

Isaac's eyes glistened as he placed a hand over his chest. "She has no idea how much I love her." Forcing his emotions back in place, he faced me. "You'll be fine. Just pretend we're at another ball."

I nodded. The knife pains in my stomach, however, were a thousand times worse than they'd been at any ball or soiree we'd attended.

Isaac's hand was steady as he turned and assisted me from the carriage. Stepping down, I took in my first view of the Old Bailey. We disembarked near the gates set into its circular walls. My father had hired men to hold back the crowds, but I still sensed that we were surrounded by a sea of humanity. Everyone called to me at once. Some whistled; some screamed.

As planned, Isaac took both Kate's and my hands, then tucked them beneath his elbows and hastened us through the gate.

En route I eyed the gallows, situated high above the crowd, where those given the punishment of death would be hanged later today. One rope hung lower, in case a child or short person was convicted. Those who came to witness the spectacle waited with baskets of garbage.

I squeezed Isaac's hand, trying to recall what Mr. Whitney had said. Theoretically, by some interpretation of the law, bigamy could be punishable by death, though Whitney had assured me it wouldn't happen.

Once we arrived in the courtyard, Mr. Whitney raced our direction, wearing a smile.

Isaac released us, stepped forward, and pulled him tight, revealing how close the pair had grown.

Mr. Whitney patted Isaac's back twice, then stepped away and faced me. His wig alone would command respect. Later that day, I counted twenty-five perfect horizontal rows, not including the large curl along his brow, nor the thousand tiny wool-like curls over the crown, nor the long constant curl that outlined the back. The expensive piece had been purchased by my father and was meant to impress the courts. It was so well-fashioned that it became Mr. Whitney's signature wig and lasted the whole of his brilliant career.

"Come with me," he ordered, and then, giving us no time, he raced off toward the massive courthouse, his black robes billowing behind him.

Isaac gathered my arm and followed. The bonnet Nancy chose had such a wide brim, I was able to block everyone else out of view as we made haste.

"The Right Honorable Sir John Bosanquet is giving you use of his parlor today," Mr. Whitney said, throwing open a door and revealing a surprisingly comfortable room.

"Where's Pierson and Simmons?" Isaac asked.

"They purchased seats in the gallery this morning. Pierson thinks it will be more difficult for the juries to go against his will if he has glowered at them beforehand."

Isaac shook his head, then drew me inside and pulled out one of the chairs from beneath the mahogany table. I removed my bonnet, sending up a prayer of thanks that I didn't have to wait with the other criminals or Mr. Macy. Thick wooden panelling lined the walls. In the winter it would have been comfortable, for there was a mosaic fireplace and a pot cupboard with a tea service on top.

"I suppose it helps to have a father who knows everyone associated with the East India Company." Mr. Whitney gave the chamber an appreciative nod. "I can't stay. They're starting sessions any moment. There are already arguments amongst counsel that the legality of the marriage needs to be determined today. They might not even require a defendant's plea from her, as the crime isn't determined until the marriage is."

Isaac nodded. "Thank you. We understand. Will you escort Kate back out the gate now? Pierson has a carriage waiting to take her to Mother."

Mr. Whitney frowned but gave a curt nod. "Yes, yes, but hurry, Kate. I'm anxious to find out which jurors are selected. Some of them are staunch supporters of my cases. I'm crossing my fingers."

I waited until the door was closed, leaving Isaac and me alone. "What is happening? I don't understand."

"Trust me, no one does," Isaac said in a soothing voice, taking a seat. "Not even the most seasoned lawyer can unknot this tangled mess. Simplified, it will be easier for the courts to know how to proceed with Edward's charges and Macy's civil suit— once it is settled whether or not your marriage to Macy stands. A criminal case, a civil case, and a charge of treason all hinge on that one legality. Today we learn whether you're actually married to Macy."

I nodded, mentally preparing to be placed in his custody. Though it wasn't ladylike, I placed my elbows on the table and buried my face in my hands. Part of me never wanted to leave this room, never to face what was coming next. And yet the other part just wanted it over.

Isaac didn't help with his next observation. "How many men do you suppose spent their last day inside this court? Must be scores, perhaps hundreds. How strange that thought is to me."

"Yes, well, thank you for that," I said into my palms.

Whereas Jameson would have laughed, Isaac must have shifted, for his chair squeaked. "I'm sorry. That's not very good company, is it? Would you care for a cup of tea? I doubt Bosanquet would mind." Then, standing without waiting for my answer, Isaac started to gather teacups. "You know, seeing Kate climb out of the carriage today made me think of my first memory. Did I ever tell you it?"

I drew a deep breath, in no mood to exchange civilities. Lowering my hands, I looked at him and was suddenly reminded of the day he'd come home from Maplecroft. He'd tried to meet privately with me so he could tell me about Edward, but my father discovered us. After my father had burned my letters, Isaac had taken it upon himself to teach me how to keep my composure during crises. How vehement I'd been as I silently declared I'd not sit idle having tea with Lord Dalry as my life fell apart.

I half smiled. And yet he was still here, still trying to make me ladylike. Regret swelled once again as I recalled that he'd been planning to collect me in Scotland. I swallowed, knowing I still barely understood Isaac. How badly I now wished I could go back and start anew. To have asked him about Ben. To have learned more about his school days. To have inquired how he'd come to live with my father.

I glanced at the clock. If Macy won, there were only hours left of our friendship, and it was too late.

Then it struck me.

It had come circular. I was here again with Lord Dalry. I blinked with the wondrous idea that it is never too late to become what we were meant to be. And if Isaac was right, I was a lady.

I gave a laugh. Yes, I thought, looking about the chamber. I would start now. Right now.

"I would love a cup of tea," I said, wiping aside a tear. What did it matter if my life was crumbling again? When wasn't it? At least I was safe right at this exact second. And at least I was with a friend—one I didn't know nearly as well as he knew me. I was tired of losing all the moments of my life to fear. "And yes," I continued, "I would love to hear about your first memory."

Isaac's eyes galvanized me as they turned in my direction. At first he only blinked disbelievingly. Then joy lit his entire face, for he understood. He laughed. Hours and hours of his tutelage had finally paid off, and I'd finally stepped into my role.

"Ah, well." He laughed again, for his voice was thicker than usual. "It was of Kate being born. It was the middle of the night, and though Mother had tried to hide it, I suspected even at that age that she had gone into labor. . . ."

And thus I spent the morning leading up to the trial having tea with London's darling. He held nothing back as though he'd waited his entire life to be seen and heard by me.

⌇

Five hours later, Mr. Whitney stuck his head inside. "Are you ready? You're needed right now." Perspiration trickled down his face from beneath his wig. His robes looked wilted. He gave us a puzzled look, as he'd entered just as we were laughing about the only time Isaac stepped on his dance partner's toes.

I stood, thankfully not overturning my tea, which had grown cold. My dread returned in panicky needles.

Isaac likewise stood and glanced at the clock. "Is Edward up, then?"

Mr. Whitney motioned for me to hurry and not ask questions.

Tears gathered in my eyes as I looked at Isaac, for the plan was that he would return to London House. My father didn't want him questioned under oath. Admitting that he'd knowingly hidden the truth would haunt his political career for life.

Isaac's face was likewise crushed with grief.

"Thank you!" I flung my arms about him, not caring it wasn't proper. If Macy won, it wasn't likely I'd see him again. "You've been a dear friend."

"Let's not say our good-byes yet," he said, squeezing me back. "There's still hope."

I nodded, then hastened after Mr. Whitney. "Have you seen Edward?"

"Yes, yes. He's next, and we best hurry. The prisoner before him is known here, and it won't take them long to convict." Mr. Whitney took my arm and started to hasten me toward the courtroom. Then, in the hall, as we jostled past those waiting in groups, "Remember, you haven't been charged with a crime, though Edward has been arrested. Right now this trial is to argue the legality of the marriage. You're being called as a witness for the prosecution—"

"The prosecution!"

"Don't panic. It's a high risk on their part, for they're counting on your testimony being damning to yourself. Stick exactly to the timeline; our legal arguments rest on it. Do you understand?"

I nodded, my feet feeling like blocks of ice. "Is there any chance the trial will spill over into tomorrow?"

Mr. Whitney looked at me as if I'd requested a rock from the moon. "Most cases take about twenty to thirty minutes. Though yours will likely outlast an hour. Steady now."

We plunged into a courtroom filled with men. While Mr. Whitney plowed forward with poise, I cringed, overwhelmed by the sheer number of people sitting at various levels. White wigs dotted the courtroom, some up high behind what looked like pulpits. The man I assumed to be the judge sat overlooking the chamber from a raised area. Though everyone was in rows, nothing made sense. There were barristers standing next to plain-clothed people. Some people sat looking thoroughly bored, while others were in deep, animated discussion.

The courtroom was abuzz with a hum as if a thousand angry flies were competing for attention.

My breath came in short pants, for it was far more crowded than anything I had anticipated. I started to look about for a way of escape, though I wasn't sure what would happen if I ran.

From across the courtroom, deep-set hazel eyes met mine. Eyes that suggested we beard the lion in his den, that we leave this courtroom breathless with the reality of who we were. Edward's face had no expression except an outward calm. But his eyes—oh, how they blazed.

I allowed Mr. Whitney to lead me by the hand, but as he did so, I met Edward's steady stare, turning my head as I went. Like a bride at a funeral, my white dress stood out in a room otherwise clad in black. One by one, the judges, aldermen, councilmen, sheriffs, undersheriffs, and barristers all stilled and observed what passed between Edward and me.

I glanced over their stern faces, realizing that if they had love for truth or justice, then they would perform their sworn duty to protect me. For was not the law created to protect the weak? These men had to know the depravity of Macy—for even Mrs. Windham's brother-in-law feared him.

Some of Edward's fire infused my soul. We scoff at those who think in terms of black and white, but at that moment I saw life as Edward did, and it stole my breath.

I saw everything in a startlingly different way. Whereas before I saw men as trees, my sight was adjusted so that I saw mere people. It wasn't about my winning or losing this case, I realized. It wasn't even possible for me to lose. I had nothing to lose. Something so much more vital was at stake, for there was a higher reality at work. I was not the one on trial. These men were. And they would pronounce their own judgment on themselves through their treatment of me.

                                      ∽

The grand jury found Edward's charge a true bill, and it was given to the clerk of arraigns and brought to open court. Mr. Whitney frowned and contested this as a strike against the argument that I wasn't married and therefore unfair. Edward, wearing leg chains, had pleaded not guilty, and Merrick opened his case by calling me first to the stand.

"State your name, occupation, and residence."

I swallowed, not certain I could form words. But then, determined to make my voice clear, I said, "Julia Josephine Auburn."

Merrick rolled his eyes. "Your true name."

My chest and stomach immediately hollowed. I saw the trap. If I said I was Julia Elliston, then clearly I was married to Macy. If I allowed glass to cut my tongue by saying my name was Julia Macy, it was an admission of guilt. If I stated I was Julia Pierson, I would be deemed a liar. If I insisted I was Julia Auburn, I would be seen as hostile.

I looked at my father, who sat without expression, and then at Edward, who calmed me with his eyes.

Lastly I looked at Macy, who leaned back in his chair, fingers laced around his knee, seemingly amused.

I drew in a deep breath, recalling that I wasn't the *only* one married under false pretenses. I bit my lip, wishing I'd pressed the matter with Whitney about what to do given the opportunity to reveal Macy's true ancestry. His answer was always the same: *"You'll never get the chance, as you won't be asked."*

"I suppose," I said quietly—and then more loudly, realizing the gallery needed to hear me, "I suppose you should call me Mrs. Augustus Rainmayer."

Merrick's wig went slightly askew as he jerked his head in surprise. "I beg your pardon!"

But by now there were shouts all over the chamber, so his words went unheard by anyone but me. Unable to help it, I glanced at Mr. Macy, but he only gave a sad shake of his head. He looked neither alarmed nor frightened that I'd used his gypsy name. My father rubbed his brow, doubtless angry that he'd had the perfect defense, and it was apparently true, but he'd not been able to plan around it.

As the confusion died in the courtroom, Mr. Macy stood. His chest heaved slightly as if he were deeply grieved. Merrick saw him from the corner of his eye and went to him.

I swallowed as Macy's hands gripped the sides of the table he'd sat at. He leaned forward, and the magnetic tones of his rich voice travelled through the chamber. It was so quiet, even I could pick up the deep concern in his voice. My heart quickened as I felt myself begin to panic again.

The loud clank of chains and irons drew my attention as Edward shifted his legs.

Once again his eyes met mine, and I calmed.

The crowd murmured angrily, seeming to take our fortitude for defiance. Though we had not been found guilty, the proper thing, apparently, was to look contrite.

Merrick rose to address the court. "Mr. Macy respect-fully asks that his wife no longer be required to testify. Clearly she's fracturing under the mental strain. He is well aware this is one of the lies she's been fed about him while living in Lord Pierson's household—that he's really a gypsy prince." He paused, allowing the chuckles that followed his statement. "Considering the grievous emotional damage that's been inflicted on this girl, I rather agree with my client. There's enough evidence to prove the marriage without her testimony."

Mr. Whitney stood. "First, I'd like to point out that Merrick is unfairly calling her Mr. Macy's wife. She is not, and her testi-mony is necessary to proving such."

The judge thoughtfully sat back. "Did your client inform you of her belief that Mr. Macy is a gypsy prince?"

Red colored Mr. Whitney's cheeks as he stood stock-still. "Yes, Your Honor, though she did not use the word *prince*."

The judge's eyes widened with surprise. "And were you planning on introducing her unique belief to court today?"

Mr. Whitney turned even more scarlet. "No, Your Honor. I thought it irrelevant."

"Irrelevant?" The judge's robes billowed as he half stood. "When there are claims this girl's mind is being poisoned?" He frowned as he looked over the courtroom as if debating what to do next. His eyes landed on Macy, who had remained standing. He visibly paled, then swallowed. "Remove the girl from the stand. I agree with the prosecution. Her testimony is of no benefit."

I gaped, then gripped the handrail of the witness stand. For I was the only person who could explain everything, and I'd just been barred from testifying. In a flash of anger, I decided not to leave. I would not. The only thing now stronger than my shame was my anger at being helpless. How many other girls were in my exact position, I wildly wondered, unable to defend themselves, forced to rely on the nearest man for their fate? I wouldn't do it anymore.

Before I could cry out, however, Mr. Whitney caught my eye with a look that was sterner than any my father had ever managed.

Trembling, and with Merrick's aid, I made my way down the steps. There wasn't anywhere for me to go except to the witness box reserved for high-class members of society. I might have been barred from testifying, but I would at least hear the rest of the trial. I picked up my skirts and willed myself to move past Mr. Macy.

My father scooted over so that I could have the nearest seat. He wore a face I'd never seen before, likely the one he used for matters of Parliament. He looked unshakable and unfazed. As I sat, he briefly placed a hand on my shoulder.

Over the next half hour, I learned that Mr. Macy had requested that his witnesses be sequestered until their appearance, as they feared Lord Pierson's wrath. Most of the testimonies were what I expected.

First the magistrate from the night I'd married Mr. Macy. Then the parish registrar, who'd allowed Mr. Macy to enter my name in the parish books on the combined testimonies of the footman, valet, and magistrate that they'd witnessed the special license and marriage.

I held in my surprise as Reynolds entered the courtroom, for I hadn't expected him. His blue eyes flashed in my direction with a look of reassurance before he took the stand.

Like those before him, Reynolds took an oath.

Merrick signalled for him to begin. "State your name, occupation, and residence. Then tell me what you know about the marriage of Mr. Macy to Miss Julia Elliston."

"I am Edgar Reynolds, the personal valet of Mr. Macy, and I reside at Mr. Macy's estate, Eastbourne, in Bedfordshire. I witnessed the marriage of Miss Julia Elliston and Mr. Chance Macy."

"Did the couple spend time alone together after the ceremony?" Merrick asked.

"No, sir. Mrs. Macy became greatly frightened of her husband when Lord Pierson arrived. Then she was forced from the property of Eastbourne by Reverend Auburn."

"Was she frightened of Mr. Macy before Lord Pierson's arrival?"

"No, sir."

"How is it that you're certain of that?"

Reynolds's voice kept its perfect lilt. "She was with Mr. Macy nearly every possible hour beforehand, sir. Even requesting audiences with him in the middle of the night when she had nightmares, sir."

"Was Miss Elliston frightened often during her visit?"

"Yes, sir. The whole staff was under the impression that she was greatly distressed. More than once we commented that she only seemed calm when Mr. Macy was at the estate."

"Do you know what she was frightened about?"

"Not exactly, sir."

"What do you mean by that?"

Reynolds's eyes narrowed as he looked in Edward's direction. "She acted rather strangely around Reverend Auburn. She didn't appear to be comfortable in the company of his elder brother, either."

"How do you mean?"

"She was very skittish, on edge."

Mr. Whitney caught my eye and gave me a look as if to ask if I knew where this line of questioning was going. I gave a slight shrug; I didn't see how any of this was relevant.

Merrick walked to his table and fetched a small wooden tray. "Do you recognize this?"

Reynolds's eyes widened with astonishment. "Yes. That is Mr. Macy's ring. I've never seen him without it."

With a nod, Merrick returned that tray and then fetched another. "Do you recognize these?"

"Yes. They are Macy heirlooms, formerly belonging to the late Mrs. Macy, his mother."

"Formerly?"

Reynolds's features softened as he viewed the various bracelets. "Yes, sir. Mr. Macy gifted those to Miss Elliston during her stay at Eastbourne."

"Did she wear them?"

"Oh yes, sir. Straightaway."

Again, Mr. Whitney turned slightly, narrowing his eyes. I

gave him an apologetic look. For the bracelets weren't on the timeline. In truth, I'd forgotten all about them.

"Thank you." Merrick signalled for him to step down.

To my surprise, the next witness he called was Mrs. Windham's hall boy. The newspapers said that both Edward and I exhibited great shock when he entered the court. Perhaps it was so, though I don't remember giving a visible hint of it.

In London, he looked twice as poor as he had at Am Meer. His bare feet were dirty and his hair was matted. He bowed his head and quickly made his way to Merrick, removing his cap. He glanced at Edward, then turned bright red.

I gave Edward a questioning look, unable to imagine what testimony this boy could give on the legality of our marriage. Edward, however, had already guessed and looked stricken.

"State your name, occupation, and residence."

"C-Caleb Hastings," he whispered. "I'm the hall boy at Am Meer in Gloucestershire, sir."

"Will you please tell the court what you saw in the woods out-side Am Meer, about a fortnight before your mistress and Miss Elliston left for Eastbourne?"

My insides curled with dismay.

Caleb peeked at Edward, then lowered his head. "I woke in the middle of the night 'cause I heard Reverend Auburn outside our cottage."

I squeezed my eyes shut, silently willing for Caleb not to say another word.

"And what was Reverend Auburn doing?" Merrick asked.

"He was throwing stones at Miss Elliston's window. When she came to the window, he demanded she come down and meet him."

"And did she?" Merrick asked.

I gave a slight shake of my head, feeling like I was about to lose my stomach.

"Aye. No one disobeys the vicar when he gives 'em an order in that voice," Caleb said.

"Did she want to come down and meet him?"

Caleb's eyes were solemn as he shook his head. "No, sir."

"And how do you know?"

Caleb cast me a quick look, then lowered his chin. "'Cause I peeked as she passed in the hall. Looked frightened to death, sir."

I placed a hand over my bodice, recalling how I thought Edward was drunk.

"Continue." Merrick placed one hand over the rail of the witness stand. "What happened next?"

"I heard her crying. Real loud like she was being hurt. So I gots up and found a lamp." He swallowed. "I thought maybe she got lost in the dark or hurt herself. When I found 'em in the woods . . ." His voice was so low it became a mumble.

"Please repeat that louder so the court can hear you," Merrick said.

"Reverend Auburn—" Caleb's voice grew strained—"was holding Miss Elliston to the ground, sir."

There was a ripple of scandalized shock through the courtroom. My father gripped my arm, though at the time I didn't understand the full implications of what was happening. I do recall, however, that Mr. Macy kept his gaze fastened on Edward the entire time with a look I couldn't quite interpret. Mr. Whitney faced me in disbelief, for this wasn't on the timeline either.

I gave him a stunned look. Of course it wasn't on our timeline! How could I have guessed Macy knew about that night?

"What happened next?" Merrick asked.

Caleb dug his toe into the wooden platform. "The vicar yelled at me to go back to bed and not look. She was crying as she ran through the hall and sobbed in her chamber too. The next day he came and told me to deliver a note to her."

"Can you describe how she looked as she read the note?"

"Aye." Caleb's head bobbed, though with sadness. "She turned real pale. Then, looking like she were about to cry again, said to tell the vicar she'd do whatever he wanted."

Ringing engulfed my hearing even as the courtroom erupted in cries. I couldn't see Edward from where I sat, because men jumped up and were shouting. But I was afforded a view of Mr. Macy. He wore the same impish smile I'd seen him wear the morning I woke on his couch in his study. Only this time, instead of looking at papers, he was staring in Edward's direction.

It chills me now to look back and understand Macy's expression. I was so ashamed of my behavior that night that I automatically assumed they were yelling because of our scandalous deed, but Macy had set up the case to make it look as if Edward had raped me. Nor did I realize that the legal ramifications of Caleb's testimony drove their excitement. Those found guilty of rape at the Old Bailey were always hanged immediately after the trial.

It took several minutes before order was established. And when the men all sat, Edward locked eyes with me again. I gave him a nod to show I was fine, still not fully grasping what had just happened.

To all of our surprise, a jeweller took the stand next. The small man with large spectacles testified, "I live on Oxford Street and own Tuttle and Sons. I do not know the prisoner, but I am familiar with Mr. Macy. He came into my shop and purchased a necklace for his missing wife during the month of April."

"Is this the one?" With one finger, Merrick dangled the necklace that Mr. Forrester had given me at Maplecroft the morning he asked me to blackmail Mr. Macy with him. It sparkled, dazzling the courtroom.

The jeweller's eyes softened as he nodded. "Yes, that is the one."

"Can you tell me its cost and purchase history?"

"Yes. Its cost was thirty thousand pounds." The jeweller had to stop, for there was a stir over the chamber. When the noise died down, Merrick signalled for him to continue. The jeweller wet his lips before resuming his testimony. "Mr. Macy purchased it. He said his missing wife had sent him a request, testing his commitment to her. He said he knew where his wife was hiding and that she was very frightened and confused. He hoped by purchasing the necklace, he'd prove his love to her and that she'd return and once more be safe with him."

Again, Mr. Whitney turned slightly toward me. All I could do was give him an apologetic look. For the thirty-thousand-pound necklace wasn't on our timeline either. His face was incredulous as if he wasn't certain he could believe I'd forgotten three such significant things.

Miss Moray testified next that she'd seen the jewelry amongst my possessions, but no, she had not known its origin.

Mr. Howell Ethan, the magistrate responsible for the investigation, testified that the jewelry was taken from my bedchamber in London House. Men's brows furrowed as they considered the evidence.

One of Macy's men testified that twice while I lived in London, I'd spent hours alone with Mr. Macy.

I settled against the wooden back of my seat, stunned by the turn of events.

Because I had lowered my gaze, needing to collect myself, I wasn't watching when the next two witnesses entered the courtroom until my father suddenly stiffened. Looking up, I found that Eaton, the butler of Maplecroft, was taking an oath, and behind him stood William, our second footman.

Eaton ascended the stand.

"State your name, occupation, and residence," Merrick intoned in a bored voice.

"Roger Eaton. I am Lord Pierson's butler at his Maplecroft estate in Bedfordshire. I was present the night Miss Julia arrived at Maplecroft. She arrived in tears, not certain where else to go. Reverend Auburn didn't want her anymore, and she feared her husband's wrath too much since she'd been forced to abandon him."

I wrinkled my nose, thinking that was an odd way to state it. "And next?"

Eaton frowned with sadness. "When Lord Pierson came home, he spent hours berating her, screaming that her husband was evil. The poor girl grew quite frightened, saying she was confused, as Mr. Macy had protected her from Reverend Auburn."

I gasped, stunned that he'd tell such a bold lie in court.

"When she insisted that she wasn't certain what to think anymore, Lord Pierson began to accuse Mr. Macy of the most horrendous crimes. Only after she began to panic did Lord Pierson threaten that if she didn't obey him absolutely, he'd return her to her husband."

"That's it! I have to object to this proceeding continuing any further," Mr. Whitney said, rising. "This is absolute fiction! My client isn't even allowed to testify to contradict this. Logic declares there's no truth here. Why would Lord Pierson risk his wealth and reputation so recklessly? Why would she run away with the man who forced himself upon her?" He flung a hand to the judge. "Is the court truly going to entertain someone so clearly and obviously a liar? Are we really going to allow such a bold mockery of justice to continue?"

"The prosecution hasn't finished with its witnesses," Merrick said dryly. "Would the defense please wait their turn to call their witnesses?"

The judge looked at Macy, who did not change expression, before frowning. "The next time you disturb us with an outburst, Mr. Whitney, I'll have you dismissed from the courtroom." He motioned to Merrick. "Proceed."

Mr. Whitney was so angry, he couldn't sit. He moved to the far end of the courtroom, where he shook his head and paced.

"Why did you not go to the police?" Merrick asked Eaton.

"I thought about it plenty of times." Eaton looked in my direction as if to apologize. "Only I feared to. I resolved to keep my mouth shut, but my conscience was heavier than lead, sir."

William's testimony was similar. He spoke about my time in London, saying that more than once he'd been present when I tearfully approached my father with my doubts about Mr. Macy's guilt. He testified that on numerous occasions I'd begged my father to write Mr. Macy, to make inquiries to see if he'd forgive me for feeling forced to run away with Reverend Auburn. Supposedly my father had even locked me within my bedchamber.

My father gave no hint of his emotions during the testimonies, though I am certain he must have felt complete shock that two members of his upper staff had betrayed him. I swallowed and glanced at Simmons, waiting to see if he planned to take the stand too. He, however, watched Eaton, seething.

My father's supposed misdeeds were of even more interest than my scandalous behavior. Here was the story the public wished to believe. The courtroom listened breathlessly. The only sound was of Mr. Whitney thwacking his robes as he paced. The more outrageous the lie, the harder he thwacked.

"How many more witnesses?" the judge asked, placing a hand over his midsection as William left the stand. "It's past lunch."

"One more, Your Honor," Merrick said.

"Is that even necessary?" the judge asked irritably. He spread a hand in the direction of the jury. "Is there any doubt in anyone's mind that the marriage is legal and consummated?"

The mixture of men shook their heads, showing they had no argument.

Mr. Whitney stormed from the back of the courtroom, his face tomato red.

Before he could speak, however, Merrick gave a slight bow. "Your Honor, my client Mr. Macy has endured extreme mental anguish as his wife has been viciously misled by her father and dominated by Reverend Auburn. You cannot imagine the torment he's been in. Dare we cut short his day in court?" He pointed at the jury. "Are these not the same men who will sit on the civil case tomorrow? This particular witness is only in London for today and is vital to understanding why Lord Pierson would choose to persecute Mr. Macy to this degree."

The judge glanced in Mr. Macy's direction with the same air a butler looks at his master with when he is trying to anticipate him. "Fine. One more witness and then a brief recess."

"When the court adjourns for a break," my father said to Simmons in a low voice, "take my daughter as planned. Leave this country immediately."

Simmons leaned forward. "Sir, she's the only witness who can clear Reverend Auburn's name now. It would mean his death sentence."

"You will take my daughter," my father ordered through gritted teeth, "and you will go into hiding."

I stared at them, wondering what sort of provisions my father had prepared for me in the event we lost. Going into hiding with Simmons had never once crossed my mind. I furrowed my brow, wanting to inquire what Simmons had meant about Edward receiving a death sentence. I was so deep in thought that by the time I registered the courtroom had grown silent, the sharp rap of a walking stick was already sounding outside in the hall.

Horror shot through me as I looked up and saw Lady Foxmore's powdered visage angrily approaching the center of the chamber.

Twenty-Eight

FROWNING FROM HER PERCH atop the witness stand, Lady
Foxmore scrutinized me. A capillary must have burst behind
her right eye, for it was completely blood-filled, which, when
set against her powdered face, was positively ghastly. As if to
accentuate the gruesome component, she lifted her lorgnette
and squinted at my father and me before turning her baleful
gaze on Mr. Macy.

His chuckle echoed through the courtroom.

Silently she promised him a slow, agonizing death. Bony
hands clutched her sable stole as she squared her shoulders.

"State your name, occupation, residence, and your testimony
in the case."

She forced breath through her nose. "I am Lady Adelia
Foxmore. I have no occupation outside of being superior to
worms such as yourself. As far as my testimony . . ." Her chest
swelled, and with a haughty expression, she glared at Mr. Macy
and me before lifting her bejewelled finger. "There sit the stupidest girl and stupidest man in the whole of England!"

Again Mr. Macy chuckled.

"You laugh," she addressed Mr. Macy, then slowly held up a letter. "But I have compartments in secret boxes in secret places you've never thought to search."

The atmosphere changed as Mr. Macy sat straight and levelled her ladyship with his eyes.

"The court may find this useful," Lady Foxmore said, handing the letter to Merrick.

If I'd ever seen Mr. Macy look murderous, it paled in comparison to the quiet dread that preyed on all our spirits as he sat forward and extended his hand for the letter. He glared at her ladyship as he flapped open the note and read it.

He passed the note back to Merrick and studied her ladyship anew, this time with a touch of confusion. Merrick opened the letter and read it, then passed it on to the judge.

I watched the white sheet of paper travel from hand to hand as people read it during her ladyship's testimony.

When Macy sat back against his seat, there was no humor in his expression.

She cackled in his direction, ignoring the fact that they were in a courtroom. "Lucky for you, I chose that letter. This is the last favor you shall ever extract from me again. Did you truly think I'd burned all those correspondences?" Her body trembled as she waited for an answer.

Mr. Macy studied her with a calculated look that would have frightened anyone with sense. My father gripped my shoulder and sat straighter with a look of hope.

Mr. Macy sliced her ladyship with his eyes and waited the span of two breaths before divesting his waistcoat of a small folded handkerchief, which he extended for Merrick to take to her.

Merrick collected the small bundle and brought it to the witness stand. She gave Macy a questioning glance before proceeding to unfold the square of cloth.

I leaned forward, straining to see.

What looked like a large pearl earring sat in the center of the cloth.

Its significance I could not guess, but it transformed Lady Foxmore. She gave it a long, hard stare before she covered it again. Her mouth stayed small and tight, but her eyes flashed. Wordlessly she flung the pearl and handkerchief onto the floor before the table where Macy and his lawyers sat.

Chills washed over me as I looked about, waiting to see what the courts would do about a witness being blackmailed before their eyes. At least two jurors squirmed as they looked at their fellows in the jury box. But everyone else either shuffled or looked at papers, pretending not to have noticed. From the corner of my eye, I saw my father's lips turn grey, as they did when his headaches came over him. He swallowed, doing his best to mask his distress.

"You want my testimony?" Her nostrils flared as she addressed Macy. "Fine! Here is what I know. I chaperoned that girl's mother in Bath, where Lord Pierson became infatuated with her despite the fact she was engaged to William Elliston. He learned that Mr. Macy was a guest in my house and recruited Mr. Macy to help him seduce Lucy Cames by arranging for me to be gone during certain hours of the day."

Her words were like hammer blows, for I'd expected her to talk about Eastbourne, not my father. I recoiled. Several men cast dubious looks in my father's direction. Macy's jaw stayed locked as one finger tapped the table.

"One morning I found Lucy lying across her bed, sobbing. She was with Pierson's love child and the whole story tumbled from her. Lord Pierson was already engaged and assumed she understood their relationship was pleasure only."

I stared, unable to breathe. Though this had nothing to do with my marriage, and though her words were awful, I wouldn't have stopped her testimony for all the gold in the world. I'd spent my life wondering what was so terrible that Mama could never bring herself to reveal it.

"Go on," Merrick said dryly.

"Macy was furious when he learned what had happened. He confronted Pierson, but Roy was finished with poor Lucy. Macy had to pay Elliston to wed her. For nothing would convince Lord Pierson to provide for the girl, not even as his wife in watercolors."

There was a general shock from the men that she'd used that term, for likely they had no idea any woman knew its meaning. My father cringed and placed his hands on either side of his head.

"It angered Macy so much," Lady Foxmore continued, "that he's thwarted Pierson's every attempt to obtain a mistress ever since, though from what I hear, he's tried."

Simmons stood, along with many of my father's cronies, who were dotted about the courtroom. There was shouting and arguing, but I felt too sickened to move. I pictured Mama frightened and alone with child. I felt tears sting my eyes. No wonder she had been so sad all the time.

"The counsel will take a fifteen-minute break," the judge ordered.

My father grasped my wrist. His face was screwed tight with pain. "Take her. Now."

Simmons frowned, looking over the scene. I followed his gaze. He watched Mr. Whitney, who had finally been handed the letter that had circulated through the courtroom. His expression was one of confusion.

"Now!" my father managed, looking ready to fall over from pain.

Simmon's grip was a vise. He pulled me after him, but instead of heading toward the doors, he made a straight line to Mr. Whitney. "Theoretically speaking," he said, approaching my barrister, "if Mrs. Auburn were to disappear right now and never be found again, what would happen to Reverend Auburn?"

"What?" Mr. Whitney said, looking up from the paper.

I glanced at Edward, who watched us from the dock.

"If she were to disappear," Simmons said, speaking very quick and low, "what would happen to Reverend Auburn?"

Mr. Whitney looked furious as he placed the letter on the table. "Don't ask me theoretical questions that I can see through."

Swallowing, I turned the letter so that I could read it for myself. The date showed it to be from the same time period he'd written my mother.

Adelia,

How can I but write? Who else will be as diverted by the twist fate played me? You will crow. I'm in love, and at first sight too. I endure your laughter, knowing my arguments against the possibility of it all these years. She's an angel. She's divine. She's a result of my misdeeds, which endears me to her all the more. Do you remember the summer Lord Pierson had that addiction to that girl under your care? It is their child I intend to collect as my wife. I imagine your shock. I am all gratitude to you. You always hoped to find me a wife, and you have finally succeeded, though unintentionally. Who knew Roy purchased my future happiness with his bribes for more time? Do you remember his pleadings?

The girl's mother visits your neighborhood. Someone by the name of Windham. Learn who they are. Add them to your circle. I'm going to give this girl the most advantaged, overindulged life. Start my wooing for me. Make me mysterious. It's a common weakness amongst your sex.

Chance

"How can you even look at one more word that man says?" Simmons said between his teeth.

I glanced up and found both Mr. Whitney and Simmons staring at me. Realizing that they looked expectant, I said, "I'm sorry; did you ask me a question?"

Mr. Whitney grabbed my arm and pulled me toward the doors. "I need to know how much of what was said was true," he whispered. "Hold nothing back from me."

From the dock, Edward paid rapt attention.

I squeezed my eyes shut, just trying to think. "The jewelry and the necklace, that's true."

"A thirty-thousand-pound necklace!" Mr. Whitney's whisper was incredulous. "You forgot to mention that?"

I nodded. "Yes, it . . . didn't seem important."

"You went into a jeweller's and tested Macy's love and commitment to you by asking for a thirty-thousand-pound necklace, and that didn't strike you as important?"

"No. It was Forrester. I didn't do it. I'd forgotten I'd even had it."

"What?" Perspiration trickled down Mr. Whitney's brow.

"We blackmailed Mr. Macy together," I whispered, crossing my arms, and got the facts out of order. "Only he ran away. Before we did, though, he tested Macy by pretending he was me and asking for the necklace."

"Forrester! I knew it!" Simmons swore beneath his breath, then looked at my father, who still cradled his head in pain. "And that testimony about you and Edward?"

"True," I whispered.

Mr. Whitney's eyes bulged. "He forced himself on you?"

I felt my face turn beet red. "No, of course not."

Mr. Whitney placed his hand on his hip, and when he spoke, it was clear he worked to keep his temper. "Where is Dalry? I need someone to interpret for us."

Simmons turned to me. "We're leaving now."

"I'm not leaving Edward," I protested. "I won't go into hiding, not if it endangers him."

"What a clever trap," Mr. Whitney said, then looked at Mr. Macy with a sort of amazement. He turned back to us. "I don't know how he did it, but he outmaneuvered us in every way." Then, incredulously, "He is Adolphus. He truly is."

"We're leaving." Simmons wore a stricken look as he mentally bade good-bye to England. "Tell Pierson that I said she'd be taken care of, on my honor."

"I'm not going," I said. "I swear to you, I'll run to Macy right now over allowing Edward to be sentenced to death. That is what's happening, isn't it?"

"You're going." Simmons's grip was strong.

Though I dug my shoes into the floor, they only slipped over the surface. Panicked, I glanced over my shoulder at Edward. His face was marked with love as he nodded approval to Simmons and farewell to me.

"No," I said, my face crumpling. "No, no!"

Simmons walked with determination, straight through the heart of the Old Bailey, dragging me behind him.

I tried to grab hold of a pillar and even one passing magistrate, who threw us an offended look. Simmons wasn't deterred. Within a minute sunlight blinded me and I had to turn my gaze to the ground until my eyes adjusted. Hudson hastened toward us.

"Prepare the horses. We're headed to the docks." Simmons shielded his eyes and took in the position of the sun. "We shouldn't have a problem with the tide, at least."

"Let me go," I begged. "You know as well as I do that I need to remain here."

Simmons made no reply.

"Haven't you ever been in love?" I asked.

"No," was his curt reply.

I shut my eyes, desperately trying to think of anything that might work with this man. But here was another soul I didn't truly know. I'd taken no pains to get to know him. In fact, I'd misjudged him and believed he was Macy's spy.

Apparently he was exceedingly loyal to my father.

Trying to hold back my despair, I rose on tiptoes and looked about. Everywhere people stared at me, but no one I recognized. Yet wasn't Macy bound to have his men nearby?

Wildly, I dug through my brain for any name I'd ever heard Macy use. "Rooke," I screamed as loud as I could. "Snyder!" I moved on to the names that Forrester had once tried to ask me about. "Dillyworth!"

"Will you please stop?" Simmons turned his head. "You don't even know who that is. Trust me, you wouldn't call for him if you did."

"Rooke!" I screamed again.

To my astonishment, someone did respond to my call. A nearby prisoner jerked his head in my direction, and I found myself staring at a man with an eye patch and a scarred cheek. I recognized him from the day he'd placed me in Macy's carriage with Rooke. He recognized me too. He must have thought it would be of benefit to come to Macy's wife's aid, because he roared and ran toward us, even though his hands and feet were bound in thick iron chains. Some of the jailors guarding him shouted and lifted their clubs.

Simmons startled with shock at the sight of a brawny man in chains racing toward him. It was all I needed. I tugged hard, throwing him off-balance, and then turned and ran back to the courthouse. Simmons wasted no time recovering.

I tore up the steps and shoved past two clerks in conversation. Simmons's footsteps pounded behind me.

Near the courtroom, I spied the doors still open and threw all my energy into crossing back into that chamber. All at once, Mr. Macy leaned into view and grabbed me by the arm. He yanked me to a halt. He assessed me for a fraction of a second, betraying nothing.

My body recoiled from his touch.

His glittering gaze scanned the scene behind me, narrowing on Simmons as he approached.

"You will release her," Simmons ordered, raising his fists as if prepared to fight.

Mr. Macy's look would have felled anyone. "I better not find that you put one mark on her, Simmons." Then, as if drawn to where my father's steward had clamped my arm only seconds ago, Mr. Macy picked up that wrist and examined its redness. His expression grew so baleful that fear undulated through me.

Even Simmons took a step backwards.

"Where was he taking you?"

I felt so miserable, I glanced toward the hall I'd just run down.

Mr. Macy stared at me with intensity. "Where—" his tone was iron—"was he taking you?"

"To the docks. That's all I know."

Mr. Macy lifted one brow at Simmons, angling his head. "Leave and do not come within a rod's distance of my wife again."

Simmons hesitated, but I gave him a quick nod of permission to leave. Macy was serious.

Mr. Macy watched until Simmons entered the courtroom, then slowly returned his focus to me. "Obviously the docks didn't suit you. Where do you wish to be?"

Once again I tried to remove his hand from my arm, but he held tight. "You know where I want to be," I pleaded. "With Edward."

He gave me a queer look, but then a ghost of a smile softened his lips as if he was amused. "No, dearest, I'm afraid my patience in that direction has ended." His eyes narrowed in thoughtfulness before he pulled me toward the gallery. Mr. Macy led me with a firm grip, then signalled for Rooke to stand and join us.

Mr. Whitney's eyes lifted to us from the floor of the courtroom with a look of disbelief.

Beyond him, Simmons tenderly knelt at my father's side. I couldn't tell you what I felt at that moment, for I'd just heard testimony that he'd viciously used and abandoned Mama, yet even from a distance, as Simmons informed him that he'd lost me to Macy, I felt pity. He gripped Simmons's arms with anguish and great pain washing his countenance.

"Has there been any sign of him?" Macy asked.

Rooke shook his head. "None."

"Nobody outside has spotted him either."

"Are you still certain he'll come?"

"Oh, he's out there somewhere." Macy's feral gaze swept over the courtroom. "Of that there's no doubt. I can practically feel his moody presence."

I tucked one arm over my stomach, realizing they were talking about Mr. Greenham. I cast them a guilty glance, wondering if Macy knew Greenham had managed to contact me through Nancy.

"Take her to my house," Mr. Macy instructed Rooke. "Do not leave her side." He grinned. "She's bold enough to slip through people's hands today. She's already escaped her father's steward."

"Wait," I pleaded, my eyes still fixed on my father as his face tightened into silent grief. Watching as he mourned the loss of a child hurt me deeply, too, though I knew he mourned an illusion. For what relationship had we? "They still haven't declared whether or not our marriage is legal. There's still a chance."

Amusement filled Mr. Macy's eyes.

I shifted my gaze to Mr. Whitney, who flipped through his voluminous pages, preparing his cross-examinations, and then to the various counsel spread throughout the chamber. Most eyes were on Macy, like trained hounds watching their master, ready to take orders. Though it hurt, I swivelled so that I could see Edward.

Chains did not suit him. He wore the fierce look of a warrior, as he had that night at the opera as he watched us.

"I want to stay," I said, turning my attention back to Mr. Macy, "until the verdict."

"Fine," he decided, his gaze sweeping over the men again with dissatisfaction as if he was angered that Mr. Greenham hadn't stood up from the crowd and revealed himself. "But not here. She spent the morning in the Lord Mayor's parlor. Take her back there."

He placed my right arm in Rooke's hand as if I were a package being passed on, then started away.

"May I make a request?" I found myself saying to Macy's back.

He turned, one eyebrow arched.

The words were like chewing gravel. "If they decide we're married, will you make certain Edward isn't harmed? For me? And . . . and I don't want to go straight to your house. I want to be allowed to return to London House to pack my own belongings." My voice choked during that speech, for in truth, I wanted to ensure that I packed the shirt that still smelled like Edward. "Please."

Macy considered me, saying nothing. Then, with a flick of his eyes, he told Rooke to remove me.

⁓

I sat in the corner of the chamber that Isaac and I had occupied earlier that morning. The feel of two solid walls against my back and the solid floor beneath me was comforting. What did it matter if all emotional, relational, and spiritual realities shifted around me? At least the physical ones were still the same.

I drew my knees close and sat silently praying for what felt like hours.

I thought of all the Old Testament stories where God displayed his hand and rescued his people. Surely, I reasoned with God again and again, without him I had no escape.

Rooke waited near the door, arms crossed. The few times I glanced at him, he paid no attention to me, though all his senses appeared heightened as if he considered himself in danger.

After an eternity, the door clicked open.

Paling, I lifted my head, not certain who would walk through the door.

"Are you Rooke?" Mr. Whitney's voice asked.

Rooke eyed him suspiciously.

"I'm to pass." Mr. Whitney held up his hands. "I'm to say that my boots are clean."

Rooke frowned but jerked his head for Mr. Whitney to enter. "Where's Macy?"

Mr. Whitney did not answer him but fastened his sorrowful gaze on me.

I hugged myself, already knowing the outcome. Mr. Whitney wouldn't have learned one of Macy's signals unless we'd lost the trial and Macy had sent him. There was no panic while inside that chamber. Instead I felt like a battle-weary veteran.

Mr. Whitney seemed scarcely able to find the words, though twice he attempted to open his mouth.

I decided to spare him. "We lost."

He simply nodded. Then, with an expression of one gathering courage, he curled his fingers into fists. His eyes darted in the direction of Rooke behind him. Thus I perceived that he thought it his duty to save me.

Not wanting him to do anything rash, I determined to keep him occupied by making demands upon him as a lady. I held up my hands. "Will you please help me stand?"

He obliged.

As I dusted off my skirt, I looked about the chamber. "My bonnet and parasol. Please, I need them. Do you see them?"

He frowned, debating as if torn between obeying a lady's request and tackling Adolphus's organization single-handedly. As I hoped, years of good breeding overruled everything else, making it impossible to do anything except search the seats of the chairs. He handed me my bonnet.

"And my parasol!" I demanded, though I knew full well it was in the witness box of the courtroom.

"Rooke," Macy's voice sounded from the door. "Take my wife to London House. Keep two men at each door there while she packs. I'll collect her myself."

And with that, Macy was gone. Two other men entered the chamber, preventing any attempt to aid my escape. Mr. Whitney looked grim as he stood and considered the men.

"It's all right," I whispered to him. "I think it's in the witness box."

His eyes remained fastened on the men, making me wonder how a man of position felt when he suddenly realized he was powerless. The men who entered the chamber paid no mind to him but eyed me uncertainly, in a strange reversal of roles.

To be united with Macy, I realized, was to be equated with power.

"Your names," I said, emotionless. The next time I needed to scream for help on the streets, my list would be longer than three names. Furthermore, I knew that my ability to survive in Macy's organization would increase if I appeared more powerful.

Both men hesitated, so I eyed them for all I was worth.

Rooke laughed. "If I were you, I'd tell her your names."

"Holt," the broad-shouldered man said dubiously.

"Ostlere," the other supplied.

I was aware that Mr. Whitney watched me with mute astonishment, for I must have seemed like a completely different person to him, but if I allowed myself to touch upon his thoughts,

I knew I'd dissolve. So I refused to acknowledge him. Instead I displayed my newfound clout and gave orders to Rooke next. "You will take me to London House. Now!"

Survival is different from healing. Instinctively I knew it was necessary to take advantage of position and leverage, the only rule of law in Macy's kingdom. Thus the newspapers were not altogether inaccurate to report that I left the Old Bailey in the company of three men, each with a ruthless and calculated look.

Rooke grinned at my newfound determination as Macy's carriage jostled through the streets. Ostlere, however, studied me with a wary look. Less than a block from the Old Bailey I turned an envenomed gaze in his direction, warning him that I didn't wish to be studied.

The whites of Rooke's teeth flashed as he advised, "I wouldn't upset her."

Our lives are littered with what-ifs. In order to stay sane, we tell ourselves to leave them scattered where they lie on the floor—never to wonder, never to turn and try to sweep them up—for they are impossible to transport to the rubbish bin. The past is sealed, and looking back only unmakes us. Yet in writing my story to you, I have already turned back.

And here my hand trembles.

What would have happened if I'd never returned to London House?

My entire life hinged on that simple request made in the courtroom of the Old Bailey. All for wanting to be able to breathe in the scent of Edward one last time, I unleashed a series of unalterable events.

At London House, I found myself looking up at the massive brick structure for what I believed was the last time, and my determination faltered.

The door swung open and Jameson's dazed face appeared at the top of the steps. His horrified expression told me he'd heard the verdict. My knees weakened as I grasped the wrought-iron fence, for I realized that, in stark contrast to the man who sired me, this man was a true father to me. His own look of stricken dismay proved it.

And as painful as healing had been, now that I was cut off from it, I saw I desired healing above anything. More than power, prestige, privilege. I wanted relationships, not dominance. I wanted the ties of love that the Dalry family possessed, the beautiful humility of Jameson. What was the carnality of Macy compared to the fire of Edward? Jesus walked the earth declaring that the Kingdom of God was at hand. One taste of that Kingdom is enough to make all else unsatisfactory.

I felt my face crumple as I looked upon Jameson. Then, knowing I couldn't let Macy's men see me weak, not even for a moment, I hastened up the stairs.

"What happened to Edward?" Jameson breathed. "I learned the verdict, but not the sentence."

I stared at him, horrified, for I didn't know either.

And with that, I was unmade.

In the short span of time it took to secure my foothold in Macy's syndicate, I'd lost sight of the only person who mattered. And if I lost sight of that, then who was I? Surely I'd become the proverbial salt underfoot. The memory of Edward as he'd walked amongst the girls at the orphanage, the way he'd studied Jacob Turner's plight with the deepest compassion, and how he'd glared at my father as he declared himself deaf to him until he honored me—all played through my mind, unravelling me. There were only two sides here. One that sought position and one that bound up the brokenhearted. I'd pledged myself to the wrong side before I had any awareness of what was truly at stake.

As I stepped through that doorway, the weight of all that I'd lost crushed me. I tore off my bonnet, then ripped out the pins holding my hair. The horrified expressions of my father's staff surrounded me, but not one dared to approach. The loss was mine alone to bear. I wept as I gave the order for someone to go to the Old Bailey and learn the fate of Edward and to fetch my father, who was in great pain.

I have no memory of how I made it to my bedchamber, but I do recall the agony of entering it. Wildly I looked around the space, as I accepted the realization that there was nothing but endless days of loss ahead of me.

I screamed and screamed all the pent-up frustration of being helpless. Catching sight of myself in the mirror, I picked up the nearest object and smashed the looking glass. My grief was so wild that I tore through the drawers of my vanity for scissors, determined I would chop off my hair at the scalp. If Macy wanted me, then let him find me in ashes and sackcloth. When I was unable to find a pair, I curled in a ball on the floor, where I alternately sobbed and screamed.

Elsewhere in the house, I'm told, Isaac lifted his head, hearing my hoarse and anguished cries. His face was grieved as he softly said, "Upon my word, James, her pain rends my heart to its core."

To the footman's surprise, Isaac did not immediately rise. Instead he closed the book he'd been reading and bowed his head, allowing the volume to touch his forehead. He kept this prayerful repose until my shrieks quieted, and then he stood in a fluid motion.

He gestured to his correspondences. "If I'm occupied when Lord Pierson arrives home, would you please see he receives these letters straightaway? He'll want to address them immediately. There's also a letter from Forrester he needs to see. It's on his desk."

A minute later Isaac cracked open my door and slipped into my chamber. Had he entered a moment sooner, I wouldn't have been able to endure another soul touching me, but I was spent by the time he gently placed a hand on my shoulder.

As I turned my face toward him, my anger drained, leaving me with clean grief.

My sobs quieted into a plaint over all that was lost. Not just for me, but for everyone. After all, what soul is equipped to handle what has become the human experience?

As only he could, Lord Dalry comforted Rachel as she grieved her shorn dreams and her dead children.

He held me tightly against him and wept.

I cried until exhausted and then started trying to plan out my next step, knowing that Mr. Macy would arrive any minute. I would quit this place having caused more harm than good. It was so unbearable.

"I didn't know." I struggled to make my thick voice legible. "I didn't know. I'm so sorry, Isaac. My understanding was marred, and I didn't see you. I didn't know." Realizing I wasn't making sense, I tried again. "Forrester put that story in the paper, not me. I thought he was going to reason with my father. And then your face! I have nightmares still about it—"

"Shh. No, don't cry. Edward was a good choice. Be forever free from that dream. There's nothing to forgive."

"Promise me, promise me you'll marry Evelyn and be happy. You must swear that; you must! When I'm at Eastbourne, I need to be able to picture a happy outcome for at least one of us. Or I can't do this! I won't be able to survive this. I can't."

Isaac shifted so we could face each other. His face was expressive but with an emotion I couldn't read. "Think upon Evelyn, then, when you need that picture, for she is going to have her happy ending. Just wait and see."

I nodded and squeezed my thanks into the sleeve of his coat.

Thoughts follow no direct course when under duress; they take random, senseless paths, becoming as splintered as we are. My mind switched from Isaac to the fact I still didn't know what had happened to Edward, to the fact that any minute I'd find myself back in Macy's care. Each facet of my being, each thought, and each emotion was shattered, fracturing me to the very essence of my soul.

"I have to pack," I said, feeling desperate again. I scrambled from the floor and tottered to the wardrobe, where I started to claw through its contents for Edward's shirt. "Where's his shirt?" I began sobbing anew. "Where is it? I must find it!"

Isaac, gentle as ever, managed to collect my thoughts and emotions for me and seal them up. He shrugged off his frock coat, then held it out for me. "Come with me."

I shook my head, for he didn't understand. I returned to emptying the wardrobe. When my fingers finally located the roughened fabric, I held my face to it, but my nose was so swollen from crying, I couldn't even breathe, much less smell it.

"You're more overwrought than you realize," Isaac whispered. "Come, allow me to read you to sleep. You need it more than you know."

I gestured to my belongings, shaking my head, too worked up to speak.

His gaze followed the motion of my hand before it took in the strewn contents of the wardrobe, and he became riveted. The book I'd brought from Maplecroft lay amongst the items I'd tossed out. His eyes stilled with wonder and disbelief as he revealed the hidden painting. "How on earth did this get here?"

I ran my fingers through my hair, sobbing anew. "I stole it. It wasn't Eaton's business. He's a liar! He's . . . he's . . ." Then, looking at my belongings scattered about my chamber, "I need to pack. Macy will be here soon."

Isaac placed his coat about my shoulders. "Let the servants attend this. Come be with me instead."

I buried my face in my hands, for it was too overwhelming to release the only thing I knew for certain I was supposed to do. "I need to pack. I have to. You don't understand. It's . . . it's . . ." I hiccupped, realizing I couldn't form a good reason for why I had to pack right that second—though the notion pounded against my brain that it was the most crucial thing in existence. Then, recognizing I wasn't making sense, "I'm sorry,

Isaac. I don't know what I'm doing. I can't even trust myself right now."

"Then trust me. Listen only to my voice. Just breathe. You're safe. Think of nothing outside this moment. I will keep you so nothing will happen to you." He placed a hand on my shoulder. "Let's retire to the library."

He held my hand, keeping my arm tucked beneath his as he led me down the staircase. More than one servant's eyes were tinted with red, making me realize how sympathetic they were to my plight. As we made our way down the last flight, Jameson hastened across the foyer to meet us.

His gaze landed on the book in Isaac's hand before he froze and met Isaac's eyes with a stricken look. His mouth parted as he took a small step backwards.

"Will you see that no one disturbs us until Mr. Macy arrives?" Isaac asked him.

Jameson seemed unable to speak. His eyes were lachrymose as he gave a nod. His mouth swelled with sorrow, but then, clearing his throat, he gruffly managed, "Edward is fine. They tattooed his thumb and then arrested him again for ra—" He remembered himself in time and stamped his feet. "Er—on other charges. There'll be another trial."

I blinked back tears, nodding.

"Thank you, Jameson." Isaac placed a hand on the butler's shoulder and met his eyes before continuing toward the library.

Once inside, Isaac convinced me to drink one of my father's sedatives mixed with wine. Apparently my father kept small packets in his desk, for he often felt anxious before important meetings. I don't remember taking the drug, though I have a clear memory of Isaac's thoughtful face as I handed him back the glass.

He took up Lady Josephine's book, which he had carried into the room, and in his serene tone, he began reading. His pleasant voice filled the corners of the chamber and inspissated the atmosphere with a heavy, rich peace.

Still clutching Edward's shirt, I eventually rested my head against Isaac's shoulder. Though I'd intended to remain awake, I realized that Isaac had given me a stronger dose than I expected. It was as if roots of sleep grew out of me and deepened and spread through the down-feathered sofa and through Isaac's peerless body, gripping and pulling me downward. The weight of slumber pressed upon me as I sank into the unfathomable levels of consciousness. I shut my eyes, allowing myself to finally breathe as if sleeping.

I have lived and relived this memory so many times in my life, bookmarking certain facts, that now I only remember what I've told myself happened. The memory is not real; it is only the memory of a memory.

Here is what I've told myself.

Just before I plunged into the deepest stage of slumber, Isaac stopped reading and clasped me tight.

Twenty-Nine

I AWOKE TO THE SOUND of James's garbled weeping.

The slam of heavy doors was followed by the noise of more weeping—women's voices this time. Intuitively I knew it was the maids. The sedative became a brick wall I had to break through in order to wake. Leaden weights sat upon my thoughts and limbs, making even the simplest ideas slow.

But eventually I managed to open my eyes, and I spied the library's magnificent ceiling. I blinked, dazed, not quite certain what I was doing there. Forcing myself to wake, I turned my face toward the door.

James crouched just inside, unable to stand. He pressed his back against the wall, covering his mouth. His face was marred. His eyes met mine, but he couldn't speak. Behind him, I caught the refrain of weeping throughout London House.

Chills ran along my arms and legs as I managed to stand.

My head felt weighty and my legs hollow as I stumbled into the hall. There, a maid sat on the floor, sobbing into her apron, and farther down the hall, two upper maids sagged against the walls, crying and staring at me, too horrified to speak. My breath came in hard pants. Panicked, I picked up my skirts and rushed past them.

Suspecting the truth, I shook my head and begged God—not this! Not this!

Outside the smoking chamber, a stableman stood, clutching his hat. He turned at my arrival, his face stunned with disbelief and pain. It was the look Sarah wore after Mama died.

It's not Isaac, I assured myself. It couldn't be. God could not permit such a possibility. *He isn't allowed,* I thought frantically, *to give people more than they can bear.*

As I raced toward the chamber, the stableman tried to take me by my arms. "Do not enter, miss."

I violently threw off his hand.

Heart pounding, I gained the threshold. At the farthest end of the chamber, Mr. Macy lay dead, a frozen look of malice and consternation upon his face. Scattered about him were overturned chairs and tables, broken glasses, and fractured pictures, as if he'd tried to stave off the demons as they gathered to collect his soul.

I sagged against the doorframe in complete disbelief. At first my mind wouldn't even register the combination of impossible thoughts—that Macy was dead, and that Macy was in my father's smoking chamber. But he was dead! I clutched Mama's locket, feeling a visceral pain that I couldn't even label if I tried.

Only then did my ears note the soft gasp of someone weeping quietly. Turning toward it, I caught sight of Isaac's polished black shoe. It extended into view just beyond the large sofa. My stomach plummeted.

Feeling vertigo, I stepped forward. And my world stopped.

Jameson wept as he cradled Isaac's head.

I had thought the hour England declared me Macy's wife, nothing worse could ever happen to me. But there is always the possibility of a deeper, more acute pain.

I gasped in horror, starting to cry, then rushed to him.

Isaac's lifeless eyes stared up at me. In his right hand, he held a brandy snifter. A wet stain spread out over my father's Turkish carpet. I shook my head, denying this, though I saw enough to envision what had happened. His silk cravat stirred as I dropped on my knees beside him. I laid my head on Isaac's chest and listened, but it was silent. "No," I pleaded in a whisper. "No."

He couldn't hear me, and he couldn't respond. Death already marked his handsome face. There was nothing I could do. Nothing I could say.

"You may not leave me," I shouted, pounding on his chest, screaming through tears. "I do not give my consent. You may not! You will live! You will not do this for me!"

"Lass." Jameson stayed my hand. "He's gone."

"No!" I jerked my hand away. "No! No, he's not!"

I laid my head upon his breast, already knowing I wouldn't hear a heartbeat. It wasn't Isaac anymore. It was only his body.

How dare he! I wanted to scream at him. *How dare he!* I wanted to beat his chest and force his heart to start pumping again. This should have been my death. How dare he decide to sacrifice his own life? I hadn't asked him to, nor wanted him to do this. It was the cruelest, most unfair twist of the universe. He'd waited so long to win my trust and friendship. And now that he had it, he was gone.

I dug my fingers into my hair. Never again would that soothing presence walk into a room. Never again would his calm face sit across from me at the breakfast table.

I pressed my face into his chest, willing his soul to return. Yet I knew that even now he was meeting his Maker.

"Please, Isaac, please." My voice was muffled and stretched with pain. "Please don't leave me."

Two magistrates arrived and stood aghast in the doorway as they took in the scene.

I gave them a desperate look, begging them to do something.

They say my gaze kept travelling over Isaac's body as I rocked—as if I were unable to comprehend what had just passed.

But I comprehended. Oh, but I comprehended.

I was escorted with Jameson to the hall, where we were ordered not to leave until our statements could be taken.

Once again, London House became the scene of an investigation. The crowd who had gathered outdoors to applaud Macy's success in reclaiming his wife found themselves front-row spectators to another scandal.

Tears streamed down my cheeks as I sat and watched the police file in and out of my father's smoking chamber. I made no attempt to abate my sobs. I wanted to stop feeling. I wanted numbness. I wanted the blurry indifference that I'd walked in most of my life. But it wouldn't come.

Within the hour my father arrived. His face had no color as he staggered toward his smoking chamber. Simmons followed. He alone glanced at me, seemingly befuddled and frightened. I shut my eyes. They'd somehow heard the news but like me had refused to believe it. I tensed, knowing this would devastate my father, for Isaac was the lifeblood of our house.

To this day I am haunted by the excruciating and inarticulate cry that issued from my father as he discovered his beloved son dead.

⁓

I saw the value of a man like Simmons during those agonizing hours that followed Isaac's death. He alone managed the unmanageable. Macy's estates and wealth were now mine, and Simmons handled them as he likewise managed my father's and the Dalrys' affairs. He made cut-and-dried decisions that the rest of us were too overwhelmed to address.

The irony was that as Macy's wife, it was my duty to sit with his corpse that first night. I shall not, however, describe that gruesome task, except to say that my thoughts remained with

Lady Dalry and Evelyn, who took the first nightly watch over Isaac's body.

Death is profound. The absence of a soul is felt in the very fabric of our universe. Each one of us gives life or pain to others—though we often fail to recognize the life givers until they've departed.

But then how we languish without them.

There are certain harrowing moments one must undergo with any death, moments that force us to relive the loss and plunge us back into the landscape of darkness. The following morning, when James set down the newspapers with Isaac's death splashed on every front page, was one. The chair across from me never felt so barren.

My father was more ashen than I'd ever seen him as he realized he couldn't discuss the papers with his protégé. The malady came over him, forcing him back to bed.

Afterwards, I sat by the window, missing Isaac with an ache so fierce I thought I'd never recover. Gone was the velvet way with which he moved through life, and it angered me that anyone could gather outside London House in curiosity on such a tragic day. I watched the nursemaids stand chatting with their charges on their hips. Sad-faced men discussed Isaac as if they felt his loss. But had they truly loved him, they'd be home grieving, not relishing the spectacle. Isaac's absence punctured the fabric of all that was true and right. So much good had just been removed from England—from her present and her future. And people milled about gossiping over it.

When I could take it no longer, I left my window seat and confronted the place where I could grieve in earnest. I found in Isaac's snuggery traces of his presence. I covered my heart as I took in the familiar scent of this chamber.

He has to be alive, my spirit cried. There over the back of the chair was his favorite jacket, for heaven's sake. How could he not be coming back? How was it possible he wasn't about to cross under that doorframe with his benign expression that hid the vast greatness of his soul?

I picked up the coat, wanting to scream my agony into it, but my throat was already raw from the previous day. Instead I took in his chamber—the notes in his handwriting, the portraits of his family. I'd done this before. I knew this path. Right now I could remember him vividly. I knew who he was. I knew him. But he would fade as surely as the scent on his clothing would.

It is a blessed relief that memories and raw emotions fade, for which one of us could ever survive every wound remaining open? But at that moment the mercy felt more like a horror. I didn't want to forget all but the fragments of Isaac. I didn't want to see him dissipate in the haze of time that swallows the mundane remembrances as well as the painful. I wanted to retain everything.

I crumpled his jacket against my chest, wishing I might never leave this spot. For here I still knew him and still retained every memory. And when I left, he'd be truly gone.

I hadn't heard Jameson enter the chamber, but as he slowly placed a hand on my shoulder, I turned my tear-streaked face toward him.

Grief and compassion lined his writhen face.

For a moment I felt comfort. Had he not also lost Isaac? Did he not consider Lord Dalry amongst the brood of hurting fledglings that he'd gathered beneath his protective care? Yet another part of me wished to give Jameson a cold shoulder. For he was elderly and soon to pass, and I dreaded to suffer any more losses. I swiped the heel of my hand over my eyes, shaking my head. "I can't do this," I finally said, my voice thick and ugly. "I can't do this anymore."

Jameson considered my comment a moment, then said, "Isaac believed you could, and so do I."

I clutched Isaac's coat tighter but acknowledged Jameson with my gaze. "How could he have done this to me?" My voice broke. "I didn't want him to die for me. If I had to choose, I'd rather have him alive, even if it meant my being with Macy right now."

"It was his gift to you, lass."

I'd cried so much, it hurt even to tear up. "It wasn't his decision to make."

"He prayed long and hard over it," Jameson said.

I glanced at him, sensing that Jameson knew far more than he was telling me. My breathing stilled. "Please tell me you didn't know."

The haunted look Jameson gave me made my blood run cold. He gave a slight nod. "I knew. About a week before the trial, Mr. Whitney sent a request for books from your father's library in the middle of the night. He needed so many that when Dalry found I was still awake, he recruited my help. On our way, as our carriage waited for a flock of sheep to pass, someone opened the door and joined us in the carriage."

Jameson's face looked dour. "The man kept his face hidden. He was tall, though—so much so, he had to bend to keep his head from mashing against the top of the carriage. He was so stealthy, not even Hudson realized a passenger had climbed in with us."

Stress needled my stomach as the name of John Greenham arose. He'd killed Mama for Mr. Macy. The idea that he might have had something to do with Isaac's death made him all the more loathsome. "What did he say?"

Jameson shook his head. "Not a word. He handed Dalry a note with a vial, then, after giving me a look that chilled me, exited the carriage. That night, Dalry came to my office. I knew something in that note had changed him, because he sat for ten minutes, looking disturbed, before speaking."

I shut my eyes, hugging Isaac's coat.

"He showed me the vial and said if we lost the case, he had the means to kill Macy. According to the letter, Macy wouldn't touch any food or drink unless the person offering it partook first, making it difficult to poison him." Jameson met my eyes. "Master Isaac was advised to give the vial to you. Macy apparently trusted the food in his own household."

My blood ran cold.

"Master Isaac had already rejected that option. He didn't want you to risk being hanged for murder; neither did he desire you to live with something like that on your conscience. He also feared what would happen if Macy found it on your personage." Jameson's countenance broke and he removed a handkerchief to wipe his nose, taking a minute before continuing. "He wanted to know if I thought it was a mortal sin to poison Macy together with himself."

"Jameson." My voice came out strained. "What did you tell him?"

"I didn't know." Jameson spread his hands. "How could I answer a question like that? How could I say yes or no? Edward is the one with training. Rather than leaving him burdened with such thoughts, I tried to steer him to a better frame of mind. I recommended he lay a fleece before the Lord. I suggested he pray that if he were allowed to do it, then Mr. Macy would come here to London House after the trial, so he'd be less suspicious if Isaac invited him to drinks. But then, fearing that Macy might not be able to resist the opportunity to gloat his victory over your father, I suggested that Isaac also pray for a very clear, unmistakable sign."

I covered my mouth, recalling Lady Josephine's book.

Jameson's eyes grew red and glassy.

"You knew," I whispered, remembering the way Jameson had gasped and stepped backwards. "Didn't you? When we came downstairs and you saw the book in his hands?"

Though he blinked hard, his face screwed with pain. "Yes, but there was also a chance it wasn't that poetry book. Yesterday when he came home from court, there was a letter awaiting him from Mr. Forrester."

Afterwards, I learned that Forrester had located Ben Dalry.

Mr. Greenham hadn't sent him on a wild-goose chase after all. Years prior, Ben had disappeared while helping Mr. Forrester transport a witness—a prostitute who was ready to testify against Macy. Apparently I wasn't the first person whom Greenham had taken pity on. Instead of killing the pair, as ordered, Greenham had forced them aboard a ship heading toward America. Papers had been forged stating that he was an indentured servant. So great was her fear of Macy, the prostitute had been more than willing to go along with the story rather than return to England. When Forrester failed to checkmate Macy with his Gypsy heritage, Mr. Greenham sent him another means of destroying his foe.

Had Isaac taken the reappearance of Ben as a sign? It was possible, for right after he read Forrester's letter, Isaac had pondered a bit, then sat down and penned a series of letters to his loved ones.

Later I also learned that my father's associates prevented his being at London House while Macy collected me. Whether Isaac had orchestrated that too, I do not know. Thus, when Macy arrived, it was Isaac who greeted him, and Isaac who showed him where I slumbered in the library. Only James witnessed what unfolded next. I'm told that Macy knelt beside me, and with great care he scrutinized every inch of me as if making certain I'd not been harmed in any way. Then, with an expression of kindness, he gently kissed my brow and thanked Isaac for calming me. He spoke of how difficult the past months had been for him.

Even with his prior knowledge of Mr. Macy, James's gut was wrenched with sympathy. He likely thought Isaac felt the same emotion, because Isaac in turn invited Macy to partake of cigars and drinks and discuss other ways to ease my transition. As they tapped their way down the hall to the smoking room, Isaac offered his hopes that this entire affair hadn't forever marred his chances of one day becoming prime minister, that he deeply regretted the fissure that this entire scandal had created between him and Macy's cronies.

Isaac played his role so flawlessly that even Macy, who guarded himself every waking moment, thought himself safe.

I ache to think of Isaac's final performance. Of course Macy fell for it. He viewed life as a power struggle for wealth and prestige. It would have made perfect sense to him that Isaac would scramble to ingratiate himself to the winning side. Isaac was irresistible bait. Here was a chance to not only steal Lord Pierson's daughter, but his protégé as well.

Jameson's hands shook too much for him to dare remain in the chamber; thus he passed the tray to James, then took a place outside in the hall and waited with tears streaming down his cheeks. Throughout the years, I've wondered what thoughts and emotions coursed through Isaac's head as, smiling, he lifted his glass in a toast to Macy and then took the first sip. James tells me that Isaac confessed many frustrations about Roy as they drank, which I believe he did as bait to keep Macy indulging in conversation and partaking of his laced drink. Isaac manifested no signs of being poisoned until well into the third drink, when it was too late for Macy as well.

"He wasn't afraid." Jameson's voice came out strained. "It was the bravest death I've ever had the honor to witness. Right at the end, he wore the same expression as that painting on the book. He kept saying that you were finally free now. That he'd accomplished it."

I collapsed to the seat, wishing Isaac had consulted me. For I never would have allowed any of it.

With stiff movements, Jameson removed a letter with Isaac's seal from his waistcoat and placed it in my hands. "I'll leave you alone to read it, but if you want company afterwards, I'll be in my office."

Some things are sacred, and what Isaac wrote will remain

sealed, for I've never spoken of it to anyone—not even to Edward, who had his own letter, which he read later beneath the ancient oak at Maplecroft. There he sat and pondered Isaac's last words to him for hours afterwards.

For the sake of this narrative, however, I will reveal two things Isaac wrote. For without them, I might be misunderstood.

Isaac wrote to me about my father. He said that it is man's way, not God's, to limit how long it should take someone to change. He urged me to not grow weary. For he still believed that someday I would reap a harvest there.

He also communicated that he needed me. For that morning at the courthouse, he had deposited into me all the stories and memories that would best comfort those who'd grieve him most. He bade me not weep, for if I didn't step forward and take this mantle, no one else would, and those dearest to him would be left lost and broken.

Thirty

✦

I STOOD OUTSIDE my father's bedchamber with Isaac's words burning within my heart, though his last letter to me was safely tucked away. For several minutes I could only stare at the ceiling, waiting until my need to cry had passed.

Then, determined to honor Isaac, I gathered my courage and faced the thick door. As I placed my fingers on the handle, I felt the same sensation I had standing before Mr. Macy's bedchamber. What, I wondered, would it reveal?

An oil lamp was keyed low, washing the room in the weakest possible light. I paused, amazed by the intricacies of the chamber. It was every bit as regal as my father. The gloom made it difficult to see the dark wood ceilings, but I could tell they were cunningly crafted. The silhouette of a massive brass chandelier stood guard over the chamber. The carpentry along the walls looked as though it belonged in a castle, with the wardrobe serving as its gate.

A groan on my right forced me to step into the masculine room. I grew aware of the pleasant scent of pipe smoke. I gave a weak smile, uncertain why it touched me to learn that my father smoked a pipe before bed. I pictured him in a quilted robe, allowing smoke to curl about his head while he pondered.

His bed was at least twelve feet in height with steps leading to it. In the flickering shadows, he looked delirious with pain. Thoughts of Mama crowded my mind, and how he'd abandoned her, leaving us penniless. The cold manner he constantly showed toward me. I splayed my hands over my stomach, tempted to leave, yet knowing that Isaac would have proceeded.

I was uncertain whether my father knew of my presence. He held his eyes as he moaned. Pity struck my heart, for as horrific as Isaac's death was to me, the agony must be tenfold for the man before me. He'd just lost the only person in whom he'd invested his life. Whereas I at least had others.

Half-afraid, I crept to him and knelt on the top step, the folds of my dress puffing around me.

"Papa?" I whispered.

With one hand he reached, and I gave him my hand.

His pain was so great, he clamped his fingers over mine. I closed my eyes, hating pain of any sort. I pressed his hand to my forehead and felt his strained knuckles. A lullaby that Mama used to sing came to mind. This was ridiculous. It hurt him to speak, to open his eyes. I couldn't sing to him. Yet his hand tightened over mine, and I knew another knife of pain had split his head.

How can I sing for him? I thought wildly. He'd abandoned me, left me with a cruel stepfather and then a murderous husband. My throat ached. He'd tried to force me to marry someone besides Edward. He'd ranted, yelled, and raved, making my life miserable.

Like a small child, my father sank back into his pillow. His face was grey as he moaned.

I bent my head, realizing that this, too, was part of my healing—accepting the unacceptable. He wouldn't love me, but it didn't bar me from loving him. A vicar's wife would forgive. And a Dalry sister would sing.

So I did, trying to keep my words susurrant. As I crooned the lullaby, my voice warbled. Yet I sang words that bade him to hush, that said I was there to protect him and love him. Words Mama used to rock me to sleep with. Words he didn't deserve. And all the while, I kept in mind that I hadn't deserved Isaac's love and protection either.

My father's breathing grew shallower and his face relaxed. Eventually, even his clamping fingers loosened. With a gentle hand, I stroked his brow. For a moment I saw all the potential in him that Isaac had. My father was Lord Pierson. He'd risked his reputation, his career, his lifework trying to protect me. Within him were the seeds, even the shoots, of greatness. Already he was benevolent. He fed orphans, gifted large sums of money to charities. He was influential, but not without a heart. Maybe not noble . . . but maybe, just maybe, if enough people saw what he was meant to be and breathed that truth into him . . .

The mattress sank beneath my hands as I stood, then tipped forward and kissed his brow, something I'd never be allowed to do if he were awake.

I left the bedchamber free of my father. I no longer needed his love. I'd found my own.

ᕲᕲ

I never learned whether my father was conscious of my presence that afternoon. But the following day at the breakfast table, after being stabbed by another headline with Isaac's name, he unexpectedly took my hand and just held it.

Isaac's request for me to resist tears was far more challenging than releasing my father from the debt he owed me. Whereas before I would have sat and lamented my loss, all I could think was that I owed Isaac anything he desired. He had given his very life so that I would know freedom.

When the Dalrys came to me, I wondered how he could have asked something so cruel. He knew me. He knew I had no other vent than tears. What did one even do with oneself if not allowed that luxury? For to lie down in a heap and give up did indeed seem like a luxury.

But as Lady Dalry and Kate arrived, my heart broke.

Kate was inconsolable. She'd not calmed since his death, and not even Lady Dalry could soothe her pain. I found myself compelled to go and wrap my arms about her. "Did you know," I whispered softly, pulling her close, "that you were Isaac's first memory?"

She sniffled and gave me a strange look.

"His very first memory is of the day you were born. Your mother had tried to hide that she was in labor," I continued, trying to ignore the discomfort of having more than one set of eyes upon me, "but Isaac was so excited to meet you, he sat up all night waiting. When he heard you cry, he hurried from his bed so he could be the first to hold you."

Kate's sobs softened enough to listen.

"And outside of the midwife," I said, "he was first. She tried to shoo him from the chamber, for not even your mother had seen you yet, but he refused to leave. And then, once they placed you in his arms to be rid of him, he still refused. For you captured his heart and he wouldn't let anyone remove you until he eventually fell asleep."

Kate's eyes were swollen as she faced Lady Dalry. "Is that true, Mama?"

Lady Dalry laughed and cried as she slipped an arm about my waist and pulled me close. Her voice was laced with pain, but she likewise forged on. "Yes. And when he woke, he wouldn't even touch breakfast until he saw for himself you were safe in your cradle. Not even Ben could convince him to come outside and play. He would guard you from being snatched by faeries—an idea the midwife gave him when he refused to hand you over. She teased that a fay was planning to snatch you away and give us a changeling in your stead."

Kate forgot her tears. "He believed that?"

My heart eased, as I knew my actions would have gained Isaac's approval.

When Evelyn Greenley arrived, our eyes met and we clasped hands before tightly clinging to each other. We drew immeasurable strength from one another. Because Ben had been found, she was as jolted and on as strange a ground as I was. We both had been engaged to Isaac while in love with another, which left a strange mingling feeling. There was a relief to have another who understood emotions that had no label. Like twin sisters in sorrow, grace, and mercy, we spoke words of comfort and lightened each other's burdens.

That afternoon as I trudged after Isaac's coffin, people jeered and spat in my path. They were angry, and I couldn't blame them, for they only had one version of my story, and it was a lie—the legacy Mr. Macy left to me. But by that time, I'd found my inner strength. I fixed my eyes on Isaac's coffin, which was draped in crepe and piled with white roses, and knew that I had been loved, that Isaac held my value, and he regarded it in such high esteem, he'd given his life.

But in the grand irony and absurdity of life, someone screamed at me so loudly it drew attention from even the pallbearers. Mr. Whitney looked over his shoulder and found that I had slowed my steps, separating myself from the mourners so as not to distract. He paled, knowing my story better than anyone else in the world. To my amazement, he abandoned Isaac's coffin and hastened to me.

How could I not have been visibly touched? Thus began the rumor that in addition to my other crimes, I'd seduced and had liaisons with my barrister. The fact that we were both too grieved to care what anyone else thought anymore, and that we weren't inclined to lose a friendship forged in the depths of the refiner's fire, didn't help matters either.

There was also the matter of Macy's vast wealth, now my

inheritance both by birth and by marriage, neither of which were strictly aboveboard.

Macy's civil suit against my father was pressed because of Merrick's efforts. Macy had signed a contract giving Merrick the right to represent his estate in the event of his untimely death. I doubt either of them believed Macy would die when it was signed, but it gave Merrick the right to continue the fight.

Despite his influence, my father lost the suit and as Macy's wife I was awarded the lion's share.

Edward's rape charges were dropped after Macy's death. His thumb had been tattooed, marking him a bigamist, even though technically I was the bigamist.

Dust trailed in the wind as he was escorted across the courtyard between two guards to the gate where Jameson, my father, and I awaited him.

That morning as we departed London House, dread had seized me that too much had happened since our parting. What, I wondered with quiet dismay, would Edward make of the changes that had been wrought in me? For I felt like a completely different person.

Yet one look at Edward's eyes was enough to dispel fear. He, too, had matured during our separation. He fixed his unwavering stare on me, assuring me of his unfaltering love, as the guards fumbled with the locks on the chains binding his hands and feet.

The dreamlike quality that had surrounded Isaac's death finally shattered as Edward pulled me against him and lifted me from my feet. I gave a wild sob of joy as I clung to his neck and then kissed him, forgetting that my father and Jameson were present. We remarried the same day, though I kept propriety by continuing to wear mourning for Macy for a full year.

When the pain lessened enough for us to jest about that season of our life, Edward was wont to remind me that he'd suffered greatly for me—he'd been accused of rape and bigamy—and his reward was being marked, so that if I were to die, no one else would ever marry him. Jameson would laugh and tell him those were light consequences for marrying a faerie, and he should thank me instead of complaining. Our children and our grand-children flourished. Our foursome survived, of sorts. Henry and Elizabeth hadn't undergone the same testing as Edward and I had, so for a while we thought them juvenile and they thought us tiresome bores. Eventually life tempered them too.

Those acquainted with the undercurrents of the criminal world have probably well guessed that John Greenham was the famous Lombard Street murderer, who was credited with hun-dreds of murders during Macy's reign of terror. And yes, it is true that I visited him in prison. And yes, I likewise shouted words of courage to him as he was pushed to the gallows. For God's healing extended even there. Was his mistake any different from mine? He'd chosen the wrong path and was unfaithful with the life given him. But the door for healing and change is open to all.

Immediately after he turned himself over to the law, I used my wealth and position to gain an audience with him. There were questions I wanted answered about Macy. There, I learned that the day Mr. Greenham murdered Mama was the day his self-loathing took over. He dealt out death for Macy's crime syndi-cate, but to murder fellow malefactors was quite different from murdering a gentlewoman. Even as she died, Mama pleaded with him to keep me from Macy. Apparently her letter to Macy, grant-ing him permission to marry me, was written under duress. And all those tearful letters were correspondences between her and my father as they tried to figure out a solution for me. When I asked Mr. Greenham if Mr. Macy had ever loved me, he rubbed his eyes, then gave a grim chuckle. He said that when it came to evil, it never ceased to amaze him that every person thinks they're the exception, that their story is different.

"There are no exceptions," he told me, "only consequences. Only fools believe anything else."

It was strange being entrusted with Macy's onerous accumulation of wealth and influence, for it was extracted from human suffering. The girl whom Edward had ministered to at the orphanage, for example, started her life in one of Macy's brothels. There was no way Edward and I could sort through the priceless artifacts and bank records to determine who the rightful owners were. Our only option was to figure out how to use them to bring healing to the people Macy had damaged. Thus his brothels were turned into refuges, his studies in botany entrusted to hospitals. There were orphans and women in need of protection at every corner.

Who can resist the perils that come with fame and fortune, unless such things are already but dung to them? Had Edward and I not suffered to the degree we did before being placed in such a great position, I cannot believe it would have done otherwise than bedevil our lives.

Pain, it seems, was God's sharpening tool.

People may decry God when all is lost—screaming from the wreckage of their lives, demanding answers, unable to comprehend why. Yet who are we to tell a master painter the shades and colors we approve of and the ones we don't—we who are unskilled, and who have no cognizance of the painting's subject matter?

Of course there is always more to the story—parts that I'll never learn. For example, I know not who took advantage of the emerald mine, whose paperwork I'd lost in the carriage, or why my father abandoned Mama. Nor, to my great dismay, why Benjamin Dalry refused to ever meet me. I lost a true friend in Evelyn Greenley. Occasionally I'd spot her at the opera or a soiree, her face beaming with joy as she strode beside her beloved Ben; upon spotting me, her eyes would shine with unfailing love in my direction, though her husband's wishes made any contact impossible.

For each one of us, could we see our individual motives and reasons laid before us, they would make little sense. Reason does not always rule, nor does love, nor does nobility—no matter how desperately we wish to believe it. But shall we judge the path of another? Shall I so easily accuse Forrester of being a beastly coward for running away? Was I there as his houses were burned, his family put in peril, his businesses destroyed? Or dare I call the new Lord Dalry callous, when it was my actions that brought about his brother's death?

Are our own paths truly less tangled?

What would have happened had I obeyed my father and married Isaac? Or stood by my convictions that Mr. Macy wasn't making idle threats when he made it clear he considered me his legal wife?

No one can know. Like everyone else's, my choices were made one at a time, without full knowledge of how they would unfold.

But of what matter? For there is One who is good.

And I know my time draws near, and I can scarcely wait to greet Isaac and tell him that I did not waste his gift, that I learned to love. Soon, soon, I shall greet him and Edward again. Flooded by heaven's light and joy. We shall be united—equals at last, each one of us pure and clean. And how we shall laugh and laugh, knowing that we overcame. How shall we handle so much joy after so much pain?

But this I know, even on this side of life's veil: my heart fairly bursts with love. I have so much. I have been so richly blessed. I am a river, as it was promised.

At long last, like Mr. Macy, I feel no shame for who I am.

I have become the adulteress dragged before Jesus' feet. What does any opinion matter, save his?

Willingly I spread wide my arms for those who cast stones. It is their own jaundiced eyes that keep them hurling jagged rocks. It is their own souls they cut to ribbons.

With such dreadful truths ruling the universe, it is no wonder that grace and mercy are all that is left us.

ACKNOWLEDGMENTS

I AM SO GRATEFUL TO:

My daughter for sharing her time with Julia yet again! This is it. You won't have to share with her anymore!

My incredible editors: Caleb Sjogren, Stephanie Broene, and Karen Watson. Thank you so much for the thoughtful attention you gave to this story. I cannot tell you how blessed I am to work with you!

Chip MacGregor, the incredible agent man.

Lawrie for the beautiful and incredible desk that you gave me years ago. It gave me fuel to keep writing, and it has become my workstation regardless of where I am.

Anna and Howard for the incredible support you've been and continue to be.

Colleen Hollis at Christ Church in Nashville, for your teaching on the cost of healing that spoke life into darkness.

Joshua, Sarah, Joy, and Brian for all your amazing support. Thank you!

Lastly, I want to acknowledge Kate Leary. She passed away before she could finish this series. She took such pride in these books and did everything she could to spread the word. Kate, I miss you more than you know. Thank you so much for the friendship we shared.

DISCUSSION QUESTIONS

1. How has Julia changed throughout the three books, and what have been her steps along the way? Consider the following areas of her life: attitude toward God, interactions with others, self-confidence, self-worth, and hopes and expectations for her future.

2. One of the themes in the Price of Privilege series is that a person's daily life decisions ripple outward, resulting in long-range consequences and repercussions. As one example, how do Lady Josephine's decisions play a role in Isaac's downfall long after her death? In what ways might your choices continue to have weight beyond your own lifetime?

3. Isaac's thread is the shortest on Julia's timeline, yet his life has an inordinately significant impact on hers. Can a brief meeting—perhaps even an unspoken meeting—change the course of someone's life? Can you think of someone who may not have been part of your life for very long but had a lasting impact on you? Why do you think they affected you so deeply?

4. Julia bemoans the waste and excess in her father's household, yet when she and Edward find themselves in

need, they are willing to live under Pierson's roof. How do you feel about the scene in chapter 14 where Edward takes a stand and refuses to wear the requisite finery? Do you agree with any aspects of Edward's argument, and if so, which ones? Do you find Isaac's counterargument persuasive?

5. How does Macy use his wealth and influence? Lord Pierson? Isaac has no great wealth of his own, but how does he utilize the resources at his disposal? Consider what Jesus says about wealth in Matthew 19:23-26. What words of caution do these verses have for the materially wealthy? What hope do they provide for the wealthy—and for all of us? How can a person avoid getting mired in possessions and financial concerns?

6. In chapter 26, Julia considers what might have happened had she submitted to authority rather than trying to take matters into her own hands. Would this have been a better course for her? For Edward? When is it right to wait, and when should a person take action? What is your typical response when faced with an unwanted or uncertain situation?

7. At one point in the book, Edward believes himself called to the orphanage, as does Jameson. Julia believes the opportunity in South Africa may be God's provision. How well are we able to determine what God is doing in our lives based on what is currently visible to us? (Consider the biblical story of Joseph, especially Genesis 50:15-21.) What are the dangers of judging others or ourselves based only on the circumstances we can see?

8. Edward chooses a radical path, refusing to be boxed in by rules and societal expectations, while Isaac opts to learn from and obey them, working to influence the system from

within. What are the advantages and disadvantages to each of these paths? How should a person determine which one to follow?

9. Jameson and Edward treat Julia differently than she's been treated in the previous two books. These relationships, combined with Isaac's sacrifice, transform Julia. As a reader, did you react differently to Julia in this book because several characters acknowledge her value? Does how we treat someone really change them and the way they are seen by others? What, then, is our responsibility to the broken and downtrodden?

10. In Julia's society, expectations of men were very different from expectations of women. What aspects of Julia's struggles in this series are a direct result of Victorian constraints on women? Have you ever felt at a disadvantage because of your gender?

11. Though restricted in many ways by Victorian gender roles, Julia exhibits her own gender bias when she arrives at Maplecroft and winks at the menservants' state of unreadiness but is stern with the female staff. Like Julia, are we at times blind to biases in our own culture? Where do you witness double standards today? (Consider areas of education, career, media portrayals, parenthood.) Have you ever knowingly or unknowingly perpetuated these double standards? How can we recognize and break these cycles?

ABOUT THE AUTHOR

JESSICA DOTTA has always been fascinated by the intricacies of society that existed in England during the Regency and Victorian eras. Her passion for British literature fueled her desire to write in a style that blends the humor of Jane Austen and the dark drama of a Brontë sister.

Jessica lives in the Nashville area. She is always happy to accept tea invitations from book clubs, especially when they serve Earl Grey and scones. Visit her online at www.jessicadotta.com.